ONE NATION UNDER GODS

REESHI RAY

Book Cover design by B&J
Book Interior Layout by CirceCorp Design

PUBLISHER'S NOTE

For those who keep going

THE LAST PRESIDENT

The president gripped the document tight and scanned its grim contents. In the last twenty-four hours, the list of names had grown longer. As he read, he forced himself not to picture the faces of the dead.

Vice President Amelia Jordan. Assassinated. Midair ambush of Air Force Two.

Speaker Orrin Vasquez. Brain-dead (hospitalized at 49th Combat Support Hospital). Air raid on Capitol Building.

President pro tempore of the Senate Daniel Whitman. Assassinated. Safe house ambush in Naples, Florida.

Secretary of State Anisha Gupta. Presumed dead. Last known location: Antler Labor Camp, North Dakota.

Secretary of the Treasury Sergei Valley. Presumed dead. Captured at Siege of Manhattan.

Secretary of Defense James Lionel. Dead. Suicide via gunshot.

The president didn't finish reading. He put the list down and looked at the sea of clouds outside his airplane window. They resembled a vast, blue mountain range touched by the moonlight.

"Lionel's dead?" he asked.

"That's correct, Mr. President," Admiral Grover answered from the seat across the aisle. "Our plan was to extract the SecDef to Baja via Crescent City on a Navy cutter. The boat was scheduled to leave two nights ago, but a spec hunter-killer team found his safe house the morning of departure. They killed the Marine unit guarding him and forced their way into the home. By that time, Secretary Lionel and his wife had already taken their own lives. ONI sent confirmation."

All dead. The president rubbed his eyes. They had killed every person in the presidential line of succession. He was the last one.

The only one they were hunting now.

"Mr. President, did you hear me?"

President Mathias turned away from the window and looked at the broad, serious man sitting in the seat across from him. He was wearing a dark jacket and slacks instead of his uniform, but Admiral Grover still projected the authority of his official role as Chairman of the Joint Chiefs of Staff. This was not his first war, yet the president could see in his exhausted eyes the inhuman toll this one had taken on him.

"You'll have to repeat yourself, Admiral," the president said, feeling every inch of the Admiral's exhaustion.

"Mr. President, we don't have any other options. It's time to activate Omega Rex."

The president tipped his head back against the chair and closed his eyes. Here in his private airborne office, he let himself just listen to the engines as they carried him to exile.

This was what it had come to.

"At this point, sir, we have no viable defensive line," Grover continued. "Our communication network has been compromised, and the Armored Infantry is in full retreat. The Manhattan siege was repelled." Grover paused for a moment. "And the NSA reports that he has escaped."

He. The president fumed. That murderous Traitor who had somehow managed to bring the world's greatest superpower to its knees.

"No," the president said flatly, his eyes still closed.

"Sir?"

The president opened his eyes and even he was surprised by the force behind his words. "I will not bring another monster into this world."

"Mr. President." The Admiral chose his words carefully. "Omega Rex is different. We would have complete control—"

"That's what they told me about the Specials. We have complete control of them. Look at us now." The president flung the papers off his desk. "*What control do we have now?*"

Grover sat back in his chair and held the president's glare.

"I'm sorry, Admiral," Mathias said, taking a moment to breathe. "Is Joanna safe?"

"Yes, Mr. President. We received a report just an hour ago. Your daughter was extracted by the JSOC team to a Seawolf-class submarine in the Atlantic. She will be in European waters in approximately twenty-four hours."

For the first time in years, Mathias felt relief. "Thank you, Admiral."

He stood up, and his vision swam. He steadied himself on the cabin wall.

"Sir, shall I call your physician?" Grover asked.

"No. I just need sleep."

Almost seventy-two hours he hadn't slept. Ever since abandoning the safe house in Denver—one of seventeen he had shuttled between in the last year—he had only snatched a few hours of sleep a day, mostly in moving vehicles.

Grover nodded and left the cabin. The president walked over to the small couch across the airborne office and stretched out.

The plane rumbled on through the night. Mathias couldn't sleep. The sofa was lumpy, and the Boeing's jets droned in his ears. They had done their best to replicate the comforts of Air Force One, but ever since the Specials had bombed it off the runway at Andrews, he had been forced to take these lesser jets to avoid detection.

There were seven other planes like this flying in different directions tonight, he knew. Decoys all of them, filled with people who knew that they would probably be shot out of the sky as the spec hunter-killer teams swept the country, searching for him.

They want my head on a stake. They want the world to see me fall.

"Fucking specs," the president grunted under his breath. He didn't remember exactly when he had started using that slur, *specs*. In the first days of the Emergency, (*Has it been nine years already?* Mathias wondered) the bigots had spat that word out as invective. A cutting word, a dividing line between the past and a terrifying future.

Mathias had always thought himself better than that. He had always thought he wasn't afraid of the future.

It was the past that kept him up at night.

The Specials had spiraled out of his control so fast. He had unleashed the full might of the US military on them and somehow, led by that blue and gold Traitor, they had smashed his lines. For the first three years of his presidency he had tried to assimilate them. He had stood shoulder to shoulder with the Traitor on the Rose Lawn after signing the Special Homeland Act. "A new era of peace between our two peoples," he had said to the press cameras.

He'd never wanted war.

Mathias rubbed his brow. Sleep was far away, and old, dark thoughts swept through his mind.

I could have stopped this.

*

Mathias walked out of his office, having given up on sleep. He passed Agents Dillon and Hauser, his two Secret Service sentinels guarding the door. They smelled of sweat. Their suits, usually pristinely pressed, were torn and stained. He knew Agent Hauser, that straw-haired Minnesota titan, was still nursing the shrapnel wounds in his side from their close call in Provost. Both men had been by his side since he'd put his hand on the Lincoln Bible and taken the oath of office eight years ago.

They followed him silently as he walked through the main cabin, passing the snoring gauntlet of aides and advisors who would accompany him to Europe to begin their government-in-exile. As long as the Executive Branch survived, the Specials would have no legitimacy.

Some of his aides in the cabin woke up as he passed. One tried to stand, but he put a hand on her shoulder.

"Go back to sleep," he said quietly.

He turned to Hauser outside the door of the private sleeping cabin in the back.

"Is she awake?"

"No, sir. Not for the last two hours."

Thank God. He couldn't take another fight with her in his wretched state. He reached for the doorknob.

"Sir?"

He turned. It was Dillon this time. He was touching his earpiece, which always seemed to be beaming bad news from central command.

"What is it?"

"Mr. President, we've lost contact with Decoys One, Three, and Six."

"I see."

"We have to presume that they've been brought down."

"And if they've been brought down, that means that they've searched them."

"Yes, sir. They know you're in the air. Their search field is narrowed, but we still have four more decoys in play."

"How many people were on the planes?"

"Twenty-one total," Dillon said like he was reciting a grocery list.

"Mr. President," Hauser chimed in, "we just passed over Flagstaff. We should be over the border in an hour. I'm not here to make assumptions, sir, but I think we'll be out of the woods soon."

"Thank you," the president said. "I appreciate that."

An hour before they entered Mexican airspace. Followed by a covert landing in the desert and a change of planes for a final dash across the Atlantic toward government-in-exile.

The bedroom was dark and cool. He could make out Annabelle curled up on the left side of the bed, her orange pill bottle on the bedside table.

He sat beside her. Annabelle's hand touched his.

"Is it over yet?" she whispered.

He stroked her hair, the long brown strands brittle and knotted. He remembered the way they slid through his fingers like silk the night they met at their first Yale graduate mixer.

"Yes. It's all been a bad dream," he smiled at her.

She nodded vacantly. "Joanna?"

"They got her out."

Annabelle squeezed her eyes tight and covered her face. "Oh God, if anything happened to her . . ."

"Our little girl is safe."

She faced him, her eyes sharpening with hostility. "I don't know how you could do it."

"Do what?"

"You're responsible for all of this." Her bony finger jabbed at him in the dark. "You."

Mathias's jaw tightened. She knew, even drugged-up, where to stick the dagger.

"I'm going to fix this."

"Hmm." She closed her eyes again and caressed his cheek.

He lay down next to her. He tried to remember when it was that their marriage had fallen apart—and whose fault it had been.

The media had branded them as America's Couple when he'd won the election. His come-from-behind victory had left them all breathless. The young, dashing president with his brilliant federal prosecutor First Lady. Hope was high in those days, and a country teetering on the edge had looked up to them as saviors.

It took a monumental effort to hide the fracture in their marriage that had started so many years ago over things he couldn't remember now. On their wedding day, he'd ignored that nagging feeling that there was an entire continent inside her that she'd kept hidden from him. At this moment, as everything fell around them, Mathias realized with a painful clarity that he had been alone his whole life.

He thought about Joanna, sixteen years old and holed up in a cramped submarine, far away from everyone she knew. He wondered if she was afraid and then laughed at the notion. His exceptional, iron-willed daughter, afraid? Ludicrous.

Thinking about her made the clouds part for a moment. He had failed his country and his people. But he would not fail Joanna. Somehow he would salvage this. This war was not going to be his legacy. Somehow, he knew as he fell into sleep, he was going to make this right.

*

The screaming alarm woke him.

For a second, Mathias thought it was part of his dream. But then he heard Hauser's voice above him.

"Sir, we need to get you off the plane. *Now!*"

Strong arms grabbed him and pulled him off the bed. Annabelle screamed his name. Six agents dragged him into the main cabin, where he saw his aides stumbling around in panic.

"What is going on?" Mathias demanded.

Mathias's stomach lurched as the plane suddenly fell into a dive.

The alarm kept shrieking. The plane leveled out and tipped hard to the right. Mathias felt terror claw inside him. His socked feet dragged across the carpet as the agents carried him like a child.

Crack!

The air around the plane snapped in half, and pressure waves rang in Mathias's ears—a sonic boom.

They were here.

The agents were moving as fast as they could, hands on weapons, moving him toward the cockpit. Toward the escape pod.

The president struggled against the six much larger men. "I'm not leaving my wife!" he yelled.

He twisted his body and wrenched free from Hauser and pushed back toward the bedroom. "Annabelle—"

The plane dropped fast again, a moment of sickening weightlessness.

They had found him so fast.

Inhumanly fast.

"Let me through!" Annabelle ran through the cabin, clawing at the agents. The president gripped her hand in the scrum. The plane twisted left, tossing everyone to the ground. Still, Mathias held his wife's hand.

"Sir, we have to go now!" Dillon yelled at him.

"I'm not leaving her."

"The pod only has room for one."

"*Then we fucking surrender.*"

The agents froze. Even Mathias was stunned at his own words.

He stood up and straightened his suit. Annabelle was looking at him, her eyes clear, as if seeing him differently for the first time in decades.

"I'm going to surrender," Mathias said simply.

Hauser bristled. "Sir—"

"If they wanted to blow us out of the air, they could have done it from miles away." The president looked at the terrified faces around him. "They want me alive."

"They'll execute you," Hauser said.

"Maybe. But they'll spare you all." He looked at his wife.

"Gabriel," she said, her lips trembling. She broke through the shell of agents and held him tight. The smell of her hair made him smile.

Crack! Another Special shot by the left wing, supersonic.

The pilot released the flares. Dove hard to the right.

The second Special cracked overhead.

But this one was different. Its wake was like a bellow torn from the depths of the earth, impossibly powerful and implacable.

It was *him.*

The Traitor in blue and gold himself. Coming to take the head of Mathias personally.

The president turned to Hauser and Dillon.

"Get me on the speakers. I'll surrender myself if they spare the plane."

It was his last move. The last order of the president he was, not the one he wanted to be. After so many years of being afraid, here and now, at the end, he would finally make his stand.

He smiled at Annabelle. "Tell Joanna . . ." He choked up. "Tell her . . ."

Annabelle nodded, squeezing his fingers.

He let go of her hand and walked toward the cockpit. He had made it halfway when they tore off the tail fin.

The plane spun violently. Up became down, and bodies tumbled through the cabin like balls in a lottery cage. Mathias's head hit something hard, and stars filled his vision.

They tore the right wing off next.

Fire and smoke ripped through the jagged hole in the fuselage, icy air spinning through the chamber like blades. The president watched in horror as Hauser tumbled through the hole.

Mathias grabbed the legs of a seat and hung on as the plane spiraled. Oxygen masks fluttered above their heads. He heard the screams of his aides, watched as their bloodied bodies were sucked into the night.

Where's Annabelle?

Mathias couldn't see anything. Somebody crashed into him, loosening his grip on the chair. It was Admiral Grover, a shard from the fuselage embedded in his neck.

"Annabelle!" Mathias cried into the spinning darkness.

A large silhouette appeared in the breach.

The Special stood calmly in the storm of death. It was here for one reason and one reason only.

Mathias searched desperately for a weapon.

The Traitor walked into the cabin and grabbed Mathias by the collar.

It was an otherworldly force. A strength unmatched by anything in human history. Mathias's torso scraped across the carpet, and suddenly the world was calm again. Only clouds above and clouds below.

He watched the plane hurtle toward the horizon, a flaming missile.

He was falling. Or maybe he was flying.

He was Gabriel Constantine Mathias. The last president of the United States of America.

QUOTES

President Mathias was dead for only three hours when crowds began forming in bombed-out streets across America, chanting "Long Live Patriot Gold." From New York to Los Angeles to Albuquerque, they celebrated their otherworldly leader, who after five years of war had finally emancipated them.

Amid the celebrations, the magnitude of the moment was all too clear. The race of Specials, who had been the target of so much persecution and exploitation since their existence had been uncovered ten years prior, had managed to do what no one thought possible: they had toppled the world's last remaining superpower.

The speed with which the world order changed startled even the most jaded observers. That the American empire, the country of Washington, Lincoln, and Roosevelt, could be erased from the map so quickly left the world stunned. Most would have pinpointed China as the most likely candidate to remove the US from its perch atop the geopolitical pyramid—perhaps Russia.

But not the Specials.

The Specials were supposed to cement American dominance, not destroy it. Created in military laboratories with classified technology, they were designed to be weapons—black-ops soldiers with capabilities that could sow devastation across the lands of America's enemies. In hindsight, we should have all known how this modern-day retelling of Pandora's Box would end.

Ten years ago, the technology used to create the Specials escaped the government labs in Salt Lake City, Utah, and spread like an airborne virus across the western United States, infecting millions of people. Overnight, men, women, and children were transformed into beings with extraordinary powers. Powers, as it turned out, that could not protect them from what came next—protests, violence, segregation, a hopeless pursuit of peace, betrayal, and finally, inevitably, war. The grim momentum of mankind's age-old response when faced with encroaching minorities.

This is what we know about the history of the Specials. But this reporter, and I'm sure much of the world, has no inkling as to what they will do next.

So we wait. And we watch. And maybe the clear-eyed among us will spend time pondering the lessons of the American Collapse.

This strangely gifted and terrifying race, once a hounded minority, now rule over the ruins of the last great empire. But the Specials' role in the collapse is only a fraction of the real story. As the history of the Ottomans and Romans has taught us—and as the plight of the former United States again proves—the mightiest of empires have always been destroyed from within.

—EXCERPT FROM AN EDITORIAL PUBLISHED IN THE *LONDON TRIBUNE*, FIVE DAYS AFTER THE END OF THE IMMORTAL WAR

The United States of America and all its institutions of oppression are hereby dissolved. We declare this land under sovereign rule of His Majesty, King Patriot Gold, the Firstborn; the Resurrected One and the Savior of our Peoples; Master of the Lands from the Atlantic to the Pacific and from the Cascades to the Rio Grande. There is no king but the Risen King. Raise your eyes to the sky and behold the Golden Kingdom.

—ROYAL DECREE, NEW YORK CITY, TWO WEEKS AFTER THE END OF THE IMMORTAL WAR

We have uncovered a wide array of crimes against humanity committed by the so-called Golden Kingdom, a military state where impunity and martial law reign. The policies of this rogue nation continue to violate every constitutional tenet of the United States government it overthrew fourteen months ago. The gravity, scale, and nature of these violations reveal a state that does not have any parallel in the contemporary world. Their crimes against humanity are numerous and widespread, and include the enslavement of human prisoners of war; murder and imprisonment of political dissenters; mass executions of suspected enemies of the state; brutal crackdowns by Crown-controlled secret police; and the continued and vigorous persecution of all those not considered "Special"—i.e., humans. For these reasons, this Commission calls on the Security Council to refuse to consider the Golden Kingdom as a possible member to our community of nations and to adopt targeted sanctions against this violent regime.

—EXCERPT FROM A UNITED NATIONS HUMAN RIGHTS COMMISSION REPORT TO THE UN SECURITY COUNCIL, ONE YEAR AFTER THE END OF THE IMMORTAL WAR

TEN YEARS AFTER
THE IMMORTAL WAR...

1

The woman looking for Houston Holt was having trouble finding him. It was Thursday night and Katya knew that usually meant he would be in one of the upscale bars on Bloomfield Street, cutting deals in smoky rooms and pretending like he wasn't a criminal.

But tonight, there was no sign of him.

So far, Katya had checked the Black Bird, River Haus, and the Willow with no success. Even though Houston wasn't out tonight, it seemed like every other person in River Town was.

What a madhouse, she thought as she passed by the drunk, singing crowds celebrating the news that had spread like wildfire through the settlement four days ago.

Ceasefire. Katya shook her head in disbelief. After ten years of living under Special occupation, the thought of peace was too overwhelming for her to comprehend. Instead, she focused on the task ahead of her—locating and recruiting Houston.

After striking out at Cantina Social, she realized there was only one place left where he could be.

Goddammit, Houston.

Her palm instinctively brushed across the corded leather grip of the Star-Spangled Hammer—the big-bore .50 caliber revolver tucked into her belt. It was her staunch sidekick, more of hand cannon than a handgun and better suited to shattering the structural integrity of armored vehicles than marksmanship. The scumbags of River Town all respected the Hammer. Katya had no love for guns, but in her line of work it was a necessary evil.

And if there was any place in this town where she would need the Hammer, it would be the Lowlife Quarter.

The Lowlife Quarter was what the locals called the stretch of nightlife on Fifth Street between Bloomfield and Grand. It was gang territory—a cluster of dive bars, casinos, and strip joints seething with violent rivalries. Katya was well-known around there, albeit not very popular. Over the last five years, she had arrested half its denizens.

Long story short, she wasn't expecting a hero's welcome.

She slipped her shield—a five-pointed brass star—into her coat pocket. Although she wasn't afraid of the Quarter's goons, tonight was not the night to pick a fight. As much as she hated to admit it, she needed Houston's help, and that would require finesse.

On Fifth Street she was greeted by a wall of noise. In the early spring warmth, all the bars had spilled out onto the sidewalk, where the criminals drank and gambled in the open. She adjusted the hood of her raincoat over her head, covering her face and recognizable red hair. Silently, she wove her way through the crowd to The Stillery at the end of the road.

A dangerous bar to visit at any time of day, The Stillery was the chosen watering hole for the town's lowest rung of criminality. A dive she knew well from her early days in River Town—a period of her life she didn't dwell on.

What am I doing back here?

Despite the hood shielding her face, she still felt a dozen hungry eyes on her.

She pushed open the wooden door and stepped inside the gloomy bar. The Stillery had been in business for over fifty years, one of the few establishments to survive the air raids intact. She didn't remember if it was her side or the specs that had bombed this half of town into oblivion, but she wondered why they had spared this shithole. Sawdust shifted under her boots. The low ceilings and weak lamps gave it all the charm of a damp cave. The clientele were a mass of ominous silhouettes, vibrating with hidden violence. She couldn't see them, but she could *feel* the armory of guns and sharp blades hidden inside every jacket and boot holster. The first time she had met Houston had been at this bar. Back then, he had fit right in.

We both had, Katya remembered.

Through a thicket of shoulders and lecherous glares, she charted her way past the bar and the broken jukebox into the narrow hallway where the restrooms were. At the end of the hallway was the door to the cellar, where, just as she expected, a goon stood guard.

He studied her with rodent eyes, openly carrying a semiautomatic on his right hip. He was a scumbag she hadn't seen before. Not that it mattered. They were about to be introduced.

"Ladies' room is behind you, princess," he sneered at her. "Turn that ass around so I can see it walking—"

Thunk! Katya came up with the Hammer in one swoop, from her shoulder holster to his jaw. The heavy barrel rattled his skull, snapping his head back so hard it bounced off the door with a loud *crack*. He crumpled at her feet.

She stepped over him, opened the door, and tiptoed quietly down the dim stairwell. She heard male voices below her, cursing over the clang and scrape of moving metal—the soundtrack of illicit activity in River Town.

At the bottom of the stairs, she slid to her right and pressed herself against the wall, her left shoulder an inch from the open doorway. The voices were louder now, and she heard, without question, the husky tenor of Houston Holt's voice locked in an argument.

"You don't want to pay my prices? Then take a walk," Houston said.

"What do I look like to you, a fucking fool?" another voice, gruff and smoke-stained, demanded.

A tense pause. Then, Houston deadpanned, "Yes."

"You got balls, asshole," the gruff man hissed. "But you can't count. I got two guys with me and one upstairs. That's five guns, including mine. You only got the one."

"I still don't like your odds," Houston said, an edge of iron in his voice.

Katya had heard enough. Pivoting on her left foot, she swung into the room, half of her body still blocked by the wall.

"Freeze!" she yelled.

The room exploded with movement. A flurry of men spun to face her, whipping out firearms. Her own gun barrel swung between the three gangsters. The lead gangster—the speaker, she guessed—sported a sickle tattoo on his bull neck. His eyes darted to the haul of green consoles on the table.

Across the table from the three lowlifes, she spotted Houston Holt.

If his three business associates were so grimy they looked like they had been pulled out of a drain pipe, Houston was their polar opposite. Relaxed and wiry, he wore dark jeans and a navy windbreaker over a spotless white oxford. Every time Katya saw him, she couldn't help but feel like Houston was slumming it in River Town, a temporary visitor from a better city. He was almost elegant until you saw his face—a nose flattened on the bridge, framed by two dark, penetrating eyes. His black hair was cut short, and a shadow of harsh stubble lined his jaw. It was the face of a boxer, a schemer—a survivor.

He was easy on the eyes. It was his personality she couldn't stand.

"Christ," Houston grumbled when he saw her.

"I'm shooting her," the wiry gangster behind Sickle Tattoo yelled.

"Not yet," Houston said, lowering his Swiss-made SIG Sauer pistol a few inches. "What are you doing here, Katya?"

"Yo, man, this be a setup," the third gangster chimed in.

"You know this bitch?" Sickle Tattoo looked at Houston, aghast.

"Shut your mouth, dirtbag!" Katya aimed at Sickle Tattoo's head.

"Unfortunately, I do," Houston said, glaring at Katya. "But there's no need to shoot her. The esteemed lady simply made a wrong turn on the way to the ladies' room. Didn't you, Katya?"

"With all due respect, Mister Holt, I fully intended to be here."

Houston shrugged. "Okay. Shoot her."

"No, *wait!*" Katya took a step back as the three gangsters lined up their shots. "Wait, wait, wait. I'm here for Houston only. With an urgent request. For tonight," she said as her eyes scanned the military-grade technology on the table, "and *only* for tonight, I can ignore any . . . *questionable activities* being conducted in this basement."

Houston watched her for a few moments, as if he was unsure he could believe anything she said. Finally, after what felt like hours to Katya, he locked his SIG into his steerhide belt holster.

"Gentlemen," he said, addressing the three gangsters who were still drawing beads on Katya's head, "let's wrap this deal up before the lovely lady here blows all our heads off. Fair?"

*

"You shouldn't be here," Houston said when they were in the alleyway outside the bar.

"Neither should you." Katya scowled at a mangy drunk snoring next to the dumpster. "I didn't think you'd fallen this far."

"You going to arrest me, girl scout?"

"I should," Katya snapped, annoyed. She had come here on a mission and here they were, bickering about his life choices again. "You want to be one of these miscreants tearing apart our town? Go ahead. I'm not going to try and stop you."

"Lies. Every time I see you, you try to stop me."

"You could do better with your life."

"You should be out solving the case of the Sixth Street falafel thief."

She ignored him. "What were you selling those guys?"

"Don't ask about my business."

"Those scumbags were a little rougher than your usual clientele."

"I follow the market."

"I've seen those guys around," she said. "That buffalo with the sickle tattoo. He's in Kilin's crew. You know what they do right?"

He put a hand on her shoulder. "What are you here for, Kat?"

"I have something for you." She reached into her jacket and pulled out a tattered paperback. Houston took it, shielding it from prying eyes. Certain books were illegal in River Town, and being caught with one meant a lashing or worse. He studied the face of the austere man on the cover, and then read the title. "The Last Giant."

"One of the last biographies of Rockefeller. Written right before the war."

"I've been looking for this. Where did you find it?"

Katya smiled. "Being a cop has its perks."

"You're not a cop."

"I know a few dirtbags sitting in a cell right now who would disagree."

Houston slipped the book into his jacket. "This feels like a bribe."

"It is."

"Not necessary."

Katya shrugged. "Figured you could use a pick-me-up."

"What does that mean?"

She tensed, regretting that she'd brought it up. "Nothing. I've just been hearing things."

"Like what?"

Katya leaned in close. "The Sultan's looking for you."

"Rumors." He changed the subject. "What're you here for?"

Katya hated asking, but she had no other choice. "There's a guy out there. A real sicko that needs straightening out."

Houston frowned. "A sicko you can't handle?"

"This one's different."

Houston stepped closer, his face darkening. "Did he hurt you?"

An argument erupted at the end of the alley. Katya looked toward the commotion for a moment before turning back to Houston.

"No." She shook her head. "Not me."

2

Houston followed Katya out of the alleyway and together they headed north on Garden Street. After a few blocks, they crossed a dank patch of ground covered in tents and surrounded by the husks of firebombed brownstones. Feral dogs scowled at Houston as barefoot street urchins chased each other through the maze, fizzlers sparkling in their hands. Above them, bottle rockets popped in the air. Houston could hear the thudding drums of the parade from all the way down on Washington Street.

Everywhere he looked, people were celebrating.

It was only four days ago, on Monday morning, that the king had announced the ceasefire from the balcony of the Golden Fort—all hostilities with the human rebels, the Redbloods, were suspended until a peace treaty could be hammered out. And then, in only a matter of hours, River Town had transformed.

This was not the River Town that Houston was used to—the River Town of pitched gun battles in the streets and hopelessness as the King's secret police tore through the town, uprooting subversives by their fingernails. That city had seemed constantly choked by oppression, a refugee settlement ripping apart at the seams.

No, Houston thought as they passed by a Greek family dancing on the corner of Seventh. *This is a whole new town.*

It used to be called Hudson County. The center was here in the former Hoboken, but the entire settlement of River Town stretched from North Bergen all the way to the southern tip of former Bayonne.

The Strip, as it was called by the inhabitants.

A stinking, low-rent stretch of displaced dreams, connecting delinquents, losers, and killers through their shared rootlessness—an impotent rage that had sharpened over the decade into a blistering pace of criminal activity.

Houston knew this town in his bones. It had infected him with its failure, its stench.

He wouldn't call the Strip home. True, he had lived within its borders since he'd tumbled out of the war ten years ago. But it was not home. Not even close.

Houston had washed up in River Town at twenty-five, a broken Immortal War veteran. Shoeless and seething, he was an outsider with no people, no juice, and no hope for survival in this outlaw sprawl.

By twenty-eight, he had his hairy fingers around the town's throat.

His plunge into the underworld slipstream had been instinctive, primal—a vicious momentum that he could not name but that had followed him out of the war.

He'd started small, connecting with other veterans and clearing out old weapons caches abandoned by the defunct US military. Using a fleet of stolen trucks, he sold guns to the Redblood rebels still fighting a war he wanted no part of. His heart pumped ambition, thick and combustible like gasoline. As his empire grew, so did the list of enemies determined to take his upstart business down, from the tent-town Blade Boys to the highest steps of the criminal pyramid, the Eschevera Family.

Houston went to war with all of them.

He had clawed his way out of the squalid tent-towns by his wits and ambition alone, and he would rather die than go back.

He had none of the anchors of human life—family, friends, country, God. Out here, where the streets burned with murderous commerce, he knew they were liabilities. Vulnerabilities. In a place like this, the best way to move was alone.

*

Houston and Katya turned onto Velvet Lane, the town's bustling red-light district. The buildings were statelier here, the brick facades brightly frescoed with nymphs and chubby cupids. Escorts tempted passersby from the balconies of the pricier brothels as others danced seductively behind the frosted glass windows of the cheaper establishments.

Halfway down the block, Katya stopped dead. She stood very still as she watched a crew of men in hard hats dismantle the wooden structure that stood at the crossroad of Garden and Tenth. They ripped up the planks of wood from the platform and attacked the structural beams with hammers before hurling the splintered bones into an idling dump truck.

"Remember what this used to be?" Katya asked Houston, her voice cold.

Houston watched the heavy crossbeam come down. He nodded.

Just this morning, the bodies of five suspected Redbloods had hung from these gallows.

Their crime had been a direct violation of the first Royal Edict that the king had passed after Victory Day ten years ago—the one that saw all human churches, temples, and historical monuments razed to the ground and all the museums and "deviant" books burned. Houston had read enough world history to know the Crown was simply following the protocol of all invading forces throughout time and systematically erasing the identity of those it had conquered. The three men and two women who had been hung on corner of Garden and Tenth had operated a secret church in a tenement basement. He suspected that one of their own congregants had sold them out.

Bad luck, Houston thought. If they had eluded capture for four more days, they would've been out here, dancing with the rest of the town.

The workmen tossed the last beams into the truck and held onto the sides as it rumbled off. Houston watched them go, guessing that they were on their way to dismantle the dozens of other gallows across the Strip. For the past ten years, the gallows had served as a clear message from the Sovereign Security Directorate, or SSD, the Crown's notorious secret police: *You are an occupied people. We are in charge.*

Even though the night was warm, Houston felt a chill. The SSD, or Gray Faces as they were called because of their ability to infiltrate every inch of human life like ghostly tendrils, had caught up to him once. He had escaped—barely.

"Peace." Katya spat on the ground. "They think we can just forget."

"You'd have made a good Redblood," Houston said. Although, in all honesty, he was glad that she hadn't joined the rebellion and skipped town. Katya had been invaluable to him right here on the Strip. As infuriatingly earnest as she was—she even had the words *Land of the Free, Home of the Brave* inscribed on either side of her hand cannon's barrel—Katya had always been one of his closest allies.

Ironic, Houston mused, that she also happened to be a Badge.

The Badges had no real authority. A loose collection of vigilantes posing as lawmen, they swaggered through the Strip with their outlandish guns, brass badges pinned to their chests, pestering local hoodlums and acting like they were the FBI.

They were mostly harmless do-gooders who were hopelessly outmanned and outgunned by the outlaw hordes that ran the Strip. Houston avoided them as a rule, but Katya felt indebted to him —ever since that night six years ago that neither of them spoke about. Indebted to keep him informed when his enemies planned to move against him, to shift other gung-ho Badges away from his trail.

If it had just stopped at that, Houston would have been happy. But Katya didn't know when to stop.

She wanted to save him.

To save him from himself and his own ambitions. To pull him into her own gang of true-blue Americans who still believed in the old country and its ancient notions of justice and equality.

The good guys, she called them.

Or, as Houston referred to them, lunatics.

He tapped his watch. Katya turned on her heel and led him toward the Siren House, an old three-story fire station, converted into a pleasure house of the highest reputation, employing the most beautiful courtesans and practicing the utmost discretion. The frescoes on the brick facade were seductive recreations of Botticelli's Venus, bursting with windswept sirens lounging in the water.

Behind the Siren House, they climbed a narrow set of stairs to a wide porch. The bouncer nodded at Katya and wrapped his beefy fingers around the handle of an ornate door.

Crack!

The air split apart. Katya ducked down as the bouncer grasped for his sidearm.

"Easy," Houston said, putting his hand on the bouncer's arm.

The bouncer looked at him. The young man was in his twenties— too young to have fought in the war, Houston realized. Too young to know what he'd just heard.

"What was that?" the bouncer asked, still on alert.

Houston pointed up to the sky. "Them."

There were seven of them—muscular figures in black, gliding in a perfect V formation two hundred feet above River Town. They were decelerating, the aftershock of their supersonic flight still rattling the city.

Katya's jaw fell open. "Are those . . . ?"

"Silverbacks," Houston said.

"Wow," Katya marveled. "I've never seen them this close."

"They don't fly out in the open like this," Houston said. "They're trying to intimidate us." He looked at Katya, who was still awestruck. "Take it from me—this is as close as you want to get to them."

Houston knew firsthand the terrible price of tangling with a Silverback. They, the elite military force of the Golden Kingdom, had hammered the former United States into dust. Houston's Marine unit had skirmished with them multiple times, and he still remembered the terrifying *sizzle* as their lethal bolts tore through the air.

He took a deep breath and watched the unit glide over the Hudson River and disappear into the brilliant lights of Sovereign City.

Katya was talking, but Houston wasn't listening.

Sovereign City filled his vision, a jeweled and soaring spectacle.

That island formerly known as Manhattan shimmered like a mirage, the golden lights of its towers and domes reflecting off the black waters. The Kingspire spun up into the clouds from its center, a beam of colored light that marked the very spot where the king had accepted the American surrender.

*

Manhattan had been the last major city to fall before the King, then just called Patriot Gold, had torn President Mathias out of the sky and killed him on national television. Patriot Gold had then declared Manhattan the capital of his new empire, and the last of the US military generals were forced to wade through its wreckage to sign the Articles of Surrender.

The specs called it Victory Day.

Houston referred to it by its human name: the Debacle.

Manhattan had been decimated in the conflict. It had taken ten years and thousands of human slaves to build it back up to the architectural wonder it was now: an island fortress forged to consecrate the birth of a new world, a new era in history. The city flowed and curved, intimidated and awed, overpowering the stars and capturing the sun like an indomitable mountain range. Across the skyline one could see the colossal domes of Istanbul merge with the glass-encrusted edifices of a modern metropolis, all of it shimmering with the ancient enigma of Babylon. It was the polestar of a superior race, a big, gilded, monumental *fuck you* to the world full of humans who wanted them dead.

To an outsider like Houston who had never been within its walls, the city seemed to burn with a mysterious magic, a sense of possibility that thrummed through its towers and forts like a golden current.

They'd renamed the island Sovereign City, the seat of the king—Patriot Gold, the Firstborn and the Risen King. And from the city, his power had spread across the carved-up remains of the United States. He'd split the country into the Four Provinces—North, East, South, and West—with Patriot Gold's four handpicked governors overseeing each one. But the center of power was, and always had been, Sovereign City.

"No time for dreaming." Katya laughed, squeezing Houston's arm and snapping him back to the balcony. "Business first."

*

They had stashed the boy on the third floor in one of the smaller bedrooms. The first thing Houston noticed was the broken glass. Somebody had tipped over a mirror, and now dozens of shards lay embedded in the plush crimson rug, surrounded by broken furniture. The room had been ravaged. But it was the boy who had absorbed the worst punishment.

Jesus, Houston thought when he saw him.

He had been a good-looking kid before the attack. Now a bruise ballooned above his right cheekbone, and his left eye was swollen shut. The boy held gauze to his bleeding mouth and absently ran his other hand along the ugly purple finger marks crisscrossing his throat. He tapped his foot nervously.

Houston glared at the Siren House's elderly Madam. "You're pimping out kids now?"

"Save your outrage," the Madam sighed, bored. "He's twenty-six."

The kid mumbled.

"What's that?" Houston asked.

"Twenty-five. I turn twenty-six next month."

"What's your name?" Houston asked.

"Sebastian."

"Your real name."

The kid looked at Katya and the Madam. They both nodded. He looked back down at the floor. "Jesse."

"Who did this to you, Jesse?"

"A john."

"No shit. What's his name?"

"He didn't give me a name. He was a big bodybuilder type."

Houston looked at Katya. "Why don't you just arrest him?"

"Because he's protected."

"By who?"

"By *you*."

Houston shook his head. "That's impossible. I vet my guys."

"Did you vet Klay Park?" Katya asked. "Because that's who did this."

Houston rubbed his stubble. "Klay Park?"

"We're sure," Katya said. "I saw him."

"He was drunk," Jesse said. "He didn't want to pay. It got ugly. I hit him in the face with a bottle. Then it got worse."

Katya knelt next to Jesse and handed him some fresh gauze to hold against his mouth. "They get the first taste of blood," she said, "and they get bolder."

She spoke from experience, Houston knew. Her red hair was down now, and Houston looked at her for a long moment.

"Kill him."

The words had come from Jesse. Houston saw the boy's blue eyes flashing with anger.

"You ever kill anyone, kid?" Houston asked.

"I want to kill *him*."

"That road doesn't lead where you think."

Jesse rubbed Houston's expensive windbreaker between his thumb and forefinger. He then motioned toward Katya. "You killed for her. Led you to some nice places."

"*Jesse*," Katya hissed.

"Long time ago," Houston said.

Six years ago, to be exact. Back then, he had run into a young redhead bleeding and crying by the back door of The Stillery. He had bought her a drink and given her money for a doctor. She was just a pretty orphan back then, working the street to survive. After a few drinks, she told him about the guy who'd attacked her—one of the Blade Boys from the Marshal Drive tent-town, a sadistic enforcer they called Remo. She managed to escape before he got out his knives, but she knew he'd be back.

"I want a gun," she had whispered. "I want him dead."

Houston told her he would get her a gun the next day. He set her up in a small apartment on Willow where she would be safe for the night. She had slept soundly, dreaming of the hole she would blast in Remo's face.

But the next morning she heard the news—they had found Remo's corpse on the street. Apparently, he had taken a swan dive off the fifth floor of the China Star Casino. Suicide, they said.

Houston never said anything to Katya about it. Instead, when he saw her the next day, he handed her a black duffel bag, weighed down with the fearsome bulk of the Hammer.

Jesse looked down at his feet. "I fucking hate being a nobody."

"We're all nobodies here," Houston said.

He walked to the window and stood alone with his thoughts for a while. Trumpets had now joined the peace parade drums down on Washington. Behind him, he could feel the others' gazes burning into his back.

He turned around to face Katya. From his jacket, he retrieved *The Last Giant* and held it up. "This better be a damn good book."

3

Klay wasn't picking up his phone. After three calls that went straight to voicemail, Houston stopped by his associate's apartment building in the Jackson Street tenements. No one answered the door, so Houston picked the lock and checked inside. The small one-bedroom was messy and smelled of dirty laundry, but there was no sign of Klay.

After leaving the tenements, Houston made six short phone calls, reaching out to his most trusted informants. Five came up empty.

But finally, at a stroke before midnight, the sixth informant delivered a location on Klay Park.

Houston picked up his step and headed east until he reached Adams Street.

Even at this late hour, Little Bangkok was raucous with street hawkers, the smoky air heavy with the smell of fried pork and fish sauce. Houston felt like he was walking through a noisy tunnel of light as he passed below the glowing bulbs strung up between food stalls. He was tempted to stop by the Tuk Tuk stall for their spicy moo ping skewers, but the line of customers stretched ten deep. His stomach rumbled.

The Fight Road Gym was perched on the second story of a brick rowhouse above the King and I restaurant. Both establishments

were owned by the same woman, Miss Namwong, the matriarch
of a Thai food empire that included half the stalls on the block and
the grocery store across the street.

She was sitting at the front desk of the gym, watching a small
TV as Houston came up the stairs. Slowly, she turned away from
the screen to peer at Houston over her glasses, her wrinkled hands
never straying far from the shotgun below the desk. She studied
Houston wordlessly for a few moments before nodding toward the
sparring area across the room.

Under the crinkled posters of Muay Thai champions, Klay Park
pummeled a heavy bag with thudding punches and kicks.

When Houston had met Klay two years ago—then a penniless
refugee fleeing the violence in Colorado—he had brought him
here to Fight Road, hoping it would do for Klay what it had done
for Houston when he had first arrived in town: provide sanctuary
from the desolation outside.

Klay didn't look up as Houston approached, his club-like fists
shaking the bag. Houston noticed the bandage across his nose.

"Chin down," Houston said. "Snap the right."

Klay glanced at him. He reset his feet and lowered his chin. He
jabbed lightly with his left and then snapped out a thunderous
right. He drilled it three more times before backing away and
unraveling his hand wraps. Houston studied his calloused hands,
which were as large as mallets. Perfect for the specialized work
Houston usually hired Klay to do.

As Klay stepped closer, Houston smelled the tequila on him.

"You got a job for me?" Klay asked.

"No."

"Figured," Klay said, tossing a hand wrap to the floor. "We still
on hiatus?"

Houston pointed to the bandage on his nose. "Walk into a wall?"

"It's nothing."

Klay stood with his hands on his hips and watched Houston.

He waited.

"When I hired you, what was the first thing I told you?" Houston asked.

"This an interrogation?"

"Answer me."

"Walk alone. Stay alive."

"Walk alone. Stay alive. You stay detached from everything. From *everyone*. We make money quietly and move on."

Klay crossed his thick arms across his chest. "Get to the point."

"You were at Sirens tonight."

"I'm there a lot of nights." He walked past Houston and drank from the water fountain.

"Why did you bust up the kid?"

Klay laughed, spitting up water. "You the SSD?" He turned away from the fountain and faced Houston. "Or is business so bad that you have to run protection for whores now?"

"Pay for the property damage. Then pay to get the kid fixed up."

Klay's nostrils flared. "That sounds like an order."

"It is. You still work for me."

"Maybe I don't work for you anymore." Klay took a step forward, towering over Houston. "Your business is in the shitter. You run guns to the Redbloods. How you think that works during a ceasefire?" Klay laughed. "The word on the street's not good for you, man. I heard the Sultan's cutting you loose. You lose his protection and then what? You're out in the open. Blade Boys. Eschevera gunners. Everybody you stepped onto get this fancy shit?" He flicked the collar of Houston's jacket. "They're gonna take a run at you, bro."

"You're taking Eschevera money now?"

"Exploring my options. I'm done playing for the losing side."

Houston held his glare for a few moments. Then he shrugged. "Me too, kid."

He turned toward the door. He heard Klay chuckle behind him.

Houston stopped. "You didn't answer my question."

"What?"

Houston turned back to face Klay. "Why'd you bust up the kid?"

Klay scratched his nose indifferently. "Cuz he can't hit back."

Houston took a step toward Klay.

"You mad?" Klay laughed. "Cuz I fucked up a little faggot?"

"No. I just wish you listened better." Houston took one more small step. "Chin down."

Klay was a half-second too slow.

Houston swiveled and crashed his fist into Klay's exposed jaw. The bigger man's head snapped back, and his legs buckled.

He hit the ground just as Houston's steel-toed boots smashed into his ribs. From his position on the ground, Klay lunged toward Houston, a giant paw reaching for his throat. Houston dodged and pistol-whipped Klay's temple. The big man crumpled onto his stomach.

Houston wrenched Klay's arm behind his back.

"Please," Klay yelped. "You're going to break my arm!"

"I intend to."

"*Fuck*—I'm sorry—"

Houston could feel Klay's shoulder joint grating in its socket. He dug his pistol into the back of his neck.

"What are you going to do, Klay?"

"Apologize."

"To the kid. And the Madam."

"Yeah, yeah. I will. I swear!"

"Pay for the room damage. Pay for his stitches."

"I swear—I will—*Christ, please!*"

Houston released his arm. Klay cradled it, whimpering.

By the door, Houston dropped a hundred goldmarks on Miss Namwong's desk. "Thanks for the tip."

She ignored him, immersed in a Mexican telenovela.

"You speak Spanish?" he asked.

She shrugged. "All the same."

He slid an extra fifty toward her. She looked at it. "For the mess," he said, motioning toward Klay's slumped figure. "Sorry about that."

"No sorry," she said, pushing back the money. She pointed at Klay. "He big asshole."

As Houston walked back down the stairs to the street, his phone rang. The caller ID read Unknown Number, but Houston knew exactly who it was.

He's cutting you loose, man . . . Klay's mocking voice again.

Houston answered the call.

It was the Sultan.

Houston listened quietly as the Sultan calmly stated a time and a location for their meeting. Houston checked his watch. "Yeah. I'll be there," he said before hanging up.

He rubbed his eyes. There was nothing left to be done now.

Houston slid through Little Bangkok. He had an hour to kill before his meeting with the Sultan.

He deserved one last drink before the execution.

*

The Sultan, now Houston's destroyer, had once been his savior.

He had shown up four years ago on the day that Houston realized he had been dealt a fatal hand.

A shipment of M-12 surface-to-air missile launchers bound for the Redbloods out west had been intercepted by the Escheveras. The truck driver was killed and the weapons left in the open—a trail for the Gray Faces to follow back to Houston.

Houston had felt the anvil drop in his gut. Gray Faces. There was no escape once the Crown's secret police got their hooks in you. Human criminals saw no courtroom, no jury of their peers. The chains clanked around your wrists and there you were, damned to the slave crews working twenty hours a day to build someone else's empire.

He was in their sights—*tick, tick, tick*—and the expiration date on Houston Holt was running out.

His finger was on the trigger, the barrel of his SIG in his mouth, when the phone rang.

Out of morbid curiosity, he had picked up.

It was the Sultan, a man Houston had only heard about—a man with the power to change lives.

"Houston Holt," he had said in a voice tinged with smoke and liquor, "I think we can help one another."

*

In the dusty confines of the Black Bird bar, Houston found himself wedged in between his fellow schemers, drinking quietly with the look of the recently bereaved. He could still hear the parade drums outside.

"Whiskey," Houston ordered from the giant bartender, Haku.

"You must be feeling good, Holt," Haku said, smiling through his missing teeth. "Never seen you drink anything but seltzer."

"I'm off the clock."

"Got something you're going to like," Haku said. He knelt down behind the bar and unlocked a cabinet. He came back up holding an unmarked bottle, the whiskey inside glowing like a campfire.

"Just came in from Tochigi." Haku smiled as he poured Houston two fingers. A burly, tattooed Hawaiian who had been slinging drinks in the Black Bird since the Debacle, Haku was a River Town legend, above the law and untouchable by any local mafia. The reasons why were lost to history. As Houston drank the whiskey, he assumed that it had something to do with Haku's uninterrupted access to foreign booze.

Houston knocked it back. "Yamazaki?"

"No, brother—Nikka. Seventeen-year."

Houston tapped his tumbler. "I'm in the wrong business, Haku. All these years I should have been bringing this in."

"Turn the sound up!" someone from the back yelled, pointing at the mounted TV behind the bar.

"Okay, okay, hold your ponies," Haku said as he turned up the volume. It was a news report from the Crown News Network. The reporter, the spec journalist Mandy Reyes, stood in a large warehouse as teams of designers and fabricators assembled massive floats behind her. Houston watched as she bubbled excitedly about the upcoming Grand Decennial Parade.

"I'm also getting word from insiders in the Royal Court that the queen herself has taken a personal interest in the design of the floats for the Grand Decennial Parade that will kick off the festivities this Sunday at midnight. And my sources tell me that Her Majesty is determined to put on a show to rival that of the Royal Wedding in size and extravagance. I can't tell you how exciting this news is. But before we get carried away, let's remember that this is so much more than just a celebration. The Decennial Parade has incredible political significance for the king as it not only marks the ten-year anniversary of Victory Day but also the beginning of what many hope will be a new era in human and Special relations. The ceasefire talks are ongoing, with Redblood diplomatic representatives and the Crown hoping to sign a full peace treaty before the ten-day Grand Decennial celebrations are over . . ."

Houston stopped listening. He watched his whisky, the way it glittered in the lights.

"You think they'll sign a treaty?" Haku asked him.

"I hope not."

"Peace is a good thing."

"Not for business," Houston said.

"More to life than business, my brother."

The delinquents around him suddenly started booing at the TV. The news had shifted from the floats to stock footage of the king smiling and waving to his subjects from the balcony of the Golden Fort, the lovely queen gleaming at his side.

"Fuck the king!" some suicidal fool yelled out from the back of the bar.

Houston felt the old pain ignite along his right flank, from his hip to his chest. He tossed his drink back through gritted teeth and raised the empty glass. "Fuck the king."

He had seen the king once in his life: twelve years ago, streaking through the clouds above a blood-soaked battlefield. Houston, his side slashed through with a bolt, had stared up into the sky and watched Patriot Gold soar. A childlike wonder had overcome him then, even as he lay wounded among the burning mech hulks and terrified screams of his decimated Marine unit. He'd wished he were up there with them, those Specials flying above the buildings like mythic birds, far from the carnage.

Houston bit down on the memory. He had survived the war—just barely. But whether or not he would survive the peace . . . that was another matter.

Klay had been right. What use was a gunrunner in a ceasefire? His main revenue stream—guns to the rebels—had been shut off like a spigot. No money coming in meant no money going into the pockets of his vast web of spies, informants, distributors, and gunmen. He would lose the only true asset he had: his mastery of this ecosystem.

The image of the Sultan, the carrion vulture awaiting him, bloomed malignantly in Houston's mind. The Sultan who saw all and recognized the rapidly depreciating asset that was Houston Holt.

Just business, Houston thought. *I'd do the same.*

"Chin up, Holt." Haku grinned as he wiped down a pitcher.

Houston looked at him. "Is this where you thought you'd end up ten years ago?"

"Ah, the philosopher returns. And only two drinks in this time." Haku rested his massive forearms on the bar, chewing over the question. It was a long time before he spoke. "Thirteen years ago,

I escaped from a bad place. A bad, bad place, brother." He turned his right forearm up so Houston could see the faded serial number tattooed there. Haku's eyes sharpened and all humor faded from his face. "I realized one thing: all I have to do is survive today."

Houston was quiet. The smile crept back onto Haku's face.

"And you, Holt? Where did you think you'd be?"

Houston lifted his eyes to the TV. An aerial camera swept over the towers of Sovereign City. Haku turned to look at the scene and chuckled. "A philosopher and a dreamer," he said.

"A useless combination."

"Relax, Holt. You're not dead yet."

"Not yet."

He paid for his drinks and left. He had ten minutes to get to the waterfront and meet the Sultan. He wove his way past the celebrations and toward the river, feeling very much like the last man to get the joke.

*

Faraz Ibrahim, the Sultan of Secrets and Lies, was already at the promenade by the time Houston arrived. He stood alone on the lonely expanse of mounded dirt and rubble that served as a waterfront. Sovereign City glittered across the river.

Perfect place for an execution, Houston thought.

Faraz leaned casually against the railing. Slim and coiled in his black suit, he watched Houston's every step.

Houston still hadn't gotten used to this new Faraz, the one who had sprung forth two years ago as a completely transformed man. The old Faraz, dashing in technicolor cravats and Ferragamo monk straps, would always stumble into their meetings perpetually late, a river of martinis in his veins, the floral scent of a flygirl rising off his collar. He was an underworld princeling who smoldered with the illicit magic of Sovereign City, always ready to fire off a bawdy joke or a tall tale. That was the man Houston had met all those years ago, the Sultan who had saved him from swallowing a bullet.

But that was before the accident. Houston didn't know the details, but he knew that two years ago, Faraz had gone off the rails in a bad way. And here he was now, a chastened yet still dangerous operator.

They shook hands. Faraz offered Houston a Murad cigarette, which Houston waved away. Faraz lit up and blew smoke toward the water.

"I heard you were at The Stillery tonight," Faraz said.

"Closing a deal."

"A very questionable deal."

"It's a different economy," Houston said. He wasn't surprised that Faraz knew about the transaction. It was the speed with which he'd acquired the intel that startled him.

"Still, this Kilin—I don't like his business." Faraz looked out at the Hudson. The jagged hulks of the Navy cutters sunk in the Siege of Manhattan rose out of the water like icebergs. "Just yesterday, three coyote boats were sunk by the Border Patrol. Twenty-eight dead."

"I can't stop people from dreaming."

"These waters are heavy with the corpses of dreamers."

"Maybe less now. I sold them the good beepers." Houston shifted. Try as he might to wave away the stench of the deal, it persisted.

The men he had closed the deal with, Kilin's gang, were coyotes. They launched inflatable dinghies into the river, each one overflowing with starving migrants who had only one hope: to make it into Sovereign City and find work as nannies, cooks, or laborers. Houston knew that even with the spec-spotting Owl Sight beepers he had sold them, most of the boats would never make it. Houston's beepers would, at best, give the boats ten seconds of warning before a Sovereign Border Patrol officer arrived and blasted them out of the water. Ten seconds to jump overboard and take their chances swimming.

Bottle rockets popped and flared above the Strip. Faraz watched them quietly.

"It is an exciting time, no?" Faraz asked.

Houston shrugged. "How's the old man?"

Faraz shifted his weight. "Not the lion he once was. These Specials don't have to worry about aging. But for us normals, it is a tragic thing."

Houston nodded. He had never met Faraz's father, Mehmet, but he knew him by reputation. As a consigliere to the gilded crust of spec society, the whisper factory pegged Mehmet as the most powerful human in the Kingdom. His operation, Ibrahim & Sons, for which Faraz worked, was the best in the world at one thing: sweeping the indiscretions of rich Specials under the rug by any means necessary. From his days in the war as a CIA turncoat to today, as kingpin of a network of human spies and hatchet men (of which Houston was one), Mehmet Ibrahim cast a long shadow over the Four Provinces.

But it was over Faraz, Houston knew, that the shadow fell the heaviest.

"In any case," Faraz continued, "it is in God's hands now."

Houston snorted.

"I forgot. God is not in your vocabulary."

"Maybe he lives in there," Houston motioned toward Sovereign City. "Not out here."

"Quite the opposite."

A silence crept up on them. They had reached the end of their pleasantries, and Houston felt the mood shift. Faraz took a deep breath, preparing himself.

Here it comes. Houston braced himself. The axe about to fall.

"How long have we worked together?" Faraz asked.

"Why are you asking?"

"I think it's been four years, almost. No? Four years ago when I heard about you. This man who came here with nothing and had somehow, against all odds, built something for himself. I respected that. A businessman in all of this." Faraz swept his arm across the ragged Strip. "It's easy to be an animal out here, but you were different. I recognized your ambition—to be something more than your environment."

Faraz went quiet as a group of dockworkers strode by, singing and carrying American flags across their shoulders—an offense punishable by death only four days ago. Faraz waited until they had turned onto Hudson Street to speak again. "Do you remember that first job I gave you?"

"Kellan Askandar."

"Kellan Askandar. He would just be another overdosed spec if you hadn't pulled him out of that drug den by his ankles." Faraz chuckled. "He loved those ladyboys like no one else I know."

That was four years ago. Houston felt the old weight of the SIG Sauer in his mouth. His finger wrapped around the trigger as the Gray Faces closed in. But then Faraz had called. He'd asked Houston to find Kellan, the heir of a spec oil-drilling fortune who had gone missing in River Town. Houston found him overdosed on Moxi in the Trunk House on Velvet Lane. He'd delivered him safely and quietly back to his family. And when it was done, Faraz had snapped his fingers, and the Gray Faces had pulled back. The mighty weight of Mehmet Ibrahim's protection had fallen around Houston like a shroud. He had become Faraz's chosen River Town fixer, the finder of lost specs.

Faraz continued, "You've always been very good at what you do, Houston. Nobody else knows this town like—"

"Get to it," Houston snapped.

"Excuse me?"

Houston's patience had suddenly hit a wall. "I get it. If this peace goes through, I lose all my juice in this town. Every door my money opens closes shut, which means I can't rescue your clients anymore. So drop this memory lane bullshit and cut me loose already."

Faraz didn't blink. His brown eyes were unreadable. He cleared his throat, and Houston tensed for the blow.

"I have an assignment for you," Faraz said.

Houston looked up. "What?"

Faraz laughed, loosening for a moment. "They can sign as many peace treaties as they want, old friend. We will always need men like you."

Just then, a cluster of fireworks popped around the Kingspire. The dome of the Golden Fort shimmered underneath the display. The Decennial precelebrations were beginning.

"Can you imagine?" Faraz asked, still watching the fireworks. "It's only been ten years since one of the bloodiest wars in history, and already they're celebrating it."

"They won. They get to do whatever they want."

"I suppose." Faraz looked at him. "What did you want when you arrived here ten years ago?"

"The same thing all the dreamers want," Houston said, looking toward the city.

"And what if I told you that, after this job is done, you will have it?"

"I'd say you're lying."

"This is a big client, Houston, with influence all the way to the top. Guaranteed Gold Stamp upon completion."

Houston had to steady himself on the rail. The fireworks felt like they were bursting behind his eyes.

The world spun.

*

A Gold Stamp.

Men killed and pillaged to get their hands on one. Whores down on Velvet Lane sold their bodies to rich specs for a taste of its power. Desperate nobodies packed themselves into shitty boats and drowned in the Hudson.

All for that one shot at a Gold Stamp.

It was neither a stamp nor gold but simply a tiny microchip the Crown Naturalization Service embedded under the skin of your left shoulder. The chip identified its carrier to all Border Patrol checkpoints as one of the naturalized, a chosen human allowed to live and work freely across the entire Kingdom, granted all the same liberties and rights as the Specials.

When they had first met, Faraz had dangled that carrot in front of Houston.

"Take care of our clients and we will take care of you," Faraz had said. "Our resources and your local knowledge will serve as a formidable partnership. And"—Faraz had smiled, brushing his cobalt cravat—"our top-performing assets get sponsorship—full access and working rights in Sovereign City and all the Crown's provinces. Understood?"

Houston had nodded, hungry like a wild animal, licking his lips at the prospect. Because Houston had been cursed with the worst affliction a man living under occupation could have: ambition.

The Gold Stamp burned in his dreams like a fever. It was a foot in the door, a business of his own, a rocket ship out of the slums.

It was freedom.

*

"You okay, my friend?" Faraz asked.

"Yeah." Houston wiped his brow. He didn't look at the city across the water, afraid that he would wake up and it would all crumble to dust.

"I made you a promise," Faraz said. "You thought I forgot?"

"Promises are cheap. What's the job?"

"Standard pickup and delivery—one truck from point A to point B."

Before Houston could respond, Faraz's phone rang. He checked the caller ID and moved away, holding a finger up at Houston.

"Okay, send me your address," Faraz whispered into the phone.

"What's your status? Understood. Stay put. I'm on my way." He hung up, and Houston noticed a nervous twitch in his step when he returned.

"Tomorrow night," Faraz said, handing Houston a burner phone. "I'll send you the details on this."

Faraz turned and walked away. He got five steps before he stopped.

Houston watched as Faraz took a drag of his cigarette, the rest of his body frozen as if hit by an epiphany.

Faraz dropped the Murad, turned, and walked back to Houston.

"One thing you should know," Faraz began. "This job may sound simple, but my clients have made it very clear that failure will have consequences."

"Sounds like any other client," Houston said.

Houston saw a change in Faraz's eyes, as if something cold and implacable had slithered up his spine.

"It would be dangerous to think so. This is business, but I'm telling you this as a friend: these people—they are a different breed. They play by different rules."

Houston felt the warning underneath the words—the opening that Faraz was giving him to walk away from this.

"I'll wait for your call," Houston said, holding up the burner phone.

Faraz studied him for a moment. Finally, he nodded. "Godspeed, then."

4

Veena couldn't breathe as she fumbled with the faucet. Her heart was pounding, and she thought she was in a nightmare until she felt the shock of cold water against her hands. She splashed it across her face and arms desperately. She had to get this blood off *right now*.

She looked at herself in the mirror. Her makeup and hair were ruined. There was still blood in her hair, and her camouflage-print minidress was wet with it.

"*Fuck!*" she hissed.

Outside the bathroom, she could hear the crowd cheering as the DJ switched tracks.

"Ma'am, are you okay in there?" Makini called from outside the door.

"I'm fine." Veena strained to keep her voice calm. "Don't let anyone in here."

The cold water dripped down her neck and under her dress, making her shiver. She shifted her weight, and suddenly her stilettos skidded on something wet. She looked down.

Blood had pooled by her feet, trickling outward from the dead woman splayed on the white bathroom tiles behind her.

Veena covered her eyes and sobbed.

Stupid, stupid, stupid. She rested her head against the cool wall. *We were so fucking close to changing the world.*

Four Hours Earlier . . .

They buzzed about her naked body like flies.

Veena watched herself in the mirror, studying the taut lines of her body as her four beauticians fussed over her. She tried to find the places in her face and figure where others saw beauty. The society section of the *Sovereign Times* routinely described her as stunning, jaw-dropping, and—her personal favorite—a style goddess.

Sometimes Veena believed their words. But tonight, the more she looked at herself, the more she saw things she didn't like—the way her blonde hair had to be constantly styled in bangs because her hairline started too far up her head; the fact that her eyes and eyebrows were slanted at so severe an angle that they gave her the gaze of a predatory cat.

And then there were the scars.

Knotted angrily across her left shoulder blade, she had carried them with her since before the war. A memory burned into her skin, a reminder of the day—the exact moment—when her childhood had ended violently.

Her stylist straightened her hair with an iron, running the silky strands through his slim hands. Veena's two handmaidens rubbed tinted coconut butter along her long legs, giving her body a bronze sheen. Her makeup artist slashed an aggressive coat of rosebud across her lips.

Stunning. Jaw-dropping. A goddess. She would need to be all of those things tonight.

She was entering the most dangerous phase of her mission.

Just then, Shanti rushed into the bedroom from the hallway like an anxiety attack, all jangling bracelets and clomping heels. Her black hair fell across her wide eyes, and she kept having to swat it away so she could glare at her smartphone. "Veena, we have to leave in twenty minutes, okay? I don't want you late for your own show, okay?"

Veena sighed. Of all the dead weights in her entourage, it was Shanti, her Head of Public Relations, who annoyed her the most.

"Will she be there?" Veena asked, piercing Shanti with a look in the mirror.

"That's what I'm hearing. There's a good chance she'll be there."

"A good chance?" Veena wheeled on Shanti, sending her beauticians scrambling. "*A good fucking chance*? Getting her there was your entire job."

"She *will* be there. I promise you, Veena."

Veena glared at Shanti before turning back to the mirror. "Press?"

Shanti yammered off a list of boldface names. Style and beauty editors from the *Sovereign Times*, the *SugarChic* blog, *Glam Slam*, and *InFashionated* would all be present.

"—and I have a correspondent from the *Red Nation Times*—"

"No lowbloods!" Veena snapped.

Shanti fumbled with her phone. "But I thought with the ceasefire—"

"No. Fucking. Lowbloods. I don't want to see *one* human at this show."

Shanti nodded her head rapidly. "Understood."

As Shanti tottered back toward the hallway, her phone rang. "Shit. It's the venue again." She shook her head, exasperated. "God, I need a drink!"

The room froze in horrified silence.

Shanti, realizing her error, caught Veena's eyes in the mirror.

"Oh . . . I'm so sorry, Veena. I forgot. I'm so stupid—"

"Just get out."

Shanti hurried out, her big heels clattering on the hardwood.

Dumb bitch, Veena fumed, watching her go.

Thirty minutes later, Veena and her entourage stepped out of the house toward two black Escalades.

Makini, her bodyguard, who towered over most men, stood by the first SUV. She opened the back door for Veena, who checked her reflection in the tinted window before getting in. She had to admit, she looked stunning. Her black leather bodysuit was cinched so tight that she could barely breathe. But with its slashed zippers, bandoliers, and sheer lace panels, it made her feel the way she always wanted to—unique, unforgettable, and *dangerous*.

She blew her reflection a kiss and slipped into the back of the truck alone, with Makini up front. The rest of her entourage loaded into the second truck. The big gates opened, and the trucks rolled out into the streets of Victory Island. Starlet Manor, her sprawling estate, disappeared behind her as they sped past other, even more marvelous homes glimpsed behind high stone walls. Next door to her was Melody House, home to the Songbird, the Kingdom's most famous performer. Down the road, they passed the ornate gates of legendary actor Gregory Hunt's home.

Veena wondered why people that famous would choose to live out here. Even though escaping the temptations of Sovereign City had been a necessity for her, out here in the affluent strip they used to call Great Neck in Long Island, she dreaded the quiet loneliness that came with every sunset.

It's all temporary. She lowered her window and inhaled the cool night air. *Everything is about to change.*

*

Veena was twenty-four years old and already one of the most recognizable Specials in the world.

Her beauty was legend in the Four Provinces. She had graced the billboards in Victory Square more than any other model in the Kingdom's short history. She had starred in two wildly successful dramas before the unrest out west had shut down the California movie industry. Alistair Glam, the city's most influential fashion analyst, cooed constantly about her revolutionary "militant-romantic" personal style on his famous blog, the *Glam Slam*. Sonia Casablanca, from the number one-rated morning talk show, *Casablanca Rising*, filmed Veena for a whole month just to dissect every aspect of her vegan diet and rigorous yoga practice.

Veena's fashion line, VSIX, which she launched when she was still in the Royal Design Institute, was haute couture, shockingly expensive, and sold out in minutes. Even the humans in Europe and Asia, who were banned from buying Specials goods, scoured the black markets for her slashed leather leggings and lusciously demented raincoats studded with shell casings.

Money and fame rained down in buckets. Models, actors, and athletes competed for a place in her bed. To the outside world, she was the girl who had it all.

But her addiction was crippling her.

It had started at Haughton Academy, the private school her father had sent her to after the war. She got hooked to vodka at first before accelerating rapidly into the amphetamines and benzos. By the time she'd entered the Royal Design Institute at eighteen, she was a full-on coke slag.

But it was Moxi that changed everything.

Cool, silver-powdered Moxi. Into her veins, up her nose, bursting like a field of dazzling flowers behind her eyes. It was at all the parties and all the clubs, backstage at runway shows— wherever beautiful people were.

On Moxi, Veena felt reborn.

Because in those fleeting hours of the high, she could forget the shameful reality of what she really was: a Beta Special. And all the bright lights and money in the world wouldn't change that.

*

The private ferry ushered Veena and her Escalades across the East River. Veena stood on the bow and watched as, above her, eight Specials flew across the night sky toward the city.

Fucking humiliating. Veena seethed. Every bridge onto the island had been demolished during the war, and the only ways in were to fly or take a boat. She bit down on something bitter as the cruising Specials disappeared in the glow of the skyline.

They were Alphas. Their Gift was strong.

That's what they'd begun calling it in those frenzied few weeks after the Incident in Salt Lake City twenty years ago, when *something*—to this day, nobody knew what—rippled across the western United States and brought the Gift to millions of people, transforming them into Specials, immortal and untouchable by time.

The Gift manifested in unlimited ways, magnified or dampened by some internal alchemy in its host that no science could explain. Some could fly, some became psychics and seers, and still others channeled their newfound powers into artistic creations that defied belief. The Gift created a new race, far up the ladder of evolution from humans.

But even within the race of Specials, there was a hierarchy.

The Alphas were those like the king and her father, whose Gift surged violent and majestic like a monsoon river. The Alphas had won the war, and now they ruled the aftermath.

And then there were the Betas.

Like Veena.

Those for whom the Gift was a trickle, the feeble drip of a faucet echoing inside their bodies.

Weakness—her father's term for it.

Veena gripped the ferry's railing and unclenched her jaw. She studied the skull ring on her left index finger. She focused on it intently and, with great effort, channeled her Gift to slide it off her finger and hover it precariously in the air for a few seconds. The effort exhausted her, and she had to snatch the ring out of the air before it dropped into the river.

Shame crackled behind her eyes.

She, the daughter of the second most powerful Special in history, could barely keep five grams of silver afloat without popping a blood vessel in her brain.

She was closer to a human lowblood than a Special.

A *fucking lowblood.* The thought enraged her. She hated them as much as her father did. In that way—and that way only—they were alike.

As the ferry drew closer to shore, Veena gazed upon the Silver Spear rising endlessly from the southern tip of the island. Where the rest of the skyline curved, glittered, and flowed, the Silver Spear stood monolithic and unadorned, an obsidian tower that lorded over the city—her father's fortress.

He wouldn't be at her show tonight. His office hadn't even bothered to respond to her invite. It didn't surprise her.

Not after what had happened last time.

*

Eighteen months ago, on a bitterly cold December night, something inside Veena had snapped.

Her show that evening was supposed to be her most personal yet—her magnum opus, a collection that veered dramatically away from her canon of leather and provocation and into the unblemished innocence of her childhood before the war. It was a work of reverence for a lost time, for a lost bond with the one person Veena had ever truly felt love for.

She had named the show *Memories of Mable.*

It seemed, on that fateful evening, that *everyone* in the Kingdom was in attendance.

Veena had once blamed the gut-wrenching horror of what followed on Moxi. But she knew that was a lie.

The breakdown had started a long time ago.

She had felt it coming for years—a blackness so cold it stole her breath. And on the edges of the void, she saw *it.*

The fire. Reaching out to touch her.

On that December night, as the awful failure of *Memories of Mable* sloshed around inside her, she found herself in the blank reaches of the East River Yards, the smell of gasoline thick in the air and a lit match in her hand.

She released the fire into the world.

Veena felt nothing as she watched the warehouse burn. As she listened to the screams of the women inside.

The ferry shuddered as it slotted into the docks. Veena felt her heart quicken with the sudden feeling of resurrection that the city always gave her. She gazed at the Silver Spear for some time before turning back to her Escalade.

No matter what her father thought of her now, very soon he would realize what she was really made of. She just had to hold her nerve tonight.

*

"Quick detour," she instructed her driver through the intercom as they cleared customs and merged onto the King's Loop heading downtown. "Stop off at the Shining Path."

"Yes, ma'am." The driver U-turned back uptown.

Veena's phone buzzed immediately. Shanti was already hyperventilating on the other end. "You're going the wrong direction! We're going to the West Village—omigod, Veena, we're *so* late. We—"

"Shut your flapping cunt."

Veena could practically hear Shanti's jaw hang open.

"Go to the show. Do not follow me. I'll be there soon."

She hung up. The Escalade wound its way up the East King's Loop and entered the sparkling canyon of Midtown.

The city felt strangely empty. It took a moment for Veena to realize what was missing.

The slaves.

Before the ceasefire, the city was overrun with slave construction crews laboring to raise Sovereign City from the war's aftermath. Now, in their absence, she watched small crews of human contractors hang up banners and construct the stages for the Grand Decennial celebrations. It was Thursday, May 24th, and on Monday the 28th at midnight, it would be ten years since Victory Day, and Sovereign City would become the center of the universe.

On every block, giant garlands of gold and blue hung above the streets. The stone facades of the buildings were lit up with spotlights, and everywhere Veena looked she saw the one image that had held the young kingdom together in a religious fervor—the sigil of the Risen King.

The symbol was everywhere—glowing on posters in storefront windows, hanging in drapes across the Crown municipal buildings, plastered along the sides of cars and archways. A gold silhouette of the king, his arms outstretched and his body ascending in flight against a cobalt sky. It was the flag of the new Kingdom, depicting the king's resurrection in the war's darkest hour—the moment Patriot Gold transformed from a freedom fighter into a god.

Veena snorted. After all these years, she saw it for what it really was: propaganda. She didn't doubt the story of the king's murder at the hands of the lowblood army and his miraculous resurrection. Every Special in the kingdom had seen the verified video of the event. It was not the wartime Patriot Gold that Veena questioned. It was the man he had become—weak, vacillating, and overeager to compromise with lowbloods. The Risen King was a symbol of a nation holding onto an old war, blind to the new one on its doorstep.

*

Veena had just turned fourteen when the humans surrendered. She had spent the five years of the Immortal War being shuttled frantically from one bunker to the next, dodging the massive mechs that hunted her. Every night in her twisted dreams she heard the thud of their giant footsteps, the terrifying grind of their gears as they loped over the horizon.

But the one thing she hated most about her war experience—more than the damp shelters and the terror of the mechs—was having to put up with Callista Von Arx.

Fragile, flowery Callista and her feckless older brother, Caspar (*definitely a fag*, Veena decided on their first meeting) were the only heirs of the ancient Von Arx family, the shadowy clan whose massive industrial empire had financed Patriot Gold's rebellion. They had been packed up along with Veena into a constant game of hide-and-seek with the humans, who knew their value as hostages. Veena—the only daughter of the Special's most feared warrior, the Warbringer himself—and the Von Arx children, whose capture would mean a choice for their parents between the lives of their children and their funding of Patriot Gold.

"I'm so glad I have a friend like you," sixteen-year old Callista would cry into Veena's shoulder in those dank bunkers as bombs fell around them. Veena would smile and swallow her disgust at this snot-filled little fairy who had latched onto her like a tick. Back then, she would have given anything to never hear Callista's weepy voice again.

How things change, Veena thought as the Escalade wound its way deeper into the capital. Now, like a once-lost puzzle piece slotting into place to reveal the whole picture, Callista had become the linchpin in Veena's plan.

*

"Ma'am, I should go with you," Makini said, her raspy voice clashing with the mountainous size of her frame as she watched Veena step out of the Escalade.

"Watch me from here."

"I can't protect you from here."

"Trust me, Makini. I'll be fine." Veena wrapped a gray scarf around her head like a shawl and covered herself in a black cotton trench. She traded her stilettos for flats and quickly walked out onto the Shining Path, feeling Makini's eyes on her back.

She kept her head down as her feet hit the wide paving stones. The Shining Path stretched for a quarter mile through what used to be Central Park, a picturesque walkway split lengthwise by massive marble dioramas of the Immortal War's greatest legends. Serene gardens spread across either side of the walk, dotted with benches and the amber glow of lanterns.

Such a beautiful night, Veena thought as she watched fireflies drifting in and out of the trees. She used to come here often before her rehab at Crosslake, finding solace from her hangovers in the lush, endless gardens. Being so close to the seat of power cleared her head in a way she couldn't explain.

She turned away from the fireflies and focused on the spectacle ahead of her. The white walkway led up a slope, exploding at its apex through a series of towering bronze gates into the jaw-dropping splendor of the Golden Fort.

The Fort rose above the grounds as if it had been there for centuries. Built upon a hill, it was the home of King Patriot Gold—a royal citadel within the city. The massive structure was formed of red sandstone inlaid with intricate carvings, and it watched over the island like the Hagia Sophia, golden domes flashing in the dark between four garrisoned towers.

It took her breath away this close. As she stood there admiring it, a group of tourists bumped by her, jabbering excitedly and snapping pictures.

Hillbillies. She watched them pass. She hated how these hordes from the Four Provinces, in town for the Decennial, had turned her beloved sanctuary into a rowdy bus station.

In any case, she had to hurry. Her meeting was about to start.

Picking up her pace, she headed toward the First Wall.

The First Wall—one of three circling the Fort—stood high and strong, its massive bronze gates shut. Two Phoenix Guards, the elite protectors of the Royal Family, stood watch on either side of the gate, wearing their ceremonial bronze armor and masked helmets. Veena's heart skipped even though she knew that the two soldiers were the least of her worries. Her main concern was the threats she couldn't see: the plainclothes SSD agents patrolling the grounds, hunting for heretics.

The sound of her own footsteps became uncomfortably loud. Her breathing grew ragged, and a cold sweat formed on the back of her neck. She felt naked, as if everyone around the Fort could see straight through her flesh and detect the treason in her heart.

Why would he want to meet here? To plot a revolution this close to the target—it made no sense. Another thought rose up in her like cold bile: *What if this is a trap?*

She considered running.

No. She steeled herself. *This is my destiny.*

A hundred feet from the First Wall, she reached the Fountain of Fire. Here, the bisected walkways of the Shining Path merged to form a massive circle, the fountain rising like a mountain in its center. The water tumbled down white marble slopes as underwater lights made the surface glitter like diamonds. Atop it all rose the fearsome, war-bringing figure of her father.

General Sixkills, Supreme Leader of the Silverbacks, sculpted eighteen feet high in Carrara marble and towering fiercely over the bodies of six humans. The humans—twisted, demonic beings—clawed at his massive legs. It was too baroque for Veena's taste, but she had to admit it accurately captured her father's fury on that day.

Veena had only been seven when Sixkills had, according to the historians, "lit the match that ignited the Immortal War." She remembered watching the trial of the Buffalo Six on TV;

those six angry lowbloods who had murdered Javeer Sharma, a twelve-year old Special walking home from school. When a human jury had acquitted them of all charges, it was Veena's father who had taken justice into his own hands, swept down onto the courthouse steps amid screams of terror, and executed all six in front of the cameras, immortalizing himself in Special legend under his new name: Sixkills. Veena had never been prouder of him than on that day.

She turned away from the fountain. Not for the first time, she noted that she had spent more time with this sculpture than with her own father. Pulling her scarf lower over her face, she sat on the edge of the fountain and waited. Her show was about to start, and she had five minutes to spare at the most.

The minutes ticked by. Five minutes turned to eight.

It was all a hoax. She bit her lip angrily. *All this for nothing.*

She was about to stand when he sat down beside her. The man was slim and dressed forgettably. His face was turned away from her as he placed a package between them on the ledge.

Veena looked down at the package. It was a flat black box wrapped in a black ribbon. She noticed a small pink rose logo on the top right corner.

The man shifted like a spooked bird. He put his hand on the package.

"He sends his regards," Veena said suddenly, surprising herself.

The man didn't turn. For a sickening moment, Veena thought she had said the greeting wrong.

"He Who Knows All," he replied softly, still looking away.

"He Who Knows All has shown me fire," Veena responded.

"Then let His work be done." The man stood and walked south, away from the Fort. Within seconds he was gone.

The box remained next to Veena, where he had left it.

*

The narrow lanes of the West Village were choked with paparazzi. They lunged forward from behind the barricades, their cameras held forth like weapons as they tried to capture Veena's arrival.

Veena's Escalade pulled up to the red carpet in front of the armory. Glossy banners hung across the red brick facade, reading *Seasons of the Queen ~ The VSIX Spring Collection*.

When Veena stepped out of the truck, the world exploded in flashbulbs. Makini barreled through the paparazzi like a grumpy wrecking ball, Veena gliding behind in her wake. As they shouldered past the hurled questions and lunging microphones, Veena felt the dangerous bulk of the black box under her jacket. Makini pulled her through the open bay doors, and they stepped into a dark hallway.

"Oh, thank God!" Shanti yelled, clattering down the hallway toward Veena, hands flapping in panic. "I thought you were—" Shanti's mouth fell open as her foot hit the corner of a rug and she tumbled facedown at Veena's feet.

"Don't worry about me!" Shanti pleaded from the floor. "Just get to your dressing room. Your show's about to start!"

*

Veena couldn't do it.

The trio of models had just swept off the catwalk and the music track changed, thumping across the cavernous hall beyond the curtains.

That was Veena's cue. Yet her legs wouldn't move.

She was dimly aware that she was backstage and that someone was trying desperately to get her attention. The face was blurred, the voice blathering incoherently.

Veena couldn't breathe.

She couldn't do this.

The last time she had stepped out on the catwalk had been eighteen months ago, surrounded by the horrified faces of the audience . . .

Panic surged through Veena's chest, and suddenly she was moving away from the stage, back toward her dressing room. She had to get out of here.

And then, like He had on that freezing night on the roof of the Crosslake Retreat, He spoke to her.

His voice whispered in no known language. He was simply a vibration she felt in her bones, and suddenly all of Veena's senses snapped back to high definition.

Once again, He showed her the future.

The clarity was stunning. White fire bloomed and ate the world. Veena felt the terrible heat on her skin.

And then, when the flames cleared, she was walking barefoot on asphalt, her hands chained. The bloodthirsty mob of humans called for her head, and she knew that if she did not walk onto that stage—if she shrank from her mission—that only an awful death awaited her.

"Veena, please! You have to go now!"

Veena's eyes shot open. She recognized Shanti's terrified face inches from her own. Veena shoved her away and turned to the curtains.

She ran her hand down the cool silk of her strapless gown. She remembered how she had gasped with pleasure when, locked in her private dressing room a few minutes ago, she had lifted the dress out of the smuggled black box.

It was silk, a stunning shade of peacock blue that reflected the light in wonderful ways. The corset was embroidered with intricate gold vines that swirled down the skirt into a forest of blooming orchids and prancing white foxes. It was the most beautiful dress that Veena had ever designed. And yet, up until the man had handed her the black box, she had only seen it in her sketches. It had been a wild, intoxicating creation that had eaten up a better part of the past year, born of an otherworldly inspiration that coursed through her like lava. Ever since her return from rehab, ever since He had first chosen her, the creation of this dress—this jeweled Trojan horse—had become Veena's obsession. And then, when the design was done, she did as He had instructed and handed over the designs. To whom, she did not know for certain. A crew of very specialized—and dangerous—fabricators would be her best guess.

A chill entered her bones. As beautiful as the gown looked, she would be wise not to forget what it was—a weapon.

"Veena . . ." Shanti whimpered.

Veena took a deep breath.

"Trust Him," she whispered to herself. She sucked in her stomach, rose to her full height, and strode out onto the catwalk.

The cheers smashed into her like a gale.

Camera flashes turned the world white. She couldn't see more than five feet in front of her. Around her she caught glimpses of the magical wonderland built for her show, unrecognizable to anyone who had been to her past shows. Instead of chains and strobes, there were prancing horses, shooting stars, and phoenixes soaring above the audience's head—a fantasyland built for one special person.

With each powerful step, her body felt like it was filling up with electrified air. The music boomed as she reached the end of the catwalk and then, with a flourish, dropped her chin and leveled her gaze downward. Immediately, she locked eyes with the woman sitting in the front row.

Queen Callista's face lit up in a stunning smile as she looked upon her old friend.

For Veena, the queen's circle of Phoenix Guards, handmaidens, and advisers might as well not have been there. All that existed were the two old friends encased in a silent bubble.

Veena held the pose, letting her gown blaze under the lights.

With one last smile at Callista, she spun on her heel and stalked back up the catwalk.

The cheers rose like a tsunami, lifting her until she felt like she was flying.

5

"**I**s she here?" Veena demanded again over the heavy bass line. The thunderous music reverberated off the gothic arches, threatening to rip the cavernous Tangle nightclub off its hinges.

Shanti fumbled with her phone, squinting at the screen in the darkness. "No. Not yet," she stuttered, on the verge of panic.

"You promised me she'd be here. Fucking hell, Shanti!"

"She was! The queen was at your show!"

"And she left!" Veena barked. "You were supposed to keep her there until I could talk to her."

Shanti recoiled, her lower lip trembling. "I'm sorry, Veena. She left before I could stop her. Please don't hate me—she's the queen. I can't control her schedule."

Veena tossed her cranberry juice in Shanti's face. Shanti gaped dumbly, her face and neck glistening. Before she could cry, Shanti spun around and scurried off to her boyfriend, Kormedia, who at that moment was showing a group of models his latest forearm tattoo. He grimaced when Shanti sobbed into his shirt.

Veena gripped the balcony rail and scanned the packed dance floor below, feeling achingly sober as she watched her fashion show's after-party reach its frenetic peak.

At the armory, Veena had rushed off the stage and tried to intercept Callista after the lights had come up. But the queen had already left by then, swept out of the show by her royal handlers.

Veena cursed herself for leaving an imbecile like Shanti in charge of such a fluid situation. It was her first mistake of the night and possibly a fatal one.

She felt a heavy hand on her shoulder. She turned to see Makini frowning at her.

"Ma'am," Makini rasped, "there's someone here for you."

"I thought I told you no more visitors," Veena said.

"Ma'am, this one is important."

The tone of Makini's voice made Veena's alarms ring. She looked past her bodyguard to the figure waiting by the velvet rope barrier.

At first Veena thought she was looking at a statue, so enormous was the man. He wore a navy suit, a crisp white shirt, and a navy tie. An earpiece wire curled out from his shirt collar.

The man calmly flashed a badge as Veena and Makini approached. The king's phoenix-and-sword sigil shimmered in the strobes. Underneath the sigil, Veena read, *Phoenix Guard Battalion—CPC.*

The Crown Protection Command, Veena realized with a start. This giant was one of the Royal Family's personal bodyguards.

"We need to speak to you," he growled into Veena's ear. It was not a request.

*

It was not the queen waiting for her in the club's loading dock.

Veena's stomach turned at the sight of the figure waiting for her. It was a man she knew well.

Man was not the right description for him. He was tall but foppish, grinning and gangly like an awkward teen in his garishly brocaded jacket and slacks. Now, just like the first time Veena had met him as a child, he struck her as a predatory nitwit.

"So lovely to see you, Veena." Caspar Von Arx smirked, the narrow smile missing his eyes by a mile. "You were *tres beautifique* tonight."

"Caspar. Such a treat to see you again." They air-kissed, and she smelled the lavender of an expensive French soap on his collar.

Caspar said something, but Veena missed it. Her heart was thrashing in her chest.

Breathe, Veena. Breathe.

Caspar Von Arx was the queen's older brother, the only male heir to the Von Arx fortune. And yet, on account of his impeccable taste in Moxi and lowblood hookers, Caspar securely occupied the position of family black sheep. It was a title he wasn't going to relinquish anytime soon.

"Is the queen here?" Veena blurted suddenly.

"Unfortunately, no. Queen Callista had Crown business to attend to—the Parade and all that. She did, however, ask me to relay a message."

"Really? Regarding what?"

"She loved your show." Caspar's eyes lit up, as if channeling his sister. "She felt so honored that you would dedicate an entire collection to her. Especially that last outfit. In her words, 'it struck a chord in her heart.'"

Stupid Callista.

"That is so wonderful to hear." Veena smiled.

"The queen would love to have tea with you tomorrow and thank you in person. It has been ages since the two of you spent any time together."

"It would be my honor to have tea with Her Majesty."

"Excellent. She will expect you at 5:00 p.m. at the Lady's Eye. Congratulations again on the show."

Caspar grazed her arm with his hand. He held her eyes with his, and Veena felt the sensation of spiders crawling up her spine.

He swept past her to the exit, taking the massive Phoenix Guard—and the scent of lavender—with him.

*

After her meeting with Caspar, Veena went back up to the VIP balcony to grab her coat. Her job for the night was done, and the music was giving her a headache. Coat in hand, she and Makini headed toward the private elevator. They had almost reached it when a strange woman blocked their way.

The woman locked eyes with Veena and smiled. Makini moved forward to intercept her, but the woman held up her hands.

"I'd just like to congratulate her," the woman said, looking from Makini to Veena.

Veena studied the woman. She had long raven hair with a startling streak of white across the right side. Her black dress was vintage, and her red platform slingbacks had gone out of style years ago. Veena motioned to Makini to stand down.

"Let me introduce myself," the woman said, her eyes boring into Veena. "My name is Esther Neel. Have you heard of me?"

The way she asked the question irritated Veena. "Should I have?" Veena asked, startled by the woman's crushing handshake.

"Can I buy you a drink?" Esther asked, ignoring Veena's question.

"Excuse me?"

"Don't take it personally. I just thought you were much more interesting before you went sober."

Veena stopped cold. "What did you just say?"

"I'm sorry; I didn't mean to offend you. It's just a habit, you see. People in my line of work can be quite confrontational."

"Your line of work?"

"I'm the Managing Editor for the *Red Nation Times*. That's a human newspaper, in case you were wondering. I know you don't read a lot."

Veena gasped. The woman in front of her was a Redblood. The same Redblood terrorists that had killed dozens of Specials in attacks and bombings all over the Kingdom, that had called for her and her father's heads on stakes.

How the fuck did she get into my party?

"Your king invited me, thinking that we may like your collection,"

Esther remarked, as if she had read Veena's mind. "He's so eager for all of us to just get along. To be honest, I wasn't too eager to attend your show. Your past collections were a tad too derivative of Rick Owens for my taste."

"Since when did lowbloods have taste?"

Esther's eyes narrowed at the slur. "I expected as much from you. You're like your father—a simple brute." Esther tilted her head. "It must be hard trying to forge your identity on the ashes of better people."

"You think a ceasefire will protect you?"

Esther eyed Veena from head to toe, her lips curling up into a grim smile. "The question is, Veena, do you think it will protect *you*?"

Veena's hands trembled. She was too shocked to speak. Esther Neel, still smiling, brushed by Veena and stepped inside the VIP ladies' room.

A cold fist clenched around Veena's heart.

A fucking lowblood. A fucking, insolent, mangy, disgusting lowblood—

Veena's world shrank into a black tunnel. She moved forward as if on rails. She stationed Makini outside the ladies' room door and swept in quietly.

Esther was the only one in there. She had just stepped out of the stall when Veena entered. The smirk on her face died when she saw the look in Veena's eyes.

Esther took a half step back and made a move to reach into her purse, but Veena closed the distance fast.

She covered Esther's mouth with one hand and clawed at her eyes with the other. Esther fell backward, her head smashing against the tiles. She cried out as Veena dropped her knee into her stomach.

Veena swung her fist in frenetic arcs, smashing into the soft tissue of Esther's face and throat, collapsing cartilage and bone. Blood spurted warmly on Veena's skin.

Dirty, filthy lowblood.

The human's black-and-white hair splayed out across the tiles. She tried to scream, but Veena pressed down on her mouth. Esther's teeth cut into her palm. Veena recoiled.

Something caught Veena's eye under the sink.

One of Esther's shiny red slingbacks.

Time blinked. The shoe was suddenly in Veena's right hand, her left hand wrapped around Esther's throat. Somewhere far away, she heard fabric rip.

Veena raised the heel high above her head and savored the terrified bulge of Esther's eyes before swinging the shoe down with sickening force. Again and again and again.

Esther stopped making sounds. Her head lolled to her right shoulder at an odd angle.

Veena stood over her. Every breath she took felt like fire. Her nose dripped snot, and her eyes were wet. Slowly, she stumbled over to the sinks.

Veena couldn't breathe as she fumbled with the faucet. She had to get this blood off *right now.*

"*Fuck!*" she hissed

"Ma'am, are you okay in there?" Makini called from outside the door.

"I'm fine." Veena strained to keep her voice calm. "Don't let anyone in here." She shifted her weight, and suddenly her stilettos skidded on Esther's blood.

Veena covered her eyes and sobbed. *Stupid, stupid, stupid.* She rested her head against the cool wall. *We were so fucking close to changing the world.*

She dialed a number on her phone.

Faraz picked up on the second ring.

"I need you here. Now."

"Okay. Send me the address. What's your status?"

"Tangle nightclub. Status: totally fucked."

"Understood. Stay put. I'm on my way."

6

E*xtraction.*

Disposal.

Alibi.

EDA—the acronym hammered into the heads of every Ibrahim & Sons consultant by the big man himself, Mehmet. Right now, Faraz's brain was scanning down the mental checklist as he watched massive hydraulic plates descend on Esther Neel.

Extraction. Esther Neel's body had been whisked out of the Tangle nightclub by a team of his father's men, and the VIP bathroom had been scrubbed clean after Veena had left the premises.

Disposal. Currently underway. Next to him, Jacinto, the disposal center foreman, adjusted his hard hat and watched as the compactor plates bore down on the Mazda Miata holding Esther. The same Jacinto, here in this Bronx scrapyard, who had done this very same thing to Faraz's Porsche Spyder last year.

Faraz focused on the third item: alibi.

"What you gonna do?" Jacinto asked, as if he knew what Faraz was thinking.

"About what?"

"That's one of us in there." He pointed to Esther. "Not a good time for our people to be dying, you know? Ceasefire and all."

Faraz bristled. He knew that Jacinto would never question his father so boldly. "That is not your concern."

Alibi. He would have to call Rick, the nightlife correspondent over at the *Sovereign Times.* Plug in a story about Esther Neel making a scene as she left Veena's party. Then coordinate with his contact over at the Border Patrol data station to falsify the exit logs to prove that Esther Neel left the city drunk behind the wheel.

Faraz rubbed his eyes. His meeting with Houston was supposed to have been the night's final task—arrange the covert transportation of the Sun Angel into River Town and then go home for some much-needed rest. But then his most important client, Veena Sixkills, had intervened.

The thick plate cracked down on the Miata, crunching metal and shattering glass.

Faraz took a step back. His vision suddenly narrowed and darkened, his lungs constricting.

Jacinto said something that Faraz missed as he stumbled toward the latrines. Something rose up inside him sickeningly.

He shouldered the door of the latrines open and ran for the sinks. For what felt like a long time, he doused his face and hair in cold water. Outside, the machinery still whined. It took Faraz three tries to turn the water off, his hands were shaking so badly.

It was the sound of breaking glass, the memory of it, that had shaken him.

In those moments right after he'd crashed his Spyder into a lamppost, all Faraz could think about was Nadia and Yasmin. He was upside down in the roadster's twisted shell, glass from the smashed windows everywhere.

Faraz knew he was going to die. But rather than feeling fear, all he felt was shame. The flygirl next to him was dead, her white dress doused with blood and her limbs twisted horrifically. Just a few seconds ago she had been laughing, her hand dangerously high on Faraz's leg. He didn't turn to look at her. His thoughts were only on his wife and child. His father. How far he had fallen. How he had failed as a husband, a father, and a son.

The compactor outside fell silent. Faraz dried his face with paper towels, straightened his hair, and walked back to the yard, where Jacinto was waiting for him. What had once been the Miata and Esther Neel was now sitting on the loading platform, a dense metallic cube no bigger than an armchair.

"How's your father?" Jacinto asked.

"Unchanged."

"Give him my best. He's a great man."

Faraz didn't respond. He was already walking to his car, feeling exhausted. The work of a situation consultant never seemed to end.

*

Since he had started working for her over a year ago, Faraz had wondered when exactly he would see the real Veena Sixkills.

That snowy morning two winters ago when he had pulled up to the front gates of the Crosslake Retreat, he had been surprised by the woman who had walked out.

His instructions for that day had been vague: arrive at the retreat in Saratoga Springs at 11:00 a.m. sharp and collect a passenger. He did as he was told and waited outside the stately manor, the car's heater struggling against the frosty air.

At first glance, Crosslake Retreat, with its elegant main house and green fields, looked like a charming hotel. But everyone knew that behind its resort exterior, Crosslake was really a discreet rehab clinic for drug-addled spec aristocrats. Before his accident, Faraz had shuttled at least forty specs back and forth between the retreat and the city, every one of them under the spell of Moxi, the synthetic drug flowing out of the western shadowlands.

Even humans could get addicted to it—badly addicted, as Faraz knew from experience. His blood had been boiling with Moxi the night of the crash. And Faraz didn't have the benefit of a place like Crosslake to kick his habit. He'd had to do it alone, sweating his life away in a hospital bed with a broken femur and three cracked ribs.

His passenger arrived late. At a stroke before noon, the gates of the retreat had opened and a frail woman in a dark jacket and white jeans had stepped out. Wisps of blonde hair strayed out from under her jacket's hood, and it wasn't until she slid into the back seat that he realized who she was.

He drove Veena Sixkills to her Victory Island home in silence. She gazed out the window and rubbed her arms nervously. To Faraz, it seemed impossible that this skinny, nervous thing was the same woman who had burned sixteen of her own seamstresses alive.

Faraz had kept his eyes off his sullen passenger. He was well aware that Veena had inherited her father's legendary hatred of humans. And yet, for some reason, he had been chosen to watch over her.

And so he did. He cleared her homes of all alcohol and Moxi. He deleted the numbers of all her dealers. He visited her weekly, ensuring she was focused on designing her new collection and not sneaking back out to the party circuit. She'd barely said a word to him the whole time. Her subdued, solitary persona was a far cry from the hell-raiser he had heard about. No matter how she behaved in front of him, he always worried about the day when the Veena Sixkills of old would show herself.

Well, here it is, Faraz thought as he drove away from the scrapyard, the image of Esther Neel's bloody corpse still fresh in his mind. *The real Veena Sixkills.*

*

Faraz hung up his call with his contact at the *Sovereign Times* as he rode the elevator to the seventeenth floor. One job done. Tomorrow's online edition of the *Times* gossip section would now include a short piece about how Esther Neel had been seen stumbling out of the Tangle nightclub at 2:00 a.m., hurling slurs against Specials before driving away.

The elevator doors opened and Faraz turned left, towards the entrance for a company called Horizon Ventures Fund. He scanned his ID card, waited for the heavy bolts to unlock, and then swept through the doors.

Faraz still had one more call to make. His agent at the Border Patrol was going off her shift in fifteen minutes, and he needed to ensure that Esther's name was on the city's exit logs before sunrise.

He branched deep into the secret offices of Ibrahim & Sons, his wingtips padding along the plush blue carpet. It was almost five in the morning, and the cubicles were still buzzing with ringing phones and whispered voices. The life of an Ibrahim & Sons employee, Faraz knew, was work first, everything else last.

He passed the Istiklal Conference Room with its wall of windows overlooking the Royal Design Institute. Sovereign City was still alive outside, with Specials flying between the buildings and massive Risen King billboards animating above the streets. In the gap between buildings, he glimpsed the turquoise waters of the Emerald Ring.

Yasmin loved the Ring. She would squeal with joy in Faraz's arms as the gondoliers ferried them around the dazzling canal, the breeze ruffling her hair.

Faraz shook off the memory before it could grip him. He reached his tiny office down a hallway, at the opposite end of the building from his father's command center with its big black doors flanked by golden griffins.

Not an accident, Faraz knew. The vast distance between Mehmet's lair and Faraz's backwater cubby was a subtle, yet stinging, rebuke for the crash.

He sat down at his desk in the windowless office. A framed picture of him, Nadia, and three-year-old Yasmin stood next to his laptop. Yasmin would be almost five now. He felt the urge to call Nadia. To wake her up and hear her voice. She would hang up on him immediately.

He was scanning his online database, searching for his Border Patrol contact's number, when he heard a phone ring. For a moment he ignored it, not recognizing the ringtone.

And then he froze.

It was the ringtone of his *other* phone.

Faraz whipped out the silver Nokia, his hands sweating. Only one person had the number to this cell.

*

The Nokia phone had appeared right when he was ready to give up.

His first month back in the office after the crash, he felt like a dead man walking. The other consultants averted their eyes when he passed by. No new assignments landed on his desk and his old clients were gone, poached by his more enterprising colleagues.

And every time he tried to sweep through those double black doors to visit his father, he was summarily turned away by smiling secretaries. *Mister Ibrahim is busy right now. I'll let him know you stopped by.*

The chatter was too hard to ignore. Consultants, usually discrete creatures, gossiped endlessly about the succession plan. Before the accident, it was expected that Faraz would take reins of Ibrahim & Sons once his father, in failing health, stepped down. But now, Faraz's name wasn't even on the list.

Faraz hung his head in shame when he thought about it. The entire time he had been in the hospital, only his mother had come to visit. Faraz had asked about Nadia and Yasmin. His mother had just bowed her head and handed him a note from Nadia, which he read, bleary on painkillers:

You are not worthy of this family.

Nadia, who had long suspected his indiscretions, refused to see him even when he left the hospital. Refused to let him back in their home, no matter how hard Faraz pleaded for a second chance.

Six weeks out of the hospital, he had just returned from a coffee break when he found the box on his desk.

It was flat and black, embossed with a pink rose on the top-right corner. Inside he found a silver Nokia phone and a folded letter.

The letter was written on his father's personal stationery. Faraz's heart raced as he unfolded the crisp paper. There were only two simple words floating in the stark whiteness, written in Mehmut's severe hand:

Last chance.

The Nokia had rung immediately. It was a number Faraz didn't recognize, and his voice cracked when he answered. The woman's voice on the other end was soft and clipped, the emotion stripped from every syllable. Faraz had listened, his breath quickening as he realized what this was—an assignment.

A second chance from his father.

The woman did not ask any questions. She told him very clearly what she expected of him.

Arrive at Crosslake Retreat tomorrow morning at 11:00 a.m. sharp. Pick up the passenger who leaves the front gates.

*

Faraz shut the door to his office and picked up the call. The woman's voice on the other end simply said, "Octavia Park, fifteen minutes." She hung up.

A meeting, Faraz thought, troubled.

He had never met his contact before, this mysterious woman who acted as his father's messenger. What had prompted this sudden meeting? At this time of night, it couldn't mean anything good.

Faraz shook off those dark thoughts as he took the elevator down. He hadn't had a chance to contact his Border Patrol agent, but he felt that could wait. He had a feeling his father's messenger was not one to tolerate tardiness.

Faraz hurried down the three blocks to Octavia Park on Fifty-Sixth Street. It was a narrow strip of trees and cement lanes wedged between two construction sites. In the dim lamplight, Faraz couldn't see anyone inside. But he knew this park's reputation; starving human migrants would hide here, ready to rob unsuspecting passersby.

Faraz wondered if something worse than a mugger awaited him under those trees.

He stepped inside the park, his eyes scanning warily. After wiping the surface of a bench with his sleeve, he sat down directly under the statue of Lady Octavia. A breeze rustled the leaves above him.

She sat next to him, appearing as if she had been there all along. Faraz shot up, startled.

"Sit down, Faraz," she said in her clipped tone.

Faraz caught his breath. He sat down slowly.

She wore a high-collared navy trench, upon which her hands shone a shockingly pale white. Her face was hidden from Faraz, covered in a silk scarf and sunglasses.

She was elegant, even delicate. She belonged in one of the cafes on Sky Avenue, holding a dainty teacup and watching the well-heeled shoppers.

"Why are we meeting here?" Faraz asked.

"I like it here."

"It's dangerous."

"Nonsense. Let's walk, Faraz." She stood up and waited for him to follow. They walked down winding lanes overhung with elm branches.

"Eighty-eight," she said suddenly.

"What?"

She pointed at a tree by the path. Faraz followed her finger and squinted until he saw it—a thumb-sized brass sculpture of a man wearing coveralls and a hard hat. He was climbing up the tree like it was an electrical pole.

"I've found eighty-eight so far."

"I think my daughter has found the same number," Faraz said. Yasmin used to drag him and Nadia to this park in her hunt for the hundred and twenty-four tiny sculptures that were hidden in the landscape, each one representing a Special that Lady Octavia had rescued from the US government's wartime concentration camps. It was supposed to mean a lifetime of good luck if you found them all.

"I don't want you to worry, Faraz," she said.

"I'm not sure I know what you mean."

"Your father wants you to succeed him. He is waiting to see if you are capable of doing so. So far, you have done exceptionally well. And if you continue like this, you will have your family back. Very soon." Her face was still hidden by the scarf as she spoke.

"I pray for that."

"This driver, Houston Holt. Has he been secured?" Her tone suddenly switched gears, all business. Faraz felt an odd sensation when she spoke, as if she was speaking to him through a screen—an unsettling but strangely familiar feeling.

"Yes. He is waiting for the next steps from me."

"Good."

"We had a minor incident tonight," he said, wondering if she already knew.

"Oh?"

He told her about Veena and the murder of Esther Neel.

"I worry about her. She is unstable," Faraz finished.

"It is not your place to worry. For the first time in her life, Veena has a purpose, and it is your job to make sure she fulfills that purpose. In any case, Veena's part in all this is coming to an end."

"I see."

"I know what you're thinking, Faraz."

"And what is that?"

"You're wondering why I brought you here."

She knelt down and studied the dirt by the path. She pointed to a sculpture of a young girl by the roots of a hostas plant. The girl was reading a book.

"Eighty-nine," she said softly, and stood up. She resumed walking. It was a few moments before she spoke again. "It is normal to wonder about our place in things. Fifteen years ago, a young Special with great power decided to stand up against the injustices inflicted upon him and his people by the humans. He fought back, and now we are here, in his Kingdom—one unlike any the world has ever known. But many difficult choices were made to get here. Many sacrifices. And now, if this world is to survive, we must make even more difficult choices. Especially you."

Faraz stopped. "Me?"

Her face was still hidden, but he could sense her smiling behind the veil. "Like Veena, your part in this is coming to its end."

A flash of movement. Faraz saw the glint of metal before a heavy blow knocked him to the ground.

He fell onto his side. Pain shot through his right elbow where it hit the cement. He glimpsed two dark shapes clash above him— the woman and a much larger man wielding a blade.

The woman moved inhumanly fast. She knocked the blade out of the man's hand, sending it clattering across the stone next to Faraz's head. She struck the man's throat. He grunted and fell to one knee. She swung her boot into his face, dropping him hard.

For a moment she stood over the unconscious mugger. Then, her heels clicking on the stone, she strode over to Faraz and retrieved the fallen blade. In three curt steps, she walked back to the motionless man and drove the blade into his heart.

The woman then turned to Faraz.

Faraz trembled as she swept toward him. But before she got halfway, her entire body locked up.

Something hitched in her leg, like she was caught on a nail. Her head twisted from side to side, her limbs stuttering.

Faraz tried to get up. *Run, you idiot.*

And then the woman softened and exhaled, the glitch disappearing.

She held out her hand. "The danger has passed, Faraz," she said.

Faraz took her hand and marveled at her strength as she lifted him up. Her headscarf had slipped off, and before she pulled it back on Faraz caught a glimpse of gray eyes studded with stars.

She led him to a bench and sat down, motioning for Faraz to sit next to her. He did so hesitantly now that he knew what she was.

Her inhumanly fast movements, the underwater voice, the way she seemed to be channeling someone rather than being someone—and then the hitch in her step, a resetting as her hidden puppet-master momentarily lost contact with her.

She was a Stringer. Those emotionally attuned humans who could communicate with, and be controlled by, Special psychics and telekinetics.

"Well," she said as she looked over to the mugger she had just stabbed, "that was inconvenient."

My word, Faraz thought with a twinge of fear. *I've never seen one this good.*

He knew Stringers were reflections of their controllers. Most of them were twitchy, jerky-limbed oddities—the telekinetics controlling them simply did not have the mental strength to seamlessly control another being. It was the hardest thing a telekinetic could attempt. The Specials had tried to use their top telekinetics during the war to infiltrate the US military, but the Stringers were spotted and executed immediately.

But this one was different. Had he not seen the small glitch, he would never have known. Her master was a telekinetic far more powerful than any he had come across.

"As I was saying," she started as if nothing had happened, "you have been exceptional in your duties. However, there is only one more task before your part comes to an end. Are you willing?"

"Yes."

She turned to him, and the darkness swallowed her face. "Once Houston Holt has delivered the Sun Angel, you must eliminate him."

"Eliminate him?"

"Are you friends with this man?"

"He's . . . we're business associates."

"And this is business. It is very important that he drives that truck. And it is even more important that he disappears soon after. No trace. You must arrange it. And then your father will know you are a changed man. Nadia will know it as well."

Faraz said nothing. He sat back, stunned.

She stood up and straightened her jacket. As she walked away, she stopped and pointed to a sculpture embedded in the iron fence.

"Ninety."

And then with one graceful step, she hopped over the dead man and walked out of the park, the first light of dawn catching her like fire.

7

From the outside, the Patel Brothers Bakery was like any of the other two-bit operations servicing the people of River Town. Its dingy storefront displayed a collection of grim Indian sweets, not so much to entice passersby as to keep them away—a strategic ploy on the part of the store. Amin Patel, the patriarch of this sweets empire, was eager to hide the much more lucrative trade he conducted underground.

Houston passed the storefront and turned into the filthy alleyway along its side. All around him, River Town was struggling to wake up, weighed down by a serious hangover. Empty bottles rolled across the asphalt, and confetti from last night's street party covered the Strip in a brightly hued blanket.

Houston sipped his coffee and felt every inch of the town's exhaustion. Waking up at dawn had been a habit ingrained in him since his time in the corps—one that persisted even when, like last night, he hadn't managed a wink of sleep. Every time his eyes had closed, he saw himself in Sovereign City, the Gold Stamp humming under his skin.

One step at a time, Holt. There was still work to do before Faraz handed him a Gold Stamp. Houston tossed his coffee into the trash before entering the bakery through the side door.

Houston found Amin Patel in his closet-sized office surrounded by stacks of invoices and receipts. He ignored Houston, focused wholly on his phone screen, which he jabbed at malevolently. Over the years, Amin had developed an antagonistic relationship with all forms of technology, and Houston estimated the man spent a good third of his day cursing at devices and anyone who tried to explain them to him.

"Stupid, bloody thing," Amin grumbled at his phone.

"Morning," Houston said.

Amin squinted at Houston over his glasses as if he were an intruder who needed to be shot immediately.

"Your delivery just arrived," Amin said, standing up and tossing the uncooperative phone to the desk. Amin, short and balding with a widening paunch, always seemed to be chewing over how to efficiently extract himself from whichever conversation he was currently having. Overall, his frumpy appearance deflected any suspicions as to his true vocation—the owner and operator of a far-flung network of storage depots and delivery trucks that were invaluable to smugglers like Houston.

He studied Houston disapprovingly. "You look absolutely terrible."

"Thanks, Amin."

"Don't thank me," he said as he unlocked the door to the basement storage unit. "Just stop living like a hooligan."

*

Houston's arms disappeared inside the sack of flour. A sweet white cloud puffed up into his face and made him cough.

"No coughing on the flour!" Amin reprimanded, shivering in the cold basement air. He leaned against a plastic shelving unit, which groaned under the weight of ancient baking pans, mixers, and unmarked boxes.

Houston closed his eyes and dug deeper until he felt the parcel. He pulled it out and set it alongside the two other packages on the center table. He tore open each package and laid out the contents in precise lines.

The carbine of the Colt M6 rifle came first. Next to it he set six magazines of spec-killing whipper rounds wrapped in tape, then a rifle suppressor, and, finally, four stacks of goldmarks in denominations of one hundred. If discovered, all the gear on the table would land Houston a one-way trip to the Screaming Cells.

"Everything's here," Houston said.

"Where else would it be?" Amin grunted as he closely inspected a packet of chocolate sprinkles that had somehow invited his scrutiny.

Houston pushed one stack of goldmarks across the table toward Amin. "For the new gear."

"It's extra this time."

"What for?"

"Rush fee. Minimum forty-eight hours' notice."

"You're killing me, Amin."

Amin shrugged. "Company policy."

Houston shook his head and pushed another stack across the table. Amin eyed the money for a moment before leaving the room. When he returned, he placed two devices on the table.

Houston picked up the first one. It was a camouflage-green box with molded plastic grips. A row of three buttons were set beneath a small LCD screen. The device was an Owl-Sight, able to detect a Special within a half mile—the exact same beepers Houston had sold to Kilin's coyotes. He switched it on and checked the battery. Satisfied, he turned to the second device, a Cyclops Tactical night vision scope.

"How did you get your hands on those?" Amin asked, pointing to the goggles. "Those are Israeli. Their Kidon units use them."

"Remember Swan's Island?" Houston asked, referring to the thwarted United Nations attempt three years ago to land a covert special operations force on Maine from Novia Scotia. "Found some gems in the wreckage."

Amin whistled, impressed for a full second before his scowl returned. "Hurry up. I'm freezing in this igloo."

"Wife and kids are good?" Houston asked as he packed the gear into a duffel.

Amin shrugged. "Wife is always talking. She talks my bloody ear off. I tell the girls to study hard, to make something of themselves. But what? What can they do in this world? Become a criminal like dad. That's the only way."

"We're entrepreneurs."

Amin snorted. "Sure, okay."

"They say peace is here. Maybe a homeland for us."

"You believe that nonsense?"

"No," Houston said, zipping up the duffel.

"This king of theirs—no good. I don't believe a word he says. He wants peace with us, he says. But you know what he's afraid of?"

"Frontier."

Amin nodded sagely. "And the one thing Frontier hates more than the king is us: humans. You think they will give up their slaves? Not a chance. So the king makes a deal. He gives us a homeland—puts all of us in one place like trout in a barrel. Then *boom*—Frontier has an easy target."

Houston smiled, knowing better than to get roped into one of Amin's conspiracy theories about the Frontier Nation. Nobody knew for sure what was happening out in the Western Province, but Amin's network of suppliers and drivers brought back a steady stream of conflicting intel. Some swore that Frontier had launched a full-blown civil war against the Crown. Others shrugged them off as a gang of religious terrorists agitating for a human-free homeland. The highly censored Crown News Network never mentioned the unrest, but Houston had heard enough firsthand accounts from western refugees to cobble together a picture—three years ago, a cabal of fanatical Specials calling themselves the Frontier Nation had splintered off from the Crown and were now in control of large swaths of land from Texas to California. What their endgame was, only they knew.

In the end, it didn't matter. Houston would be in Sovereign City soon. He shouldered his bag and shook hands with Amin. "I think things are going to change, Amin. I have a good feeling."

"Change your life, Houston. You look like shit."

*

Houston walked back from Amin's bakery to his apartment to deposit his illicit gear in the crawl space behind the fridge. This tidy one-bedroom apartment had felt like a mansion after his first years living in the tent-town ditches, but now, with the Gold Stamp on the horizon, it suddenly felt too small.

For the fifth time, he checked the burner phone Faraz had given him. Still no call. With nothing else to do but wait, he proceeded to thumb through the spines of his collection of biographies, military history tomes, and business books. Then Houston remembered *The Last Giant*, the book Katya had given him. He raced through six chapters before his stomach started to rumble.

Outside he heard music from the River Festival down on Washington Street. The smell of fried dough and animal fat carried in on the breeze, thick and warm.

He put his hand in his pocket. Faraz's phone sat there quietly.

Man's got to eat, he thought to himself as he headed for the door.

Most years, the River Festival was a sad affair—a valiant attempt to lift people's spirits with loud music and alcohol—but this year was very different. Houston noticed the size of the crowd first, packed shoulder to shoulder across Washington Street.

They had come from every corner of the Strip, refugees and lifers alike, speaking in a dozen languages. Balloons flew into the air like neon birds, and kids ran between stalls stuffed with candy, food, and street art.

As much as Houston hated crowds, the sight brought a smile to his face. There was hope here—something this town had never felt before.

Standing under a bamboo arch that read Peace for All, Houston wolfed down a steak gyro, followed by an espresso from the Marzano Brothers stall. The burner sat silent in his pocket.

The crowd roared over by the stage as the band launched into a nostalgic anthem. A child started to bawl somewhere.

Stomach full, Houston pushed his way toward Sinatra Drive and over to the Pier A Park. Jagged ship carcasses rose like dorsal fins along the river, and the domes of Sovereign City glinted in the sun.

Houston sipped his coffee and watched the city, remembering the skyline the way it used to be. He had been inside its borders only once, as a boy, when it was still called Manhattan.

8

They had been on the run for three years at that point.

Houston, sixteen and big for his age, felt out of place in the Ivory Room. The walls were dark red velvet, and the guests in the secret club glittered, lit by tabletop candles, their fortunes older than the street names outside.

They all faced the curtained stage at the far end, waiting for the show to start. They whispered nervously, knowing that despite all their wealth and influence, the US government could raid this illegal show at any moment, guns blazing.

"How's the suit?" Big Don asked. His large hand rested on Houston's shoulder.

Houston looked down at his custom navy suit. He had never worn anything like it in his life. It was a beauty, crafted by Big Don's private tailor in SoHo.

"Feels good," Houston said.

Big Don smiled. "When you look like a man, you deserve to be treated like a man," Big Don said as he filled Houston's glass with wine from the bottle.

"*Don*," Houston's mother, Jessalyn, reprimanded Big Don from the seat next to him. Big Don, thickset with a ruffle of silver-black hair, laughed so hard the table shook.

"It's a big night. He's a man. Let him have some," Don replied.

Jessalyn just shook her head and smiled. It was not like his mother to back away from a fight, but she wasn't about to jeopardize her relationship with Big Don—or his money—on account of a drink.

Houston drank the wine and immediately coughed it up. Big Don laughed again and squeezed his shoulder. "You'll get used to it. Just do what I do: practice, practice, practice."

Jessalyn muttered something under her breath. Houston watched as she finished her third glass of Barolo and then poured herself a fourth. Big Don studied her out of the corner of his eye.

The lights went low. The crowd suddenly sat up in their chairs, and an illicit thrill filled the room.

The show was about to start.

Houston fiddled with his collar. It was with mixed feelings that he prepared for what was about to stride onto that stage.

The curtains parted. The audience deflated perceptibly when they saw the bare platform. Having become accustomed to a higher class of sublegal entertainment in this space, they were expecting more than a microphone and a musty brick backdrop.

The crowd's mood did not change when the small boy, no older than thirteen, shuffled onto stage and fidgeted behind the microphone with the sleeves of his velvet blue tuxedo.

Houston knew that his brother, Bobby, was never comfortable in the spotlight. Even though, in the past three years on the run, he had performed on stages in every backwater town across America, Bobby had never gotten over his initial stage fright. Seventy-one performances, Houston calculated, and still his little brother shrank like a violet in the glare of opening night.

But it was only temporary, Houston knew. The crowd around him had no idea what was coming.

Bobby cleared his throat.

Houston shut his eyes and braced himself.

What came next was magic—a crisp breeze, carrying the sounds of the stars wheeling in the heavens.

Houston's feet lifted off the ground.

The walls of the Ivory Room fell away like cards. The ceiling swung off like a lid.

Houston soared up into the night sky. The air was cloudless and cool, and the city was a rug of jewels beneath him.

Air in Houston's lungs, so fresh and clean. He pierced the clouds and arrived in a whole new world.

On a moon-glazed cloud to his right, he saw their old house—the cramped cottage in San Jose with the dead fridge lying on the dense, brown lawn.

The Emergency, he remembered as he saw the tanks and Humvees roll down in front of the house. In the distance, Black Hawk choppers scoured for Specials across the hills. The mysterious outbreak of the Gift across the western US—the Incident—was only a few months old at that point, and yet that was all the time it took to turn their hometown into a police state, convulsing with fear.

He dove down closer to the house. He saw himself, twelve years old, through the window, taking the bottle of out his mother's hand as she snored on the sofa and placing a sick bucket on the ratty carpet next to her head.

Go left, he heard Bobby's voice say. Houston spun away from the scene and hovered over another cloud, thick and brewing with thunder. This time he saw the snowy flats of Ohio, their battered Sierra station wagon plowing down the dark highway. He knew what was in that car—himself, ten-year-old Bobby, and their mother drunk behind the wheel. They were all outlaws the moment Jessalyn had stuffed them into her station wagon and, against federal law, transported a Special across the Containment Line dividing the United States between west and east—infected and uninfected.

The memory of those freezing winters sleeping in that car almost dragged him down like an anchor. Three years of living like fugitives, Jessalyn profiting off Bobby's talent anywhere she could, eking out just enough cash for canned food and gas.

Houston shook off the weight he felt. *I'm free*, he remembered. A swift kick, and he was rising higher, into the next layer of clouds.

Salt in the air. Houston gasped when he saw what lay before him—a stretch of ocean so blue and endless it took his breath away. He felt the wind in his face, and he watched the sun burst over the horizon.

In the distance, on the rim of the world, he saw the island again. He kicked hard and streaked toward it. He could make out mountains rimmed with clouds and the foam of breakers smashing against stony cliffs. A volcano simmered and bubbled, blue flames spitting high into the air. The island never seemed to come closer no matter how fast he flew.

He didn't know why, but he knew he had to get there. He knew down there he would find *it*—something magnificent.

The wind rose up off the waves and found him. It lashed at his body and spun him like a feather. Houston fell toward the sea.

He smashed into the glassy surface.

He opened his eyes as if from sleep. Bobby stood on the stage, silent, tugging at his sleeves again. The song was over.

It was a full minute before the crowd rose to their feet and roared. Houston remained seated as the applause shook the walls.

That night, Big Don took him, Bobby, and their mother out to a French-Moroccan bistro he co-owned. Big Don had the best table in the house, and the waiters rushed to fill their plates with enough steak frites and lamb saddle to feed an army. Every few minutes, a new well-dressed diner would come to pay their respects to Big Don. As their mother finished another bottle, Bobby leaned over to Houston and asked, "What did you see this time?"

"That place again," Houston said.

"That island?"

Houston nodded. "It was clearer this time. Do you know why I see it?"

Bobby shrugged. "I sing what I feel, and that makes other people feel things too. It was a new song. I haven't done it before." Bobby smiled shyly. "Was it good? Tell me honestly."

"It was my favorite."

Bobby blinked. Genuinely touched. "Thank—"

"Hey, Bobby!" Jessalyn snapped her fingers across the table. "Come here. These nice people want your picture."

Bobby rolled his eyes to Houston. He left his food and shuffled over to where Jessalyn was waiting with a grinning older couple. Bobby posed for pictures as Big Don snapped away. For some reason, their mother inserted herself into every picture.

Houston knew Bobby hated being the center of attention. But once in a while, Houston believed, his brother must have enjoyed the feeling of being a somebody—a star. And in this world, there were no bigger stars than Specials like Bobby.

When Bobby sang, he created worlds. No one ever remembered the words to his songs after they were done, but they remembered where he had transported them. Some longed for that place for the rest of their lives. Some died, gripped by its mad beauty.

It was his Gift.

Houston nudged the soggy steak frites around his plate. He glanced at the wealthy diners around the room. He would never have the Gift, like Bobby. But as he looked at Big Don commanding the room like a ringmaster, he hoped that maybe, one day, he could be like him. He could become something more than a fugitive wearing a suit he couldn't afford.

Bobby returned from his photo op looking exhausted.

"You okay?" Houston asked.

Bobby shook his head. He picked up his fork to take another bite when the finger snapping started again.

"Hey Bobby! Say 'hi' to the senator here!" Jessalyn called, sloshing a full glass of Chablis all over the table.

Bobby put his fork down and started to slide off his chair.

"No." Houston put his hand on Bobby's shoulder. "Eat."

Bobby looked between Houston and his mother, whose eyes had suddenly narrowed viciously.

"Bobby," she said simply.

"Let him eat," Houston growled. Their mother's eyes grew wide, and her jaw tightened. She held the glass very still.

Houston prayed that because they were in public, this wouldn't end like all the other times.

Big Don put a hand on her arm. "Let the kid eat." He turned to the senator. "Senator, how about we stop by your table before we leave?"

Jessalyn settled back in her chair. She turned to the senator and flashed one of her brilliant smiles as he nodded and left.

Bobby snuck a look at Houston. "Sometimes I wish all I could do was fly."

Houston laughed. "You and me both."

After dinner they retired to Big Don's penthouse on Sixty-Seventh overlooking Central Park West. They spread out on the big white rug in his living room and played cards until it got late. Jessalyn had forgotten the clash over the senator and was playing along happily. Manhattan glowed warmly outside the big windows.

Well past midnight, Jessalyn knelt between Houston and Bobby's beds and looked both of them in the eye.

"It's so good to be together," she said, her eyes luminous.

Houston lay awake for some time that night, listening to the cars outside. For the first time in years, he felt like he was home.

Five hours later, in the dead of night, his mother shook him awake, madness in her voice.

"We have to go! *Now!*" she hissed.

Houston rubbed the sleep from his eyes. In the dark, he watched his mother run over to Bobby's bed and shake him awake. Bobby sat up, mumbling.

As Houston's vision adjusted to the gloom, he noticed the dark stains on Jessalyn's white nightie.

"What happened?" Houston jumped out of bed, heart racing.

She ignored him. Instead she ran to the closet and pulled out their suitcases, stuffing them with clothes.

"Start packing!" she barked.

"Where's Big Don?" Bobby asked.

"*Shut up!* Help me pack." A sliver of moonlight caught her nightie, and Houston realized that the stains were still wet.

"Did he hurt you?" Houston demanded, his fists curling.

She grabbed him by the neck. Her face was so close Houston could see the flecks of red on her cheeks.

"If we don't leave now, we're all dead."

It was only then that Houston realized that his mother was unhurt—*and covered in blood.*

His stomach twisted violently as the truth dawned on him.

Big Don's blood.

They were on the run again.

*

From the pier, all these years later, Houston could still see the spot where Big Don's old building had stood. The painted towers of the Cosmic Sky Theater occupied the space now, in the shadow of the Golden Fort. Houston turned and walked back toward the festival. The afternoon sun was bright in the sky, and it was beginning to hurt his eyes.

He had just crossed over Washington and onto Third Street when a man going in the opposite direction bumped him. It wasn't intentional; just two people pushed together by the dense crowd. Their arms slid past each other and for a brief moment, their knuckles touched.

The effect was electric. In that second of skin-to-skin contact, Houston felt a shock of energy crackle up his bones, and the air in his lungs thickened as if he had just entered a soapy bubble. A familiar warbling filled his ears, and then . . . it was gone. The man continued past him.

Can't be . . .

Houston turned and watched the man weave through the crowd. The temperature was in the mideighties, but the man wore a green duster coat and combat boots.

Houston felt his guts twist. Bad vibes hit him like a wind. Those sensations—the crackling, the warbling in the thickened air—he had felt all of them before, on a battlefield years ago. Back then, he hadn't known enough to stop the terror that was on its way.

The man slithered his way through the crowd. Houston's hand crept to the gun in his waistband.

It's nothing, he tried to convince himself.

But the longer he watched the man, the louder his alarms blared.

What Houston had felt was the man's Gift—not the Gift of a Special like Bobby, whose power flowed as gently as a mountain stream. This Special carried something sinister, an energy that bristled and gnashed its canines, thirsty for blood.

His Gift was *weaponized*.

Houston followed him, his hand slick on the gun grip. The world tightened down to a narrow tunnel, forming a string between him and the green duster twenty paces ahead.

Sound disappeared from the world. Houston heard only his heart beating, his breath quickening. The rhythm of war.

Green Duster wove purposefully through the crowd. Houston realized he was heading for the stage—the most crowded place in the fair.

Houston ripped the SIG out of his jeans.

"Holt!"

Someone grabbed him by the shoulder. Houston's instincts took over, he spun, ready to pistol-whip—

"Katya—" He quickly slipped the gun away.

"You okay, Holt?" she asked, scowling. "I wanted to thank you. Klay came by last night, and—"

But Houston wasn't listening anymore.

He had lost sight of the man.

"—we sent Jesse to the doctor, and—"

"Not now." Houston brushed by her, blood pounding in his ears. Behind him, Katya was yelling something.

Dammit. He searched the teeming crowd. *Where was he?*

He raced forward, pushing his way through the mob. He was vaguely aware of people cursing him, giving him dirty looks.

There.

Green Duster was in the center of the audience, facing the stage. Everyone around him was dancing, but he didn't move.

As Houston rushed forward, he saw the man's eyes were closed and his lips were moving.

Ice flooded Houston's veins.

He's praying.

Houston's feet slammed into the asphalt. His gun caught the sunlight. He had a few seconds at most—

He was still too far away when the man ripped off his coat.

The muscled body underneath swarmed with tattoos, venomous snakes coiling around a sunbaked torso.

"*Run!*" Houston yelled, drowned out by the crashing drums. "*Everyone run now!*"

The man spread his arms wide and looked up into the sky. A cry escaped his throat like a war bird: "*The Snake Mother Rises!*"

Houston aimed down the barrel.

Green Duster smashed his fists together.

The air vibrated, then expanded like a vicious living thing.

The blast tore Houston off his feet and into the air, the world shattering around him.

9

Houston blinked. He lay on his back, staring up at a dark sky. Thin streams of sunlight slipped through the ceiling of smoke.

He got to his feet, palms burning as he pushed off the asphalt. The air around him swirled, as hot as an incinerator. For a few terrifying seconds, he looked at the fiery landscape around him and thought he was dead.

Focus, Holt. Surveying the damage, he tried to remember what had happened.

River Festival.

Tattoos.

Bomb.

The stage had collapsed into a burning pyre. A column of black smoke spun into the sky from a blast crater ringed with twisted bodies. Through ringing ears, Houston could hear screams.

He raced toward the fire. *That smell.* Houston grimaced. The odor was like nothing he had ever experienced before. It clawed at his throat. He retched onto the sidewalk.

Time passed in jagged blinks—Houston was barely aware of himself carrying a crying woman away from the crater. Her fingernails dug into his back, her other hand clutching her shredded right leg.

How many dead? Too many to count.

Keep moving.

The pillar of smoke from the crater sparked and spit coils of flame. The coils snapped by Houston's head like vipers and charred the lamppost behind him. He watched as the flames spread, snaking their way across the street, licking at buildings.

The fire's alive.

Houston ran back to pull out more people, but the smoke filled his lungs. He fell to the ground, coughing violently. Someone grabbed his collar and yanked him up.

"Haku," Houston muttered. The big bartender from the Black Bird grinned.

"We really in the shit now, huh, brother?" Haku said.

"There's still people trapped in there," Houston said, pointing to the crater.

"Well, why are we dicking around here, then?"

They covered their noses with their shirts and ran back in. They heaved a girder off an old veteran's leg and dragged him out, the fire's coils whipping their shirts.

"What the hell is this?" Haku stared at the flames.

"Frontier," Houston said. "A kamikaze."

"You saw him?"

"Snakes all over his body. Heard him pray to the Snake Mother before he detonated."

"What the fuck are Frontier doing out here?"

Houston had no idea. Frontier's war was supposed to be out west against the Crown, not here in River Town.

"Holy shit." Haku grabbed Houston's shirt and pointed. Houston turned around to see a wall of flame by the stage, and beyond it, an unmistakable shock of red hair.

"Katya . . ."

Katya and a dozen others were trapped behind a pile of burning debris. The circle of flames tightened in on them as Katya corralled the group, searching for a way out. Houston took off toward her, Haku right behind. Within seconds, Houston was lost in the smog. He could barely make out Haku two feet away and had lost all sight of Katya.

"Katya!" Houston yelled blindly. He took a few steps forward before a hot gust blew him back.

Haku's big face streamed with tears as he pulled Houston away from the stage. "We can't help her."

Houston tore his arm away. He lunged forward a few feet and was immediately shoved onto his heels by a blast of hellish heat.

"She's going to die!" Houston yelled.

"*We're* going to die!" Haku shouted, dragging Houston back.

Houston clenched his fists, overcome with a helpless rage. He took two steps out of the smoke, watching Katya's red hair disappear in the haze.

And then he stopped cold. At first he thought he was hallucinating.

But then Haku noticed it too. "Holy . . ."

"Silver," Houston whispered.

Millions of silver particles no larger than dust motes rode in on a cool wind. The silver wind surged and wrapped around the smoke column like a python.

The silver particles swelled into a dense mass and *squeezed*.

The column swayed frantically, flames spitting and struggling to stay alight. The temperature plummeted below freezing as the silver particles thickened into a wall. Houston couldn't see his own hand in front of his face. His entire world turned to silver, his body tossed backward in the icy hurricane. He fell to his knees, gasping in the surging cold.

And then, like a giant's inhalation, the wind lifted. The silver wall dissipated into a soft flurry, and Houston could see the sky again.

The flames were gone. The column of black smoke had weakened, and the crater in the ground simmered like the mouth of a dormant volcano.

Katya stood by the stage, gasping for air. Before Houston could go to her, he heard a shout behind him.

"Look!" a young boy yelled, pointing to the sky.

"Specs!" a woman cried.

There were seven of them, gliding in formation as they came in for a landing on Washington Street. Shockwaves spread through Houston's chest as he recognized the unmistakable form of their leader.

"It's him," Houston said to no one.

The Silverbacks landed in unison and marched in perfect lockstep across the carnage. The silver particles they had created swarmed across the street, returning to surround their masters. The Silverbacks' flight suits were iridescent onyx, stretched taut over massive frames that dwarfed the humans around them. Even in the murky air, the thick silver band running down their backs from neck to tailbone shone like fire.

Houston stayed rooted to the spot dumbly, vaguely aware of others fleeing down the side streets at the sight of the warrior leading the unit: the Supreme Leader of the Silverbacks—the Warbringer himself—General Sixkills.

Haku gripped Houston's shoulder and pulled him out of Sixkills's path. Houston felt the air displace as the general strode by.

Sixkills was a giant—six foot five, two hundred and sixty pounds of rigid muscle. His tightly cropped silver hair framed a face as hard and jagged as a mountain range. From the side, Houston saw his arched brow hanging like a hood over pitiless eyes.

The General knelt next to the crater and ran one hand along the rim. The other six Silverbacks stood in a defensive circle around him as he studied the simmering asphalt.

"Damn. He's a big fella, huh?" Haku whispered to Houston.

"No shit."

"How many of us you think he's killed?"

"Thousands."

Haku whistled. "Why did he save us, then?"

Houston chewed it over for a minute before the answer came to him. "Because there's only one thing he hates more than us."

Haku looked at him. "Frontier."

Sixkills stood up and turned his massive head. The crowd shrank back as he studied their faces.

The hooded eyes fell on Houston. It was as painful as staring into the sun.

Sixkills turned to the sky and, with an imperceptible shift in his weight, went airborne. His men followed, and within seconds they were up and over the river.

Sirens rang, and ambulances rolled in from the side streets as if they had been waiting for Sixkills to leave.

"I'm out of here," Houston said to Haku.

The bartender nodded. "Stay safe, brother." He looked over at Katya, who was retching into a trash can. "I'll get her home."

Houston made it ten blocks before he had to rest against a brownstone. Exhaustion fell on him like bricks. His clothes were covered in soot, and he had to force images of charred corpses out of his head. When he finally straightened up, he saw a burnt banner lying on the street.

Peace For All.

Houston shook his head. *Not yet.*

His burner phone beeped as he stepped onto Jackson Street—Faraz.

"Are you okay?" Faraz asked as soon as Houston picked up.

"Living the dream."

"What happened out there? I'm hearing conflicting things."

"Frontier kamikaze."

Faraz swore under his breath. "Frontier? What are they doing here?"

"That's what I want to know."

"Mindless terrorists. I'm thankful that you're all right."

"Yeah." Houston paused. "We're still on for tonight?"

"Yes, of course."

Houston listened as Faraz read off the particulars of the upcoming operation. He memorized the pickup coordinates out in Ringwood State Park and the drop-off location in River Town. Lastly, he confirmed the coded greeting for the people handing over the truck.

"Got it," Houston said when Faraz had finished. He was about to hang up when Faraz spoke up.

"Houston?" he said.

"What?"

Faraz cleared his throat. "Do you have plans? After the job?"

"Not yet. Why?"

"I will be in town on other business. If you were to be at home, I could drop off the naturalization forms. I'm sure you're in a hurry to get the process started."

The Gold Stamp. It felt like a cool breeze, wiping away the sludge of the day.

"I'll be home."

"See you then, Houston."

10

Veena knew she was dreaming when she saw the veiled woman with the gray eyes.

No, she thought as she felt the chains around her wrists. *Not a dream.*

The vision. From He Who Knows All.

Veena remembered bits and pieces of the last few hours—her fashion show, the after-party, Esther Neel's bloody corpse. She was vaguely aware of all that and still completely convinced that she was *here* . . . in this nightmare, in this world that He Who Knows All had first shown her over a year ago on a Crosslake balcony as she'd prepared to plunge to her death.

Back then, behind her, Crosslake had been dark, all the patients and doctors fast asleep. Veena, however, had been awake for hours, strangely serene with a newfound realization:

There was nothing else.

Her beauty and fame had failed to rid her of that *thing* that had clung to her all these years—that stench of her lost childhood: piss, fire, smoke, and death. The Moxi had been the best salve she had found, and now the rehab gestapo had taken that away too.

The last three weeks at Crosslake had been exquisite torture. Her once glamorous life had devolved into a fog of drug tests, behavioral therapy lectures, and pointless hours meditating alongside the other dead-eyed residents. And then the nights . . . the *awful* nights as the Moxi burned out of her system inch by inch.

And not one of her friends from Sovereign had come to visit.

This is the only way, she had reassured herself as she had stepped up onto the pine balustrade and held her breath, dreading how inelegant her pajama-clad corpse would look on the grass.

As soon as her right foot had left the railing, the crackling white light had hit her. She'd gasped in shock, her eyes clamping shut against the pain as her entire body split apart.

She had opened her eyes and found herself in a new world—a nightmare which she now saw again.

Veena heard their angry chants first. They blew across her like a hot wind as the lowbloods snarled at her from the side of the road. There were thousands of them, a roiling mass of gnashing teeth and rage.

War criminal!

Fascist!

No peace without justice!

She was naked, her wrists and ankles chained. The cracked asphalt tore at her bare feet.

She was somewhere in Sovereign City, but she couldn't recognize the street. The veiled woman watched her from the crowd, a vision of white in the madness.

A rock hit Veena on the temple and she fell, her knees cracking on the cement. Blood slid coldly down her cheek. Big hands hauled her up and pushed her forward. The man who handled her wore the olive uniform of the Overwatch, the city's police force. More Overwatch officers lined the route, holding back the baying crowds.

And above her, she saw *them*—King Patriot Gold and Queen Callista, resplendent on a high balcony, following her with their royal gazes.

Condemning her.

Veena blinked away hot tears. The officer prodded her forward, toward a structure twenty feet ahead of them.

She stopped in her tracks.

The gallows stood the middle of the street. A hangman watched her silently through a black hood. Behind him were two nooses. One empty, the other one . . .

No.

Her father, General Sixkills, hung dead from the second noose. Veena retched when she saw the brutalized flesh of his naked body.

The officer dragged her up the stairs, the tops of her feet scraping against the wood. The noose chafed her neck as the hangman slipped it on.

Once again she noticed the Lady's piercing gray eyes shining in the crowd.

And then she felt a presence over her shoulder. A peaceful breath across her neck.

Only you can stop this, Veena, He Who Knows All whispered to her.

This was no dream.

She was being shown the future.

War criminal!

No peace without justice!

The wood creaked beneath her toes. The crowd swelled with bloodlust, their chants shaking the world.

Filthy fucking lowbloods, Veena thought as her stomach twisted in terror. *I'll burn you all.*

And then, just as the floor fell away, she heard the sound of a ringing phone.

She opened her eyes in the darkness, the vision fading away into the shadows. Her back was stiff and her tongue felt like petrified wood. And somewhere close by, her phone continued to ring.

Veena turned her head to locate it, and her skull exploded.

Oh, God. Cold needles of pain jabbed into her brain, aggravated by the shrill ringtone. Veena fumbled around on the nightstand, and by the time she found the phone, it had stopped ringing. The blue light of the screen assaulted her eyes.

Six missed calls. Unknown number.

She would deal with the calls later. First, she realized with a growing panic as her eyes adjusted to the murk around her, she had to figure out where the hell she was.

This wasn't her Victory Island bedroom. This one was smaller and more modern, the bare walls speckled black and gray. Outside the plush drapes, Veena could hear the familiar rumble of the city. As her head slowly cleared, she felt a glimmer of recognition.

Refuge, she realized with relief. She was in her Sixteenth Street apartment in Sovereign, one of four penthouses she owned. Refuge was her secret sanctuary, hidden from the paparazzi hordes.

Veena blinked in the gloom, still troubled. She had no recollection of coming here.

Her plan last night had been to head straight home to Victory Island after the party at Tangle. The sequence of events that had led her to this apartment was gone from her memory. Veena closed her eyes and retraced her steps.

Fashion show. The dress. The queen. Caspar. Her heart shot into her throat. The queen's brother had invited her to tea with the queen today, Friday, at 5:00 p.m. She snatched up her phone and checked the time. It was only 2:30 p.m. She exhaled. If she had missed her meeting with the queen . . . Veena shook that awful scenario out of her head, refocusing on last night.

After calling Faraz to deal with Esther Neel's body, Veena had left the club with Makini, flooded with adrenaline. And then . . . what? The driving headache gave her a clue.

"Damn it, Veena," she hissed to herself. "You weak bitch."

The Moxi hangover drummed against her skull. She was a loose cannon on the drug, and she dreaded to think what it had made her do.

The phone rang, startling her. She flung it across the room, where it smashed against the wall and went silent.

"Whoa . . . what's going on?" Kormedia asked, stepping out of the bathroom naked.

Veena spun around. "What are *you* doing here?"

Shanti's tattooed boyfriend smiled and dove onto the bed. He stroked her leg under the silk sheets. "What do you think?"

"Did you give me Moxi last night?"

He smiled and nodded.

"Asshole!"

"What? You were practically begging me for it."

He rose up to kiss her. She pushed him away and jumped out of bed, her face hot with shame. Veena wasn't bothered by the fact that she had slept with Shanti's boyfriend. In fact, before Crosslake, Kormedia had been a regular in her bed. Handsome, dumb, and discreet, he was the perfect night's entertainment, and Shanti could go fuck herself.

What really got to Veena was that she had taken a big step backward. He Who Knows All had set her on a glorious destiny, and she had failed him for a Moxi-fueled romp with this idiot.

Kormedia lay back on the bed and rubbed the owl tattoo on his chest. "You're such a spaz when you're high."

"I was one year sober, you dick."

He shrugged. "You really don't like the queen, do you?"

Veena whipped around. "What did you say?"

"Last night at Magritte's afterparty, you kept saying things like, "The queen's going to burn,' and, 'Can't wait to sit on her throne.' I had to make sure no one heard you."

Panic stiffened Veena's limbs, paralyzing her.

"Non-stop with weird stuff like that all night," Kormedia continued. "'I'm going to watch her burn in that dress.' 'Fuck all the lowbloods.' What was that all about?"

"Just the Moxi." Veena coughed the words out.

"That was one gnarly high."

Veena turned away before he could see the terror on her face. She had to change the subject fast. But before she could, Kormedia's phone rang. He frowned at the screen.

"Shanti?" Veena asked.

He shook his head and picked up. After a moment, he looked at Veena. "Yeah, she's here," he said and held out the phone to her. "They want you."

"Who is it?"

He shrugged. "Sounds serious."

Veena took the phone, her hands trembling. "This is Veena."

As Veena listened to the woman on the other end, she felt all the warmth drain from her body. A few seconds later, the line went dead.

"Damn, you look pale," Kormedia said. "Who was that?"

Veena's heart pounded. "Nobody. Work stuff." She avoided Kormedia's eyes as she raced to the bathroom and shut the door. Instinctively, she curled up in the porcelain tub and let the fear take over, her body shaking with it.

The voice on the other end of the phone had been a woman she knew well—Amanda Clark-Holler. A woman whose official title was Chief of Staff to General Sixkills.

Amanda's tone had been officious, covered in enough professionalism to disguise the cold steel underneath.

"We will be sending a car for you, Miss Sixkills," Amanda had said. "Please be ready in fifteen minutes. Your father needs to speak with you about an important matter."

*

He's going to kill me, Veena realized as the Land Rover approached the main gates of the Silver Spear.

Not once in her twenty-four years of life had her father ever willingly spent time with her. From her childhood dance recitals to her star-studded fashion shows, General Sixkills was always conspicuous by his absence. Even when he sent her to Crosslake, he never spoke to Veena directly, instead communicating the decision through Amanda Clark-Holler.

And now, on the precipice of treason, the morning after she revealed god-knows-what in her Moxi-frazzled state, he had suddenly summoned her to his fortress.

The armored Silverbacks guarding the front gates of the Silver Spear surrounded the Land Rover. Veena tapped her foot anxiously as a guard inspected the driver's credentials. The Land Rover had been waiting for her outside Refuge, and the driver, another Silverback, had driven her downtown in silence. The entire ride, Veena felt as if she were gliding in a black cocoon, watching the red bricks and gold eaves of downtown fall away as they crossed over the boundary into the darkness of her father's southern domain. The Silver Spear was the centerpiece of his massive military installation, which stretched from the east of the island's tip to the west. Unlike the rest of the city, resplendent with its domes and warm glory, the structures here were rigid and severe, all their color drained into cool blues and grays. Even the air felt heavier and thicker.

Probably all the anti-surveillance signals in the air.

The gate guard handed back the driver's papers and ushered them through.

Veena felt her insides twist. Her father's tower, home of the most-feared military machine on the planet, drew closer and closer, until its shadow swallowed the car.

*

"Veena Sixkills, please come with me," the young lieutenant ordered as he led her past the front desk. His name was Cortland, and like every other Silverback, he reminded Veena of a younger version of her father.

This being her first time in the Silver Spear, Veena thought she may have been more interested in her surroundings, with its harsh architecture and steady parade of uniformed Silverbacks, but the thought of her imminent unmasking and execution kept her preoccupied.

"Did my father say what this was about?" she asked Cortland's back.

"No, ma'am," he replied, and left it at that. His polished shoes struck the cement floor sharply as he led her through an arched entryway with a simple plaque that read Never Forget.

They entered a cavernous space that opened up around them like an airplane hangar. The lights were dim, the atmosphere as hushed as a mausoleum. Veena's pumps struggled against the uneven surface of the white cobbled floor as she followed Cortland through the great hall.

Across the long cement wall to her right, Veena noticed thousands of flanged greatmaces embedded into the surface like thorns. The maces were the primary weapon of the Silverbacks, and they wielded the bladed clubs ferociously in combat. As she studied the engraved weapons, she wondered what the significance of the display was, knowing her father was not one for art or symbolism of any kind.

As she struggled to keep up with Cortland, Veena glimpsed a series of stark exhibits locked inside tall plexiglass cases. Having lived through the Emergency and the conflicts that followed, Veena recognized many of the artifacts:

A green jumpsuit with an encircled red *S* on the armband—the uniform worn by Specials imprisoned in the Emergency quarantine camps.

A pane of glass from the Nawab Halal Meats shop. The slur *spec* slashed across the business name with spray paint, marking it as a Special-owned business and therefore un-American—a common sight before the war.

Next, they crossed in front of a child's charred tricycle. Veena was surprised by the swell of anger in her chest when she saw it. Like every Special, she knew the horrifying story of four-year-old Carlos Diaz, a Special who was riding this trike at the exact moment the Americans had hit the Hawaii settlements with a nuclear ambush.

Veena realized her hands were shaking. Whether from hatred of the humans or fear over what lay ahead of her, she didn't know.

"Ma'am, is everything all right?" Cortland asked, looking back at her.

"I'm fine," she replied. "Is this a museum tour?"

"No, ma'am. This is not a museum tour."

"Why did you bring me here, then?"

"Every person who enters the Silver Spear has to walk through the Last Memorial, ma'am."

"Why?"

"The General had the building designed that way, so that every Silverback would remember his primary duty."

"To never be ruled again," Veena recited her father's ethos from memory.

"Yes, ma'am."

"How does that work with the ceasefire?"

"I'm not qualified to comment on state affairs, ma'am."

Veena was about to respond when she noticed the monstrous shape blocking their path.

"Oh, fuck . . ." She took a sharp step back.

The machine dominated the center of the room, rising up to the ceiling. Eighteen feet in height, the black mechanical power armor reminded Veena of a skeletal bird. The head was an eyeless terror. Long and narrow, it sat on an articulated neck with a beak-like proboscis that bristled with antennae. Above both its shoulders, the mech carried two mounted sets of missile launchers and railguns that spread out like black wings. Veena's eyes ran down its rangy torso, along the battered titanium armor, toward the egg-like cockpit nestled in its belly. Big enough to fit one pilot, the cockpit was ringed with titanium ribs, some of which, Veena noticed, were broken off. On either side of the cockpit were the machine's long, spindly arms, hanging down nearly to the floor and terminating in hydraulic talons.

"One hell of a beast," Cortland said when he realized Veena was staring at the machine.

No shit, Veena wanted to say. She had spent two years of the war running from these beasts. The president had unleashed droves of these mechs onto the battlefields with one mission: kill any and all Specials. In her nightmares, she still heard their whining hydraulics.

"The lowbloods nearly wiped us out with these sons of bitches." Cortland rapped a knuckle on the mech's right leg, below a chipped stencil that read Heavy Metal Marine. "This Tin Man was piloted by Lieutenant Caleb Cross. Cross was—"

"The most decorated mech pilot in US history," Veena finished. "He killed two hundred Specials in combat."

Cortland nodded, impressed. "So you know who finally took him down?"

Veena's eyes fell on the photograph mounted on a stand next to the mech. It showed her father in full battle armor, lording over the crushed hulk of the Tin Man with his greatmace, Crossbreaker, in hand. The body of Caleb Cross lay slumped in the cockpit, visible through the smashed glass and ribs.

"Of course I know," Veena said, glaring at Cortland.

The young lieutenant nodded and tapped his right heel on one of the white cobblestones next to the mech. "This is Caleb right here."

Veena frowned. "What are you talking about?"

"This is his skull," Cortland said looking at the rounded stone. "The general wanted it close to his mech."

Veena's jaw fell as it dawned on her. Her eyes swept over the countless curved white "stones" along the floor. "You mean . . . ?"

"Yes, ma'am." Cortland nodded with pride. "The floor is made up of human skulls taken in combat. Two thousand and sixty-four exactly."

"Why that exact number?"

Cortland pointed to the greatmaces along the wall. "One thousand and thirty-two maces, one for each Silverback who fell in the Immortal War. For every one of us they killed, we took two of them."

Veena knelt down, her own danger momentarily forgotten. She rubbed Caleb's skull, fascinated. She looked up at Cortland. "I love how sick you boys are."

The young lieutenant held her gaze for a long moment before turning on his heel.

"Let's continue, ma'am. The general is waiting."

*

Amanda Clark-Holler greeted them with a smile when the elevator doors opened on the twenty-seventh floor. The smile was not a pleasant one, and the eyes that peered out at Veena from over the rims of her red spectacles were narrowed with suspicion.

Cortland held the elevator door as Veena stepped into a massive antechamber ringed with glass walls. Sunlight streamed into the room, and Veena marveled at the panoramic view of both rivers through the glass. She then noticed the thick iron door embedded in the opposite wall.

His office. Veena's stomach somersaulted. A dozen half-baked alibis ran through her mind as Amanda approached and held out her hand.

"Thank you for coming, Veena," she said.

Horse-faced twit. Veena smiled and shook Amanda's hand. Her father's chief of staff was small, prim, and unreadable. Veena couldn't be sure, but it looked like Amanda was wearing the same outfit as she had been a year ago, when she'd chaperoned Veena to Crosslake. Midnight blue pantsuit, black pumps, and no jewelry. Other than her red spectacles, she wore nothing that Veena would ever classify as stylish.

Amanda slipped her hand out of Veena's and called out to Cortland, who at that moment was heading back into the elevator. "Lieutenant, hold on. I'll need you to escort Miss Sixkills back downstairs."

"Excuse me?" Veena looked at Amanda, confused.

"Your father's schedule has changed," Amanda said. "He had to tend to an emergency. I tried calling you to reschedule, but I couldn't get through to your phone."

"Really? I didn't get any calls," Veena lied, knowing full well that her phone was lying in a cracked heap on her bedroom floor.

Amanda steepled her fingers together and leaned forward, an odd gesture that made Veena incredibly uncomfortable. "We will reschedule as soon as possible."

"What is this about?" Veena asked.

That shallow smile again. "That is between you and the general. Now the lieutenant will show you back to the car. Keep your phone close to you."

As Veena rode the elevator down, she went over the day's events. If her father knew about her plot, she would already be jailed or dead. There was no way he would let her walk out of the Silver Spear if he suspected her of treason. The tension drained from her face.

The mission was still on.

She checked her watch. It wasn't yet four. She still had time to go home, pick up the Peacock Gown, look the queen in the eye, and execute the penultimate phase of her revolution.

11

"Déjà vu," Veena muttered as armed guards surrounded her vehicle once again.

This time the four men inspecting her personal Escalade were Phoenix Guards, protectors of the iron gates leading to the Lady's Eye. Instead of the cobalt-and-gold ceremonial armor of the soldiers at the Golden Fort, these men wore discreet black ballistic suits engraved with the king's gold phoenix sigil across the collarbone. One of the guards took Veena's name and disappeared inside the guardhouse.

Veena waited impatiently, tapping the slim garment box on the seat beside her. She had just been through this entire process at the Silver Spear. Through the windshield of the car, past her personal driver and Makini, she could see the high white walls that surrounded the Lady's Eye, the queen's riverside retreat in the West Village.

The guard took his time. Once again it became clear to Veena that in all the high places of this Kingdom where the real power lay, she was still very much an outsider—a celebrity lightweight with millions of fans but no real influence. With great effort, she swallowed her bitterness.

The guard returned and leaned down by her window. Veena guessed he was in his late twenties.

"Ma'am, we're going to have to ask you to get out of the car."

"What?" Veena's hand instinctively covered the box.

"We're going to need to do an extra inspection before we can let you in."

"Inspection?" Veena sputtered. "Do you know who I am?"

"I know exactly who you are, ma'am—"

"I am an invited guest of the queen, and I will not be subjected to this harassment!"

"Then I can't let you in, ma'am. We have orders from the Office of the Crown itself. After today's events, we can't take any chances."

Veena felt she was missing a key piece of information. "What are you talking about? What events?"

The guard opened her door and ushered her out of the car. She held onto the box.

"Ma'am, please leave that in the car."

She did as she was told, placing the box on the back seat. Two other Phoenix Guards ran scanners over her, Makini, and the driver. After confiscating Makini's gun, the guard said something into his wrist mike that Veena didn't catch.

"Are we done here?" Veena snapped.

"Just one more thing."

He turned to his right, and Veena followed his gaze. The black iron gates in the wall opened, and a guard walked out, holding a German shepherd on a leash.

Shit. Veena's jaw tightened. She had been assured that the weapon she carried in the box could not be picked up by any security tech in the kingdom. As the massive dog strained at its leash, she prayed the box would stand up to the scrutiny of a canine. Her life depended on it.

The dog brushed by her and leapt into the back seat of the car. She could hear it rooting around, its paws scrabbling on the carpeted floor.

After what seemed like hours, the dog jumped out and inspected the outside of the car. When it was done, the handler gave the young guard a nod.

"You're all clear, ma'am," the young guard said. "I'll notify the house that you're on your way."

Veena stepped back into her car and the iron gates swung open. As the Escalade entered the property, Veena marveled at the beauty of the Lady's Eye. A perfect replica of Callista's ancestral home in Montagnola, Switzerland, the white Jerusalem stone of the queen's hideaway glowed in the afternoon light. Built along the former Hudson River Park, the landscape was verdant with lush gardens and marble fountains shaded under thick willows.

Veena smiled as they passed a row of stables. Year after year during the war, Callista would weep over the loss of her beloved family home—confiscated by the UN—and especially her stable of show horses. *My horses*, she would weep into Veena's shoulder. *How will I live without my horses*?

Some people can't let go of the past, Veena realized as the Escalade stopped in front of a great staircase leading up to the front door.

The driver opened her door and she slid out, her knuckles white around the box. She checked her reflection in the window, frowning at her ridiculous poppy-print dress.

If only leather and lace were appropriate in the presence of royalty.

She fixed her hair and hopped up the stairs. Not for the first time today, she felt the jaws of some hidden trap closing in on her.

Steady, Veena. Just smile and lie.

The queen's butler, Forsyth, met Veena at the door and led her to the back of the house. He opened a set of glass doors, and they stepped out onto a vast terrace with a breathtaking view of the Hudson.

Veena spotted the queen atop a short flight of stairs by a marble balustrade. Her back was to Veena and she was facing the river, her golden hair glinting in the sun.

"Your Majesty, may I present Madam Sixkills," Forsyth said.

Veena waited stiffly for the queen to acknowledge her presence. But Callista didn't move.

Forsyth gave Veena a tight smile and departed, leaving Veena alone with the queen. Veena cleared her throat loudly, but still the queen remained motionless.

Confused, Veena laid the box down on a lounge chair. She smoothed her dress and took the stairs toward her old friend.

Veena smelled the queen's rosewater and citrus perfume as she approached the balustrade. Callista was still staring straight ahead when Veena reached her side.

"Savages," the queen whispered softly. Her eyes were locked on something across the river. Veena turned to follow her gaze.

"Oh my god," Veena gasped when she saw the angry column of black smoke rising above River Town. "What happened?"

"It's those Frontier terrorists," Callista said, balling a handkerchief in one hand. "They're sending us a message by striking this close to the city."

The queen touched Veena, and Veena was startled by how gaunt her hand looked. She looked up to see Callista's emerald eyes glistening with tears.

She's changed.

When the Von Arx clan had handed their nineteen-year-old daughter over to the king, she had captured the world's imagination with her stunning beauty and grace. But now, Veena saw only fear in her eyes.

"What do they want?" Veena asked.

"They're traitors. Power-hungry traitors and nothing more." Callista gripped Veena's arm with surprising force. "You do believe my husband is doing the right thing, don't you, Veena? You believe that we should make peace?"

"Of course I do."

"I feel so much better knowing that your father is out there, fighting the Frontier."

That's why you want to throw him to the lowbloods.

"My father likes nothing better than fighting."

"Even so, we're lucky to have a warrior like him on our side. Even if . . ." Callista paused, suddenly awkward.

"Even if he doesn't agree with the ceasefire," Veena said.

"I can't blame him, Veena. After what the humans did to him in Arizona . . . It breaks my heart that he won't be at the Decennial Parade."

Veena nodded. He father would rather be horsewhipped than celebrate next to a king ready to emancipate humans.

"He means no offense to the king by it," Veena said.

"So glad to hear that." Callista smiled. "Come. The tea is getting cold." Callista led Veena to a wrought iron table set for tea.

"They're so dreadful," Callista started up again as she wiggled her fingers and levitated the teapot, pouring a cup for both of them. "I sat in on one of my husband's intelligence briefings last week. He doesn't like it when I'm there, but I hate being kept in the dark. In any case, the SSD is still trying to determine how Frontier functions. What their capabilities are. I really shouldn't be discussing this, but I don't think we should keep this a secret. The people should know." Callista rubbed her arm nervously. "Do you know what they call their leader?"

"What?"

"The Snake Mother."

"Snake Mother? That sounds ludicrous."

"Apparently, they worship her like some kind of deity, but we still don't know for sure. Three years it's been since she overthrew the Western Province, and to this day, every patrol we send out over the Rockies never comes back." She shook her head. "So dreadful."

"I had no idea it was that bad," Veena said.

Callista looked around and then leaned in conspiratorially. "You know, I've actually *seen* one of them."

Veena's eyes went wide. "Really?"

The queen nodded. "Your father caught one of them alive—one of their warriors. He was being kept in an SSD prison for questioning. An awful-looking creature with these horrible tattoos and scars all across his body, snapping his teeth like a rabid dog." Callista shivered at the memory. "I heard later that he chewed off his own tongue and choked on it to escape questioning."

"That's horrible," Veena gasped.

"That's what we're facing: extremists."

"That explains all that," Veena said, pointing to the ring of Phoenix Guards floating fifty feet above their heads.

Callista rolled her eyes. "My husband's idea. He won't admit it, but I think there have been threats on my life."

You have no idea.

Callista touched Veena on the knee. "But let's forget about this ugly business, yes?"

"Gladly." Veena raised her cup and drank the fragrant tea.

"I just wanted to acknowledge the elephant in the room," Callista began, her hands balling the handkerchief again. "When I heard about . . . about what happened to you—about you going to rehab—I wanted to reach out. To do what, I don't know. Maybe just let you know I was thinking of you. But your father didn't want anyone seeing you in there." Callista covered her face and sobbed. "I am so sorry, Veena. I've been such a terrible friend."

Veena steadied herself. She was prepared for this.

"You're not a friend," Veena said.

The queen's eyes rose above her fingertips, startled, ashamed. "Veena—"

"You're more than a friend." Veena smiled. "You're a sister. You always will be."

Callista's face lit up. She stood up and embraced Veena tightly. "Thank you, Veena. I'm so happy we're together again!"

Friends. Veena felt suffocated by Callista's perfume. *A friend who will watch silently as her husband throws me and my father to the wolves.*

Callista squeezed Veena's shoulders. "I'm so going to enjoy our time together."

Veena flashed her brightest smile. *I'm going to enjoy watching you burn, bitch.*

*

"The king must die," the Lady in the Veil had told Veena a year and a half ago in the frosted gardens of Crosslake.

Who this woman was and how she had slipped past security, Veena did not know. All she knew was that for the past six nights, from the moment the vision had stopped her from killing herself, she had seen this woman in her dreams over and over—the veil and the frozen gray eyes.

The last vision had shown her this place, the tiny Garden of Reflection, hidden away in the depths of the Crosslake compound. She had woken at dawn and trudged through the snow to the tiny clearing by the icy brook. She sat down on a bench and watched the sun rise through the scrawny branches.

Five minutes later, the Lady sat down next to her.

"What is happening to me?" Veena asked.

The woman faced straight ahead, the scarf covering her face. Veena could only see the woman's frosted breath in the air.

"You have been chosen," the woman said.

"Chosen for what?"

"Six nights ago, you were prepared to end your own life because you had lost your way. I'm here to reveal who you are meant to be."

"And how would you know anything about me?"

The woman watched a sparrow land on a branch. "Your father doesn't know what you are—what great deeds you are capable of. But he will, once you save his life."

The vision came back to Veena—the terrifying march to the gallows. "I don't understand what I saw," she said. "Why were we being hung?"

"Because the king will betray you both. Just over a year from now, he will sign a peace treaty with the Redbloods—"

"*Bullshit.* Not the king."

"He will. His enemies grow bolder by the day. The west has fallen to the Frontier rebellion, and they will not stop until their banners fly over the Golden Fort. The United Nations waits and plots, gathering their armies to cross the oceans and topple the Crown. The king knows he is under siege. An alliance with humans is his only hope. He will have a united front against the Frontier Specials and a shield against UN intervention."

"The Redbloods would never agree to peace with the king."

"They will. Patriot Gold will give them two things they want more than anything: a homeland . . . and the justice they seek."

It took a moment for Veena to understand. But when she did, a sickening weight fell in her gut. "My father."

"The humans blame your father for starting the Immortal War. He is responsible for the deaths of thousands of humans. To the Redbloods, Sixkills is a genocidal tyrant who is next in line for the throne. And the general has made it very clear what his first order of business would be should he ever wear the crown."

Human extermination, Veena knew.

"I have seen his trial," the Lady began. "A criminal tribunal where he is paraded like a dog for the cameras. I have seen yours. And you have seen what follows."

The noose once again slipped around Veena's neck. She heard the angry mob barking for her blood.

And then the Lady told Veena the bloodshed that would follow her and her father's deaths. The Redbloods would soon betray the king, Frontier would spread like a cancer, and UN nuclear bombers would darken the sky. The Golden Kingdom, the Specials' one and only homeland, would be swept into the sea.

"The king must die," she finished, "so that our people can be saved."

They sat in silence. Around them, the world woke up. The sun brought a weak heat, and snow shook off the branches.

"Are you one of them?" Veena asked. "Those psychics I've heard about from the Southern Province? Sibyls, I think they're called."

The woman smiled. "No, Veena. I am simply a humble disciple of His."

"His?"

"He Who Knows All."

"Who is that?"

"A prophet. A Special Gifted beyond imagination. And unlike the king and his corrupt court, He desires nothing—not power, not money. Simply that we, the Nation of Specials, live free forever." The Lady breathed softly. "I know it may be hard to believe. It was for me. But I have seen that His word is true, that His prophecies always come to pass. And He needs *us*—the dedicated, committed few—to hold back the coming disaster."

Veena stamped her feet against the cold. This was becoming ridiculous. She stood up, suddenly dizzy with withdrawal nausea.

"This is too much," she said. "I have to go."

"Red fox. Ten seconds."

"What?"

"Over there," the woman pointed to a snow bank twenty feet away.

Veena turned and looked. A few seconds later, a red fox peeked above the bank. It locked eyes with Veena and then scurried away.

"Have faith, Veena," the Lady said. "There are others like me—freedom fighters who can save your life, your father's life, and this entire kingdom along with it. But we cannot do it without you."

Veena shook her head.

"No."

"No?"

"I can't help you."

"Only you can help. No one else."

"Look at me. I'm in a fucking hospital. I have no fucking Gift. Even if what you say is true, how can I stop what's coming?"

The Lady's eyes held her. "You believe that being able to fly and shoot bolts is what makes one special. You believe that your worth is based on how much of the Gift you have. But the truth is, the greatest power one can have is the courage to do what's right when everyone else is afraid."

The woman rose and pulled the scarf back over her hair. "He will visit you again to show you your path."

"What does He want me to do?"

The woman smiled.

"To be our savior."

*

On the patio of the Lady's Eye, Veena and the queen talked until the sun went down and lamps flickered on around them. The servants cleared up the empty teacups and replaced them with almond biscotti. As Callista bit into one, she turned to watch the setting sun tinge the clouds pink.

Veena braced herself. It was time.

"What are you wearing to the parade?" she asked.

"Oh, who knows? I have about sixty designers begging me to wear their dresses."

"I'm ashamed to admit it, but there's going to be one more designer begging you."

"Really?" Callista raised an eyebrow.

Veena went down the stairs and brought back the slim box she had left there. She unwrapped it and, with a flourish, unveiled the Peacock Gown, holding it in front of her own body. Callista's jaw fell open.

"Oh, my. Is that the one . . . ?"

"From the show," Veena said.

"Oh, my," Callista said again, feeling the fabric between her fingers. "It's even more stunning up close."

"I made it for you."

Callista took the dress and held it in awe. Her fingers traced the gold vines woven across the corset.

"You're going to look incredible in it," Veena said.

The night after the Lady in the Veil had found Veena at Crosslake, He Who Knows All had shown Veena another vision, as promised.

The vision of her mission.

She saw Queen Callista up on the dais, resplendent in the Peacock Gown as the Decennial Parade passed below her. She smiled and waved, standing next to her husband, King Patriot Gold.

Then, somewhere in the crowd, the weapon they called the Sun Angel would detonate. The blast would send out a signal that Callista's dress—which was not a dress at all, but a finely woven mesh of electronic receivers—would recognize and amplify.

And then . . . Veena's body trembled as she remembered it.

White fire. The queen, laced with silk and secrets, would become a lightning rod for the Sun Angel, screaming as a hellish fire warped and melted her body. And next to her, King Patriot Gold would be swept off his throne by a tide of flames.

*

The Lady's Eye disappeared behind the closing gates. Veena's heartbeat thrummed as her Escalade pulled away.

She had done her part.

Tonight, the lowblood driver hired by Faraz would pick up and transport the Sun Angel into the shadow of the city. When the Sun Angel detonated three nights from now, the dominoes would fall fast.

The evidence would lead back to the lowblood driver and his Redblood connections. The pieces would fit together in the vulture minds of the Gray Faces, the conspiracy threading itself together into a vicious spider's web.

Her father, General Sixkills, next in line to the throne, would sweep his eyes over the trail of death left by the Redbloods and then take to the skies with an army built for one purpose:

Holocaust.

And she, Princess Veena Sixkills, would watch a new world rise from the battlements of the Golden Fort.

He Who Knows All had promised it to her.

Veena leaned her head on the leather seat and closed her eyes. She allowed herself a smile as she listened to the tires trundling over the streets all the way back to the ferry.

12

Something was wrong.

Houston shifted inside the darkness of his camouflage hide and scanned the forest again through the Cyclops night vision. The small clearing blazed green, circled by the black limbs of oaks and beeches.

Still no sign of the truck.

The truck will reach the clearing at 10:00 p.m. sharp and not a minute later, Faraz had told him. *The truck's ignition will be keyed to your fingerprints. They'll take your car, and you'll take the truck. Remember, ten sharp. These men don't tolerate tardiness.*

Houston checked his watch again. Ten fifteen.

He had a hard-and-fast rule about handoffs: wait ten minutes past the drop time and no more.

A breeze rustled through the treetops. Clouds drowned out the moon and darkness covered the forest like a shroud. Houston had never been scared of the woods before, but something out here in Ringwood State Park unsettled him.

Five more minutes passed.

Houston wanted to leave, but Faraz's words came back to him: *This job may sound simple, but my clients have made it very clear that failure will have consequences.*

Ten years Houston had survived in a notoriously brutal business because of his rules—the set of guidelines, procedures, and practical superstitions that nudged the odds of his survival upward. But to abandon the mission now meant no Gold Stamp, no escape hatch to a better life.

A delay didn't necessarily mean disaster. The trails here were rugged, and the truck might have blown a tire or fallen into a ditch.

Neither the Cyclops heartbeat monitor nor the Owl-Sight spec sensor showed any activity. Houston crawled out of the hide and scanned his surroundings. All was quiet.

He packed his gear into his rucksack. Using the tree line for cover, he edged his way around the clearing toward the trail.

*

It was slow going up the dark trail. He had to measure every step, avoiding fallen branches and loose stones. Usually, he could count on chirping crickets to provide cover, but there were none tonight. Other than the cries of a sullen bird, the forest was silent.

Houston approached a low hill. In a thicket of birch trees at its base, he found the first body.

Houston swung his rifle up.

Male, five eleven. Multiple gunshot wounds to the arms, legs, and torso—

The man had a thick white beard and was propped up against a birch, a silenced pistol in his right hand. Houston kicked the pistol away. Switching the Cyclops to heartbeat mode, he scanned the body. Flatline.

Back in night vision mode, Houston saw blood, broken branches, and churned dirt on the hill ahead of him.

Houston flattened out onto his stomach.

Where is the killer?

His finger grazed the Colt's trigger. The man with the white beard, who may or may not have been one of Houston's contacts, was shot somewhere over the hill. He had managed to escape his attackers and roll down the slope to here.

To his west, Houston spied the old skeet range, overgrown and littered with smashed clay birds. To his east, the black curves of the Ramapo Mountains loomed, faceless. On a clear day, you could spot the towers of Sovereign City in the distance.

His choices had rapidly narrowed: retreat and fail, or stay and die.

Or, Houston reasoned, *get up and fight.*

Houston rose to his feet and faced the bloody trail. He had no plan, but he had a gun and a job to do.

*

The box truck stood in the center of a clearing by the edge of Shepherd's Lake. It was painted gray, with a fifteen-foot cargo hold, and was shielded underneath a camouflage tarp.

Four bodies, Houston counted. Sprawled out on the dirt, guns gripped in dead hands. Two dead riders in helmets straddled off-road motorbikes. Two other men lying closer to the truck. Shell casings everywhere.

An ambush.

Houston slotted together the clues. His contacts had arrived with the truck and waited in this clearing for their rendezvous time with Houston. Then, before the men could drive down to meet Houston, two bikers had rolled in with bad intentions. The bikers would have known that the truck's ignition was keyed into the driver's fingerprints. They would have wanted to take him alive. Studying the bodies, Houston guessed the driver had been the big bald man lying closest to the truck.

The lone bird cried out in the distance. Houston watched the truck for a few minutes. With the driver dead, he was the only one who could start the vehicle—something a sniper waiting in the trees would know too. A bullet to the gut would take minutes to bleed out—enough time for the sniper to drag him into the truck and press his fingers against the scanner.

Houston looked at the open truck. He listened to the silence of the woods, hoping that something would deter him from what he was about to do next.

He took a deep breath, and then rushed headfirst into the kill zone.

Houston braced himself for the sudden crack, the scream of the sniper's bullet as it tore through the air.

He slammed into the truck, using it as cover. His heart pounded.

Dropping down to one knee, Houston untangled the dead bodies of the biker and the bald man. If he was right and baldie was the driver, he would have the truck's keys with him.

Houston turned the bald man onto his back.

Fuck.

The man's pale blue eyes stared at Houston. An unmistakable shrapnel scar ran from his left temple to the back of his neck.

Lazlo Koyle.

Houston had done business with Lazlo many times, had sold him everything from machetes to military-grade explosives—the tools of Lazlo's very specific trade.

Because Lazlo Koyle was a Redblood.

Not just any Redblood—a high-ranking officer in their elite paramilitary unit, the Redguns, responsible for carrying out a decade-long campaign of bombings, assassinations, and kidnappings against the Crown.

Houston felt a dull ache in his temples.

What was a hardliner like Lazlo doing delivering a truck to Faraz's clients?

Faraz's *spec* clients.

Houston cut off his train of thought. It wasn't his job to figure out how far down the rabbit hole this went.

"Sorry, brother," Houston whispered to Lazlo as he reached into the dead man's jacket and pulled out the truck keys. There were three keys on the ring: an ignition key, a padlock key, and a flat key that resembled a USB drive.

Keys in hand, Houston checked the rear cargo door of the truck. What looked like a simple padlock kept the door shut. But on closer inspection, Houston realized that a thin magnetic strip sealed the door to the lower frame. A flat keyhole was embedded next to it for the USB key.

Houston exhaled. The cargo was safe.

The truck cabin was cramped and smelled of lemon disinfectant. Houston slid behind the wheel, slouching below the windows as he turned the ignition key. The console illuminated, and a box below the dashboard blinked on, directing Houston to "Please place all five fingers on the screen."

Houston pressed his five fingertips onto the cool glass and waited. The box buzzed, and the truck's engine rumbled to life.

Peeking above the steering wheel, Houston hit the gas. One hand stayed on his rifle as he maneuvered the truck past the bodies and out of the clearing.

"Freaking tank," Houston grumbled as he muscled the truck onto the park's main road. His foot was heavy on the pedal, but still the truck struggled to accelerate pasty fifty.

The added weight of ballistic armor, Houston knew from experience. Somebody went through the trouble of welding blast-proof plates underneath the truck's frame and switching out the tires for bulletproof run flats. In all the handoffs that Houston had done, he had never seen this level of security. The bulk reminded him of the old, plodding Hercules mechs he'd trained on before the Tin Man models arrived on the battlefield.

He wondered how much weight the cargo added.

Houston drove with the headlights off, the world tinged green through his Cyclops scope. As he turned the truck around a bend, he heard a soft buzzing.

The buzzing grew louder and then suddenly receded, as if pulled away on a string.

Then bullets smashed into the windshield.

"*Shit!*"

Houston wrenched the truck to the right. The bulletproof windshield was a mess of impact craters, and Houston couldn't see the road. He dropped low in his seat and floored the gas as gunfire raked the hood. The strange buzzing grew louder, hovering overhead.

Houston knew exactly who—no, *what*—his attacker was.

He kicked down on the brake. The truck spun, rubber burning. Through his window, Houston caught a glimpse of his pursuer: four furious rotors, a cannon strapped to its belly.

Houston's head hit the door as the truck screeched to a stop by an embankment. The attack drone overshot the truck by ten feet. Houston watched it recalibrate itself and spin around, its red laser eye locking onto its prey—

Houston twisted the ignition off. The drone's cannon spat a wall of bullets into the passenger door.

Move.

Houston flung himself out of the truck, grunting as his knees smacked on the road. He was up, running, rifle in hand. The drone's buzzing grew distant.

Gaining altitude for a better shot.

Houston had one hope. He sprinted around the back of the truck and dove down the embankment. The ground rose up to meet him. His right shoulder bounced hard off loose rocks, shrubs tore at his shirt, and dirt sprayed into his eyes.

Thud. His ribs bore the brunt as he pinballed off a tree. Above him, branches wheeled in the dark, reaching down like clawed hands. Pain lit up his body.

The buzzing returned.

Get up. He pushed himself up to his knees.

The drone hovered angrily at the top of the embankment, its red eye flashing as it patrolled the dense tree line.

It was a Skyfire quadcopter. Houston had smuggled enough of them to know their main weakness. On an open battlefield, it could reach speeds of up to sixty-eight miles per hour. But in dense environments—like tree-lined forests—its fragile rotors could easily snag on branches. Houston flipped it the bird, safe in his thicket.

The Skyfire unleashed a frustrated volley of bullets, unable to cross into the dense forest.

Protected by the trunk, Houston checked his body. Other than scratches across his back and arms, he was in good shape. He had lost his rifle and goggles, but the truck keys still jingled in his jacket.

The gunfire ceased. A few seconds later, the buzzing disappeared.

A bad thought struck Houston. The Skyfires were remote-controlled. Their range was no greater than two miles, which meant . . .

Tires churned up dirt. Houston spun around the trunk just in time to see a motorbike bounce down the slope, its helmeted rider hunched over the bars.

He had five seconds, Houston guessed, before he was overrun. The bike threw up a rooster tail of dirt as it zagged toward him. Unarmed, Houston only had one hope—

He ripped the flashlight out of his jacket and aimed it. A blazing halo of light lit up the forest. The blinded biker fired an errant burst into a tree, his bike twisting under him. He hit the ground hard, gun clattering across the rocks.

Houston leapt toward the gun. His fingers had just wrapped around the grip when a stone hit the back of his head, sending him sprawling.

Footsteps raced up behind him. Houston spun around just as the charging rider cannonballed his shoulder into Houston's chest with an ugly *thud*. Houston tumbled down the slope. At the bottom, stones dug into his back, and his mouth flooded with blood.

The rider ran down after him.

Houston scrambled to his feet, dodged the rider's kick, and grasped the man's leather jacket. The rider swiveled and caught Houston's temple with a back fist. Houston returned fire, throwing a combination of fists and knees. Each blow felt like he was hitting a rock wall.

The rider cracked Houston across the jaw. Houston's vision turned to water.

Crack. Another blow across the back of Houston's head. A terrible weight fell on his windpipe.

The cool touch of a suppressor pressed into his cheekbone.

"Get up, motherfucker," the rider growled.

*

The rider marched Houston back up the hill to the truck, prodding him forward with his automatic pistol.

Houston was going to die. The rider would get him to start the truck with his fingerprints, and then—*thwack*. Game over.

"Move faster," the rider ordered.

"Fuck you."

The rider chuckled. "The balls on you."

Houston knew from the way the rider had fought that he was a professional, probably an Immortal War veteran working the mercenary beat.

"Picking fights with Redguns, huh?" Houston said as they stepped back onto the road. "Dumb move."

Another metallic prod on his spine.

"Redguns like killing specs," Houston continued, "but they love killing blood traitors. They have a special building for it. The Red Bitch herself designed it. You know what they call it?"

The rider spun Houston around and slammed him into the truck. The rider spoke through gritted teeth. "They call it the Bonehouse. And if you call me a blood traitor again, you won't get a bullet—you'll get the blade."

Despite the darkness, Houston could make out the rider's features: black hair cropped short, the face hard and misshapen, skin stretched taut over bones that had broken and never healed properly.

"I know you," Houston said. "You're a . . ."

The man grinned like a skull. The broken face swam up from the dark pool of Houston's memory—a moldy old kitchen, snow falling outside the windows. Guns out on the table. Lazlo inspecting the weapons. And behind him . . .

"Damian Jackson," Houston said. "What the fuck are you doing here?"

Jackson shoved him toward the driver's door. "Open it."

Houston did.

"Get inside. Start the truck."

Houston took his time looking for the truck keys. Jackson jabbed the gun into his ribs.

Houston had met Damian Jackson once in River Town, on a weapons deal with a team of Redguns—a team led by Lazlo Koyle. A team whose second-in-command was Damian Jackson. Jackson and Koyle were comrades, fellow Redguns . . .

What the fuck was going on?

A turn of the key. The console lit up; the fingerprint pad buzzed.

"Don't Redguns frown upon killing your superiors?" Houston asked. While he talked, he scanned his surroundings for a weapon or a way out. "What did Koyle do, pass you up for promotion?"

"Fingerprints," Jackson growled.

The scanner read Houston's fingerprints. The truck woke up.

Jackson pulled Houston out onto the road and marched him to the edge of the embankment, facing the dark woods. Houston heard Jackson take a few steps back from him, preparing the shot.

"Any regrets?"

"What?" Houston asked.

"I ask everyone: Any regrets?"

Houston looked up at the sky. He wished he could see the stars, but gray clouds covered them.

He remembered himself, many years ago, running for freedom through a muddy field, white mountains moonlit behind him.

He thought of Bobby. Of his mother. Of sitting in Big Don's penthouse, the city outside the windows, a pile of cards on the plush rug.

A strange thought came to him, unbidden. He was flying over the sea, toward the island he had seen in Bobby's song.

"Too many to count," Houston answered.

He closed his eyes and waited for the shot.

The bullet whispered as it left the suppressor.

Houston felt warmth spread across his bare neck. And then . . .

Nothing.

He blinked. The woods stretched before him. His heart thudded against his ribs. He was still alive. But he knew he had heard the silenced gunshot.

Before he could turn, he sensed a presence next to him, shifting above him. Within seconds, he felt it all around him—a sinuous pressure wave that thickened the air.

Houston spun around. A brass bullet hung an inch from his face, suspended within the pressure wave. A high-pitched vibration rattled his bones, and a sudden burst of white light blinded him.

The blast took him off his feet.

The force spun him around like a leaf. When he fell, grass filled his mouth.

Death. The word rose up inside him.

For a moment he was lost, spinning down a black hole. Then air reentered his lungs, and he pushed himself onto his hands and knees, the world regaining clarity.

He saw Jackson on the road, getting back to his feet. Behind him, Houston saw the truck.

The truck . . .

It levitated five feet above the blacktop, floating on a bed of stars. The stars burned so bright that Houston had to shield his eyes. Then the light grew dark and toxic, laced with a black rage. Houston felt it wrapping around his heart, his chest. *Squeezing.*

The truck touched down softly. The light fell away, and the night was still again.

Jackson steadied himself. He turned and spotted—

The gun.

Houston saw it at the same time, lying on the road.

Houston crashed into Jackson as they both lunged for the weapon in a tangle of knees and elbows. Jackson's fingers clawed at Houston's eyes. Houston strained forward, the fingers of his right hand grazing metal, curling around the rough grip—

He twisted hard. The gun came up in an arc, the suppressor lodging below Jackson's left eye.

Thwack!

Jackson jolted backward. Blood sprayed across Houston's face. The Redgun fell onto his side, the white of his remaining eye shining in the night.

Houston wiped the blood off his face with his sleeve and stood, watching the truck. A mass of dark energy roiled around it, invisible to the naked eye—but a presence that Houston could feel in his marrow.

Before he could stop himself, Houston marched over to truck, reached into the cab, and switched off the ignition. He took the keys, opened the padlock on the cargo hold, and keyed the magnetic lock.

The lock hummed. Then, with a pressurized *whoosh*, the bolts slid open. Houston gripped the door handle.

He froze for a moment. The crickets were chirping again. Birds flapped and cawed in the trees. The forest was coming alive around him. He wondered if he could ever go back, if there was any hope of return once he opened these doors.

He flung the doors open.

The hold was dark, and Houston felt a cold air slither out. He couldn't see anything in the gloomy box at first, but slowly, something began to take shape, pressed against the interior right wall of the hold.

Houston retreated, stunned.

He turned around and walked away from the truck. He walked in circles, cursing. He looked up into the sky and blinked at the clouds.

"No," he finally said. He leaned against a tree and slid down to the dirt. "No, no, no, no . . ."

13

The soldiers surrounded the king and fired.

Patriot Gold fell to the valley floor, his body spasming as dozens of whipper bullets tore through his armor. The slashing rain swirled his blood into the muddy battlefield.

I hate this part, Faraz thought as he shifted in his seat. *So melodramatic.*

On the screen, the soundtrack plunged tragically as Patriot Gold took his last breath, surrounded by his human killers. After a long war, the leader of the Special rebellion was dead.

Faraz checked his watch. Other than a few snoring drunks scattered around the tattered seats, he was the lone spectator in the Monarch Cinema, suffering through the interminable *Rise of the King 3: The Resurrection.*

Truth be told, Faraz did enjoy the first two installments in the *Rise of the King* trilogy. Those films, even though they were produced as propaganda after the war, did a serviceable job of charting Patriot Gold's course from CIA-trained weapon in the Orchid Program to civil rights activist to rebellious outlaw. But this third film was sentimental garbage. Faraz's contact was late, and he didn't know how much more of this movie he could sit through.

Business meetings used to mean a cozy bar and a cold mezcal. But since his car crash, bars were off-limits to Faraz. And due to its unpopularity and lack of alcohol, the Monarch was his best option for conducting clandestine transactions.

On the screen, the camera zoomed in accusingly on the gleeful face of Attica Corum, the Special who had betrayed Patriot Gold and lured him into the Appalachian Ambush, as history would brand it.

Faraz felt a twinge in his stomach. He was soon to betray a friend of his own.

Behind him, he heard footsteps walk down the row and the crinkle of a paper bag.

She's here.

She sat down behind him, and the smell of vodka made him dizzy. Even though Faraz no longer conducted business in bars, he could depend on Celia Jones to bring the bar to him.

"I love this part," Celia said.

"You're late."

"Got held up at the Box. New boss is a bitch."

The Box was what the Sovereign Border Patrol called their data center. Forty and thickset, Celia was a midlevel SBP officer and a longtime "independent contractor" for Faraz. As a Beta Special, one of those Gifted with inconsequential powers, Celia occupied the lower rungs of Special society. Her days in the Box were spent amid the blue glow of surveillance screens, scanning for intruding illegals—a thankless and poorly paid position.

A perfect mark, Faraz had thought when he first met her in a Catalan bar on the Bowery. Her SBP credentials allowed her to move in and out of the city without inspection. Her drinking problem and two young boys at home guaranteed she was grateful for any possible side income, regardless of the legality.

Celia Jones was the ideal person to smuggle the Sun Angel into Sovereign City after Houston delivered it to River Town.

The time now was ten thirty. Faraz estimated that Houston would be on his way back with the Sun Angel at this very moment. The drop-off time in River Town was scheduled between eleven thirty and midnight tonight.

"Why are we meeting here?" Celia asked loudly.

"Keep your voice down."

"Relax, Fuzzy," she said, calling him by the nickname he hated. "So you done with the drinkies now?"

"Yes."

"Man. Guess some people just can't handle the city."

"How are your boys?" Faraz growled. "Still fatherless and destined for a life of crime?"

Celia breathed loudly behind him. Faraz regretted his words immediately.

"I'm sorry. That was unprofessional of me."

Celia gulped down more vodka. "All good, Fuzzy. My boys are growing up to be just like their shithead dad." She drummed her fingers on the armrest. "So what's cooking?"

Faraz slipped a thick envelope out of his jacket and into the gap between the seats. Celia pulled it away.

"Details and compensation are in there," he said. Onscreen, Patriot Gold's resurrection began, his levitating body shrouded with a heavenly light as the humans retreated, aghast.

"Ooh, this scene gives me the tingles," Celia said, bouncing in her seat.

"I suggest you put a pause on the drinking," Faraz warned. "You will be required to drive to River Town and pick something up."

"Fuck," she hissed. "I hate the Strip."

"Then give me the money back."

"Chill, Fuzzy. I don't hate it *that* much."

Faraz rose and slipped toward the back of the theater. Behind him, the violins reached a feverish pitch, the angels sang, and a god was born. He took one last look back. The camera was tight on the horrified face of Attica Corum, the betrayer.

A hand clamped down on Faraz's chest. He walked out of the theater, remembering that image. A most inauspicious one, he thought. For he still had one job to do tonight: finalize the details of Houston Holt's death.

*

This is not a business for friends, Faraz reminded himself as he turned off Orchard onto First Avenue, heading uptown. Life was cheap in this new world, and Faraz could not hesitate to pull the trigger on Houston Holt.

His father wouldn't. Mehmet's empire had been built on the bones of his enemies.

As well as his friends.

And here I am, Faraz sulked, *agonizing over one River Town criminal.*

The city clanged dully around him. Workmen in a crane set up an arching banner across the avenue, which read, "The Grand Decennial Parade featuring the Songbird. Begins Sunday at midnight." The city was gearing up for a party, yet Faraz felt apart from it, a sober ghoul untouched by the festivities.

Houston had been a loyal soldier—the only person who would still work with him after his accident.

It's just business, Faraz repeated to himself. The veiled woman in the park had been very clear. Success meant Nadia and Yasmin back in his life. And for that, for his wife and daughter, Faraz would trade *anything*.

Houston was now on his way back from the pickup, Faraz guessed. An hour from now, he would park the truck containing the Sun Angel in a secured warehouse on the northern boundary of River Town. Then he would go home as Celia arrived at the warehouse, changed the plates on the truck, and drove the Sun Angel past the Sovereign City border checkpoints without inspection. Then she would drop it off at a secured garage in

Washington Heights, where it would wait until . . . he didn't know when.

He didn't know what the Sun Angel was or why he needed to smuggle it into the city. Drugs, maybe. Guns, perhaps. It didn't matter. It was a job, a challenge from his father to rehabilitate his broken life.

To his left, he glimpsed the cozy lights of the Jade Lounge and heard the laughter of the drinkers inside. Faraz's shoes hammered against the sidewalk as he raced north, pulling past the bar's gravitational field. The night of his crash, he been drinking in that bar. It was where he had met Emily, the girl who had died in his Porsche.

Faraz lit up a Murad and went over tonight's plan once again, using the simple repetition to stabilize himself.

Within the next hour or so, Houston would be waiting at home for Faraz to knock on the door with the naturalization forms. But Faraz would not show up with papers. He would be bringing something else.

There is loss in this place, Faraz thought as he reached the underground garage where his BMW was parked. He looked up at the lights of the city, at the brilliant gold plume of the Kingspire. *There are things here that look so beautiful but can crush a man.*

Maybe I'm doing Houston a favor, he thought hopefully. Maybe, when there was a knock at the door and Houston opened it to find men with guns, it would be the most merciful path his life could take.

*

When it came to hiring assassins, the Kingdom was a buyer's market.

On the surface, that wouldn't seem to be the case. The Kingdom seemed like any other orderly civilization, humming along with doctors, lawyers, executives, and bureaucrats. But those who paid attention knew that the real grease in the engine were another group of people entirely—for both inside and outside its borders, the Kingdom had never stopped fighting a war.

And what a country at war needed most were killers.

Killers to deal with seditious humans. Private militias to be wielded by vicious oligarchs in their struggle to snatch up resources. Discreet professionals hired to "vanish" troublesome mistresses and ambitious journalists.

As Faraz drove off the ferry and merged into the snarl of River Town, he knew that for every type of problem in the world, there was a specialist trained to erase it.

To solve the problem of Houston Holt, Faraz had gone down the extensive list of his options. At the top of the killers hierarchy was the Shadow Regiment, a private army of former elite Special operatives from the Immortal War. Its ranks were filled with Silverbacks, Phoenix Expeditionary Marines, Gray Face telekinetics, and even Southern sibyls. They were the Kingdom's most feared mercenaries, but the Regiment was prohibitively expensive.

At the bottom of the hierarchy was the scrabble of human freelancers, short on subtlety but willing to work on short notice at rock-bottom prices. The River Town Blade Boys, for example, who preferred getting up close to their targets with their shanks. Unfortunately, with the freelancers, there really was no quality control. Faraz preferred not to use them for a mission this sensitive.

Faraz would have to climb a few rungs higher on the hierarchy to find his "security technicians," as they were called in the halls of Ibrahim & Sons. Earlier in the day, he had reviewed the three criteria that all consultants were expected to follow in this exact situation: Competence, Cost, and Discretion—CCD, another of his father's beloved acronyms.

The men he had hired fit all three criteria. Lifelong criminals from before the war, their competence was not in doubt.

Better yet, they were locals, able to strike and disappear into the crevices of River Town in an instant.

Cost: somewhat steep, but nothing Faraz couldn't expense to his operating budget.

And finally, discretion. These were men bound by an archaic outlaw honor; they would die before snitching.

But best of all, these men *wanted* Houston Holt dead.

I probably could have gotten a discount, Faraz thought as he turned his car onto Adams Street and parked. He was early. It was only a quarter past eleven, and the meeting was scheduled for eleven thirty.

Exactly fifteen minutes later, Faraz watched in his rearview mirror as the three men approached his BMW.

They opened the doors and slipped inside. One man sat up front with him, the other two in the back seat.

"Greetings, Mohammed," the man next to him said.

"My name is not Mohammed," Faraz snapped.

"Okay, Mo." The man grinned. He was in his forties, with unsettlingly blank eyes.

His name was Como, and Faraz didn't even want to guess his body count number.

In the back seat, Griggs and Fuentes sullenly watched the street and lit up cigarettes.

"No smoking in the car," Faraz said.

They ignored him. Faraz fumed as thick smoke blew around the interior. Despite his anger, he understood their animosity.

These men were Eschevera *sicarios*.

The Escheveras had been the reigning crime family in River Town immediately after the war. Their power over the refugee sprawl had been absolute, enforced by their brutal army of *sicarios*.

Until Houston Holt had come to town.

With his military connections and burning ambition, Houston had pried away the gun trade from the Escheveras. Only the power of Ibrahim & Sons had forced the Escheveras into an uneasy cold war with Houston's network.

And they were still bitter about it.

To help ease the tension, Faraz handed the men three bulging envelopes from under his seat. Como opened his and counted the goldmarks. He smirked.

"Never thought I would get this call," he said to Faraz. "Especially not from you."

"Well," Faraz said, "here we are."

"You are a cold-blooded *A-rab*," Griggs chuckled from the back, "icing your own man."

"I've been waiting a long time to cap that fucker," Fuentes growled.

"Do you have the information I sent you?" Faraz asked.

Como nodded. Fuentes handed him a tablet computer. On the screen, a green dot blinked on a satellite terrain map.

"That's Houston," Como said, pointing to the green dot.

Faraz looked at the screen. As was standard procedure, the burner phone he had given Houston had been embedded with a tracker chip.

"What's his location?" Faraz asked.

"Still out in the park," Como replied.

"What?" Faraz scowled at the motionless green dot. He checked the time. 11:33 p.m.

The handoff had been scheduled for 10:00 p.m. If all had gone as planned, Houston and the Sun Angel should have returned to River Town by now.

"Been like that for ten minutes," Fuentes said. "Not moving."

Faraz's throat tightened as he watched the motionless green circle.

What are you doing out there, Houston?

14

Houston sat by the road and watched the truck. The cargo hold stood open like an entrance to a dark cave.

He was a target out here in the open. Redgun reinforcements would be on their way right now, racing through the darkness toward him.

He had to move.

He stood up and walked back to the truck. He peered inside.

Seven, maybe eight years old at the most, Houston thought as he looked at her.

She gazed back at him from the cargo hold, sitting on a bed bolted to the floor. The expression on the girl's face was the same as it had been when he'd first opened the doors—a serene curiosity that unnerved him, as if by seeing him she was able to unearth all his secrets. Her eyes were unnaturally bright, set off like a storm against her black skin and her tangle of curly brown hair.

Those eyes, Houston thought. They were far too old to belong to a child. They had seen too many horrors.

And then there were the colors.

Shimmering like oil in water, snaking through the air around her. Houston watched tendrils of pink, sapphire, white, and violet burn in her aura, blinking like stars.

She stood up, still looking at Houston. Then she took two steps toward him and punched him in the nose.

"Son of a bitch!" Houston stumbled back, holding his nose. "What the hell?"

"I can't help you," the girl said. "I won't . . ."

She grasped the side of the truck, her legs buckling. Her eyes rolled to the back of her head, the lights extinguished, and she collapsed to the floor.

Houston jumped into the hold and lifted her up. She felt fragile in his arms, like a small bird. He could feel a warm energy ebbing away through her skin.

He sat her up in the front seat. Her eyes were closed, and she wasn't moving.

He was reaching for a water bottle when he heard it: the woods were *roaring*.

A heavy wind circled through the treetops, rustling the leaves madly. Birds cried out and flapped their wings as beasts large and small scrabbled across the undergrowth. It was like nothing Houston had ever heard before.

Houston locked the doors. The girl slid sideways, flopping onto the seat. Houston lifted her up gently and put the water bottle to her lips. Her small hands curled around the bottle, her eyes fluttering as she took little sips.

Drugs. Guns. Even a full-grown adult he would have been able to tolerate in the back of the truck.

But a kid . . .

Using the butt of his rifle, Houston hammered the bullet-ridden windshield out of its frame. Five minutes later, they were on the road. Houston glanced at her from the corner of his eye. She was huddled against the door, wearing his jacket like a blanket—and watching him intently.

Just put her back in the hold. Then go pick up your Gold Stamp.

It was that easy.

The Redguns were willing to kill each other over her. A very powerful spec out in Sovereign was willing to hand over a Gold Stamp for her. The smartest thing to do right now was put her back in the hold, drop the truck off in River Town, and move on.

He glanced over at her. She was fast asleep.

He drove intently down I-78, the lights of River Town twinkling on the horizon. Beyond them, he saw the skyline of Sovereign.

He pulled the truck to the side of the highway. She must have felt the deceleration because she sat up and looked out the window.

"Where are we?" she asked in a soft voice. She looked at Houston. "Are you taking me home?"

The way she looked at him made him turn away.

"Yeah." Houston nodded. "Taking you home."

She shifted along the seat and lay against his arm. He could feel her energy again, that heartbeat rhythm that warmed his skin.

"Yeah," he said again, looking down at her. "We're going home."

He laid her back down on the seat. With the truck still running, he stepped out onto the road. After a quick scan with the Cyclops scope, he walked ahead of the truck and dropped Faraz's burner phone on the concrete—the one he knew was tracking his every move.

Houston climbed back into the truck and accelerated its bulk forward until he heard the phone crack under the reinforced wheels.

15

The green dot flashed across the black screen, creeping toward the articulated mass of River Town on the map, hypnotically sliding closer and closer . . .

Gone.

Faraz squinted at the map.

The green dot had vanished.

Como flicked the screen with his fingers. When that didn't do anything, he logged out of the software and reloaded it. But it was the same. No green dot.

"What happened?" Faraz asked, suddenly nervous.

Como frowned at the screen. "Signal's gone."

"I realize that. Where did it go?"

"What kind of tracker did you use?" Como asked.

"A Technica GPS chip."

"Hmm."

"What?"

"The Technicas are solid gear," Griggs said from the back. "CIA shit. They don't drop signal. Ever."

"He's right," Como said. "There's only one way a Technica would fizz out." He looked at Faraz. "The phone's been dumped."

"Dumped?"

"Destroyed," Griggs said. "Shot, stomped, blasted—"

"Okay, okay." Faraz's mind was already churning. "There is a possibility that the tracker just malfunctioned."

"A fucking small possibility," Griggs said.

"But if it did, the phone can still receive calls, yes?"

Como shrugged. "Yeah."

Faraz dialed Houston's burner phone. There wasn't even a ringtone.

Como read Faraz's expression. "He dumped the phone."

A dull ache throbbed in Faraz's temples.

Houston had destroyed the phone.

It was a betrayal. How fitting.

"What's our move, Mo?" Como looked at Faraz expectantly.

Faraz started the car. "We're going to his house."

*

The shadows slipped through the dark confines of Houston's apartment, guns sweeping.

The three *sicarios* moved like wraiths. Silently, meticulously, they searched for their prey, clearing the apartment room by room. It took them less than a minute to secure the space.

Houston wasn't home.

*

"Was he there?" Faraz asked when the men returned to the car.

Como shook his head.

"Shit," Faraz grumbled. Just then his phone rang—Celia Jones.

"Where the fuck is this clown?" she yelled when he picked up. "I've been waiting here for forty-five minutes. If this dickface doesn't—"

"Stay where you are until I call and tell you differently." Faraz hung up.

It was well past midnight. The operation was dead in the water.

No. Faraz could not walk away from this mission empty-handed.

Failure meant his father's disappointment.

Failure meant Nadia and Yasmin were gone from his life.

Sweat trickled down his back and soaked his shirt. Failure meant the wrath of Veena Sixkills.

Houston had a thousand places to hide in the Strip, and if he wanted to disappear, it would be impossible to find him.

But, Faraz realized with a flash of relief, he had planned for this.

As per the Ibrahim & Sons guidelines, he had drafted a contingency plan for just this situation. The rulebook was clear on this point: *never trust only one asset.* If they go rogue, you're screwed. Diversify your people. Keep your assets working for you, and better still, working against one another. A natural balance would form with everyone watching everyone else.

And he had someone watching Houston from very close.

Faraz dialed another number. It rang twice before the person on the other end picked up.

"I'm looking for a mutual friend," Faraz said.

"We have a few mutual friends," Klay Park replied.

"This one you work for."

"Used to work for."

"What do you mean, 'used to'?"

Klay grumbled, "Fucker broke my orbital last night. Over some Velvet Lane whore."

Faraz pressed on. "In any case . . . do you know where Houston would go if he was in danger?"

"A lot of places," Klay replied. "But if he's in *real* danger . . ."

Faraz waited, the phone pressed to his ear.

"Then he'll go to one person," Klay said. "Find the redhead."

16

Her name was Lily.

Houston hadn't asked her for her name; she'd just offered it up on the drive back to River Town. Her strength had returned in the truck, and along with it came the questions.

"What's your name?" she had asked.

"Not important."

"Why?"

"We don't need to know each other's names."

"Mine is Lily."

"Not important."

When Houston had pulled the truck into River Town, she had gasped at the lights of Sovereign City across the water.

"Are we going there?" she had asked.

"One of these days."

He dumped the truck in a warehouse by Bayside Park and swept every surface clean of prints. Lily followed him, toting her small backpack, as he led her into Curry Gardens, the Indian stretch of River Town's southern tip. He took the long route to the safe house, bypassing the cluster of late-night restaurants on Newark Avenue. He was on the border of Eschevera territory and being spotted was not on his to-do list.

At one point, lost in his own thoughts, he looked back and saw that Lily wasn't there. In a panicked rush, he raced around the corner to find her kneeling over a snoring drunk on the sidewalk, rifling through his pockets. She slipped out his wallet and walked back to Houston.

"What are you doing?" he asked her.

She shrugged and held up the wallet. "Do you need money?"

"No."

"Good." She pulled out a wad of goldmarks and tossed the wallet. "More for me."

Now, sitting in the safe house, watching her eat, Houston realized what a huge mistake he had made.

He got up and left Lily with her bowl of soup. He paced down the hallway of the apartment. It was a two-bedroom place on the second floor of a house that Amin owned. The pantry was stocked with canned foods, and the fridge held water and a bottle of Crown Royal. A collection of burner phones was locked in a wall safe for emergencies, and a hand-drawn map hidden in a desk—a map that Houston had memorized—outlined all the secret escape passageways and weapon stashes in the floor plan. This one time, Houston was grateful for Amin's paranoia—this was a place for desperate men.

He went back to the kitchen, poured himself a glass of Crown, and sat on the couch. He took a big swig and weighed his options.

Going home was out of the question. Houston had already ignored ten calls from Faraz on his personal phone. Alarm bells would be ringing all across Ibrahim & Sons.

A thought crept up on him suddenly: *Did Faraz set me up?*

He gulped down more whiskey, not even tasting it. He had no patience for speculation. His mind wrapped around the facts, the things he knew so far.

The Redguns had been involved. That was bad news. Infighting among the criminal lowlifes of River Town was expected, but the

Redguns were different. They were trained soldiers—dedicated rebels. Not once had Houston ever heard of Redguns killing each other. It just didn't happen.

So what *had* happened?

Lazlo Koyle had been delivering Lily to Houston, which meant that Lazlo was working with Faraz's spec clients. Damian Jackson had been sent to take Lily back from Lazlo. So if Lazlo was working with the specs, then it would be logical to assume that Damian's mission came directly from the Red Bitch herself.

Houston had something the Red Bitch wanted—and she always got what she wanted.

By bringing Lily here, Houston had pissed off not only one of the most powerful criminal dons in Sovereign City but also the leader of the ruthless human rebellion.

"Well done, Holt," Houston muttered, toasting himself. "Well fucking done."

Walk alone, stay alive. Nothing holding you back. No wife, no kids, no family. Because that was what it took to survive in this world.

But that was gone now. His code was dead the minute he opened that truck.

He was dead the minute he opened that truck.

His phone was in his hands, Faraz's number on the screen.

Call him. You can still fix this.

His thumb hovered over the dial button.

He heard Lily get up from the kitchen table. She walked into the living room and stood there.

"You have any more food?" she asked.

"You just finished two cans of soup and three energy bars."

"I'm still hungry."

"Go buy something with the money you stole."

She blinked at him, her eyes shimmering like submerged lights. She scratched her nose and waited.

Houston dug into his pocket and pulled out another energy bar. "I'll give you this under one condition."

"What?"

"I have two rules. Follow those rules, and things go smoothly."

Lily squinted, suspicious.

"Rule number one: no talking in the house."

"But—"

"You're already breaking rule one."

She crossed her arms and glared.

"Rule number two: no talking in the house. Nod if you understand my rules."

Lily held his gaze, her eyes bright and unflinching. Then she turned and walked into the hallway. Houston, still holding the energy bar, heard the bathroom door close.

Weird kid. Houston drained his whiskey and went back to the kitchen for another. But the bottle of Crown was missing. He rooted around all the cabinets, but the bottle had disappeared.

In the living room, he found Lily on the sofa, thumbing through one of Amin's old *National Geographic* magazines.

"Where's the whiskey?" he demanded.

"I hid it."

"Why?"

"So you don't drink it."

"Give me the bottle."

"Drinking won't solve your problems."

"My only problem now is I need a drink and I can't get one."

"You sound like my dad."

"Where is your old man?" Houston pulled out his phone. "I'll give him a call right now. Get you off my hands."

"He's dead."

"Mom? Friends? Who'll come get you?"

"All dead," she said.

"You don't have *anyone*?"

"I have you."

Houston shook his head. "You don't know me, kid."

She shrugged. "You're a thief. And you're afraid."

Houston smirked. "You're a spec psychic. Congratulations."

"No." She grimaced. "And I hate that word."

"Psychic?"

"*Spec*. Don't call people that."

Houston took a breath and sat down next to her. "I just need a drink."

"And I need some more food," she said.

Houston handed over the energy bar. She devoured it. She wiped the crumbs off her face and then leaned over, rubbing her nose against his sleeve.

"What are you doing?"

"My nose itches."

"You have hands. Scratch it."

She fixed him with her big, stern, yet childlike eyes. "Weirdo."

"You're the weirdo here."

She stood and walked to her backpack against the wall. She pulled out a sketchbook and colored pencils, sat on the floor, and started to draw. From time to time she looked up at Houston like a painter studying her subject.

Houston glimpsed a black bracelet on Lily's right wrist. He had seen it in the truck but had thought nothing of it then. But now, in the light, he saw its crystalline surface, a black lattice that glimmered like spiderwebs.

That wasn't a bracelet. It was a Clamp.

The last time he had seen one was back at Camp Olympus.

During the war, Camp Olympus was a sodden pit of despair up in the Cascades. After being wounded in Chicago, Houston had been reassigned to guard duty there.

The inmates called it the Freezer.

The Freezer was where they sent powerful spec prisoners of war.

Technically, it was an interrogation camp, but none of the captives were under any illusion as to what their ultimate fate was. After their "interviews" with the CIA, the prisoners were trucked out to death camps in Wyoming or Utah.

And all of them wore Clamps.

The Clamps were military hardware. They locked around a spec's wrist and, using magnetic suppression technology, muted the prisoner's Gift, rendering them temporarily powerless.

Houston watched Lily intently. Only an extraordinarily powerful Special would have been able to stop Damian Jackson's bullet while wearing a Clamp.

"What are you?" he asked her.

"You're breaking your own rules."

"Look at me."

Lily put her pencil down and looked at him.

"What are you?"

She glanced at the Clamp on her wrist. Her attention wandered, and her eyes peered into a place that Houston couldn't see. She remained very still, as if her soul had left her body.

"Lily?"

She blinked and turned to him. "A lot of people think that I can save them with my Gift—that I *want* to save them. But they're wrong. And if you're thinking that I can save you, you're wrong too."

"Right now, I think you're a problem."

She smiled. "*That* I can handle."

She went back to her drawing. Houston watched her for a moment before pocketing his phone and walking in the master bedroom. He shut the door. There, he sat on the bed and dialed a number.

*

When he was done with his call, he didn't move for a while, unsure if he had made the right choice.

He had sealed her fate. Both of their fates.

When he went back to the living room, Lily had moved her art studio onto the coffee table. She drew intently, her array of colored pencils spread out across the glass.

"You can drink if you want," she said without looking up. She reached into her backpack and pulled out the bottle of whiskey.

"Maybe later," Houston said. He watched her draw for some time. Her hand moved gracefully across the page—far beyond a child's jagged technique.

As he watched, a question sprung to mind. He didn't want to ask it, but he had to know.

"You lied," he said.

Lily kept drawing. "Hmm?"

"You said you couldn't save me. But in the woods, you stopped the bullet."

The pencil stopped. She looked up at him.

Houston asked, "Why?"

Lily put her pencil down and looked away, head tilted, eyes far away, listening to a melody that only she could hear. For a moment Houston thought she had forgotten the question. But then she refocused on him.

"Because you have something left to do before you die."

Houston leaned forward, certain he had misheard. "What?"

Before she could answer, the intercom buzzed.

Someone was at the front door.

"Come with me." Houston took Lily by the hand and put her in the bedroom. "Wait here. Don't make a sound."

He went back out and checked the intercom camera feed before buzzing the downstairs door open.

The visitor stomped up the stairs. Seconds later, a knock hit the door so hard the hinges rattled.

When Houston opened the door, he could tell Katya was pissed.

"I knew it," she growled, bursting into the room. "I knew this day would come. You're in a pickle you can't get out of, and now you call me at the ass-crack of dawn for help. How badly did you screw up, Houston? How—"

She keeled over in a fit of coughing so violent that Houston was afraid she would collapse.

"Jesus," Houston said. "You start smoking again?"

"No, dumbass." She stood up, her eyes watering. "It's from the fire."

Houston felt like he had lost all sense of time. The hellish fire from the Frontier suicide bombing had only been hours ago, yet it felt like an episode from a past life.

"You got cough syrup?" she asked.

"Whiskey."

"Good enough."

Houston poured her a finger, which she shot back eagerly. Then, emboldened, hands on hips, she investigated the living room. Houston noticed that even though she had been asleep when he'd called, she'd taken the time to put on her ridiculous uniform: fatigue pants tucked into military boots and a shiny star pinned to her leather bomber.

"So what did you do?" she asked. "How badly did you fuck up that you need the help of a—what do you call me—a 'tin-badge sheriff'?"

"I didn't call you that."

"I think you did."

"I said you were a tin-badge lone ranger."

"You think I'll help you?"

"I remember doing you a favor not too long ago."

She scowled but said nothing.

"Also," Houston continued, "I tried to save you from that fire."

"General Sixkills saved me from that fire." She cringed. "God, it gives me the willies just saying that."

"Do you still work with that children's shelter?"

"I didn't say I would help."

"Do you?"

"It's a school. And yes, I help out there sometimes. Why?"

Houston was about to answer but he noticed Katya's expression change. Her gaze fell behind him, and her eyes grew wide.

Houston turned to see Lily standing in the bedroom doorway. "Shit." He looked at Katya and shrugged. "Katya, meet Lily."

17

The *sicarios* gathered underneath the cover of a white oak and prepared for war. They shut off their phones, strapped extra ammo to their kevlar vests, and hung flash bangs along their webbed belts. Griggs hummed to himself as he chambered rounds into his shotgun.

The more guns the better, Faraz thought. Because Houston Holt was the ultimate survivor.

Faraz looked at the target house down the block and took one last draw from his Murad before crushing it under his shoe. The cigarette had done little to calm his nerves. For the most crucial phase of the upcoming raid would be the one he was responsible for.

Like Klay Park had said, the redhead had led them to Houston. Fuentes had followed her from her apartment near Velvet Lane straight to a three-story house in Curry Gardens. He had called in the others, and they had parked a block away from the house, out of sight.

Faraz had hoped that what came next would be simple. The *sicarios* would break in, do their work, and Faraz would wait in his car until it was over.

But there was a hitch.

"They have cameras everywhere," Fuentes had reported upon returning from his reconnaissance. "No back entrance. Iron bars on the windows. The only way in is the front door, and that's got a recessed camera and reinforced frame. Can't get to it without tripping an alarm."

Houston had chosen his hiding spot well.

Como punched Faraz's shoulder. "Relax."

Faraz nodded, his neck tight.

"Tell me the plan again," Como said.

"We've been over this."

"This is a fight," Como said. "Everybody has a plan till they get hit."

"Ring the bell. When the door opens, go inside and put this"—Faraz held up a thin strip of aluminum—"between the door and the frame to stop it from locking."

"Good. Then what?"

"Go upstairs and pretend to offer him a deal."

"But really do what?"

"Confirm the location of the package."

"And then you just have to say the magic word."

"Godspeed." The word that would transmit through the pin-sized microphone hidden in Faraz's belt and bring the *sicarios* racing through the unlocked front door and up the stairs, guns firing.

"Just hit the ground when you hear us coming. Got it?" Como asked.

Faraz nodded.

"Just don't take your pants off and you'll be fine." Fuentes snorted, listening to the belt microphone's feed through headphones.

Como grinned and turned to Faraz. "It's time, Mohammed."

Faraz straightened his suit. He took a deep breath and walked out into the middle of the street, every footstep exploding like a bomb blast as he approached the target house.

18

"I think I'm having a stroke," Katya said, her face pale. She held the cold glass of whiskey to her forehead.

"Do you have numbness in your face?" Houston asked.

"No."

"Are you having difficulty moving an arm?"

"No."

"Then it's not a stroke. You're just being dramatic."

She glared at him. "Who is she, Houston?"

"I told you, her name is Lily."

"Why do you have her?"

"There was a misunderstanding."

"Are you trafficking kids now? Because if you are, I swear to god I will pistol-whip that fat melon head of yours so hard—"

"No," he snapped. "I don't touch that kind of business."

"Not yet." She drank. "So how *did* you end up with her?"

Houston raised an eyebrow. They had an agreement going back years—an uneasy alliance between lawman and criminal that depended on neither knowing too much about the other.

"I need you to take her," Houston said.

"What? Take her where?"

Houston looked to make sure that the door to the bedroom where Lily waited was closed. "To the school. And then out of town."

Katya frowned. The school was a house hidden away in the depths of River Town. In addition to providing a free education to kids, it housed battered women and orphaned children—anyone who wouldn't survive another day in the open.

"I never thought you could be involved with people like this," Katya said. "People who would hurt a child."

"I'm trying to get her away from those people."

"Look at you." She snorted. "You should have been a Badge."

"Didn't like the uniforms."

"Be a smart-ass. You still need my help."

"And a long time ago, you needed *my* help."

"I didn't ask for it," she snapped.

"You didn't have to."

They sat quietly for a moment, neither looking at the other as they tried to shoo away the memory of the dead Blade Boy—the debt that hung between them.

Katya spoke. "These people looking for her—are they looking for you too?"

"I can handle that part," Houston said.

"I can protect you."

Houston laughed. "Okay."

"I'm serious. If you're in trouble, the Badges can—"

"Katya, stay away from this. These people would kill a Badge without blinking."

Katya slammed her glass down on the table and jabbed a finger in his face. "Screw you, Holt! I told you where this would all lead. I warned you over and over."

"Don't start this shit again," Houston warned.

But Katya wasn't listening. "You could have been more than this. You had choices—"

"I had no choices."

"That's bullshit and you know it. All you ever gave a shit about was the money."

"I chose to move forward," Houston said, "because I realized what you didn't."

"Spare me this lecture."

"We only get to be as good as they let us."

Katya waved that off. "We get to be as good as we choose to be."

"America's dead, Katya. It's easier if you just let it go."

Katya watched him. "So there's nothing you won't leave behind?"

He didn't say anything for a moment. Then he sat down, letting the anger drain from his shoulders. "Take her, Kat. She won't make it here with me."

Katya drained her drink. "I can get her to the school tonight and arrange a transport out for tomorrow morning. There's another school further out, up in Minnesota, run by the Reds. A big farm with good teachers, from what I hear. That's as safe as I can get her."

"That's good enough." He stood up and spread his arms. "Wanna hug?"

She flipped him off. "Hug this." She turned to the closed bedroom door. "Her name's Lily?"

"Yeah. You should go meet her."

"Don't tell me what to do," she grumbled as she walked by him to the bedroom. Halfway down the hall, she keeled over in a coughing fit. "I'm fine," she snapped before entering the bedroom and closing the door.

Katya always had that annoying habit, Houston thought, of seeing the best in him. He wondered if he could ever cure her of it.

In any case, at least Lily was taken care of. His own fate, however, was still up in the air.

Houston sat in the living room and finalized his plan. Faraz could sniff out liars in his sleep, and the smallest misstep would be fatal.

He would tell Faraz a simple story, most of which was even true: Houston had arrived at the handoff site in Ringwood State Park on time. But after his dance partners didn't show, he went looking for them. That's when he found the truck and the dead Redguns. On his way out of the park with the truck, he had been ambushed. The truck had been stolen by another team of Redguns, and Houston had barely escaped with his life. The cargo was in the wind.

He was about to call Faraz when he heard the bedroom door open behind him.

"Houston?"

It was Katya. She sounded worried.

He turned to see her standing in the doorway, ashen. "I think you should take a look at this," she said.

*

Lily was sitting at the desk, drawing. Katya stood next to her.

"What?" Houston asked, a bad feeling in his gut.

"Show him," Katya said to Lily.

Lily put down her pencil and raised her right sleeve. A red snake coiled on the inside of her forearm, wrapped around an engraved black circle.

Houston had seen a tattoo just like it this morning—engraved on the chest of the Frontier kamikaze.

"Where did you get this?" Houston held her arm in his hands.

"From the Snake Mother," she replied, as if it were obvious.

Houston's head spun. Lily wasn't just a spec—she was a Frontier spec. And in the eyes of the Kingdom, every Frontier spec was an enemy combatant. Harboring one was treason, punishable by death.

Houston let go of her arm, and Lily went back to her drawing. He sat down at the edge of the bed and looked at the floor.

"Houston." Katya interrupted his thoughts. "We have to—"

The intercom buzzed.

Houston stood up, his hand tracing his pistol grip. Both Katya and Lily were looking at him.

"Who is that?" Katya asked.

"Wait here," he said before leaving the room.

On the intercom screen he saw a familiar face waiting outside: Faraz.

"Shit."

Houston ran to the kitchen and cleared away the dishes. He straightened out the living room. If his story was going to work, there could be no evidence of Lily's presence here. When he was sure there was none, he opened the front closet and scanned the security monitors linked to the cameras around the house.

The intercom buzzed again.

Houston ignored it. He checked all the feeds. A team of hitmen could be waiting in the shadows. As soon as he buzzed Faraz up, they could come swarming in.

The cameras revealed no one else on the street.

"Are you alone?" Houston growled into the intercom speaker.

On the screen, Faraz raised his hands, showing his empty palms. Houston buzzed him in.

Faraz's footsteps rose up the stairs. The staircase camera feed showed him approaching alone. His shadow darkened the space beneath the door. Houston unholstered his SIG.

Standing to one side, Houston flung open the door and pulled Faraz inside before slamming the door shut and bolting all six locks.

Houston turned to Faraz, keeping his gun held loosely by his side. Both men glared at each other.

"I have to search you," Houston said.

"You know I never carry weapons," Faraz said, his expression dark.

"Standard protocol."

"For your friends?" Faraz asked. "Or your enemies?"

"Neither."

"Ah. Of course. Just business." He raised his hands. "Let us get on with it, then."

After patting Faraz down and finding only a phone, cigarettes, and keys, Houston ushered him toward the sitting area. They sat down across from each other, Houston with his back against the wall. Houston noticed Faraz's eyes flick into the kitchen and then into the hallway.

"Can I smoke?" Faraz asked. Houston nodded. Faraz lit up and exhaled. He watched Houston through a curtain of smoke. "Do you have an explanation?"

"How long have we worked together?" Houston asked.

"I remember asking you that question quite recently."

"Four years. Four years with no mistakes," Houston said.

"And you made one tonight?"

"I'm saying my record entitles me to a fair hearing."

"We pay you *not* to make mistakes. It is the expectation. It does not entitle you to anything," Faraz said.

"Listen to what I have to say. Then decide."

Faraz leaned back. "Fine. Explain."

Houston told him the edited story. When he was done, Faraz let it sink in, his expression worried. "Redguns?"

"I was set up."

"By who?" Faraz crushed his cigarette into a tin ashtray.

"Maybe you," Houston said.

"Is that why you hid—why you destroyed the burner and didn't pick up my calls?"

"Did you set me up?"

"If I wanted you dead, Houston, I could have done it long ago and with much less effort."

"I told you four years ago: I don't get involved in politics," Houston said. "I don't take sides."

"You haven't."

"Whatever was in that truck was Redblood property. I was the pickup guy for something they didn't want taken. The Red Bitch would see that as taking sides."

"And what about your clients, Houston? What about me?" Faraz leaned forward. "Your behavior tonight—the loss of the cargo—that could be seen as taking sides against us."

"We can work something out."

"That's true; we can. A good place to start would be by handing over the cargo."

A silence fell between them, charged with volts. Houston scowled. "I told you I don't have it. The hijackers took it."

"Are you alone here?" Faraz asked, glancing toward the bedrooms.

"Yes."

"Then you won't mind if I search the house?"

Houston's hand tightened around the SIG's grip.

Faraz shook his head sadly. "I can help you, Houston."

"You think I stole the cargo?" Houston asked.

Faraz shrugged. "I work with you because I know what to expect. You are dependable. Predictable. But tonight is an anomaly. In my business, I have come to despise anomalies because they always are caused by the same thing—weakness." He clasped his hands together. "I have been down that road, Houston, so believe me when I tell you it leads to nothing."

Houston put the gun on his knee. "You try to put me in a box, Faraz, and this isn't business anymore."

"You can threaten me all you like, friend, but I am trying to help you. Kill me, fine. But then what? I am simply an emissary. And the people I answer to—well, I don't think you can truly comprehend the kind of enemy they can be. You are not suited for that type of combat. We are talking about people who count their fortunes in the hundreds of billions. Do you know how many bullets that buys? How many assassins? If you steal what is theirs, where is it you think you can hide? They will hunt you, and they won't unleash the half-breed hounds on you—the amateur killers. No, Houston, they will reach into the darkness and bring back the nightmares."

Faraz put his hand to his heart. "Let me help you, Houston. We can fix this together—before the monsters become a part of this."

Houston didn't move, but his grip loosened on the gun.

"You seem to think that I am your enemy," Faraz pleaded, "but I vouched for you. If you break the contract and run, they will come after me. After my family."

"I don't have a lot of choices here."

"You have one good choice. I don't care what the cargo is or why you took it. Maybe with your business faltering you thought you could sell it—"

"Hold up." Houston was surprised. "You don't know what the cargo is?"

Faraz shook his head. "Just an emissary, remember? But it doesn't matter. As I was saying, you have one good choice left." He paused before adding, "I have the papers in my car."

"The papers," Houston repeated.

"The citizenship application forms. You sign them, and with my sponsorship, this time next week, you'll be moving into a loft overlooking the Emerald Ring."

And there it was: two choices.

One would lead Houston to freedom.

And the other . . .

He slid the gun away.

"I'll be back," he said.

When he entered the bedroom, he saw Katya standing with the Hammer unholstered, Lily behind her.

Katya raised an eyebrow. "What's going on?"

"C'mon," he whispered to Lily. "I'm taking you home."

"What happened?" Katya asked, insistent.

"It's handled," he answered.

Katya saw the truth in his eyes. "No," she warned, rushing forward to block his way.

"Get out of my way, Katya."

"Don't do this." Her finger slid across the Hammer's trigger.

"Shoot me," Houston dared, locking eyes with her.

"Whatever they're offering you, it's not worth it."

Houston walked forward. Katya raised her gun.

"No," Lily said. She tugged at Katya's jacket and shook her head. "No."

She walked out from behind Katya and stood next to Houston. Katya put the gun down as Houston knelt next to Lily.

"There is a man here who will take you home," Houston said.

Lily looked at him, her eyes placid and deep. "And what about you? Can he get *you* home?"

"Close enough."

She put her hand in his. Houston stood and walked her to the door.

"You asshole," Katya growled behind him.

They were almost out the door when Houston felt a tug on his hand.

"Wait," Lily said. "I need to get something." She ran to the desk, where her pencils were. She grabbed a handful of them along with her sketchpad and returned to Houston.

"I drew this for you."

She ripped a drawing out of her sketchpad and held it up.

An intense blue sea. Birds, drawn in the childlike curves, soared above massive cliffs. And in the center, partly obscured by fog, a volcano unleashed blue flames into the sky.

The memory hit Houston right between the eyes.

He was sixteen again, deep in Bobby's dream, his little brother's song freeing him, launching him into the sky, where he flew above a turquoise sea, the island on the horizon. The black cliffs waited for him, and through the veil of fog he saw the blue flame—*felt* it in his chest—a vibration that called his name.

"What is this?" he asked, his hands shaking as he held the picture.

Lily shrugged. "Home."

Katya was now standing over them, watching Houston with a strange look on her face. "Are *you* having a stroke?" she asked.

Houston stared at the drawing for what felt like hours. When he looked up, Lily was smiling at him.

She'd known all along.

There were no coincidences with her, no random events.

You have something left to do before you die.

He looked at Lily. "Do you know where this place is?"

She nodded. "It's where I was born."

Houston folded the drawing and handed it back to her. "The man outside—he's not taking you back there."

"I know."

"What else do you know about him?" he asked.

She turned to the door, listening to a hidden tune. "He's lying to you."

"Houston, I don't like that look on your face," Katya said.

Houston got up and crept toward the windows, staying hidden as he scanned outside. The streets were empty, but that didn't mean that there wasn't anyone there.

It meant he was dealing with professionals.

He called Katya over to where Lily couldn't hear.

"What?" she whispered.

"Do you trust me?"

"Not at all."

"I have a plan."

Katya glanced back at Lily. "How deep are we in it?"

"There's probably a team of men outside waiting to kill us."

She rolled her eyes. Then she unholstered the Hammer, checked the cylinder, and slapped it back in. "Never an easy fucking day in the Strip," she muttered.

19

Faraz stood up and blinked when Houston brought the girl into the room.

Is this some kind of a joke?

The girl was not even ten—a black girl with wild bushels of curls and eyes that pinned him to the spot.

"What is this?" Faraz sputtered.

"What you asked for."

The girl didn't look away from him. He couldn't tell if she was upset or curious.

This was the Sun Angel—a child only a few years older than Yasmin. Maybe many years older. It was hard to pinpoint her age. Every time Faraz glanced at her, she seemed to change. It was the sensation of glancing upon a field of shooting stars—bright, brilliant, and elusive.

He hid his shock and took the girl by the hand.

"Wait here," he said to Houston. "I'll bring the papers."

Outside the house, Faraz exhaled. He had succeeded. The aluminum tape was still on the doorframe, preventing the door from locking behind him.

The girl followed him quietly. He strapped her into the front seat of his BMW, avoiding eye contact. He had spent much of his adult life around specs, but never one that made him feel this unsettled.

Soon she would be off his hands and everything would fall back into place—Nadia, Yasmin, his father. It was like glimpsing the shore after being lost at sea for years.

He made a scene of searching through the back seat for the Gold Stamp papers in case Houston was watching. When he was sure Houston couldn't see him, he spoke in a voice loud enough for the *sicarios* to hear through his belt microphone.

"Godspeed."

He watched as Como, Griggs, and Fuentes melted out of the shadows around the house and poured through the door.

Faraz slid behind the wheel, feeling the strange girl's eyes boring into him. He ignored her.

It would all be over in a few minutes.

He started the car. At least he wouldn't have to see the blood.

*

The *sicarios* raced up the stairs, their hunting boots soundless on the wood. Como and Fuentes braced on either side of the second-floor door while Griggs smashed it in with a battering ram.

Como tossed in a flash bang. In the blinding explosion of light and smoke, the killers breached the apartment, guns sweeping through the haze.

"Clear!" Como yelled in the empty living room. Fuentes tossed another flash bang in the hallway. The men bulldozed through the smoke and into the bedrooms. They checked in the closets, under the beds, and behind the shower curtains.

"Fuck," Como growled after searching the last bathroom.

The apartment was empty.

"Check this," Fuentes yelled from down the hallway.

Fuentes stood in the doorway of the laundry closet, glaring at the washer-dryer unit. He gripped the unit and swung it away from the wall like a door, revealing an escape chute leading downstairs.

"Son of a bitch!" Como snarled. "Move!"

The *sicarios* raced back down the hallway toward the stairs. Como had just reached the living room when Houston sprung his trap.

*

Padding down the stairs from the third floor, Houston took aim with his M6 rifle. When the killers appeared in the living room, they were lined up like bowling pins.

His first shot landed flush.

Griggs's head snapped back in a red mist. Como dove to the floor while behind him, Fuentes squeezed off one shot before Houston's whipper rounds tore through his body armor.

Como rolled between the dead bodies of his two men and fired back, driving Houston behind the railing as his high-caliber rounds tore up the banister.

Metal clanked on the wood. Houston glimpsed a black disc bouncing up the stairs.

Frag grenade.

Houston launched himself over the railing. His arms and feet broke his fall on the stairs below. The explosion shook the house and he grunted in pain as splinters of wood pierced his skin. His ears rang.

A bullet skimmed his shoulder. He sent three rounds back and stumbled down to the front door. Shouldering it open, he ran out into the night, coughing up dust and hoping like hell he wasn't too late.

*

Faraz shifted the BMW into drive and had just touched down on the accelerator when he felt a tank cannon press against his face.

"Park it, dickface," a woman ordered.

Faraz dropped his head. He put the car in park. From the corner of his eye he could see the streetlight catch on the woman's red hair and the mountains of dust on her, as if she had crawled through a crypt.

He considered trying to reason with her, but the gargantuan barrel digging into his cheek left him with no illusions.

The little girl touched his arm.

"I know what it's like," she said, her voice soft, "to miss my father. She hasn't forgotten you."

She unbuckled her belt and jumped out of the car. Faraz watched her go.

The gun jabbed into his temple. "Your phone and keys," the redhead demanded.

Faraz handed them over. The redhead pocketed them and, with one final dig of her gun into his face, picked up the girl and ran into the night.

Before the despair came, all Faraz could think of was the glowing warmth where the girl had touched him. What she had said.

*

The last killer was still alive.

If he hadn't been sure in the house, the bullets now whizzing past Houston's ears were confirmation.

Houston ducked behind a trash can and fired back. The killer dropped behind a car, bullets *pinging* off the hood. Houston raced around the corner toward the intersection of Magnolia and Baldwin, where Katya was supposed to be waiting for him with Lily.

Katya had not gone down the washer/dryer escape chute lightly. She'd nearly choked on the dust and had complained the whole way down. At first, Houston wasn't sure she and her Hammer would both fit in the cramped tunnel, but somehow, miraculously, they both had.

A fence post exploded in splinters next to him. He zigzagged down the street. Just as he reached the intersection, he crashed into something and went sprawling. On his knees, he looked up to see Katya holding Lily.

Katya was saying something to him.

"HUH?" he yelled, his ears still ringing from the grenade blast.

Katya grabbed him and lifted him. "*Run!*" she screamed in his face.

Together they bolted through the neighborhood. Behind them, Houston saw their pursuer reloading.

They needed a car, fast. Katya could have taken Faraz's car, but it was probably loaded to the gills with trackers.

A bullet tore off a tree branch inches from him.

Katya handed Lily to Houston and fired back. The Hammer's blast shook Houston's skull.

Lily held onto him tight as his feet pounded the road. His lungs burned, and his old war wound lit up his right side like a web of fire.

They turned sharply onto Wells Street. He heard Katya curse.

"Gun's jammed," she grunted.

Houston searched desperately for a car, each step burning his side. Every single car he saw had a club on the steering wheel. All around them, lights turned on in the windows. He heard people yelling.

Then came the dogs.

Small dogs and big dogs, skinny mutts and shaggy bears, barking at them as they passed, leaping over fences to join them. They grew in number until there was an entire pack circling them like a phalanx of bodyguards.

Katya looked around at their furry chaperones. "What the hell?"

Houston could feel the air humming, a charged cloud expanding from Lily's body. He heard her laugh.

Houston's foot hit a pothole. He stumbled forward, his knees thudding on the pavement. Katya skidded to a stop and came back for him.

The killer closed in. Houston braced himself for the bullet coming his way any second now—

He heard a surprised cry behind them.

Houston turned. Twenty feet down the street, the dogs swarmed their pursuer. The man backpedaled and screamed, dozens of jaws clamping down on his arms, legs, and throat.

"Get up," Lily whispered in Houston's ear.

With Katya's help, he got to his feet. They kept running, Houston still trying to process what had just happened.

"Left," Lily said in his ear.

"What?" He looked at her as they faced the cluster of alleys and streets ahead of them.

"Trust me. Go left," she said again. Her voice was like a shock to his system. It had changed from that of a child to something else, reverberating with authority.

He turned left.

They raced down Rose Lane, the barking behind them mingling with the bellows of confused neighbors and shrieking car alarms. Houston could feel the sweat cooling his back. Ahead of them, the Kingspire glowed like the dawn—red and pink with traces of blue.

"Here," Lily said. "Stop here."

Houston stopped. They had reached the mouth of a road leading to a construction site piled with debris—a dead end.

"Why are we stopping?" Katya panted.

"I don't know," Houston answered.

The dogs caught up to them, wagging their tails.

Houston set Lily down. "There's nothing here, Lily," he said angrily.

She looked away from him, quietly gazing up at the sky. "That's what you think."

"Fix your gun," Houston said to Katya. He reloaded his SIG. Their pursuer might still be alive. He might have called reinforcements.

"Look," Lily said, pointing.

A red Mustang careened down the street. Houston spun around and aimed for the driver.

"No," Lily said. "Don't hurt him."

The Mustang screeched to stop outside a house three doors down. The driver, a young man in a Knicks hat, stumbled out drunk and, having exhausted the last of his motor skills, keeled over a garbage can and collapsed onto the lawn.

"Told you," Lily said.

The Mustang's door was open, and the engine was still running.

"Son of a bitch," Houston muttered.

They jumped into the car, Houston sliding behind the wheel. Before his door was even shut, he hit the gas and the Mustang roared down the block. Behind them, the dogs chased after the car, howling and barking joyously. Lily watched them through the back window, waving goodbye.

20

"Anorexic ditz," Veena mumbled exhaustedly. Her fingers were numb from pinning and cutting all night, but finally the Peacock Gown contoured to Callista's twiglike frame.

Rising from her knees, Veena stretched her aching neck and took a step back from the gown, appraising it coldly as it draped over the tailoring dummy molded to Callista's exact proportions that the queen's messenger had delivered a few hours ago.

"The queen would like her first fitting tomorrow at three. Can I tell her you accept?" the messenger had asked with a flourish. Veena smiled through her teeth and, even though she knew the task would take her all night, she had agreed.

Because one did not refuse the queen.

Now Veena stood very still and studied her work. In the glow of the studio spotlights, surrounded by taped-up *Vogue Italia* spreads and David Bowie posters, the Peacock Gown shone, exquisite and terrifying.

Veena's fingers grazed the silk of the skirt, the embroidery and tiny jewels of the corset. She tried to decipher its secrets, but nowhere could she find the places where its fabricators had hidden the mechanisms of death.

The Lady in the Veil had convinced her that it was harmless on its own, that Veena could cut, sew, and pin it to her heart's delight—the gown would only awaken in the presence of its trigger: the Sun Angel.

A shudder rose up Veena's spine. Not for the first time, Veena felt both giddy and uneasy as her eyes swept over her creation. Her gaze shifted slowly from the jeweled dress to the studio's windows. Her studio was in the west wing of Starlet Manor, overlooking the fir-lined lawn that led to the waters of the Long Island Sound. On a clear night, from her private pier, she could see the lights of Sovereign City far in the distance, shimmering under the Kingspire.

What would remain of that wondrous city once the Peacock Gown finally awoke?

Veena switched off the lights and stepped out. She would have preferred to celebrate with champagne and oysters, but out here in her exile, mineral water and leftovers would have to do. Veena padded down the dark staircase to the kitchen, passing through shafts of moonlight that dusted the long halls of the manor.

This home used to terrify her. Other than Makini and the hired help, Veena was alone out here. She missed the city like a dancer missed the stage. In her first weeks here after Crosslake, she would wake up screaming in the middle of the night, the sound of angry cries in her ears and the heat of a fiendish fire on her skin. She *hated* sleeping alone, starting at the smallest sounds, keeping one open eye on the dark corners of her bedroom, convinced that something vile glared back at her from the shadows.

Veena found a box of kale chips in the fridge and munched on them as she wandered around the house, stretching her stiff limbs. Her circuit took her through the foyer and the formal living room and into the sun room, with its arched windows overlooking her pristine hedges and the moon-dappled waters of the Sound. The stillness of every room felt ice cold, like a preserved corpse. The mansion held an entire tapestry of silences within it—thousands of them, each one different, each one raising the hairs across Veena's skin.

But silence could be her friend too—a cocoon in which to grow and change.

You were once beautiful under the lights, but here in the shadows you will become the savior we need, the Lady in the Veil had told her once. *Be patient. Be brave. The shadows are your ally—your weapon.*

In the long hallway leading to her spa, Veena stopped in front of the only picture in the house that wasn't of her. She kept it hidden away here, unwilling to look at her father's face every day.

But her mother deserved better.

Both the general and Veena's mother, Mable, stared down at her from the framed portrait. Her father loomed in his United States Army greens, an armada of medals shining on his chest. Mable sat in front of him, her hands crossed on her lap, effortlessly elegant and roguish in her rose leather jacket and white sundress. Sixkill's giant paw rested on Mable's shoulder, and together they formed the impression of a jagged cliff face brushing up against a warm ocean.

Even though Veena had tried for years, she still failed to find any traces of her own face in her mother's beauty. Mable's eyes were a spring lake, alive with a loving presence that—even though Veena had only been a baby when Mable had died—connected her to her mother's warmth every time she looked upon them.

It broke Veena's heart that this portrait was all she had left of Mable. It was the only one that had survived when the lowbloods had tried to burn her alive.

Her eyes were drawn away from her mother to the picture frame. She scowled at the dark patches of soot that stained the edges of the wood. Veena could have replaced the frame a long time ago, but she wanted to remember.

She lived here now, in the desolation of Victory Island, because He Who Knows All had promised her salvation from the one thing she feared most, the one thing the lowbloods had taught her that terrible night in her family ranch in Millsap, Texas—a lesson lacerated across her shoulder blades with scar tissue and pain.

They had taught her the price of being powerless.

*

For weeks, the men and woman who came for Veena's life had gathered in the dark places of the country and plotted.

They wore no insignia or uniforms announcing their allegiance. They were nurses and engineers and veterans who melted out of the rhythms of daily life and transformed, as if passed through a poisoned sieve, into an army of retribution. Night after night, this shadow army congregated to assemble the machinery of murder, for they were honor bound by the code of the Native Sons Militia to avenge the deaths of their own, to retaliate for their brothers and sisters torn apart by Sixkills on the courthouse steps.

The general had sent a message to the world. They would send one back.

Time had run out on the craven politicians cawing from their podiums, promising change but delivering nothing. Their patience was gone for the biased media parading their collection of integrationists and bleeding hearts who squawked on inexhaustibly about pluralism and diversity, too caught up in their own intellectualizations to name the threat in their midst.

But the Native Sons harbored no illusions. The Specials were an invading army, a cultural cataclysm, and the militia would protect their country from them by any means necessary—even if that meant hunting down a child on the night of her eighth birthday.

The day of the attack began like any other for Veena. In the study of her father's Millsap ranch, she spent the morning struggling with her tutor as he tried and failed to coax the Gift out of her.

Veena trudged through these excruciating classes dutifully, half listening, mostly daydreaming about all the fabulous people who would be at her party tonight. She had cycled through six tutors already, and it would seem that no matter how hard she tried, she would never match her father's prowess. He had channeled his

Gift—*trained* it—into an earth-shattering force, a Gift as brutal as war itself. No one had any doubts as to what her father was capable of—not after the command performance of violence he'd unleashed five weeks ago in full view of the world's media.

Veena was lucky if she could get her Gift to crack open a window.

But she was young, and like all children, the future was vast and hopeful before her, and what she lacked now she believed she would find later.

As the tutor led her through a series of breathing exercises, Veena's attention kept being drawn away by the big men outside her windows, moving in teams across the vast shrubland of the property with hulking rottweilers on leashes. They were a small army of Specials that patrolled the ranch day and night like sentries in a besieged castle.

Which, in a way, they were—because Veena was the daughter of Sixkills, the most wanted man in America.

Along with her maid, Flora, Veena been watching the news on TV five weeks ago when *it* had happened. The Buffalo Six had stood on the courthouse steps, celebrating their "not guilty" verdict for the murder of teenage Special Javeer Sharma, their fists raised as they smiled smugly into the cameras.

And then Veena's father had arrived from the sky.

With mute fascination, Veena had gawked along with the rest of the world as her father tore into the lowbloods and etched the name of Sixkills into the history books with blood and terror.

Veena knew little of the events of the world, but she knew enough to realize that her father probably wasn't coming to her birthday party tonight.

After the tutor left, Veena bounded into the hallway, locked herself in her bedroom, and flung open her closet door.

There, draped in plastic and magic, was her dress—the dress Flora had custom made for her. The dress for her big, fabulous birthday party tonight.

She reverently pulled it off the rack and lifted the plastic. It was pink with embroidered roses. It was a dress her mother would have *loved*.

For her whole life, Veena had only known this home and its inhabitants: Makini, Flora, and a string of frustrated tutors. Her father was an occasional visitor at best. The people in her life were dutiful, silent, and serious.

But her mother . . . her mother *shone* from every corner of the home.

The clues were everywhere, like a trail of petals her mother had left for her to find, leading Veena to the remains of a magnificent civilization that had once stood on these grounds, a world of beauty, music, and pure, unsullied enchantment. Every day Veena looked upon Mable's pictures on the walls. In every frame, her mother seemed buoyed by some graceful spell—laughing at galas, in repose on a sunny beach, or surrounded by friends and admirers. Veena marveled at how her mother seemed so alive in every picture, like she was about to reveal a marvelous secret.

Flora would tell stories about Mable all the time. "She was so beautiful, Miss Veena," she would say. "She was a light, shining wherever she went. When she was gone . . . it felt like we had lost the sun."

Veena would often imagine her mother walking through these lonely halls with her. She would *hear* her voice.

You look beautiful, Mable would say when Veena slipped on her mother's string of pearls.

Stunning, she would remark, clapping her hands when Veena's tiny feet swam inside Mable's embellished Gucci sandals.

And when Veena burned with a fever in her cavernous bedroom, Mable would hold her hand and sing a song that brought tears to Veena's eyes.

Whatever remained of her mother in this home, Veena drank it all in, desperately thirsty for beauty, for love, for *life* out here in the long, dense silences of the sun-baked plains.

But the most mesmerizing feat of Mable's—the one that held Veena in thrall—was the effect she'd had on her husband.

Mable had died in a car crash before the Incident, when Veena was still a baby. Mable had remained human until her death, and yet Sixkills had loved her more than he loved anything. *Still* loved her. Veena could feel his loss in those rare moments when he was here—in the way he looked at the pictures of his dead wife and something vital stirred within his hooded eyes.

In her father's study, Veena would gaze up at the official portrait of her parents and wonder endlessly how Mable had solved the riddle of Sixkills's heart when no other living thing could.

And she did it without the Gift. *That*, Veena understood, was true magic.

Night came, and Veena's birthday party descended on the house like a glittering freight train. It was raucous, effervescent, *glamorous*. Every room bubbled with the laughter of titans and society queens. No matter that the only people *physically* in the home were Veena, Flora, and Makini, circled around a pink cake with eight candles. In Veena's imagination, Mable sat by her side, and the world around them danced.

The crowd sang happy birthday and cheered when Veena blew out the candles with a single breath. After Veena had eaten her slice of cake, Makini went back outside to supervise the guards, and Flora packed the rest of the cake into Tupperware for later.

The party ended. Evaporated.

Veena wiped pink and white crumbs off her new dress, went back to her room, and closed the door. She wrapped her pink dress back in its plastic and gently hung it in her closet.

She fell asleep listening to her mother's lullaby, a whispered song that opened her heart and carried her into a dream.

She slept with a faint smile on her face, oblivious to the world outside, where a clan of killers gathered outside her gates.

*

Her eyes snapped open.

She was flung out of sleep in an instant, landing in the alien darkness of her bedroom so suddenly that she gasped. Every cell in her body screamed in alarm.

Something had woken her—something *very close*.

She knew it was there, watching her. She knew it, knew it, *knew it* with a certainty that sickened her. While she had been asleep, something vengeful had crept in and now roved its eyes across her body. She lay ramrod straight in bed, hoping that if she just ignored it, if she didn't move a muscle, maybe it would go away.

It rustled.

Veena jolted up in bed, her hands flying to her mouth. Her bedroom was long, and in the dead of night it was an ocean of dense shadow and threat. At first she saw nothing. The long cavern of the room seemed suddenly foreign to her, like the hollowed-out spine of a treacherous beast. Before her eyes grew accustomed to the dark, her ears picked up the sound.

It wasn't a natural sound. Not the fall of a foot nor the scrape of clothing against the walls nor the whisper of a person's breath.

It was inhuman—a dry rasping that crept along the far wall. Veena shrank back in fear as the gloom cleared and something appeared: a pale horror, white as bone in the dark.

A boy, she realized in shock. No more than twelve years old, scrawny and shirtless, covered in a sheen of sweat. The boy was curled up on his knees, his entire body straining and trembling against an invisible oppressor. Veena thought about screaming, but he seemed so wretched that her first instinct was to help him.

He raised his head, and in his eyes she saw a world of unfathomable pain.

"I'm sorry," he sobbed. "They forced me . . ."

He opened his mouth wide.

Sound bubbled out of him like the breath of a submerged leviathan—a muddy vibration that clogged Veena's lungs, taking shape between them as something rank and vile and *alive*. A trembling maw opened up in the air, born of a foul Gift, stretching wide and disgorging something.

No, not something. Veena recoiled in horror when she realized what was emerging from that awful portal: an arm, a foot, a leg, a shock of white hair—*someone.*

She fell onto Veena's bedroom floor, birthed through the hellish canal, black and glistening.

A sick fascination, a belief that she was still in a dream, held Veena's tongue as the woman stood to her full height, wired with muscles and dressed in black camouflage, her ivory hair pulled up in a severe bun. Veena gawked at her face, streaked in war paint so dark that all that remained were the whites of her eyes, burning like stark, pitiless moons.

"Darling," the woman whispered in a voice so soft, so reasonable, that Veena forgot her peril. "Darling, darling, darling . . ." she took two steps forward, her hand slipping across her belt and sweeping out the serrated blade holstered there. "I have been *dying* to meet you."

It was too late to scream. The woman was upon her, the rough leather of her gloved hand clamping across Veena's mouth. The woman's weight dropped across Veena's abdomen, punching all of the air out of her lungs.

Then that vibration again. Veena could sense more of those awful portals opening as the pale boy birthed more terrors into her room.

It's just a nightmare, baby, Mable whispered to her. *There's nothing to be afraid of.*

Three more attackers fell upon her, war painted and grinning. Veena writhed madly as they held her down. She gagged when they shoved a balled sock between her teeth.

They're hurting me . . . The thought was stupid and useless, and Veena knew, with terror burning her throat like bile, that they intended to do a lot more than just hurt her.

One of the attackers filmed the scene with a small camera, focusing the spotlight on the white-haired woman straddling Veena like a priestess. The woman smiled into the camera and spoke in that soft, reasonable voice.

"This is retribution for the crimes of the spec terrorist Sixkills. You murdered our brothers and sisters. Now we, the Native Sons, patriots and the true blood of this land, take one of yours."

The woman licked her lips and whispered in Veena's ear, her breath warm and as sweet as honey, "You will not replace us."

The woman leaned back and raised the blade above her head with both hands.

Veena arched her back and screamed into the sock with every fiber of her body. In that moment, time slowed, and she felt her Gift awaken, felt it tear out of her pores and burst forth like a startled deer and slam into the woman above her.

The woman screamed, more out of shock than pain. The knife trembled in her hands, and for a moment, Veena felt hope—a hope that was dashed immediately as the woman recovered and refocused her murderous glare on Veena.

"Nice try, spec," she cursed, unhurt. Veena's puny Gift had, at best, only stunned her. She felt the woman's weight shift on her stomach and, blinded by the camera light, caught only a glimpse of the blade as it streaked down toward her heart.

Heat.

Burning, scouring heat.

Veena sensed it passing over her body, leeching away her flesh, blood, and soul. Warm liquid spurted across her chest, and sharp shards cascaded across her face and neck. She smelled charred flesh as the woman's weight fell off of her.

She opened her eyes.

The woman above her was gone. No—Veena blinked, and the scene became clearer—only the top half of her body was gone. The other three attackers were in various stages of spinning around, shouting, clamoring, reaching for weapons, reacting to the threat in the doorway—

Thwoom! Thwoom. Thwoom!

The Native Sons fell like axed trees, suddenly small against the fury of Makini's Gift as it burned through their bodies in great, bellowing blasts.

The rottweilers barked madly outside. Veena blinked and trembled, covered in bloody corpses.

Makini swept her out of the bed, her hands still warm from her Gift's afterburn.

"Don't cry, Miss Veena," Makini grunted as she carried her out into the hall. "You're safe."

She wanted to tell Makini about the boy—the pale, wretched boy who had brought the nightmares here—but as they fled the room, Veena realized the boy was no longer inside. He had escaped, and yet, Veena knew, he was still somewhere close. She could still feel his Gift in her lungs. She tried to warn Makini, but her voice was little more than a croak as Makini swaddled her and raced down the hallway.

And then Makini stopped so suddenly that Veena nearly tumbled out of her arms.

That awful rasping grated through the air. Veena pushed her head out of Makini's biceps and peered into the gloom.

Slithering portals opened around them.

One . . .

Three . . .

Five . . .

Veena gaped in horror as *dozens* of portals opened their slick wet mouths across the house, defiling every room, every hall, of what had once been her home but in the blink of an eye had rotted into a crypt. And in the places where her mother's magic had once sparkled and danced, the horde descended—a savage mob of face-painted monsters, wielding flaming torches and knives, tumbling into the house like a flooded river. Their rage was so thick that it turned the air to sludge.

"Kill the spec!"

"You will not replace us!"

Makini gripped Veena tight and ran. Together they hurtled through the madness, turning this way and that, Veena's stomach lurching with each hairpin turn. In the chaos, she caught glimpses of firelight across the long walls.

They had set the house on fire. Torches flew in through the broken windows and ignited the curtains first. The flames ate across the furniture, the rugs, the walls.

Veena gasped.

The *pictures . . .*

They were alive with fire—every picture of her mother, every memory of Mable and her beauty, devoured by the flames. Veena felt a sob catch in her chest as she watched her mother blacken and die right in front of her.

Crack! Makini cried out in pain, and Veena came tumbling out onto the floor as her giant bodyguard collapsed. Veena banged her head hard on the floor and lay there, stunned, for a few dizzying moments. Slowly, she picked herself up and blinked in shock at the sight of Makini on her hands and knees, huffing like a wounded bear. The mass of muscle between her neck and shoulder was blown out, a plume of blood soaking her white shirt.

More gunshots erupted behind them, shattering the windows.

Veena grabbed Makini's arm and pulled, struggling against her inert weight. The Native Sons streamed across the house, their voices growing louder and closer.

"Makini, we have to go!"

Makini grunted and struggled to her knees. Before she could rise to her feet, Veena felt a tingling along the hairs of her neck. She spun around.

A portal belched open twenty feet down the hall behind her. The man who emerged wore his hair long, his beard even longer. In his right hand he brandished a Molotov cocktail. He exhaled loudly and shook off the birthing fog before his gaze fell on Veena.

He was close enough that Veena could see his eyes. What she saw in them she would never forget for the rest of her life.

The man threw the Molotov.

Veena spun away as the bottle shattered against the wall, the long fingers of its liquid flame clawing outwards and carving into her back.

Pain exploded across Veena's body.

It was an agony wrenched from the depths of hell. It tore Veena's legs out from under her and made her scream until her throat was raw. The fire *ate* her, embedding its teeth deep into her boiling skin. She screamed and screamed as she burned alive. Behind her, the man unsheathed a blade and charged. She was powerless to fight back.

Thwoom!

The great thunder of Makini's Gift shook the world, and the man's head fractured into a foaming pulp.

Veena remembered little of what happened next. Later she would be told that Makini had funneled her out of the home through the underground tunnels her father had built long ago. But in that moment, all Veena could recall was screwing her eyes shut against the agony on her back and crying into Makini's bloody shirt.

Behind her eyelids, in the smoky darkness, she saw her mother's face devoured by flames, her depthless emerald eyes burning until they were black and empty.

From that day until the end of the Immortal War six years later, Veena had been on the run. Hunted.

Powerless.

Veena wiped her eyes. She touched the portrait of her parents and remembered.

The fire had followed her out of the ranch. It had hidden inside of her, dormant, until it had finally escaped eighteen months ago.

Memories of Mable—it was supposed to have been the couture show to end all shows, more expensive and extravagant than any other in the Kingdom. Veena had conceptualized it as an otherworldly ode to her mother's memory.

Otherworldly . . . and misguided.

No. Veena clenched her fists. Her intentions were good. Her execution, however, was poisoned by delusion, by blindness.

By Moxi.

It wasn't until Veena had swept out onto the catwalk, when the fog of Moxi lifted from her eyes just for a moment, that she realized what she had done.

The crowd grinned at her like a row of skulls—forced smiles, desperate eyes. They couldn't be seen disapproving of the Warbringer's daughter, but Veena could sense their discomfort, so thick and suffocating was its stench. She looked down at the gown she wore, at the gowns of the other models behind her on the runway.

Tacky.

Kitsch.

The work of a designer who was too high to realize her own foolishness.

She had brought her mother back to life, not as the regal, beautiful presence that she was, but as *this*—horrible, shabby, polluted and, worst of all, *ugly*.

Veena had raced off the stage in a storm of tears and humiliation and careened away from the venue in her car, sunglasses darkening her eyes against the burst of camera flashes from the circle of paparazzi vultures swooping down on her. That night, unable— unwilling—to face her failure, she did the next best thing: she obliterated it.

Moxi and more Moxi. So much Moxi it blew the top of her head off. Under its spell, she ventured out into the cold night, and—to this day, Veena didn't remember how—she found herself at her atelier in the East River Yards. The drug screamed like a fighter jet through her veins as she chained and padlocked the doors and poured the gasoline.

"I'm sorry." She whispered it over and over again, the hushed words gliding over her boiling shame. "I'm sorry," she said to her mother. "I'm so sorry."

She lit the match. Her seamstresses—the twenty slaves who had crafted her revolting designs—pounded on the heavy doors, screaming and wailing. Veena felt no anger toward them, no hate. She just knew that everything she had done, everything from her past, had to die.

The fire bloomed against the night sky. Fearsome and beautiful, it warmed Veena's skin and made her cry and laugh so hard that she barely felt the rough hands pull her away from the terrible flames.

*

The burned frame prickled underneath Veena's fingertips. One day very soon, her mother would reside in a place worthy of her grace—the halls of the Golden Fort.

The Sun Angel would arrive in Sovereign City tonight. He Who Knows All had shown her its power, but he had not revealed what it was. A weapon, she was certain. A very special weapon.

An Unholy.

The only thing powerful enough to kill a king who had conquered death once before.

The Sun Angel, magnified by the Peacock Gown, would turn every soul within five square miles of the parade to ash.

And ash doesn't resurrect, Veena mused with a smile.

A phone rang—the burner Faraz had given her.

"I must see you," Faraz pleaded over the phone. "The situation has changed dramatically."

*

They met on Asharoken Beach. Cool sand slipped into Veena's sandals as she approached the breakers rushing against the shore. Behind her, Makini stood outside the Escalade, watching her go. Veena had wanted to come alone, but Makini was having none of it. Makini had not only tagged along but had also brought two of her men with her. After the Frontier attack on River Town, she wasn't taking any chances.

Faraz was waiting for her by the lifeguard chair at the ocean's edge.

"What happened?" Veena demanded.

Faraz bowed his head. "I must apologize. Tonight has been—"

"*What happened?*"

Faraz looked out to the water. "We have lost the shipment."

"Lost the shipment?" Veena sputtered.

He nodded. He then proceeded to tell her everything, ending his tale with the sight of the Mustang—and the Sun Angel—fleeing into the night as the streets erupted with alarms and barking dogs.

"It's a girl?" Veena asked, bewildered. Of all the things she imagined the Sun Angel to be, a child was not one of them.

"Houston Holt has her," Faraz said.

"Fucking lowblood!"

"I will make it right," Faraz said. "There are men I can hire to track them down. The very best professionals. Very discreet." He inhaled on his cigarette. "I will make it right."

"Then why *aren't* you making it right?" Veena hissed. "Why are you here?"

"Ah." He crushed his cigarette underfoot. "There is the matter of . . . resources. You see, I was allotted a budget for this operation, and that has been depleted as of tonight."

"Ask *her* for more money."

Her—the Lady in the Veil. The suggestion seemed to put Faraz back on his heels. He shook his head.

"I think it would be best if she were kept out of this."

Veena's eyes narrowed.

"You see," he continued, "this could easily be misconstrued as a failure on my part, and—"

"It *is* a failure on your part."

"Not yet, Miss Veena. I would like the opportunity to make this right—before making this slight mishap an *official* matter."

"How much?" Veena couldn't believe she was agreeing to this.

"Not an insubstantial amount, but an excellent value for the caliber of services these men render."

Veena looked at him in the dark.

She knew she should never have trusted a lowblood.

*

On the drive back home, Veena tried to corral her racing thoughts. She was furious, terrified, and frustrated all at once. Without the Sun Angel, the Peacock Gown was useless, their plan hopeless.

She clenched her fists until her palms were sore. Why couldn't it just be simple? Why did everything have to be so hard for her?

They were a mile from Starlet Manor when the Escalade encountered an obstruction. Veena felt the truck slow down. In the front passenger seat, Makini leaned forward, one hand on her hip holster.

"What now?" Veena asked Beckett, the bald bodyguard next to her.

"I'm sure it's nothing, ma'am," Beckett replied. He tapped the driver, Suarez. "What are we looking at?"

"Roadkill," Suarez replied.

Veena craned her neck forward. A dead doe lay in the middle of the road, ghostly white in the headlights.

"Move it," Makini ordered.

"Fuck," Beckett moaned. "Those things have ticks."

Makini turned in her seat and stared Beckett down. "Do you need gloves for your delicate hands?"

"Do you have some? That would be great."

"Move it," Makini growled.

"Fine," he grumbled, "but it's a two-man job."

The truck idled as Beckett and Suarez marched into the headlights and lifted the dead animal. Straining under its swollen weight, they carried it into the darkness.

Veena waited, staring out into the night. The woods were heavy and wild here. The blackness outside the headlights was absolute, home to an unsettling silence.

Veena checked her watch. "What's keeping them?" she asked Makini.

Makini keyed in her wrist mike. "Beckett, report."

They waited. The radio was silent.

"Suarez, report."

Silence. Makini shifted in her seat, hand on her gun.

Something shot out into the headlights. Veena screamed.

"It's Beckett," Makini said.

Beckett dusted his hands as he approached the truck.

"Where's Suarez?" Makini asked when Beckett opened the door.

"Taking a leak."

"He couldn't hold it?" Veena grumbled.

Beckett shrugged and climbed into the truck, closing the door. The moment he sat down next to her, Veena felt something . . . strange—a rustling in her gut, like a subconscious alarm.

It was then that Beckett slowly turned his head and Veena felt his gaze land on her. It felt as cold and ghastly as death.

She faced him, and her breath froze in her lungs. Beckett was smiling at her, but something was horribly wrong with his face. It took her a second to realize what it was.

His eyes.

Oh, god.

Becket's pupils, once brown and dull, were now pulsing black orbs shimmering with a predatory hunger—the eyes of a monster beneath the waves.

"What the—" Veena's words died in her throat as Beckett whipped out his pistol and blew Makini's brains all over the windshield.

The blast echoed in Veena's ears. She leapt back, banging her head against the window.

Beckett turned to her, his face as blank as a porcelain mask.

Veena's hands clawed for the door handle.

Beckett raised the gun.

And with a flick of the wrist, jammed it into his own mouth.

The shot emptied his skull. He tipped over, his blood sloshing over Veena's bare feet.

The smells of death and cordite overwhelmed her. Her hands slammed down on the door handle, and she fell hard onto the road.

Move, you dumb bitch!

With a burst of will, Veena inched across the black road on her arms and knees, terror running loose in her mind.

Glass crunched behind her, and she spun onto her back.

She was being watched. *Hunted.*

Dust motes drifted in the headlights ahead of her. On the edge of the light, something moved.

Glass shattered. The headlights went dark.

In pitch blackness, the predator announced itself. Veena choked on its animal scent—blood, iron, and leather—scorching the back of her throat.

Fur rustled in the wind. She felt the monster's shadow, tall and seething, fall over her.

It was only then that she found the strength to scream.

21

As the lightless road stretched out ahead of the car, Houston couldn't shake the feeling of déjà vu.

He was on the run again.

Fifteen years ago, it had been his mother driving, fists curled around the wheel, an empty wine bottle by her feet. Bobby slept in the back while Houston, thirteen years old, kept himself awake, too afraid to sleep while his mother was behind the wheel.

Houston turned to his right. Katya snored next to him. Lily slept in the back.

Fifteen years, and no change. Only struggle ahead and chaos behind.

Driving down the turnpike out of the Strip was slow; it was a stretch of bomb craters and junk barricades set up by roving bandits. He spent as much time off the highway as he could, driving without headlights. The longer route gave him enough time to truly appreciate the mess he had left behind in River Town.

He could never go back.

Do you know how many bullets a billion dollars buys? How many assassins?

More than he could survive.

And all for her. He watched Lily in the rearview mirror. The whole drive she had struggled with some dark dream, shuddering and shifting under its weight.

Walk alone. Stay alive.

If he had no pressure points, his enemies had no leverage. The fight would be on his terms, using his rules. His Gift, he liked to joke to himself, was the ability to stay alive.

It was all blown to shit now.

Sleep crept up on him suddenly, like a thick fog behind his eyes. He blinked and stretched his jaw. The sun ignited over the horizon. It would be another fifteen minutes at most before they arrived.

He may be hunted, but he wasn't dead yet. And he had one last card left to play—a long shot, but that was the life of an outlaw. All you had left were long shots.

Houston gripped the wheel. So far, they had avoided the bandits on the road and the spec patrols that cruised the skies. But would they survive the Mad Fox?

They were about to find out.

*

The first rays of sun dappled the Carnegie River as Houston drove across the stone bridge. A group of bohemians sat on the bridge parapet and passed around a pipe, grooving to the beat of a bongo player.

Lily shifted and opened her eyes. Houston watched her rise up from under his jacket and blink at the passing scene.

"Where are we?" she mumbled.

"This," he said, "is Seekers Port."

"What kind of people live here?" she asked.

"The worst kind," Houston replied as he watched the dancing tribe by the water. "Hippies."

Depending on who you spoke to, Seekers Port was an experimental artists' community, a religious way station, or a neutral zone where the laws of the Kingdom held no sway.

As Houston got out of the car with Lily and Katya and passed a gaggle of Golden Flock disciples, he knew that there were only two reasons that the Port had turned into a boomtown.

First, the town formerly known as Princeton, New Jersey, was one of the few picturesque hamlets that had survived the war relatively intact. After the war, humans had settled here in droves.

Second, the Port occupied prime real estate on the journey from the king's birthplace in Jacksonville, Florida, to Resurrection Mount in Vermont, where Patriot Gold had risen from the dead. The fervent Golden Flock disciples, golden-robed and celibate, stopped here en masse on their yearly pilgrimage, and wherever the religious crazies went, merchants followed. Corner preachers and artifact hawkers arrived in droves to take the Flock's money. Seekers Port vibrated with both commerce and faith, a neutral zone that was allowed its eccentricities because of its importance to the Flock.

That neutrality made it a perfect hiding place for a certain type of criminal. The Mad Fox had chosen his lair well.

"Your friend lives here?" Katya asked as they passed a store selling ceramic busts of Patriot Gold.

Houston nodded. He had made sure to give Katya only the bare-bones version of his plan. He didn't mention how, depending on the Fox's mood, they all had a fifty-fifty shot of surviving the day.

"This place is so weird," Katya said, looking around.

"I love it," Lily said, hopping up and down as man on stilts lumbered past them. She gasped when they came up on a jungle gym created from the painted hulks of old Marine mechs. The metal giants towered like dinosaur carcasses, studded with ladders and coated in brilliant shades of pink with hand-painted daisies.

Lily looked between Houston and the mechs, waiting for him to say it was okay.

"Go on," he said. "Be quick."

She squealed and ran toward the jungle gym, tripping over her own feet on the way but rolling back up, unfazed, and clambering over the hulking ruins like a spider monkey.

Houston rubbed the scar along his side. At the height of the war, the life expectancy of a mech pilot was two weeks. *Guess I got lucky.*

Next to the mechs, a merchant tended to his pet stall, feeding brightly colored birds in their cages. The birds flapped their wings and chirped, suddenly stirred by Lily's presence. The noise was tremendous, attracting the attention of the other merchants.

Houston pulled Lily off the mech.

"Buzzkill," Lily groaned.

"We can't let her be seen," Houston whispered to Katya as they crossed into an alley of canvas tents. "They'll have people looking for her. Plus," he added, "this place is crawling with Gray Faces."

Katya whipped around. "What? Gray Faces here?"

"Keep your voice down."

"What are Grays doing here?" she whispered.

Houston motioned his head toward a large group of caravans. A ragged family stood on the grass, next to a sign that read, "Refugees from Frontier. Please help."

"Those poor people," Katya said. "What do the Grays want with them?"

"Frontier terrorists sneak in among the refugees."

After the Frontier Nation had overthrown the Western Province, Seekers Port had become a shelter for humans fleeing the brutal culls that convulsed the western states. They became trapped in limbo, unable to return home and blocked from entering any of the other Provinces.

Lily watched the refugee family. "I'm sorry," she whispered.

Houston realized then that Lily was just like the family—an exile from Frontier rule with no home and no hope. But he didn't let himself dwell on it, not even for a moment. Once he started thinking about how unfair her life had been, he wouldn't be able to go through with what had to happen next.

Houston kept walking. Katya was slow to follow.

"They're suffering," Katya said.

"Then you should leave them alone," Houston said. "Being around you won't help."

As they crossed town, Houston glimpsed his destination, its blue facade rising above the rooftops.

"Get something to eat," Houston told Katya, handing her twenty goldmarks.

"I don't need your money." She pushed the cash away.

"There's a diner two blocks down—Schillers. Don't talk to anyone. And get her a hat," he said, looking at Lily. "Cover her up."

"Anything else?" Katya raised an eyebrow.

"Don't draw attention to yourself like you usually do."

"Sure. As for you, try not to ruin any more of my life while you're gone."

"I'll call you when I'm done."

Katya took Lily and headed down the street. Houston watched them go, scanning the space around them. If anyone was taking an undue interest in the two, he couldn't spot it.

The Wonder Emporium sat off of Hamilton Avenue, dead center in the Holy Quarter. A sprawling warehouse painted blue, its shadow draped over the quiet streets of a neighborhood where clattering stalls gave way to prayer houses and an observant quiet.

The woman who greeted him at the Wonder Emporium doors was stunning. She smiled at Houston. "May all your blessings come to life."

Inside, the first thing Houston noticed was Patriot Gold flying above his head. The bronze sculpture was fifteen feet tall, intricately carved, and suspended from the ceiling under a sunlit glass dome like a gift from heaven. It was a perfect replica of the Risen King's symbol.

The rest of the emporium was a retail warehouse, its heavy-duty shelves bursting with a massive collection of plaster and wax sculptures of the king. Part museum, part superstore, Houston watched as throngs of customers bustled through the wide aisles with overflowing carts.

Houston took a moment to marvel at the larger dioramas set along the far wall. Each one illustrated a major milestone in the king's life: his resurrection on the sodden plains beneath Resurrection Mount; standing victorious in the hollowed-out core of the White House; mourning his fearsome ally, Titan, where he fell in the New Mexico desert; the Fall of Chicago.

Houston froze.

It was a half-scale diorama in plaster and oil paints of the king battling a Tin Man mech. The pilot inside the egg-shaped cockpit was visibly terror stricken as Patriot Gold smashed his machine.

Houston's old wound throbbed. He had been in that battle. He didn't know at the time that it would be his last.

He studied the diorama. Patriot Gold was lean and coiled like a panther, the gold phoenix sigil on his chest armor and gauntlets sparkling in the lights. The Fox's artisans had carved an expression of righteous fury on his face.

"Quite unsettling, isn't it?"

Houston turned to the man who had appeared beside him. "What?"

"The sculpture. They do incredible work here." The man was slim, with serene brown eyes beneath blue-rimmed spectacles. But it was his clothes that made Houston's stomach knot up.

The man wore a simple workman's outfit of jeans and a green field jacket. On his lapel he wore a yellow hibiscus.

"Chicago was a hard battle," the spectacled man continued, facing the sculpture. "There were many hard battles in the war. They glorify them here, but as beautiful as these sculptures are, they always give me pause."

Houston took a small step away from the man. The man didn't seem to notice, his eyes still on the king. "They," the man said in a lowered voice, indicating the Golden Flock shoppers in the nearby aisles, "would like us to believe that the king is a god. But I don't know if I can believe in a god that does this." His hand swept across the violent diorama. "That would make him no different than us."

"I'm not interested," Houston said suddenly, an edge of iron in his tone.

The man gazed at him placidly and then looked at his hibiscus as if he were noticing it for the first time. "Oh, don't mind this." He laughed. "I'm not recruiting."

"What *are* you doing?"

The man shrugged. "Sometimes a conversation with a stranger can be enlightening. It can make you see the world differently." He dusted his hibiscus. "I've always believed there was something more to this life, something larger than war and kings and bloodshed—a truth too profound to be wrapped up in a tidy myth. I often wonder if I'm alone in believing this way."

The man's eyes shone behind his lenses, fixing Houston to the spot—waiting, as if his words were an invitation, a coded message.

Houston took another step back. "Like I said, not interested." He turned and walked away from the man. His heart pounded as he left, feeling the man's eyes on his back.

A long arm reached out from his past and gripped him by the shoulder.

The simple uniform, the yellow hibiscus—the man was one of the Ohana, a missionary sent out to convert the lost, like they had his mother.

Like they had tried with him.

After killing Big Don, Jessalyn had fled with Houston and Bobby to the mountains of West Virginia, to the only place that would take her—the Last Shelter. It was home to a group of peaceniks and foragers that called themselves the Ohana—a cult of pacifists, as Houston saw them, hiding from the world in their encampment that swarmed over the green ridges and valleys, a sanctuary for the broken and hopeless.

The Ohana did not judge or condemn Jessalyn's past. They only offered forgiveness and a fresh start. For Jessalyn, it was the home she had been aching for.

For Houston, it had been hell.

Jessalyn had tried to spread the faith to her sons. She'd succeeded with Bobby, but Houston had never been a believer. Even back then, the only faith he'd had was that the world was divided between those who had power and those who didn't. So he had run.

He'd abandoned Bobby and Jessalyn as the clouds of war darkened on the horizon. Eighteen and alone, he joined the only family that would take him—the Marine Corps.

Five years later, the corps was gone, and Houston was alone again.

Leaving the Ohana man in the blue spectacles behind, Houston passed the Emporium Café and slipped through a door marked Employees Only. He entered an elevator, tapped in a code, and rode up one floor.

The doors slid open, revealing a small vestibule and an unmarked door. He turned the handle and went in without knocking.

He immediately wished he had knocked.

Weed smoke enveloped him in a cloud. The floor was covered in crossbows, and on the bed, the Mad Fox lay naked with a blue-haired salesgirl draped over him.

The Fox raised his head very slowly and blinked, his right hand still curled around a bottle of Cuervo. He squinted at Houston.

"If you're looking for customer service," he growled, "it's downstairs."

"Christ." Houston shook his head. "Put some fucking pants on, you maniac."

22

If Katya's job was to keep Lily under the radar, she was failing miserably.

They had been in the large tent for ten minutes, searching the shelves for a hat that could shield Lily from prying eyes. Lily had spent most of that time investigating everything *but* hats, much to the irritation of the goateed shopkeeper; she lifted and dropped the small pottery, inspected the hand-dyed scarves, and rang the metal chimes.

"Stop touching the merchandise, little girl," the shopkeeper growled as he stocked the shelves with candles.

Lily rolled her eyes.

"What about this one?" Katya held up a straw sun hat. Lily looked at it and shook her head. She pointed to a hat on a hook out of her reach.

"That one."

Katya lifted the brown leather aviator cap and goggles set off the hook.

"Really?" Katya asked. "It's very Amelia Earhart."

"We can share it," Lily said. "It'll look good on you."

"No thanks." Katya checked the price tag. "Jesus." She waved the cap at the shopkeeper. "Forty-five goldmarks? Seriously? This isn't even real leather."

The shopkeeper sniffed. "Perhaps you should browse the budget stores down the road."

Lily scowled at the man, then impishly began tossing a fragile snow globe from hand to hand.

"Little girl, if you don't stop touching things, I will *make* you stop."

"Try it, asshole." Katya took a step forward. Lily gripped her arm, stopping her.

The shopkeeper smirked and turned away to deal with another customer. When his back was turned, Lily winked at Katya.

Then she slid soundlessly behind the shopkeeper. With one swift movement she lifted his wallet out of his back pocket and glided back to Katya. She took out forty-five goldmarks and shoved the wallet onto a shelf of picture frames.

"We'll take it," Lily told the shopkeeper, holding up the cap and the money. "It's perfect."

*

"You shouldn't have done that," Katya said as they left the tent. "It's illegal."

"It's illegal to steal from Specials," Lily said, the cap down over her wild hair, the big, ridiculous goggles bouncing on her nose.

"That's not the point. It's wrong to steal from *anyone*."

"Houston stole a car to get here."

"Whatever you do, *don't* use Houston Holt as your guiding light."

They crossed the street. Katya could see the Schillers Diner sign above the rooftops.

"Who taught you to steal?" Katya asked.

"A thief." Lily left it at that.

"Have you stolen anything else since we got here?"

Lily looked down at her feet.

"Lily?"

Lily reached into her backpack and pulled out a wallet embroidered with a five-pointed star.

"That's my wallet!"

Lily shrugged and rubbed her nose on Katya's sleeve. "You're lucky I got it and not someone else. This place is full of thieves."

Katya was about to respond, but a mob of marching protesters nearly trundled over them, storming onto the sidewalk from a side street.

"They'll bomb us next!" one of the protestors shouted. Like the dozen others marching with him, he was older, and his face was contorted with rage. "Refugees out!"

Katya and Lily stopped and watched the marchers pass, many of them waving signs painted with the Frontier snake sigil slashed through with a big black *X*.

This town needs order, Katya thought. She made a mental note to send a strongly worded letter to whoever was in charge here about the possibility of—no, the *necessity* of—starting a local Badge chapter in Seekers Port.

The mob passed, and Katya and Lily continued on. Katya was already drafting the letter in her head when she noticed a face in a plate glass window. It appeared for a second and then was gone—narrow face, dark coat—a face Katya had glimpsed before in the crowd back by the mech jungle gym. She had seen him again browsing in the stalls while Lily had tried on hats.

Two times could have been a coincidence, but now Katya knew they were being stalked.

The man reappeared across the street, checking his phone.

"Lily," Katya said as calmly as she could, "we're going to walk fast. Can you keep up?"

Lily nodded. "Giddyup."

They hurried forward and turned right. Together they wove through a cluster of tattoo parlors before cutting sharply onto a quieter street lined with storefronts.

In the window of a pipe shop, Katya saw that narrow face again—but now she noticed the second stalker: a dark-haired woman approaching them from the opposite side. She didn't look at Katya, but she didn't look away, either.

Katya tensed. They weren't being followed; they were being *herded*.

Nothing the Hammer couldn't solve. But Katya's hand stopped by her holster. These people were probably armed, and Katya couldn't risk a firefight on the street.

The dark-haired woman was twenty feet away. The man closed in fast from the opposite direction.

"We should run," Lily said, watching the two approach.

"Good idea." Katya lifted Lily. "Hold on."

Katya spun and made it three paces down a cramped alleyway when a third stalker came up behind her.

She saw him too late, just as he slipped out of his hiding spot in the pipe shop. A large hand clamped over her mouth, and Lily was ripped out of her arms. A bolt of lightning hit her at the base of her spine, and she watched with a dull curiosity as the pavement raced up toward her.

The last thing she heard was Lily calling her name.

23

———————

"**W**eed?" Otis Flynn asked, offering the joint to Houston. "Pass."

"Good call, boyo," Otis said, settling into his armchair and taking a hit. He grimaced. "The strains are all shit now—nothing but Sinaloa skunk since those Frontier nutsuckers grabbed California."

"Otis." Houston pointed at the older man's robe where it had parted rudely, gracing Houston with a view he would rather forget.

"Sorry." Otis covered up. "We run things a little loose around here."

That he did, Houston thought. Even though Otis "the Mad Fox" Flynn had the shaven head and long graying beard of the Golden Flock, he was no disciple of any god that Houston knew. Boston Irish by birth, opportunist by nature, Otis Flynn was no longer the same man that Houston had met in the war. Back then, he looked like the CIA agent he was—clean-cut, watchful, and mostly sane.

Otis picked up a compound crossbow from the floor and wiped down the stock with a rag. "This a social visit?"

"Work," Houston said.

"Houston Holt, never off the clock. What do you need?"

"Need to get your temperature on something."

Otis looked up at him. "Hardware?"

"Not exactly."

"Pfft." Otis went back to his crossbow.

"I can get you hardware, but your people aren't buying."

"The Reds aren't my people," Otis growled.

"Since when?"

"Since they stopped buying our guns." Otis slotted a bolt into the groove and pulled back the string until it latched. He poured himself a shot of tequila and tossed it back.

Houston kept his eye on the weapon. "You still talk to them?"

"Depends," Otis said, "on who you want me to talk to."

He took another tequila shot and then snapped up the bow and aimed it at Houston's chest. Before Houston could move, Otis swiveled the weapon to his right and fired out the open window.

"What the fuck?" Houston yelled.

Otis burst out laughing. He ran to the window and looked out. "One day I'm going to hit one of those Flockers right on their pointy, bald heads."

"*You* have a pointy, bald head."

Otis waved him away. "Cost of doing business in Suckers Port."

Houston knew that Otis's transformation was not spiritual in nature but simply a survival mechanism. He dressed like the Flock and sold them memorabilia, but—having worked with Otis over the years to smuggle guns to the Redbloods—Houston was certain that the only cause Otis still believed in was profit. It was why Houston trusted him.

Otis sat down and scowled at Houston. "You in trouble?"

"Depends on how this conversation goes."

"Motherfucker." Otis tugged at this beard angrily. "You better not have brought your bad mojo up into my house."

"If I did, you have other houses to hide in."

"Yeah, well, I like this one," Otis said as the blue-haired salesgirl exited the bathroom and walked past them into the kitchen. "The location is good."

"When we met, you were living underneath a bridge."

"Bringing up the past again—one of your worst qualities, boyo."

"Just reminding you that we made serious money together, and if some bad mojo did follow me here . . ." Houston left it at that.

Otis looked at the girl in the kitchen, then back at Houston. "Walk with me."

They went to a small studio at the back of the apartment, behind glass doors that Otis closed behind them. A ring of work tables was set up along the walls, covered in half-finished clay figurines and wood tools. Conceptual sketches bristled along the walls like scales, each one a different study of the King.

Otis sat at a table and continued a sketch in progress, scratching his pencil across the thick paper.

"Who do you need to talk to?" he asked, still drawing.

"The Red Bitch."

Otis laughed. "Seriously."

"The Red Bitch."

"You're as dumb as you look if you think I can arrange that."

Houston sat down. It was time to play his only card. "Have you heard of the Sun Angel?"

Otis kept drawing. "No."

Bullshit.

Otis had been trained to deceive for half his life, first in military intelligence, honing his skills in the quagmire of the Syria, and then—when his work had resulted in enough dead jihadis—in a government division that did not officially exist: the Orchid Program.

Hidden from the public, the Orchid Program—or Orcs, as they called themselves—were an elite unit that had spearheaded two very important missions for the CIA: create Specials and then unleash them on America's enemies.

After years of experimenting, the Orcs had succeeded in creating one Special—the Firstborn, Patriot Gold. Protected from congressional oversight, the Orcs were launching their one-man assassination squad into foreign soil long before the world knew what a Special was.

And then the Incident in Salt Lake City blew the lid off the entire program. One theory—the one that Houston believed to be the most plausible—claimed that the Orcs, experimenting to create new, deadlier Specials, had lost control of whatever fiendish engine they had used to create Patriot Gold. That technology had scoured western America, triggering the end of the country they'd fought so hard to protect.

When the Immortal War ended, the last remaining Orcs—a hardened, violent core of survivors—coalesced to form the leadership of the Redblood rebels. The Red Bitch was a former Orc—and a former colleague of Otis's.

"You know exactly what the Sun Angel is," Houston pressed.

"Sounds like a tanning machine. And if you came all the way out here to convince the Red Bitch to buy a tanning machine—"

"I have it."

Otis's pencil scratched loudly across the paper.

Finally, Otis looked up. He yelled out the door, "Izzy, give us the room."

Izzy, the blue-haired salesgirl, peeked in from the kitchen, wearing only a cutoff tee, her slender arms shining with geisha tattoos. "But I just started the vaporizer," she protested.

"Get out."

"Asshole," she muttered as she stormed out and slammed the front door behind her.

Otis jabbed a finger in Houston's face. "You dickface," he growled. "What kind of shit tornado are you bringing my way, huh? Look at this." He marched around the room, grabbing fistfuls of sketches. "You see this? I have collectors in China and Lithuania commissioning pieces now. Lithuania! I'm making so much money that I'm running out of walls to hide it in."

"Why are you telling me this?"

"Loyalty. Do you know what that word means? You gave me guns; I gave them to the Redbloods. It was a good business, but I don't need the money anymore. I did it out of fucking loyalty. And how do you repay me? Huh? Like *this*!"

Otis dropped down on a bench and tugged at his beard, steaming. He picked up a serrated blade from the table and twisted it in his hands.

"What kind of shit did I step into, Otis?"

"The kind that drowns you." He stabbed the blade into the bench. "They want the Sun Angel back. Bad."

Houston paced, thoughts jangling in his head. "I didn't steal it."

"And yet the Reds say it was stolen. And you have it. Do you see how that looks?"

"It looks like a Red civil war."

"The fuck you talking about?"

"I found the Sun Angel in a pile of dead Redguns. You know who killed them?"

"Don't care."

"Other Redguns."

"Bullshit."

"I'm like you, Otis." Houston sat next to the older man. "I don't have a cause. I don't want trouble with the Reds."

Otis shook his head. "You think the Reds are your only problem? Six weeks before the ceasefire, a Silverback unit bombed out a Redblood installation in Raleigh. Eighty-seven Reds killed. Forty-three taken prisoner."

"Yeah, I heard about it. So?"

"Four days later, Redguns tried to retaliate with an RPG attack on an Overwatch station in Nashville. They hit the target, but the rocket doesn't detonate properly. Luckily, it wasn't our hardware. But there were no spec casualties—mission failed. Over the past year, it's been playing out the same way all over. Specs hit us hard, we swing back and miss. You know why that's strange?"

"No."

"Because the Reds were *losing*. The king had them on their heels. If the Silverbacks weren't diverted half the time by Frontier, they would have wiped the Reds off the continent by now." Otis leaned forward, his voice lowering. "So why, at the edge of his victory, does the king suddenly call a ceasefire?"

Houston looked at the pictures on the wall for a long time. The answer came to him, settling heavily in his gut.

"The Reds have something the king needs."

"Bingo, boyo."

"The Sun Angel," Houston said slowly.

The Risen King, the most powerful being on the planet, wanted what he had: Lily. Big-haired, strange-eyed, thieving little Lily.

"Why?" Houston asked.

"Don't know. Don't care. But he wants it bad enough that he's willing to go against his own people to make peace with us."

It was starting to make sense. The Red Bitch was delivering Lily to the king, and in return, she would get a human homeland.

But something had gone wrong, Redguns began killing Redguns—which meant that Houston was on the wrong side of not only the Red Bitch, but the king himself.

"You know," Otis said, studying Houston's expression, "the way you look now, I could sculpt you." He began sketching on a scrap of paper. "Your energy so constricted, so tightened. I'd call it 'Constipated Man in a Conundrum.'"

Otis's phone buzzed. He checked it, then put it away. "Get rid of it, Houston," Otis said, suddenly serious. "These people do not fuck around."

"I've heard that before."

"This is no joke."

"No. It's business."

Otis's brow furrowed. "Are you fucked in the head? You're thinking of selling it?"

"Otis—"

"The Bitch will have your balls." He began pacing, rubbing his temples. "I knew it when I met you. I said to myself, 'Otis, this dickface is going to be trouble.' You scheming fuck!" He kicked over a table.

"You done?" Houston asked.

"I'm not fencing the Sun Angel. Even I'm not that crazy."

"*Otis!*"

Otis blinked, snapped out of his spiral.

"This isn't a sale. It's an exchange."

The Mad Fox's eyes narrowed. "An exchange?"

"Get me a meeting with her."

"If your motives run counter to the hers . . . it's the Bonehouse."

"Nobody's running counter. She gets her Sun Angel back."

"For free?"

Houston paused. "Not exactly."

"The Bitch doesn't respond well to demands."

"Not a demand. Simply a guarantee."

"Guarantee of what?" Otis asked.

"Freedom."

"Freedom?" Otis squinted. "Doesn't look like you're shackled up."

"When the peace treaty goes through, I want a Gold Stamp."

Otis laughed. "A Gold Stamp?"

"That's right," Houston said.

"Why would you need it? I've heard the latest draft of the peace treaty already gives us a homeland—Tennessee, maybe. Or Georgia—one of those warm places."

"That'll take years. And then what? Starting all over again in some tent town."

"I see your dreams, boyo—a shingle with your name on it right on Victory Boulevard: Houston Holt Enterprises. A fantasy. It's not all roses in Sovereign."

"Tell that to Mehmet Ibrahim. I heard he pulled down twelve million last year."

Otis smirked. "Twelve mil in the bank buys a lot of things, but not what *you're* looking for."

Houston stood. "That's my offer. If the king wants the Sun Angel that badly, he can cough up a Gold Stamp."

"Maybe you should negotiate with him."

"Not a bad idea."

Otis noticed Houston stretching the stiffness out of his side. He pointed to Houston's ribs where his scar was. "How's the old girl?"

"Keeps on trucking. Like a bad marriage."

"What do you know about bad marriages?"

"Only what I learned from your last three."

"Fucking truth." Otis ashed his joint. "The Red Bitch isn't going to jump on a wagon and hightail it over here for you, but I can get you a meeting with one of her people. Someone with authority."

"When?"

"Right now."

"*Now?*"

Otis raised an eyebrow. "You got other plans?"

Otis led Houston out of the apartment and downstairs. "We usually don't get a lot of Reds around these parts," Otis said as they walked down a private hallway leading to the back of the Wonder Emporium. "But today you're in luck."

"Why?" Houston asked.

"The Red diplomats stopped by last night on their way to Sovereign for negotiations."

"You trust these guys?"

"Fuck no. But you don't have the luxury of trust right now."

Otis unlocked the rear doors and led Houston into an alleyway piled high with cardboard boxes.

"Where are they?" Houston asked.

"Nassau Inn. You better hope they're still there."

They reached the end of the alleyway and turned into another, narrower alley. Out here, Houston realized, he couldn't hear the sounds of the Port anymore. They were moving away from the town center.

In the opposite direction from the Nassau Inn.

"Otis—" he began before he heard the car engines.

A black van shot up into the mouth of the alley and blocked it. A gray sedan blocked the entryway behind them.

Houston had his SIG halfway out when he felt a sharp jab in his back.

"Sorry, boyo," Otis said, digging the serrated blade into Houston's ribs.

Houston put his hands in the air. Otis confiscated his gun. The door of the black van slid open, and two men and a woman stepped out and strode toward them, armed with pistols.

"Loyalty, huh?" Houston glared at Otis.

Otis shrugged. "You made a severe miscalculation: you thought this was still business. And for a while it was. But somewhere along the way, when you weren't looking, it turned back into war."

The woman, short haired and young, reached Houston. She smiled at him like an old friend before driving a crackling tazer into his gut.

24

Don't open your eyes.

The words echoed in Veena's head as she swam up out of the darkness.

Her throat was parched. At the top of her skull she felt the rumblings of a hideous headache. She needed water.

But she knew enough not to open her eyes. Because then she could convince herself it had all been a nightmare—the deafening gunshots in the car, Makini's brains painting the windshield, Beckett's blood warming her skin, and that . . . *thing.*

The scent of it hunting her in the dark, blood and fur and savagery.

All a nightmare, she told herself. *You'll wake up and find yourself back in your bed, safe.*

She opened her eyes.

"What the fuck . . . ?" she gasped.

She *was* back in her bed in Starlet Manor. Outside it was morning, the overcast sky filling her bedroom with an eerie gray light.

She blinked rapidly, trying to clear the cobwebs. She pinched her arm.

How was this possible?

"Hello?" she called out. There was no reply.

She slid off her bed and looked out the window. The garden was empty. Both her saltwater pool and the waters of the Sound were the color of the concrete sky.

As she stepped away from the window, she caught sight of her reflection in the glass.

"Oh, god . . ."

She was wearing a white sundress—one that had hung in her closet, untouched, since she had moved in.

She hadn't been wearing this dress last night.

Which meant . . .

A cold terror slithered up her spine.

Someone had *dressed* her.

She spun around, searching the dark corners of the room, suddenly certain that she was not alone.

It was only now that she smelled the patchouli on her skin, the unmistakable scent of coconut oil in her hair.

Veena's skin crawled. Some psycho had lifted her off the road last night, cleaned her, dressed her, and posed her like a doll on the bed.

What if he was still in the house?

She raced around the room, looking for her phone. She couldn't find it anywhere. She tried the landline, but there was no dial tone.

And then she remembered the gun.

Heart racing, she sprinted into her cavernous wardrobe. There, in the lockbox, she found her tiger-print Ruger pistol.

It felt like some measure of power in her hands as she swept out of the bedroom and into the hallway. She strained to hear anything out of the ordinary, but the house was silent. She checked the first two bedrooms, finding nothing. The next room was her studio.

The door was closed. Veena put her ear up against it.

Someone was moving around inside.

Veena gripped the gun, her palms sweaty.

You can do this.

Before she could back out, Veena grabbed the door handle and flung it open. She leapt into the room, gun sweeping.

The room's two inhabitants looked up at her and wagged their tails.

Veena watched dumbly as two black dachshunds trotted over and sniffed at her feet.

"Scat!" Veena yelped, shooing them away. The dogs haughtily padded out of the room. Veena watched them leave, utterly confused. Before she could even try to guess where the dogs had come from, she noticed something else amiss in the room.

Everything from her work session last night was still in the studio: her needles, thread, sketchpads, papers . . . everything except the Peacock Gown.

No . . .

The gown and the queen's mannequin were gone. The linchpin of the plan—the part she was responsible for—had been stolen from under her nose.

Panic rose like bile. The Sun Angel had been stolen by a lowblood, she had been attacked by something vile, and now *this*.

"Son of a bitch!"

She remembered the gun in her hand and felt a surge of power. Some suicidal fool had taken what was hers and dressed her up like some lowblood whore in her own home.

Veena ran down the stairs to the foyer. She was the daughter of the Warbringer, and his blood ran in her veins.

If the thieves were still in the house, she was going to kill them all.

The foyer was empty. She went into the living room. Nothing there. Same in the kitchen.

A sound behind her made her spin. It was the dachshunds again, watching her with their heads cocked. They lost interest quickly and padded down the hallway and into the sun room.

Veena followed them. From inside the sun room, she heard low voices. Her finger wrapped around the trigger.

Steadying herself against the wall, she counted down from three.

Three, two, *one*—

She spun into the room, gun aimed.

"Hello, Veena," Faraz said.

"Faraz?"

He sat on the wicker sofa, facing her with a cup of tea in his hand. His suit was torn, his face bruised.

"Faraz, what the hell is going on here?" Veena demanded.

Faraz said nothing. He put his tea down on the table and glanced nervously to his right.

It was then that Veena saw him. He was sitting on the armchair, facing away from her. From the doorway, she could only see his hands—spindly white fingers wrapped daintily around a teacup.

"Who the fuck are you?" Veena barked.

Faraz's eyes grew wide. The other man said nothing.

"Don't ignore me!" Veena yelled as she circled around the chair. The man came into view piece by piece—the sleeve of a mauve herringbone jacket, a band-collar shirt. Then his long nose and skinny mustache.

"Caspar!" she gasped.

"Hello, darling," Caspar Von Arx purred. "Please have a seat."

Veena didn't lower the gun.

Caspar smiled.

He flicked his fingers, and Veena yelped as a crackling heat seared her hands. A magnetic force yanked the Ruger out of her grip and guided it through the air into Caspar's waiting palm.

"Sit down, Vee," Caspar said, holding the gun. "You and I have *so* much catching up to do."

*

The Peacock Gown glimmered on the queen's mannequin in the center of the sun room.

Caspar studied the dress from his chair. "It is truly stunning, Veena. I thought it was beautiful at the show, but up close, it is sublime."

Veena sat next to Faraz, her hands trembling. The brother of the woman she planned to kill was sitting in her house, holding a gun. Veena felt like throwing up. She knew what the Von Arx family did to their enemies.

Caspar turned to Veena and ran his eyes up her body, studying her dress. "White suits you," he said. Veena shuddered. Caspar leaned forward, concerned. "I hope you're not upset. After what happened on the street—how messy it got—I just couldn't leave you in your old clothes. I had Hanna, my maid, take care of you. I assure you, I took no liberties."

He smiled in a way that made her want to gag. How had she survived five years with him in the wartime bunkers? He was a noxious gas draped in finery.

"What am I thinking?" Caspar interrupted her thoughts. "You both must be famished. I know *you* are," he said to Faraz. "I've been listening to your stomach growl all morning. Hanna! Nourishment, please!"

Within moments, his elderly maid, Hanna, rolled in a cart laden with covered platters. She didn't make eye contact as she set down one of the platters on the table and lifted the lid. Underneath was a mountain of melons, blueberries, bananas, and peeled oranges. Hanna brought another platter, heavy with croissants and sugar tarts. Finally, she set down a china pot of steaming coffee.

Despite all the food in front of them, Veena noticed that one covered platter remained on the cart, untouched. Hanna returned to the cart and stood next to it, motionless.

Caspar munched on a banana while the dogs circled his feet. "You two"—he swung a finger between the two of them—"have been busy, busy bees."

Veena suddenly found her voice. "Do you realize what you're doing? You're holding the daughter of General Sixkills hostage. Do you realize the amount of *shit* you're in?"

"And how much shit would that be?" Caspar asked. "The same amount you are in, or less?"

"This is all a misunderstanding," Faraz stammered. "I assure—"

"Shut up," Veena snapped. She turned to Caspar. "Release us immediately, or you're going to find out firsthand why they call my father the Warbringer."

Caspar gazed lazily toward the gown and then back at Veena. "My sister is going to look fabulous in that dress—right up until the second it burns her to cinders."

Faraz gulped.

Veena managed to sputter, "You are out of your mind. How dare—"

"Vee, please." Caspar put up a hand. "This is not a courtroom."

In the doorway behind Hanna, two giant men in burgundy suits appeared. They looked like twins, with matching shaven heads and deep blue eyes. Veena's stomach wrenched into a knot. The men's hands were the size of oars.

"Please," Faraz pleaded, "we were only—"

Veena slapped Faraz across the face. "*What did I tell you?*"

Caspar giggled at Faraz's expression. Veena glared at Caspar.

"If you're thinking of hurting me, I won't make it easy."

"Hurting you?" Caspar dropped his half-eaten banana on the table. "My heavens, no! No, no, no!" He stood up and waved his arms. "Why on earth would I want to hurt you, Vee?" He mock bowed. "After all, you *are* our savior."

"Wait, *what?*"

"Where, oh where, did you think the money for your little scheme was coming from?"

Faraz burst out with a relieved laugh. He leaned back on the sofa and took a deep breath. "You're funding us?"

"Of course," Caspar said. His heeled loafers knocked on the tiles as he walked around the sofa and came up behind Faraz. "It's okay," he said, massaging Faraz's shoulders. "Relax. Release that tension. We're all friends here."

But Veena wasn't convinced. "You're lying."

"I can assure you I am not. The Lady in the Veil, the Sun Angel, He Who Knows All . . . I was the one who convinced Callista to come to your show. I'm the one who bankrolled everything. We've been working together this whole time to make your father king. Exciting, isn't it?"

Veena scowled. "Then why did you attack us last night?"

"Alas," Caspar replied, his face changing, "with the loss of the Sun Angel, it seems we have reached a juncture in our path to liberty—a critical juncture, where everything unnecessary must be . . . trimmed."

Caspar tilted his head slightly toward Hanna. In response, she lifted the lid to the remaining tray on her cart. From where she sat, Veena couldn't see what was on it.

Faraz looked at Veena as Caspar squeezed his shoulders. He didn't see Caspar lift his other hand and spread his fingers wide.

The air hummed. Metal flashed through the air, racing from the tray into Caspar's open hand. His long fingers wrapped around the hilt of a carving knife, and he brought the blade down and slashed it across Faraz's throat.

Faraz's eyes bulged and his body arched, his hands struggling to stem the fountain of blood pouring from his ruined neck. He fell to his knees, looking at Veena in terror. He tried to scream, but it came out as a croak that rung in Veena's ears as loudly as any cry for help.

He collapsed on the tiles, legs kicking. Caspar wiped the blade on Faraz's jacket and sent it back through the air, landing it gently on the tray.

"Hanna," he said, "please have this room spruced up. And," he added, frowning at the bloodstained sofa, "have this sofa replaced. I think the burnt rose sectional from the De Mora spring collection would look divine here."

Hanna nodded and wheeled the cart out of the room. The two guards stood silently at their posts.

A drumbeat pounded in Veena's ears. She stared at Faraz's lifeless eyes. The dachshunds licked at his blood. Caspar turned to her, his hands stained red.

"Well, how about that, Vee? It looks like it's just the two of us now. How *delightful*."

25

Veena couldn't stop staring at the spot on the floor where Faraz had died.

The bloodstained sofa and corpse were gone, carried out by Caspar's burgundy-suited bodyguards. Hanna had swept in soon after with a mop and bucket, and Veena had watched silently as she took soapy water to the tiles and erased the last traces of blood.

Sick to her stomach, Veena tried to breathe.

It had all gone wrong so fast.

Faraz dead, a red gash smiling across his throat.

And Caspar. She watched him swimming outside in her pool, under the clouds. He had left Veena to stew in the sun room, watched over by the bodyguards, who Caspar had called Willem and Karl.

They were Von Arx Militiamen, Veena realized. Sired in the Alps, the Militiamen had been trained since youth to protect the ruling branch of the Von Arx clan. At Caspar's command, they would not hesitate to snap her neck.

The door from the patio flew open and Caspar waltzed in, wearing one of Veena's bathrobes and drying his wet hair.

"The water in your pool is divine," he said. "Although you may want to have it drained—a little bit of Faraz seeped in."

Veena had felt many things about Caspar over the years—revulsion, pity, hatred . . . but never fear.

Not until now.

"The more I look at this," Caspar said as he studied the Peacock Gown, "the more I see your inspirations—Dolce and Gabbana, some McQueen. All of my mother's—and thereby, my sister's—favorites."

Veena reached for the glass of water in front of her, but her hands were shaking too badly. She put it back down.

"Are you all right, Veena? You look sickly."

"Fine," she mumbled. She caught herself imagining what the cold blade would feel like against her throat. Would she thrash the way Faraz had?

"I truly am sorry for all the theatrics," Caspar said, "but extreme measures had to be taken."

He touched her shoulder with his wet hand. Veena screamed and leapt away from him.

Caspar laughed. "Oh my, Vee. You still don't trust me, do you?" He snapped his fingers. "Willem, have Hanna bring the bridle." He turned back to Veena. "You're going to love this."

Hanna brought in a black box with a pink rose logo. Caspar opened it like a jewelry case.

Veena sat forward. Inside, nestled in blue velvet, was a thin black harness with metal clasps on the front and back.

"This," Caspar said, "is the yin to your dress's yang."

"What are you talking about?"

"You've heard of the Northern Gears, yes?"

Veena searched her memory. "They're engineers or something."

"Much more than that, my love: magicians—sorcerers with the microchip and steel alike, holed up in their mountain workshop, tinkering away day and night, devising contraptions that you and I cannot even imagine.

"Obviously, I was worried when she made me hire the Gears."

Caspar pointed outside, where the Lady in the Veil appeared through the trees. Veena watched the woman glide toward the pier.

"Loose lips sink ships and all that," he continued, "but they're really quite discreet. Their only loyalty is to what they build—and they will build *anything* for the right price."

He pointed to the gown. "They took your design and wove in their magic. But the dress is simply a receiver. They needed to build a transmitter."

He held up the bridle. Veena noticed it was child sized.

"The Sun Angel will wear this during the parade tomorrow night. Once she is in position, we simply do this." Caspar reached into his pocket and pulled out a slim detonator. He pressed the single button on its surface.

"What does that do?" Veena asked.

"It activates the bridle. The Northern Gears have assured me—and they have run numerous tests, you know—that the bridle will then trigger the Sun Angel's enormous powers—"

"Powers? Faraz told me the Sun Angel is a kid. How the hell does a little girl have the Gift to kill the most powerful Special in the world?"

Caspar smiled. "You should know more than anyone, Vee, that looks can be deceiving. This little girl wields a surprisingly . . . *calamitous* Gift, I am told. Don't you worry. In any case, where was I? Oh, yes. When we press this button, the little girl will detonate, and then, *voila!*" He did a little spin and ended up next to the Peacock Gown. "The queen's dress will funnel the Sun Angel's energy into a concentrated blow." Caspar tap danced. "Then the king and queen blow up, and we all live happily ever after."

Veena looked up at him. "Why?"

"Why what?"

"Why do you want to kill your own sister?"

"Not just my sister—my parents too. Remember, they'll be up on the dais as well."

Veena couldn't hold it in anymore. She shot to her feet and slapped Caspar across the face.

Willem charged forward.

Caspar put up a hand to stop him.

Veena seethed. "You killed Makini! You nearly killed *me* last night!"

"It was her call," Caspar said, pointing to the Lady in the Veil outside. "Our plan had been compromised, and therefore, an executive decision had to be made. Faraz was expendable. And honestly, Veena, you were never in any real danger."

"Fuck you."

"Now then, that's not called for. I'm sorry to have kept you in the dark, but we felt it was best if you knew less."

"Keep *me* in the dark? He Who Knows All spoke to *me*. I am the Savior."

"He spoke to me as well," Caspar said, grinning. "Does that make you feel less special?"

"Does killing your family make you feel like less of a fag?"

He grinned and massaged her right knee. "No need for epithets. And I wouldn't classify myself as a fag. I would say that I am . . . fluid."

Out by the Sound, the Lady in the Veil watched the gray waters. Dark clouds slipped across the sky.

After a long time, Veena finally said, "Answer my question: Why are you a part of this?"

Caspar's smile melted away. He sat with the question for a few moments before answering. "Because," he began, "I realized that even Specials can be slaves."

And then he told her about Miami.

26

One night two years ago, Caspar had stood on the roof of his Miami penthouse and wondered how his life had slipped so quickly out of his control, how the only choices left to him were so exceedingly grim: he could smuggle himself out of the country; he could overdose on Moxi and die like a rockstar; or he could go home and marry fat Frieda.

Caspar, my dear boy, what happened to you?

He looked down at his black suit, his dull blue tie, and the two Xanax in hand. Was there anything left of Caspar Von Arx, or had he been wholly—unwittingly—assimilated into the family machine?

It wasn't as easy for him as it was for Callista. She was an easy mark, soft-headed and dreamy. She wanted—no, she *craved*—security. The family had airdropped her into the king's bed, and she couldn't have been happier.

But Caspar dreamed of other things—the Unlived Life of Caspar Von Arx, as he liked to call it. He would paint and spend his days as a flaneur in Paris. His oil canvases would hang in galleries across Europe. He would share his life with someone beautiful, who could talk him off the ledges he so often found himself on.

Art, beauty, culture, and love—these were the things Caspar dreamed of.

The real life of Caspar Von Arx, however, was quite different: endless gray offices and dreary suits—the life of an Executive Vice President at VAX Holdings, Inc., the family company. As the only male heir, he didn't have a choice in the matter. As soon as his schooling was done, he was indoctrinated into the family business.

And what a business it was—ancient, sprawling, vicious, *enduring*. Caspar's own responsibilities lay in the luxury goods subsidiary—fashion, fragrance, cosmetics, wines, and spirits.

Sure, it all sounded exciting and glamorous when his parents had slotted him into the division. They weren't blind; they knew Caspar's talents did not lie in numbers or strategy. This was their compromise. There was no way in hell their only son was going to spend his life covered in paint like some—god forbid—*bohemian*.

And so Caspar trudged through the life of a corporate drone. It was Fashion Week in Miami, and he expected to suffer through a few corporate presentations, shake some hands, and get drunk at the shows (including Veena Sixkills's buzzy Burning Wonderland collection).

He didn't expect his life to suddenly get *worse*.

He had just been informed that his parents had found him a suitable bride. The photo of Frieda was still up on his phone. He felt like retching. The burden of producing another Von Arx heir had fallen on him.

This is all Callista's fucking fault.

Had she been able to deliver a royal heir, at least Caspar would have had some breathing room. True, the child wouldn't have been a Von Arx, but he *would* be the future king. That would satisfy his parents for at least a handful of years.

But it had been eight years, and still no child. Maybe the king was sterile. Maybe Callista was. Maybe they just weren't fucking. Whatever the reason, the torch had now been passed to Caspar.

Babies. He shuddered.

Caspar left the roof and drifted downstairs to his bedroom. He wrapped himself under his covers and tried to block out the world.

This was a new level of depression, Caspar realized—not the vague, murky terror that he had medicated with Xanax and pink rose his whole life.

I thought I had more time.

Freida was a "suitable girl," the youngest daughter of another corporate clan. It was a business match, a joining of two families and two product pipelines.

Fat cow, Caspar had immediately thought upon seeing Freida's picture. There was nothing beautiful about her. She was an overfed corporate princess—doughy, pale eyed, and dull.

That night he woke up in terror, soaked with sweat and hounded by nightmares of what his life was about to become: marriage and duty, years of children's birthday parties, watching Frieda and her dim-witted friends stuff their faces with cake.

He was tempted to run for it. To jump off the roof. To inhale a mountain of Moxi and die in tragic glory. But he knew he was too much of a coward for any of that. Resistance against the family was futile.

It was over, he realized.

It was time for one last hurrah.

*

Caspar had planned out his last day of freedom meticulously:

Start drinking early.

Keep drinking.

Fuck someone pretty.

For tomorrow he flew back to Sovereign City, into the fleshy arms of his future wife.

That evening, accompanied by Willem and Karl, Caspar's first stop was the Fortis Gallery in Wynwood.

In the elegant space, Caspar drained glasses of Prosecco and studied Gallian Wen's aural paintings in awe—white canvases dotted with bright chiffon-like swirls that Wen had created by passing his sonic Gift through shallow pools of paint.

Loneliness, disenchantment, imprisonment—the paintings spoke to Caspar in a way that nothing else could. He felt suddenly overwhelmed by a surge of emotions—a sense of loss that weakened his knees.

"So much tragedy," someone beside him said. Caspar turned, and his throat tightened at the sight of the beautiful young man next to him.

The man's skin shone like copper. His eyes were dark and warm, and under his slim white suit, Caspar could make out the sleek muscles of his shoulders and chest.

"Excuse me?" Caspar stuttered.

"Wen," the man said, pointing to the painting. "I've never encountered an artist who could capture an unlived life like him. He's shamefully underrated."

Caspar found his voice. "I agree."

The man's eyes gleamed. He held out his hand. When Caspar took it, he felt the strength of the stranger's grip.

"My name's Guillermo. Art consultant by day."

"And what is that you do at night?" Caspar asked with a boldness that he didn't know he possessed.

Guillermo smiled.

*

It happened fast, breathlessly—from that first meeting, Caspar and Guillermo ended up spending the next three nights together, never leaving the other's sight. Caspar skipped his flight back to Sovereign. He ignored phone calls from work. His entire life had shrunk down to just the space around him and his new lover.

Throughout his life, Caspar had been with many men and women. This one felt different. Guillermo was beautiful and worldly, a successful art consultant who flew around the country digging up rare pieces for his billionaire clients. He had once been a sculptor, a dream he had shelved years ago.

They would stay up all night poring over illegal back issues of *Aesthetica* magazine from before the war. They spoke excitedly of all the places they loved—the waters off Capri, the Canal Grande of Venice, and of course, "la ville spectacle," Paris. They yearned to unshackle themselves from their lifeless jobs and travel to Europe together, where real artists still flourished.

Whenever Caspar spoke, Guillermo would gaze at him quietly. His expression would change like a passing landscape depending on the story Caspar told. *He's listening*, Caspar realized with a shock. The sensation was so new to him that it felt overwhelming at first. Nobody had listened to him before. Nobody had taken him seriously, not even his parents. Rudy and Briga Von Arx had only responded to him with frozen glares, their disapproval meted out with horrifying silences.

His sister, who had once idolized her big brother, now rushed him out of her royal chambers as soon as she could. He wasn't sure exactly when she had lost all respect for him, but he suspected it was after his third DUI.

And the boys. The girls. Countless beautiful, blank young things, happy to take his money, share his bed, share his drugs. Caspar remembered none of them fondly.

But Guillermo—he was real, genuine, loving.

And human.

It tore at Caspar's insides. A man of his breeding, Caspar knew, could *never* be seen with a human. He could fuck them, of course— abuse them, enslave them, rob them, kill them—but never love them.

At first, they met secretly. Caspar would send a car at night to pick Guillermo up and bring him back to one of his five homes in Miami metro. In the morning, a different car would whisk him away. None of the maids saw him. Only Willem and Karl knew, and like the rest of his personal, eighteen-strong Militiaman unit, he trusted them with his life.

The secrecy was suffocating them. Caspar could see it in Guillermo's eyes—the hurt at being shuttled like an embarrassing secret from tryst to tryst.

And Caspar's parents were leaving him angry voicemails. "Frieda is waiting. Where are you? Come home at once!"

He couldn't go back, and he didn't know how to move forward—not until Guillermo made him an offer.

"Can we ever be free?" Guillermo asked one fateful night as they holed up in Caspar's Sunny Isles penthouse.

"We are free," Caspar said.

"We're always . . ." Guillermo searched for the right word. "Surrounded."

"This is part of my life, G," Caspar responded, feeling a swelling in his chest as if he were about to lose something that he could never recover.

"None of this is you," Guillermo said, angry. "This is your prison. You are so much more than this. What about Paris? What about your art?"

"That's a dream."

"No. You can have it."

"I can't."

"You can have Paris. You can have Florence. *We* can have it. And I know how."

Caspar sat up. Guillermo was looking at him intently.

"How?" Caspar asked.

Guillermo smiled. "Let me show you."

*

Many of Guillermo's clients were American exiles in Europe who had hired him to locate and return their abandoned artwork. As part of his job, Guillermo worked with a network of smugglers that moved contraband across the Atlantic on a daily basis.

Tonight, Caspar and Guillermo would rendezvous with a smuggler who ran fast boats from Miami to Cuba. From Cuba, a former CIA pilot would smuggle them into Ireland, and from there, Paris.

Paris. Caspar's toes tingled at the thought. He could feel the tentacles of the Von Arx organism slipping off him.

Oh, God, it's all going to go tits-up. Panic gripped him, and Caspar was suddenly hyperventilating. Leaving the Kingdom was treason. Betraying the family was worse.

The image of fat Frieda rose like bile. Escaping her clutches was worth any risk. Being with Guillermo, sharing his life with him in a charming apartment in the Haute Marais, was worth *every* risk.

Losing Willem and Karl had not been easy. It had involved changing outfits in the men's room of the CheckMate nightclub, rushing through the crowded dance floor in a black wig, and sneaking into the back alley where Guillermo was waiting for him in a Civic.

Together they drove away from the lights of South Beach. Caspar's hands were shaking with excitement. Also fear, he realized. At any moment he expected Willem and Karl to drop down from the sky and block the road, their fists crackling with red fire.

Caspar cracked the window open and felt the cool breeze on his face. Guillermo's hand found his, and they drove like that for some time.

Eventually, they entered a human neighborhood in North Miami.

Caspar's heart pounded in his chest as they drove through the murky streets, passing by dilapidated ranch homes and junk-strewn yards.

They pulled up to a darkened house. Behind it, Caspar could see the black waters of the canal.

"Where are we?" Caspar asked, getting out of the car.

"The moon," Guillermo joked. "Relax. My friend runs his boat from here. Come."

"I don't know."

"What's the matter?"

"It's all happening much too fast."

Guillermo held Caspar. Caspar could feel Guillermo's heartbeat.

"It's okay. I'm scared too," Guillermo whispered, "but I know one thing that gives me strength."

"What is that?"

"Love is freedom." Guillermo kissed him. "Do you believe me?"

"Love is freedom."

Guillermo took Caspar's hand and led him into the house. They stepped into a gloomy foyer.

"Wait here," Guillermo said. He went down the hallway.

Caspar waited. The living room was unfurnished and cramped. Through the windows he could see a small boat bobbing on the canal.

"Babe," Guillermo called from down the hall, "come on in."

Caspar followed Guillermo's voice toward the room, his thoughts racing. He wasn't looking forward to the long boat ride and the even longer plane journey ahead of them. He wondered how his parents would react. If they would even miss him.

Love is freedom.

He stepped into the bedroom. Guillermo was waiting for him, but he wasn't alone.

Caspar stopped in his tracks when he saw the four men in ski masks.

"Surprise," Guillermo said with an expression that Caspar had never seen before. It was as if his beautiful face had been surgically removed, revealing the abhorrent truth beneath.

"What—" Caspar sputtered as the men closed in around him.

A fist crashed into his stomach. A hand clamped over his mouth. The men snapped a Clamp around his wrist and stripped him naked. They wrapped chains around his arms and hung him from a ring in the ceiling. A warm stream of piss trickled down Caspar's leg.

"Help me," he cried to Guillermo. "*Please!*"

But Guillermo was gone. All traces of the man Caspar loved had vanished, replaced by a smug, cold stranger.

"What are you doing?" Caspar moaned, his stomach burning.

A masked man with startling green eyes faced him.

"Caspar Von Arx," Green Eyes said calmly, "you are now property of the Red Bitch." The man laid out Caspar's predicament like a bored server at a restaurant. The men were Redbloods, and Caspar was now their prisoner of war. There was nothing he could say or do to change his situation. He would be held until his parents gave in to certain demands. If they refused, there would be consequences.

"Consequences," Green Eyes said, "that will be excruciating for you. Do you understand what I have told you?"

"Guillermo . . ." Caspar blubbered. "What is happening?"

The men laughed. Green Eyes leaned forward. "What is happening, Mister Von Arx, is a simple exchange. You specs stole our country, and we're going to get it back, even if we have to kill every single one of you half-breeds to do it." He turned to Guillermo. "Right, Guillermo?"

"Kill 'em all." Guillermo smiled.

"No!" Caspar burst out. "You don't mean that, G."

The men laughed again. Guillermo stepped forward. He leaned in close and brushed a hand across Caspar's cheek.

"I'm sorry," he whispered into Caspar's ear. He grabbed a fistful of hair and yanked Caspar's head back hard. "I'm sorry that fucking specs like you are allowed to live in luxury while better humans die in the shadows everyday."

Guillermo smashed Caspar across the jaw. He spat in his eye. "Filthy spec freak."

"Easy." Green Eyes held him back. "Don't break the merchandise."

The men spoke among themselves, but Caspar wasn't listening. His face stung. Urine pooled at his feet. He thought of the turquoise waters off Capri, the gondolas on the Canal Grande, and the Haute Marais.

The men unchained him and dropped a black bag over his head, confining him to darkness. He heard Guillermo laughing behind him as they dragged him down the hallway, his feet scraping against the tiles. Someone kept kicking him in the ass and giggling.

The men stopped abruptly. The laughter died.

Caspar felt the hands around his arms tighten their grip. And then he felt something horrible.

Thick liquid encased his limbs and penetrated his body with a cold so noxious he convulsed.

The hands holding him peeled away. He heard the Redbloods croaking, their voices stolen.

The cold inside him burned like fire. Worms crawled across his skin, and a pressure wave pushed him down to the floor. He fell backward, but right before he hit the tiles, he landed on a cushion of freezing air.

Something horrifying passed above him, inches from his nose—a crackling wave infused with slithering monsters. The wave passed. Caspar heard Guillermo rasping incoherently.

Feet pounded the floor, racing toward him. The hood was lifted off his head.

"Oh my lord," Caspar gasped when he saw the scene around him.

Guillermo and the Redbloods were pinned to the walls and ceiling like starfish, held aloft by an unseen, crushing weight. They struggled to suck in air, their eyes bulging.

The newcomers surrounded Caspar, studying him. Their bodysuits shimmered like oil in water, and their black visors absorbed the light, reflecting Caspar's shocked face back at him. They were men—or women; it was hard to tell—but they moved like spiders across the house, skittering and scurrying on all fours. A venomous Gift smoldered across their bodies, shimmering the air around them.

The spiders parted for a woman in a gray coat. Her black hair was tied up in a tight bun, and her eyes were cool and calculating. She held out her hand to Caspar. "Caspar Von Arx, you are safe now. My name is Corporal Zenia Alloway, and I am with the Sovereign Security Directorate."

Caspar looked up at her in shock.

The SSD—Gray Faces.

*

"Do you understand what has happened here?" Zenia Alloway asked him from across the steel table.

Caspar looked at her. They were in a local SSD safe house where, for the past hour, Zenia had debriefed him.

"Yes, I understand," Caspar said. He took a drink of his water. His skin still felt clammy where the Gray Face "spiders" had touched him with their Gift.

"You were never in any real danger," Zenia said.

"Funny, it felt like I was."

"My team was watching you the entire time."

The entire time. The SSD had been watching him and Guillermo from the shadows. They had photographs and surveillance videos of everything he and Guillermo had done together—*everything.*

Zenia, wielding the standard Gray Face Gift that allowed

her to precisely discern shifts in a person's energy, sensed his embarrassment. She approached the situation delicately. "Of course, all our recordings are for official purposes only and will be destroyed immediately upon the resolution of Operation Magic Rod."

Caspar had to laugh. "Magic Rod? Is that what you all are calling this fiasco?"

"The names are randomly generated by a computer."

"Oh, please," Caspar said. "You knew what you were doing. Please don't insult my intelligence by pretending otherwise."

"As I said, Mister Von Arx, you have been a kidnapping target ever since the war. Your family's fortune underwrites this empire. With you in hand, the Redbloods could extract blood from your parents and thereby His Majesty, King Patriot Gold."

"I understand your motives. It's your methods that don't sit well with me. Why was I kept in the dark?"

"As I explained before, we were not dealing with amateurs here. This Redblood cell had been evading capture for years. They were highly trained and focused on one mission: bring down your family by any means necessary. They were motivated, effective, and untraceable. The only conceivable strategy to draw them into the open was to present them with a target they could not refuse."

"Me."

"Yes, Mister Von Arx, you." Zenia pulled out a tablet PC from her briefcase. "Now, unless you have any more questions, I have forms I will need you to sign."

"Forms?"

"Official paperwork. These operations are highly classified, and we need your assurance that you will not divulge any of the . . . *sensitive details* that you were privy to."

"Details such as—oh, I don't know—that the SSD manipulated the son of the most powerful family in the kingdom to catch a pack of filthy lowbloods? That they let him be—be physically *used*—

by a criminal night after night? Are we talking about those kinds of details, Corporal Alloway?"

"You are upset, and that is understandable, but I'm afraid that your signature on these forms is mandatory." She slipped the tablet over the table, a dense document loaded on the screen.

Caspar stewed in his seat, remembering the bite of the chains across his wrists, the air leaving his lungs when they punched him.

"Mandatory? I think not, Corporal Alloway. Wait until my parents hear about this." Caspar stood up. "They will have your badge when they find out how you risked their only son."

If Caspar expected Zenia to tremble with fear, he was sorely disappointed. She held his gaze levelly, and Caspar detected what looked like pity in her eyes.

"Mister Von Arx," she said, "your parents have known about this for some time."

Caspar's mouth went dry. He fell back down on his chair. "You're lying."

"They signed off on your involvement at the initiation of Operation Magic Rod. We are, after all, protecting their interests."

"My parents?" Caspar sputtered. "They *knew*?"

"Of course. Do you know how much money they have lost due to this cell's sabotage? They gave us carte blanche in our tactical scope."

"Was it their idea to use me?" Caspar asked.

"I am not at liberty to say."

"Go to hell!" Caspar smashed his fist into the table. "Was it my parents' idea or not? *Answer me!*"

Zenia clasped her fingers and gazed silently at Caspar. The answer was clear.

Caspar shut his eyes. He had been hollowed out, betrayed by his family—and Guillermo.

"What happens to the Redbloods now?" Caspar suddenly heard himself ask.

"Standard processing and questioning," Zenia said in a way that made Caspar's blood turn to ice. Whatever was going to happen to them, Caspar knew it was not going to be "standard."

"What about him?" Caspar asked.

"Him?" Zenia raised an eyebrow.

Caspar looked down at his hands.

"Oh. Well, Guillermo—not his real name—is not a ranking member of the Redbloods as far as we know. He is what we call a collaborator—a civilian recruited and trained for a specific mission."

"He's not a Redblood?"

"Technically, no. The Redbloods ran a sophisticated psychological profile on you—the archetypes you were attracted to, your sexual . . . *habits*. Based on the profile, they recruited a suitable operative."

Zenia sipped her coffee and then continued, "It's not hard to find men like him. There are literally thousands of angry young humans out there with an axe to grind against us. The Redbloods stoke their fire, promise them money or glory, and then use them as cannon fodder. Like most collaborators, Guillermo was given just enough information to perform his mission. That way, if—when—he was caught, he couldn't expose any Redblood operational intel."

"And once caught, what happens to these collaborators?"

"Public execution."

Caspar drummed his fingers on the table. Over the past few hours, he had felt everything from love to terror to fury, but all of that cleared away now, replaced by something new—something cold. "Corporal Alloway," he said as calmly as he could, "I believe I have been cooperative, wouldn't you say?"

"You have."

"And that my—albeit unwitting—assistance in this matter has been of great service in your mission to take down this terrorist threat. Am I correct?"

"You are," Zenia said, growing suspicious.

"So it seems the only thing you need from me now is to sign those forms."

Zenia looked at the tablet and then back at Caspar. "What are you getting at?"

"I'm just saying that if I do refuse to sign those forms—if I choose to reveal to the world what happened here—there is very little you can do to me. I am, after all, a Von Arx."

"Are you threatening the SSD?"

"Heavens, no. The Von Arx don't threaten, my dear. We simply negotiate."

Caspar pulled the tablet toward himself. "I will sign your forms. However, before I do, I require a favor from you."

Zenia's eyes narrowed. "What kind of favor?"

*

The man that Caspar knew as Guillermo was sitting on the edge of his bunk, his arms and legs shackled to his cell wall. In the light of the recessed halogen, he looked sunken and old.

Caspar stepped into the cell, an SSD guard at his back.

Guillermo glared at Caspar, venomous.

"Was it all a lie?" Caspar asked, his voice quavering.

"What do you think?"

"I think—I thought—you loved me."

Guillermo cackled. "You're ugly. And you disgust me."

"I suppose that you had me fooled."

"You're easy to fool."

"I'm aware of that," Caspar said. "And the worst part is that I tend to fool myself most of the time."

"Don't pity yourself. Don't you dare. A spec with your money doesn't get the privilege of self-pity."

"Is that why you hate us? Because we have money?"

"I hate you because I had to watch my family die in your war.

I hate that the world gave you the powers of gods but the judgement of apes." Guillermo spat on Caspar's loafers. "Get the fuck out of here."

Caspar said nothing for a moment. Then he took a step closer.

"I will. But first, I have to thank you."

"Thank me?"

"Yes. You taught me something that I will never forget."

Caspar sat down next to him on the bed. He whispered in his ear. "You taught me that love is freedom."

Caspar seized Guillermo's throat with both hands, and with every ounce of his might, he *squeezed*. Guillermo's shackled limbs flailed, the chains clanking against the bed as his eyes locked onto Caspar, alive with terror. Caspar could feel the younger man's body struggle for air under him. The Gray Face guard watched silently. Caspar squeezed until his knuckles turned white. In the last seconds of Guillermo's life, Caspar leaned forward and whispered in his ear, "Thank you for setting me free."

*

Veena shifted in her seat as Caspar finished his story.

"After that," Caspar said, "I returned here. My parents never spoke to me about it."

"What about Callista?" Veena asked.

Caspar shook his head. "We're not the type of family to sit around a Thanksgiving turkey and air our feelings."

"And fat Frieda?"

"Ah. There was no fat Frieda."

"What?"

"Remember how the Redbloods had run a psychological profile on me? Well as it happened, my parents and the SSD had run their own before the operation. Apparently, the profile deduced that I would be most susceptible to the charms of a handsome, artistic stranger if my own life was about to be curtailed in some way."

"Your parents are devious. I respect that."

"Don't forget Callista. She signed off on it too." Caspar watched as the Lady in the Veil left the pier, her scarf blowing in the wind. "He Who Knows All spoke to me three days later."

"What did he show you?"

"A new world—a world where your father is king and I am free." He turned to Veena.

"Have you seen Him?" Veena whispered.

Caspar shook his head. "No. But I've felt his power."

"Me too." Veena watched the Lady outside. "She told me He's a prophet—a Special like us, except he's Gifted beyond imagination."

"He's more than a prophet, Vee," Caspar said. "He's a liberator. His followers are people like you and I—those who have been lost and broken and who have finally, by his grace, been awakened to our true path."

"And we have to wake the others," Veena said.

"We must. For while the king has slept, the Frontier and the lowbloods have crept into our camp. We are at war, and we need a wartime leader." Caspar turned to Veena. "Your father must be king."

"My father *will* be king."

"And when he is, the Warbringer's banner will fly over every corner of the world."

Veena suddenly understood. "And then you'll have Paris."

"Yes." Caspar smiled. "*All* of it."

"Aren't you forgetting something?"

"Am I?"

"We lost the Sun Angel."

Caspar waved a hand. "It's being handled. As we speak, that thieving lowblood is being hunted."

Veena's neck prickled as the memory unfurled again—the tall demon rising over her as she crawled through glass, the smell of blood and fur in her nose. "The man from last night?"

Caspar shuddered. "A scary fellow. Awful, really. I'm not sure where our veiled friend found him, but I'm happy not to be on his naughty list." He held Veena's arm. "So take a deep breath and calm yourself, darling. This lowblood thief of ours will not get very far—not very far at all. The darkness will find him. There is no other way."

27

The sound of a small airplane snapped Moriko's attention away from the sword in her hand.

Cessna, single engine. She listened to the gruff chatter of its propeller until it faded away. She knew what it meant: death had arrived early.

Couldn't he at least wait until after breakfast? Moriko had thought that she would have all morning to work on her latest project. The katana in her hands was still raw, the *tamahagane* steel dull and bent. It required straightening, and Moriko already had her hammer out, prepared to spend the day banging out the blade's imperfections.

For as long as she could remember, Moriko's life had centered around the blade.

Her life was here, in this dark workshop at the foot of the mountains where pine charcoal dust coated everything—the floors, her skin, her lungs. This was her home, amidst forge and fire, steel and darkness.

Outside, she heard the wind die in the trees. The serene stillness of the mountains had returned.

He's landed.

It annoyed her when he dropped in on her like this. Not that she would ever voice her disapproval to his face—not to a man like *him*.

Moriko studied the katana one last time, focusing on the previous night's work, the *hamon*—the hardened martensite steel along the cutting edge curved and bounded like Pacific waves, dark carbon against the softer *kawagane* body. Moriko placed the katana in the vise. The blade was sharp and strong.

And, she mused, *completely useless.*

The katana would be finished in a beautiful *koshirae*, a lacquered wood scabbard and a manta-skin hilt. And then it would be mounted like a dead animal on the wall of a Sovereign City industrialist, lifeless and neutered—a conversation piece for socialites. Far from the place where it truly belonged: the battlefield.

Trained in the Quiet Forge, the mountain citadel of the Northern Gears, Moriko had honed her Gift to read metal, stone, water, and fire, all in the service of war. With the Gears, she had built the weapons that had shaped this Kingdom—Silverback greatmaces that could crush a mech's titanium shell with one blow; Phoenix Legionary poleaxes that could magnify their Gift by a factor of ten and slice a skyscraper in half.

Moriko's memories were bitter. It had been almost a year since she had been expelled from the Gears, but she still felt the pain acutely. A heretic, they called her. Too individualistic.

She stood and dusted herself off. The weapons she designed now were glorified cutlery—commercial work to fund the projects that truly mattered to her: blades that would see war. Blades for him—the visitor.

She stretched her neck and was surprised to feel a thrill run up her leg. If she was being honest, she was excited that he had come. She left the workshop, listening to the birds chirp as she made her way into the woods, toward the secret chamber. On her right, she passed the cabin of Hamato, her sword polisher. To her left, she glimpsed the smaller cabin shared by her two young *sakite*, who hammered the hot steel and dreamt of forging their own swords one day.

Deeper in the woods, near the base of the mountain, she reached the meeting spot. She sat on a fallen elm and waited.

The crow arrived first, landing on the branches above her. He arrived seconds later.

A cold hand gripped her heart. The air in her lungs turned to lead, and even though every fiber of her body screamed in alarm, she could not move.

It's all right, Moriko. He won't hurt you, she repeated over and over to herself. *He won't hurt you.*

She stood and turned to face the hunter they called Longhorn.

He loped into the clearing with long, silent strides. The crow cawed, announcing its master and—even though Moriko knew it was absurd—she thought she saw the leaves of the forest around him *shiver*.

Moriko held her breath. Though her swordsmith's eye was exacting and she had seen him numerous times, she still had trouble assembling a clear picture of the man in front of her.

It was as if he were moving even though he stood still. His long, hard body seemed hewn from the bones of the earth, and within his stillness was the coiled tension of the cobra, a submerged violence that bristled and waited.

A breeze swept in from the forest, brushing over his green field jacket and powerful shoulders, ruffling the thick fur collar that crowned his sinewy neck. From what beast that fur came, Moriko did not know—something monstrous and savage that had died fighting. She noticed Longhorn's mouth twitch, a grim line bordered by coarse black stubble. The top half of his face was shadowed by a black Stetson hat with a curled brim, hiding a pair of eyes that the light feared to touch.

Moriko felt a stab of terror as she realized that his hidden eyes were probing her flesh, pinning her like a butterfly to a board. She felt them studying her bare throat, the unguarded curves of her chest and stomach—the terrain of his trade.

Moriko took all of this in within a few seconds, knowing it would dissipate from her memory like gossamer once he had left. But his hands . . . those she would never forget. They were heavy as hammers, the skin crisscrossed with ridges of scar tissue, a stark history of a brutal life—the hands of the reaper.

Longhorn bowed his head slightly. Moriko bowed in return and tentatively turned her back on him. Under the shade of an elm tree, Moriko swept leaves and stones aside, revealing the keypad. She punched in the thirteen-digit code and stood aside as the magnetic trapdoor slid open.

She climbed down the ladder first, descending into the musty darkness. He came down above her, his feet soundless on the rungs.

Her hand found the light switch. Small spotlights bloomed along the cement chamber. The air was cool and, once again, it reminded Moriko of a museum. Pristine blades, daggers, and axes hung from the walls, serenely lit behind glass—each one built for a different battlefield, a different enemy. None of the weapons had ornamental designs or mountings. When Longhorn had found her a year ago, she knew his needs were practical, not decorative. His weapons had to be light, concealable, and easily cleaned.

He opened a display to her right, the one holding the tomahawks. Longhorn studied the twin axes. With a flick of his wrists he whipped the tomahawks around in a cutting arcs, the air around the blades crackling with black energy. His Gift responded to natural materials. In the Quiet Forge, Moriko had learned how every warrior's Gift could be magnified by certain substances— silver plating for the Silverback maces, gold cores for the Phoenix Legion poleaxes. But for Longhorn's weapons she used only pure NightAlloy steel melded with bison blood, and hilts forged of reinforced bison bone and leather.

Longhorn lowered the tomahawks. Satisfied, he slipped them into their scabbards and strapped them to his back, underneath his jacket.

He placed a brick of goldmarks on the table. Moriko stood still as he passed by her like a cold wind and left the chamber.

When she climbed back up the ladder, he was gone. Leaves rustled softly, and she felt that she should return to her work.

On her walk back, she wondered again about this visitor—this Special they called Longhorn.

She had heard his voice only once, when he had pulled her off the streets after her expulsion and charged her with building the tools of his trade. She asked Longhorn no questions, but her sword polisher, Hamato, had wrung his hands nervously and warned her about the things her new client was capable of. She took Hamato's stories with a grain of salt, but some of them had the unsettling ring of truth—like the one about how Longhorn had worked as a tracker for the Gray Faces during the war, tasked with hunting down President Mathias, the first lady, and their young daughter. Her metal supplier vehemently disagreed with Hamato and asserted that Longhorn had once been an assassin on the payroll of the Mexican cartels. The most outlandish tale Moriko had heard—this one from her scabbard maker, Yoshi—was the rumor that Longhorn had once been a Warborn, one of the Snake Mother's elite bodyguards.

Tall tales, hearsay, and fantasies. Whatever Longhorn once was, he now walked the black line between living and dying, where distances were measured in heartbeats.

As Moriko approached her workshop, her mind turned to the tomahawks he had left with. It thrilled her that they would see battle, but it gave her no pleasure to dwell on the detail that they would be used to end someone's life.

So be it. Her blades decorated walls, but that was not their purpose. In Longhorn's skilled hands, they would find their true life.

Moriko entered her darkened workshop and shut the door. In here, she finally allowed herself to breathe. Her hands shook violently, and she quickly gulped down the rest of the cold tea she had left behind.

Her blades would taste blood.

Longhorn was hunting.

28

The blindfold bit into Houston's temples. In his little black world, all he could feel was the tension in his shoulders, the chafing of the cuffs on his wrists, and the sting in his ribs where the Reds had tazed him. The van jolted on another bump, sending shockwaves up his tailbone.

When you weren't looking, this turned back into a war. Otis, the old bastard, had betrayed him and sold him up to the Red Bitch on a platter. Houston couldn't blame him.

He had regained consciousness about an hour ago on the floor of the moving van. By then he knew they were far away from Seekers Port. He could only hear the van's tires rumbling over asphalt and the slow, measured breathing of his captors—three of them. He remembered their faces—two large men and a pixie-haired women. None of them spoke.

They were professionals. Redguns.

Possessing stolen Redblood property qualified Houston as blood traitor *numero uno*. Anyone who had helped him would be marked for death and booked for an indefinite stay at the Bonehouse.

Including Katya. If she had been caught . . . he didn't even want to think about it.

Houston listened to the breathing of his captors, the roll of the tires over the road. The moment he had opened the truck door last night and peered into the darkness, he knew—in some ancient, lizard part of his brain—that it was over. If Faraz didn't get him, the Reds would. If the Reds missed, the Gray Faces would swoop in.

You have something left to do before you die.

Lily's absurd words echoed in his head. He wanted to laugh.

*

They changed vehicles twice, muddying up their trail in case anyone was following. After another half hour, the car pulled off the smooth asphalt onto rough gravel. They dragged Houston out of the car and took off his blindfold. He blinked up at towering hemlock trees around him and a lonely road stretching out over the hills in the late afternoon sun.

The female Redgun with the pixie hair was glaring at him. The driver stayed in the car, and the two large Reds smoked silently off to the side.

"Water?" Pixie asked. Houston nodded. She reached into the car and threw a bottle at him. It bounced off his chest. She smiled. "Drink up." She turned to the other two Reds. "Time check."

"Sixteen twenty-three."

"Mark." She set her watch. "Two minutes and fifteen seconds."

Pixie leaned against the car, watching Houston. She had piercing green eyes and caramel skin. Her short black hair swept artfully around her face.

"I like your hair," Houston said. "And your tazer technique."

She spat on the leaves. "The man you shot yesterday? Damian Jackson? He was my training officer."

"It was either him or me."

"The better man lost."

"This world takes the better men first," Houston said.

"And leaves us with the dregs," she said. She checked her watch. "Thirty seconds."

The men confirmed, "Thirty seconds."

"Thirty seconds to what?" Houston asked, a knot tightening in his gut.

Pixie smiled without warmth or pity.

A rumble broke the quiet. Gears shifted, and a heavy engine grumbled in the distance. Houston watched as a massive cargo truck rose up the incline into view, downshifting as it approached them.

Pixie held up five fingers and counted down. "Five, four, three, two, *one.*"

At the exact moment Pixie finished the word *one*, the truck's brakes hissed, and the gargantuan vehicle lurched to a hard stop in front of them and opened its rear doors. The two men grabbed Houston and marched him into the freezing cargo hold.

Pixie remained on the road. She gave Houston the finger as the doors closed and the truck rumbled down the road.

Houston's blinked at his gloomy surroundings. His feet sank into plush wool rugs, haphazardly laid on top of each other. The glow of dozens of screens assaulted his eyes, clustered like flower petals from the ceiling to the floor, burning with colored data. The other people in the freezing hold took no interest in him.

Three young men sat at workstations, absorbing the vast reams of data on their monitors. Houston tried to read what was on their screens but couldn't even hope to decipher the organic forms he saw there. And behind it all, an electric bass sound cocooned everything. He had the uneasy feeling that the screens were tracking some sort of life form—something inhuman.

Was this the Bonehouse? He saw no torture devices or patches of dried blood on the floor. Houston was almost relieved until he noticed the ominous shape in the center of the hold. It was a brass capsule with clawed feet, riveted with studs and lined with wires. It resembled a coffin crossed with a bomb.

"What the hell, nerds?" a Red called out from behind Houston to the techs. "You're running behind."

Houston noticed that every screen had a clock on the bottom that read 16:26 p.m., coordinated down to the millisecond. The monitors around the room came alive, sliding vertically and horizontally along rails, slotting into new configurations. The coffin gurgled like a car engine kicking over loudly but refusing to start.

As Houston's eyes acclimated to the hold, he realized that there was a fourth person inside, seated in the far corner. She stood up and approached Houston. "Mister Holt." She read his name on the tablet computer tucked into the crook of her arm, the screen illuminating her lined face. "We have to go over some of the ground rules. Once you are inducted into the system, you will have a total of ten minutes—six hundred seconds—inside. Do not panic. The first time inside can be unsettling. It is normal." She studied the tablet. "It says here you have combat drive training?"

Houston tried to process what she had just said. "Wait, inducted into *what* system?"

She ignored him. "Your training will help. Remember to breathe slowly and deeply and keep in mind that your behavior will be monitored at all times." She peered at him. "I assure you, Mister Holt, any sort of hostile behavior will reflect harshly on her final judgment. Her decision is final, and—"

"Her?"

The woman's eyes glittered in the gloom. "You know who I'm talking about."

"System ready," one of the young techs called out.

Houston turned to see the lid of the coffin swing open. Inside, he saw a twinkling blackness.

The woman smiled as one of the Reds behind him pricked his left arm with a syringe.

Houston tried to ask a question, but his voice box closed up and his body turned into a wet sand. The Reds stripped him and carried him into the coffin.

The black water wrapped around him. The Reds closed the lid.

He floated in the blackness for a few seconds before *it* arrived—something alive but not human, a humming presence that stepped up behind his left shoulder and exhaled softly. Houston's eyes closed, and his body disintegrated. It was too late to be terrified.

29

The banquet hall had the feel of a secret—a jewel box hidden away in some tower, buzzing with white-coated waiters ferrying trays of uni toast to the masters of the universe.

Houston stood apart from the power brokers and Ivy League clans. Their tuxes and dresses were custom, their pedigrees old and untouchable. Secret Service agents guarded the perimeter of the room.

Houston felt a cold sheen on his skin under the silk of his tuxedo.

The coffin, he remembered, as if it had happened long ago and merited no more thought.

He walked into the crowd, realizing that no one could see him. He waved his hands in front of a dignitary's face to no response. The waiters floated by him.

Breathe. Relax.

He made a slow circle of the room, feeling the weight of the accumulated wealth. He had experienced a fraction of it in the underground Manhattan clubs where Bobby had once performed, surrounded by hedge funders and media CEOs. But that was money. This was *power.*

The presence from the coffin lingered behind his shoulder. He turned but saw nothing there. It was a shadow across his back, intangible and dark. He was keenly aware that he was a guest—or a prisoner—of a superior intelligence, one that cared little if he lived or died.

He noticed her by the bar. She was looking at him, beckoning him over with her eyes.

Stunning was the only word Houston could use to describe her. She watched him approach over the rim of her wineglass. Her dark hair was pulled back, revealing high cheekbones, bronzed skin, and onyx eyes. Her hard arms and shoulders were bare above her strapless violet gown.

She was not the most beautiful woman here. Trophy wives dotted the room, dolled up and shining, but the woman in front of him had something none of the others could even touch: the certainty that when her looks had faded, she would still retain her power.

Houston reached her. Up close, she did not look like the most hunted woman in the world.

"Hello, Houston," she said in a voice that was as plush as velvet. "I'm Carmen Vega." She shook his hand, strong and curt. "But you know me by another name."

"I don't feel right saying it to your face."

"Don't feel embarrassed. I used to hate it, but I've grown quite accustomed to being the Red Bitch."

"I'll just call you Carmen."

She looked at him like she was unlocking a dense algorithm. "Do you know why you are here?"

"I don't know where 'here' is." He looked around. "Is this hell?"

"Possibly. Although at one point I believed it to be the *other* place."

"You don't strike me as religious."

"We all have our gods. Once upon a time, I did too." She pointed into the crowd. "Do you recognize that man over there?"

Houston turned to see a man commanding the attention of a crowd.

He was in his forties, tall and vibrating with charisma. His pretty wife stood by his side, her arm linked through his, beaming at her husband the way all political wives were trained to do. The man finished his story, and the circle burst into laughter. Houston had only ever seen his face on a TV screen, the last few times on emergency broadcasts in the final days of the war. The face had been a lot older then, drawn with tension, hair almost fully gray. This was not that man. That man had been defeated. This one had just triumphed.

"Mathias," Houston said. "President Gabriel Mathias."

"Governor Gabriel Mathias," she corrected him. "Democratic presidential nominee Mathias. He won't be president yet for another seven months."

"How is this possible?"

She placed her empty glass on a passing waiter's tray and checked her watch. "Before you became an outlaw, you were in the First Mechanized Raiders, correct? The Iron Vikings out of Camp Lejeune."

"Are we trading resumes now?" he asked.

"If we were, mine would put yours to shame."

"I'll bet."

"My parents were very proud of my accomplishments: Harvard Law, Military intelligence, Special Security Advisor to the president. Immigrant parents love it when their children become part of the establishment. Not so much when we try to burn it down."

"It's not easy telling your friends your daughter is a militia leader."

She cracked a smile. "You're not like the others."

"The others?"

"The others who have been in here. The accused."

"Accused of what?"

"In your case? Theft. Murder of a Redgun officer. Extortion."

"Sounds like I need a lawyer. You accepting new clients?"

"You should consider yourself lucky. People who act counter to our interests have a very short life expectancy. The same fate was scheduled for you. However, I'm willing to give a mech pilot the benefit of the doubt." She raised her glass. "You grunts nearly won the war for us."

"I know. We all got participation trophies."

"The war's not over."

"Keep fighting and maybe you don't have to admit that they won."

"What happened to *semper fi*?"

"Same thing that happened to the corps," Houston said.

"Speaking of the corps, do you remember this feeling? Behind you."

Houston felt the hairs prickle on the back of his neck as the presence hung on his shoulder. There was something familiar about it—a connection he couldn't yet make.

"Think back to the moment you plugged into your mech before entering battle."

It came to him in a flash—strapping down in the molded seat of the Tin Man, slotting the trodes into his spinal column, and then the rush of frigid data through him, a link to an omnipresent intelligence.

"MAC," Houston finally said.

Carmen nodded. "Where you are now? It is simply an evolution of that program."

MAC—or Marine Automated Controller—had saved Houston's life more times than he could remember during the war. It was an artificial intelligence inside each mech that connected to the pilot's nervous system to provide split-second battlefield data and awareness.

"Houston," Carmen said. He looked at her, and she did something strange, tipping her head to the side and blinking rapidly. "Please try to breathe deeply. Your cortisol levels are rising."

"You forgot to put doctor on your resume."

"It's not me analyzing you."

Houston looked around at the glittering hall. "No AI I've seen can do this."

"That's because you've seen very little. Five months from now, Governor Mathias will become President-elect Mathias on the strength of his pledge to bring peace between Specials and humans. However, six months later he will—in secret, as a sealed Executive Order—green-light an unprecedented experiment—the development of a weapon that would act as a counterbalance if the Specials ever went rogue."

The presence clicked and hummed on Houston's neck. "A sentient AI," he said.

"A fully weaponized superintelligence, a heuristic evolutionary program, designed and capable of fighting—and winning—a war against Specials in over a trillion individual scenarios." She waved and smiled at someone in the crowd before settling back on Houston. "The boys at DARPA codenamed the intelligence Omega Rex."

"That doesn't make sense. We would have won the war, then."

"We would have, but Rex was never launched."

Just then Governor Mathias passed very close to them, trailing a train of starstruck acolytes. Carmen watched him pass. "*He* lost his nerve at the final hour."

Carmen's eyes lingered on Mathias and his wife as they sat down to dinner. At their secured table he saw their young daughter, Joanna, sitting bored and alone. "We spent years trying to find Rex after the war."

"Wait," Houston said, "this place isn't Rex?"

"No. This is simply the basic technology we could salvage after the war. We call it Midnight Rider."

"Does it warn you when the British are coming?"

She smiled. Houston reached out and touched her arm. She stiffened, surprised by his boldness. He held her above her elbow, feeling the warmth of her skin.

"You don't feel like a simulation."

The party continued around them, and for a few moments, they enjoyed not saying anything. She checked her watch. Houston removed his hand. He realized then that she was a woman for whom the passing of time was a palpable sin, and he understood why: she was a human fighting a war of attrition against immortals.

She straightened up. "It's time we began your trial."

"And I thought we were becoming friends."

"Perhaps in another life." She turned toward the glass doors. "Come. Let's get some air."

She led him out onto the balcony. Below them, the lights of Washington DC glittered in the night, the White House and the Capitol Building rising like the bones of an old empire. Carmen plucked a whiskey from the bar and handed it to Houston.

"We are going to have a conversation," she said, "and at the end of that conversation, I will decide whether you live or die. Fair?"

"Do you decide, or does the computer?"

She pointed to a service doorway. A waiter went through it, and for a few seconds, Houston glimpsed a familiar scene behind it—a dark forest and a box truck surrounded by dead bodies. Ringwood Park. The door swung closed, and when it opened again, he saw only a kitchen.

Carmen spoke. "Midnight Rider allows me to run simulations and behavioral models to gauge exactly what happened last night. The current model states with eighty-eight percent certainty that you killed my men and stole my property for profit."

"Property?" Houston felt his back tense. "Her name is Lily."

"Strange." She smiled. "The models did not catch that."

"Catch what?"

"Lone wolf, ambitious, highly developed self-preservation

instinct—all that we knew. But your attachment to the child is surprising."

Houston drank and watched the cars below.

"We know a lot about you, Houston. We tried to recruit you a few times."

"More than a few times." He looked at Carmen. He liked that she didn't look away. "Maybe I've reconsidered," he said. "If it helps my case."

"That ship has sailed. What would help your case is your version of events." She set her watch. "You have two minutes and thirty-five seconds. Tell me everything that happened, and then I will make my decision. Remember, Midnight is monitoring all your vitals, so if you lie, it will result in an immediate guilty verdict. Understood?"

Houston nodded. He inhaled the cool night air and told her his story, from his meeting with Faraz by the Hudson through the bloodshed at Ringwood to him showing up at Seekers Port with Lily, hoping to strike a fair deal.

Her eyes never left him the entire time. Her impassivity was unsettling, and he wondered if that was just the computer's filter or if that was how she really was—how she had to be.

"I was bringing her back to you," Houston finished. "It was business."

"A Gold Stamp." She looked confused. "Why does it mean so much to you to be a citizen of a nation that despises you?"

"I prefer it to being a nobody in a nation that despises me."

"I find it odd you could believe that even with a Gold Stamp, you would be anything more than a house slave."

"Well, I wouldn't be in this predicament if *you* and your CIA Orcs hadn't created the specs."

She looked shocked. "Your history is wrong. We did *not* create the Specials. We *discovered* them, and . . . it doesn't matter. In any case, I will not be lectured by a two-bit criminal too dumb to realize the gravity of his situation."

"A dumb criminal who you happily bought guns from—at a discounted rate, no less."

"That doesn't change the facts of this case. You killed Damian Jackson."

"After he had killed Lazlo Koyle, and after he nearly killed me."

"And that's the part that I don't yet understand. You said that Lily saved you?"

He nodded.

Carmen looked puzzled. "Did she explain why?"

He shrugged. "She said I still had something left to do."

Once again, Carmen's head tilted, her eyes buzzed. "That child is a puzzle we have yet to solve."

"What is she?" Houston asked.

"An answer."

"To what?"

"Depends on who's asking the question. The Gift is harder to study in children. Adults can harness the Gift, filter it through the lens of their will, and shape it to their ends. Unfortunately, most adults operate on a single program—fear.

"But a child," she continued, "does not fear like we do. They flow with the Gift, for they engage with it in the way most children engage with the world—through love. And that is not a power that I"—she pointed upwards, as if to some watching deity—"we, can predict."

Her watch beeped. Once again her eyes became like hard stones. "Your time is up, Houston. I have rendered my judgment."

The presence skittered behind Houston, and he felt very cold.

"Your crime is severe," Carmen said. "Stealing from the Redblood Army. Working in opposition to our interests. Aiding and abetting. Larceny. Murder of a Redgun officer. We are sixty-forty in favor of your death, Houston."

"I've survived worse odds." He finished his whiskey, then flung the glass out into the city. "Maybe if I went to Harvard Law, things would have been different. But I made the choices I had to."

"And I make the ones I have to. I'm sorry, Houston. My verdict is guilty."

"Go to hell."

She touched his arm. "This was simply business."

He looked at her. "Another place, another time, I think I might have asked you out."

She smiled.

"How will you do it?" Houston asked.

"Bullet to the back of the head."

"Right after you ask me if I have any regrets?"

"Excuse me?"

"Damian. Back in Ringwood, he asked if I had any regrets before he took the shot."

"Damian was archaic in that way." She fixed him with her eyes, the lights of the city alive in them. "Do you have any regrets?"

Houston stared at the stars. "I don't know about regrets, but that night I thought of . . . of *them*."

"Your loved ones?"

He nodded. "My family. But just at this one moment in time, when we were together, where it felt like I was . . ."

"Home?"

He nodded.

"That's normal."

"My family wasn't normal."

She looked at her watch and then turned to the party still going on inside. For a long time, she remained quiet. Then she said, "I come back here for the same reason."

"This isn't your home."

"No. Here inside Midnight, there are a million places I could be. But here . . ." she touched her smooth skin as if it were an alien artifact. "Here I can remember what I once was. This was where I felt that things could be different."

Her fingers slipped over Houston's wrist, her grip sensuous and strong. "Your family—do you want to see them again?"

*

He was back in Big Don's living room, watching from the corner. There they were all here: his mother, sixteen-year-old Houston, and thirteen-year-old Bobby, sitting on the plush white rug and dealing from a deck of cards.

Big Don's laugh boomed from somewhere in the cavernous apartment. They were high in the sky, the endless windows curving around them as they lorded over the jeweled sea of Manhattan.

A few hours from now, his mother would kill Big Don. A year from now, Houston would be racing away from the Ohana Last Shelter, his mother and brother gone from his life forever.

The scene grew jagged edges and shuddered. It shifted and rotated, and Houston saw that the disturbance was centered on Bobby. The presence behind Houston sniffed and raised its hackles.

Something was wrong.

The perfect image fell apart for an instant to reveal the ice-blue code underneath.

"What's happening?" Houston called out.

The room fragmented around him. Behind the walls, Houston saw things to which he couldn't assign color or shape. It was simply a void without end.

Bobby remained, pulsing with light, floating in the nothingness.

"What's going on?" Houston yelled out into the collapsing world. The scene receded through a pinhole, collapsing in on itself.

When he returned, it wasn't to the party.

Carmen stood across a concrete cell from him, wearing a slim black overcoat and leather stiletto boots. A desert sun filtered in through a narrow window near the ceiling.

"That was your brother?" Carmen asked.

"Yes," Houston replied. He saw the change in her face, a look of disbelief. "Why?"

"He wasn't in our files." She frowned. "What happened next? After New York?"

"My mother killed her boyfriend. We fled to hide out with the Ohana in West Virginia."

Carmen's eyelids fluttered as she consulted Midnight. "And then you left for the Marines. And Bobby—" she refocused on Houston, her eyes shining as if she had slotted the final puzzle piece into place. "Bobby became something quite extraordinary."

Houston said nothing. Carmen approached him, her towering heels *clacking* on the stone floor.

"You should have told me who your brother was." Carmen fixed him with her eyes. "I've revised my verdict."

Houston couldn't believe his ears. "What?"

She checked her watch. "Don't get your hopes up. We've simply hit pause on this discussion pending a follow-up meeting."

She opened a door that hadn't been there a moment ago. "Goodbye, Houston. We'll always have DC."

Before he could follow, she was gone, and the world broke apart.

30

Veena had seen excess in her life. She knew what it looked like, having grown up around the nouveau riche of Texas with their immense homes and plate-sized jewelry. Her social circle in Sovereign was populated by some of most spoiled heirs in the Kingdom—namely, her lech of a coconspirator, Caspar—and she herself had spent millions on clothes alone. She thought she had seen it all.

But she had never, in all her life, seen anything like the House of Azaleas.

From the outside, it was a windowless brick warehouse on the Williamsburg waterfront, large enough to fit a battleship.

But inside . . .

Oh lord, *the inside.*

As Veena carried the Peacock Gown in its garment bag and followed the queen's handmaiden through the warehouse, she thought she had died and gone to couture heaven.

Crystal chandeliers hung from towering stone arches, and floor-to-ceiling shelves covered the walls, lined meticulously with enough heels, Birkin handbags, and jewelry to clothe half the debutantes in the city. As the handmaiden trotted ahead of her, Veena noticed the rooms on either side, hidden behind glass doors like wine cellars, each one with a plaque next to it—evening wear, florals, abstract patterns, formal hats. She caught glimpses of wonders through the glass, flashes of overstated finery—a room lined with Burberry raincoats; another filled with hundreds of silk scarves on hooks; and another bursting with classic Galliano sundresses: chartreuse, lilac, and pearlescent. Veena's eyes glazed over as she followed the line of glass doors down the length of the warehouse. There were over forty rooms.

Envy sloshed around inside her like gasoline as the handmaiden led her upstairs to the lattice of walkways and suspended glass rooms that glowed above them like Japanese lanterns.

"This entire building is the queen's wardrobe?" Veena gasped, imagining what a truly glamorous woman like her mother, Mable, could do with clothes like these.

"This," the handmaiden answered, "is the House of Azaleas. Her Grace houses only her spring collections here. The House of Leaves, the House of Sun, and the House of Snow are where she keeps her garments for the other seasons."

As if Veena didn't have enough reasons to kill the bitch.

"Sweetness!"

Queen Callista stood on the balcony of a suspended glass room above. Her cheeks were flush, and she held an empty champagne flute in one hand. Veena curtsied, realizing immediately that the queen was well and truly drunk.

"Oh, enough of that," Callista giggled. "Come up, come up. We've started the party without you."

*

Veena waited inside the huge circular room decorated to resemble—and Veena was guessing here—the inside of Callista's brain: soft and dreamy, with lilac paint, gilded mirrors, and horse-shaped vases erupting with pink azaleas. A fitting room stood off to the side behind pink curtains.

The pink curtains parted, and Callista swept out of the changing room into the mirrored parlor, the lights catching the intricate gold vines of the Peacock Gown. The blue silk shimmered like a haunted sea. The foxes and horses came alive as the queen moved through the room.

Callista saw herself in the mirror. For a moment, her eyes lifted out of the fog of alcohol. "It's magical," she whispered.

Her four handmaidens nodded.

"Oh, Veena," she said, turning, "you've outdone yourself!"

Veena curtsied. The queen twirled. The stupor of the alcohol left her limbs, and her face opened up into a smile so bright that it filled the room.

"What do you think?" Callista asked Veena.

"You look stunning."

"Stunning?" Callista asked, suddenly very still. "Is that the same as beautiful? Tell me you find me beautiful." The last word trembled out of her mouth.

The room waited on pins. Veena looked to handmaidens for help but found only averted eyes. She gathered herself and smiled. "You are even more beautiful than on your wedding day."

A sharp intake of breath, a straightening of the spine, and once again, Callista came undone. "Do you know how long it has been since *he* told me that?"

All four handmaidens suddenly found something fascinating to stare at on the floor. Without warning, Veena found herself trapped in a messy, emotional moment she didn't have the stomach for. Callista stood in the middle of the chamber, a forlorn fairy, tears streaming down her face, bubbled gasps escaping her throat.

Veena willed herself forward and held Callista. Callista sobbed into her shoulder, and Veena tried hard not to grimace. When the queen pulled away, Veena saw her eyes were glistening and red.

"Where is my head?" Callista said, embarrassed. "Two years of etiquette school, and here I am blubbering about my husband."

She tried to laugh, but it came out as a squeak. She flitted her fingers, and the bottle of champagne flew across the room into her hands. She shook it, frowning. "Oh my. Dry as a bone. Lana." Callista turned to her handmaiden, holding up her empty glass. "I need a refill from downstairs."

"No," Veena said a touch too quickly. "let me get it."

Once downstairs, Veena exhaled.

Design and deliver the dress that kills the king and queen—that much she could manage. But she was on the verge of becoming a marriage counselor, and that was a bridge too far. Surely there were simpler ways to kill the king—a rocket-propelled grenade from the rooftops, a pack of wild dogs, highly trained carrier pigeons strapped with explosives—something, *anything*, that would be easier than this.

Veena grabbed a bottle of Prosecco from the bar and, wiping the queen's snot off her blouse, started back upstairs. She had just taken her first step on the staircase when she heard the piercing shriek.

Veena stood very still.

Glass shattered upstairs. Another shriek followed—a cry of anger, not pain. A small distinction, but one Veena knew well. Within seconds, the four handmaidens came rushing down the stairs in single file. They soundlessly disappeared behind a heavy door.

Now would be a good time to leave. A very good time.

The bottle was in her hands, frosted and sweating. The front door beckoned, but Veena knew she couldn't leave now. Slowly, she headed up the stairs. When she reached the dressing chamber, she knew immediately she should have left.

Callista's sobs were gurgling, wet gasps that bubbled up from her chest. She was wearing a white robe, crying into her hands on the ottoman. Her bare feet bled into the rug, surrounded by the shards of a broken flute. She sensed Veena's presence and peered at her through her fingers.

"Oh, Veena, I'm sorry. I get like this when I drink too much. What would my subjects say if they saw me like this?"

They would say you deserved to die, Your Majesty.

"Your subjects adore you, my Grace."

"Oh, hush with the formalities."

Veena stepped around the broken glass. "What's the matter?"

"What a mess I've become. What a . . ."—she willed out the word—"*fucking* mess." She cursed like a child, ashamed and exhilarated by the word's taboo power. "I wish I were like you, so free and loved."

"Callista, that's not true."

"No, it is. I know how men look at you, how they *desire* you. I've seen you on TV. In the magazines." She gripped Veena's wrist and pulled her down with surprising strength. "How does it feel, Veena? To be loved so."

I wouldn't know.

"I want you to tell *me*," Veena replied. "I want you to tell me how it is to be loved by millions of your subjects. To have the love of a king."

"It's not like you think it is. It's not at all how *I* thought it was going to be. That he would be so . . . so far away from me."

"I know something about distant men. I'm the daughter of General Sixkills."

Callista laughed a little. "That can't be easy."

"It isn't. But people show their love in different ways."

"They do." Callista nodded.

Veena watched for a second, thinking of all the people who "loved" this queen. *Me, her only friend*, who had designed a dress that would incinerate her. Her parents, who had married her off as a child bride to cement their power. Her own brother, who giggled while he plotted her murder.

"You are loved," Veena whispered, struggling not to choke on the words.

"Really?" Callista's face flushed.

"Yes. I—"

The kiss landed on Veena's lips, wet and desperate. Callista's tongue pushed into her mouth, and her hand slid up Veena's thigh, reaching underneath her dress. Veena yanked herself away, revolted, and almost fell to the floor as she leapt away from the ottoman.

Immediately, she realized her fatal error.

Callista's eyes went wide—wider than normal—until they were milky blue moons. For a second, they held that way, then snapped down, her painted lids shutting but not quite all the way, revealing the cold blue slits of her pupils. Shock boiled down to humiliation and sharply froze over into hostility.

"Callista—" Veena reached forward.

The queen pulled away, edging to the far end of the ottoman. It felt so cold that Veena expected her breath to frost the air. The queen composed herself and, remembering her etiquette school manners, painted a tight smile across her face.

"Always a pleasure, Veena. We should do this again soon."

"I'm sorry," Veena began. "I was—"

"Nonsense! No need to be sorry. Reginald!" Callista called out. A Phoenix Guard filled the doorway. "Please show Miss Sixkills out."

Reginald waited for Veena to leave the room. He would not wait long.

Veena turned to go, her insides a pit of snakes.

"Oh, Veena?"

She whipped around, a burst of hope. Callista raised a lazy finger toward the rack, where the Peacock Gown hung in its garment bag. "You can take that with you."

"You can't be serious."

"It just doesn't capture my imagination like it once did." Callista swung her feet over the puddle of broken glass and, with her back turned to Veena, slipped out of the mirrored cave and into the curtained darkness of the fitting room.

*

Fuck.

Veena's teeth gnashed together so hard she felt something pop in her temple.

Fuck, fuck, fuck, FUCK!

The House of Azaleas grew small behind her as she stomped down the street. She had no idea where she was going. Cold gray rain streamed down, casting a curtain across Brooklyn, soaking through her dress and spattering on the Peacock Gown's garment bag. She had been exiled without so much as the courtesy of a car ride back home.

She took shelter under a deli awning and tried to breathe away her nerves the way her yoga instructor had taught her. It didn't work.

The plan was thoroughly fucked.

Veena swallowed down bile. It couldn't end like this—not when He Who Knows All had chosen her.

The rain fell harder. She needed to find a ride home. Veena dialed a number, then immediately hung up. She had just called Makini out of habit.

The bodega owner glared at her through the window. Veena dialed Shanti, but her Head of Public Relations didn't pick up, which Veena found odd because Shanti *always* picked up her calls, panting and eager like a lonely dog. Next, she dialed Shanti's boyfriend, Kormedia, but that went to voicemail.

In the distance she saw Overwatch patrols gliding above the Sovereign skyline. Border Patrols swept over the river, gunboats bobbing in the churning water.

Out of desperation, she called Caspar's secure phone. He picked up after two rings, and she immediately bombarded him with the details of their current predicament. When she was done, Caspar was silent for a long time.

"Did you hear what I said?" Veena asked.

"My lord," Caspar said. "Stay where you are. I'm sending a car."

He hung up. Across the street, Veena spotted a construction scaffolding sheltering an entire stretch of sidewalk from the rain. The bodega owner was still watching her, and his store awning provided her with little protection.

She waited for the rain to let up for a moment before running across the street. As she stepped onto the far curb, she felt a large presence materialize on her right—tall, broad, buzzcut. She took in the stranger quickly, but her alarms didn't ring until the second man flanked her from the left.

Like a cornered animal, Veena leapt off the curb to flee when a black Jeep Wrangler blocked her path.

The giants gripped her upper arms, and her feet left the ground. The rear door of the truck opened, and Veena caught sight of a face inside that made her gasp. The men shoved her into the back seat and shut the door. The woman next to her smiled.

"Miss Sixkills," Amanda Clark-Holler greeted her. "Your father has not forgotten you. It's time you went to see him."

"What is this?" Veena demanded.

Her father's chief of staff tapped out a quick email on her phone.

Veena grew flustered. "I'm extremely busy. This will have to be rescheduled and—"

"The general does not reschedule." Amanda pressed a button. The windows blacked out, turning the truck into a coffin. Amanda held out her hand. "Your phone, please."

"Are you crazy?"

"It will be returned when your meeting is over."

Veena didn't move.

Amanda sighed. "Either you give it to me now, or you wait for your father to take it from you."

Veena reluctantly handed over the phone. Amanda passed it to the Silverback driver and then stepped out of the car.

"What's with all this spy bullshit?" Veena huffed. "I've been to the Silver Spear before."

Amanda popped open a black umbrella and peered in at Veena from the street, her eyes pure stone behind her red-rimmed glasses. "Who said you're going to the Silver Spear?"

She slammed the door shut.

31

Tommy shifted in the cramped space of Crow Nest Four and peered down the sights of his mounted SAW machine gun, prepping the shot.

He scanned the road twenty feet below him, intermittently checking his laptop screen, which displayed the Reaper drone camera feed of the approaching Yukon.

Tommy's platform was one of four crow nests along the winding road leading to the Redblood compound on the mountain. Each one of the crow nests was set high in a tree a mile apart from the others and outfitted exactly the same—machine gun alcove, mobile radio, and computer banks set in what was basically a treehouse. Any visitors coming down this road would have to confirm their identities with separate codes at each crow nest and then with a fifth code to enter the front gates of the estate. Until a vehicle confirmed the approach codes, Tommy was to consider it hostile.

He was secretly hoping it *was* hostile, that it had somehow slipped past the first three crow nests and was now racing toward him filled with spec combatants. Maybe then he would get to fire this beastly gun in combat. And even if Tommy somehow missed with the machine gun, any unauthorized weight would activate the shaped charge mines under the road and blow the hell out of any trespasser. But that wasn't even Tommy's favorite gizmo in the arsenal. If a spec attack came from the air, Tommy's laptop became a targeting and firing system for the anti-spec missile array hidden in the bush. In the four days he had been out here, he often daydreamed that he was Caleb Cross, shooting down Phoenix Legionaries from the cockpit of his Tin Man mech.

Tommy's walkie-talkie buzzed. "Status rep, Crow Nest Two. Incoming vehicle, code authenticated. Heads up, Crow Nest Three." Tommy glanced at the Reaper feed. The black SUV had just passed through Crow Nest Two's zone and had entered Crow Nest Three's territory.

"Affirmative," the watcher in Crow Nest Three, replied. "Putting eyes on target."

The vehicle was getting closer. Tommy's heart pounded. He couldn't mess this up. Tommy had been brought up from the minors for this one job—guard the compound at all costs.

Because inside that compound—and it made his head spin just thinking about it—the Red Bitch had set up her command station.

The Red Bitch! And I'm protecting her.

Six days ago, he had been transporting messages between Redblood cells in Philadelphia, which might as well have been the moon for its distance from the real action. But then a posse of Redguns rode into town and shuttled him to this compound under cover of darkness.

They gave him his orders and put him up on the platform. Something big was going down here, and they needed the most loyal Reds on watch—people they could trust.

You couldn't trust anyone these days, Tommy figured. He'd realized that the moment he saw the executions—four of them, two men and two women, all Reds, lashed to poles and shot through with a suppressed Colt carbine. The Red Bitch had pulled the trigger herself. Traitors, he was told—Reds who couldn't stomach peace with the specs.

His radio crackled.

"Status rep," the watcher said. "Crow Nest Three. Incoming vehicle, code authenticated. Heads up, Crow Nest Four."

"Ah-yeah. Oh, shit." Tommy stumbled. "I mean, affirmative. Eye—putting eyes on target."

Moron. He slapped himself. *Learn how to speak.*

He watched the Yukon approach on the Reaper feed. He keyed in his radio to the preset channel and confirmed the approach codes with a woman in the vehicle.

A minute later, he spotted the black Yukon hauling ass. Through his gun scope, he caught a glimpse of five hard faces inside. A woman with short hair sat next to the driver. Behind her, two Redguns guarded a blindfolded man who looked like he had just eaten a shit sandwich.

Another traitor. Another execution.

The vehicle disappeared around the bend in a rooster tail of dust. It was quiet again.

Tommy had six hours left on his shift.

32

―――――――

"That's a big house," Houston muttered.

As soon as the Reds had parked the Yukon, they'd whipped off Houston's blindfold and marched him up a gravel drive toward the Victorian mansion. The house was set inside an estate so large that Houston couldn't see the boundaries. For a moment he thought the grounds around him were empty, but then he noticed the security.

Between the trees, Redguns in woodland camo patrolled in small teams. Reaper drones skimmed the bellies of the dark rain clouds above, and on the tiled roof, anti-spec gunnery units hid beneath thermo-camouflage tarps.

And that was just the security he *could* see.

The air was thick with moisture, and Houston exhaled with relief when they entered through a side door into the blasting air-conditioning. They passed through a service hallway into the bustling main hive of the building.

Houston looked around. *Who the hell are these people?*

Scrubbed, clean, and dressed in dark suits, the men and women swarming through the wide halls were a different tribe than the grizzled Redguns outside. They strode through their makeshift offices as if they were very late for a momentous event, their noses buried in their smartphones. They all ignored Houston, focused on their mysterious tasks. Houston had seen this kind of energy before, back in the corps. It usually bubbled up right before a general arrived at camp.

The Reds marched him up the stairs to the second floor, away from the chaos. As they led him past a series of closed doors, he noticed the watchful eye.

They had hidden it well, mounting it high up on the arch of the ceiling. Black as a pebble, Midnight Rider's small camera swiveled on its gyros to track his movements.

The Reds tossed him into a storage room at the far end of the hallway. It contained a barred window, a few chairs, and pile of dusty junk in the corner. Houston saw another pebble eye mounted in the corner.

"What am I supposed to do here?" he asked.

"Shut up and stay put," Pixie said. "You have a meeting in"—she set a digital clock on the wall to count down—"one hour and forty-eight minutes."

A man in a blazer came in behind her, hung a garment bag on a hook, and set a shoebox beneath it. He disappeared back out the door without looking at Houston.

"Forty regular, waist thirty-two, inseam thirty-two. Shoe size ten and a half," Pixie said.

"I feel violated," Houston said.

Pixie pointed to the adjoining bathroom. "Clean up. These are important people you're meeting with."

"Are Lily and Katya here?"

"Yes."

"Let me see them."

"No." Pixie clasped the door handle and went to close the door.

"I'm sorry," Houston said. She stopped and looked at him. "About Damian," he said.

She scowled, nostrils flared. "You know he's still out there? In Ringwood, where you shot him. We can't retrieve his body until it gets dark out. He's fucking lying out there alone in the *fucking dirt*." Her eyes bored into Houston before she slammed the door shut and locked it from the hallway.

Houston looked out the barred window. He had a view of the rear lawn with its artificial lake and cement helipad. The pebble eye watched him from the corner, humming.

Houston searched the room. Amid a pile of discarded suitcases, he found a heavy punching bag. The hook was still bolted to the ceiling a few feet away. Houston dragged the bag across the floor and grunted under its weight as he slotted its chain onto the hook.

He set his feet and punched the bag until a sweat broke, until the demons came forth and took shape in front of him. He thudded home hooks and straights, one after another after another. He felt the impact jarring his bones, shooting all the way up to his brain, wiping it clean.

Thud, thud, thud.

The machine watched him.

Eventually, barking broke his focus. The door swung open, and he immediately tightened into a defensive stance, convinced they had set the dogs on him. Wolves raced inside, white and gray, barking and yapping.

Not wolves, huskies, he realized as they circled around his legs and wagged their tails. After inspecting him thoroughly, they loped back to the door, where someone was standing.

"Lily," Houston said.

She smiled and entered the room, her arms weighed down by heavy books. Halfway into the room, she tripped over her feet and fell forward, the books scattering. Before Houston could help, she was back on her feet and smiling.

"Katya said you like books," she said.

"You okay?" he asked.

She nodded. "You okay?"

"Been better."

"You bastard." Houston looked up to see Katya walk through the door. "Don't smile at me," she said. "Not after what you put us through."

"Did they hurt you?"

"Well, no, but they put blindfolds on us and *kidnapped* us. It was—shoo," she waved the curious huskies away. "It was highly irregular."

"Do you want to hit me?" Houston asked Katya.

She seemed to be thinking it over. "I do, but this place is amazing."

"What?"

"Have you seen all their gear? Their organization? The things we Badges could do with these resources. I mean, they go a little overboard with all the clocks and timing, but they get things done. They're *effective*." She smiled and then rocked Houston's shoulder with a stinging punch.

"What the hell?" Houston bellowed.

"I don't want you to think that I'm happy here."

They both turned to look at Lily. She was gathering up the spilled books and compiling them into neat piles. She had showered and changed into dark jeans and white shirt, her hair still wild. Houston noted that she still wore the Clamp around her wrist.

"You hungry?" Lily asked Houston. She handed him an energy bar from her pocket. "Took it off one of the people downstairs."

"Lily, what did I tell you about pickpocketing?" Katya said.

Lily shrugged. Houston bit hungrily in his bar and gave her a thumbs-up. She returned the gesture and went back to piling the books. He and Katya watched her for some time.

"Are we in trouble?" Katya whispered to Houston.

"I don't know. I have a meeting where I'll find out." He pointed to the countdown clock. "In one hour, fifteen minutes."

"Something big is going down here," Katya said. "I've been asking around, but no one's talking."

Pixie showed up at the door. "It's time to go," she said to Lily and Katya.

Lily stood up. "I want to stay."

"Too bad," Pixie said.

"Just a little bit longer," Lily pleaded.

Pixie looked at Houston, who shrugged.

"Fine." Pixie relented. "But not for long."

Katya gripped Houston's arm. "Be careful, Holt."

She turned and followed Pixie outside. Before the door closed, Houston heard Katya officiously announce to Pixie, "I have more questions for you." He heard Pixie groan through the closed door.

Houston watched Lily flipping through the books. "You don't have to stay here with me," he said.

"I don't like those people outside. Also," she said as she unloaded a pile of goodies from her pockets onto the floor, "I got their stuff."

"Is there a lockpick in there?"

"Two watches, a wallet, and a pack of gum."

"I'll take the gum."

She handed it over.

"Thanks for trying to help me," she said. "Back in River Town."

"Looks like I just brought you back to where you started."

"You get an A for effort."

She read the titles of the books out loud. Biographies of Genghis Khan, Eisenhower, and Caleb Cross. "They have a big library here," she said. "I've read most of these."

"Yeah, right."

"I have," she insisted. "I spent a lot of time with these people. They carry their books with them." She noticed the heavy bag. "You box?"

Houston nodded. "Clears my head."

She stepped up to the bag and punched it.

"Focus your shots," Houston said. "Picture the people that make you mad."

Lily raised her fists and focused on the bag, drilling holes through it with her eyes. She slammed two big punches into the leather.

"Better," Houston said. "Who are you picturing?"

"Everyone." Lily pounded the bag. "I'm mad at everyone."

Houston held the bag for her. "You and me both, kid."

*

Houston punched the bag, Lily by his side, mimicking his moves. They were both in the bubble now, in the flow. The jabs, the hooks, the crosses. He moved his feet around, showing her the footwork. What she lacked in technique she made up for in ferocity and grit.

"Not your first time fighting," Houston noted.

"No."

"Who taught you how to fight?"

"Some guy."

"Same guy who taught you how to pickpocket?"

"Yeah."

Her punches flew harder at the bag, her face darkening. Her form fell apart as she burned off a toxic memory. Suddenly there were tears streaming down her cheeks. Houston put a hand on her shoulder.

"Take five," he said.

Lily stepped away from the bag, hands on her knees, breathing deeply.

"Sometimes I want to hit them all," she said. "Everyone who wants something from me."

For a moment, her aura reappeared. It was pinched tight to her body, held in by the Clamp—a crackling cloud of black and blue, pulsing with thunder. She blinked and shook her body, and the cloud dissipated. She went back to the bag.

"Round two," she said.

"Want to learn something cool?" Houston asked.

She nodded.

"When you meet the king, if he pisses you off, hit him right here." He slammed a punch into the bag at groin level. "Right in the noodles. *Bam!*"

Lily giggled. "Like this?" She nailed a fast right into the same spot.

"Like that. *Bam!*"

"*Bam!*" Lily was laughing now, throwing pinpoint blows. After she had exhausted herself, she looked up at Houston. "Who do you hit?"

"What do you mean?"

"When you hit the bag—who do you picture?" Her big eyes bored into him, channeling through his skull.

He looked at her, sensing the vast *knowing* beneath her gaze. "Sometimes I get the feeling you ask me questions you already know the answers to."

She scratched her nose and grinned.

Houston sat down on an empty crate and wiped the sweat from his forehead. He watched her watching him, *reading* him. Her eyes drank in the light of the fading sun, but her look held no judgment.

"I don't blame you," she finally said, "for being mad at your family. The people who are supposed to look out for us end up hurting us the most."

Houston felt a twinge in his neck and broke her gaze, suddenly desperate to escape her eyes. He still felt them on him, brushing across his skin like feathered smoke as he pressed his sore knuckles. "My family's long gone. I don't think about them anymore," he said.

She accepted that, walked away from the bag, and looked out the barred window. "They call them the Sonorous, by the way."

"What?"

"Your brother. He's one of the Sonorous. People think they're just entertainers, creating fantasy worlds. But the most Gifted of them, like your brother, show people what their soul *needs* to see."

"Why are you telling me this?"

She reached into her pocket and pulled out a folded square of paper. She opened it to reveal the island she had drawn in River Town. "There's a reason your brother showed you this. There's a reason you found me in that truck. Everyone wants my power for themselves, but I think you might be the only one who can get me back home."

In that moment, she reminded Houston of Bobby—small, vulnerable, and infuriatingly *connected* to something he didn't understand.

And just like Bobby, he couldn't save her.

He looked at the countdown clock. Forty minutes left.

"I've got a meeting I need to get ready for," he said. He left her there, holding the drawing, and shut himself inside the bathroom.

Houston showered and changed into the navy-blue wool suit the Reds had left for him. He buttoned the crisp white shirt over his bruised body, painful reminders of his encounters with the Redguns and the Escheveras—a map of his entire life up to this point.

Lily was reading when he came out. He stepped on a piece of paper. It was the drawing, discarded by the door. He picked it up and studied the island.

Lily continued reading. He could feel her disappointment thick as a wall between them.

"Where is this place?" Houston held up the drawing.

She turned a page and buried her face deeper into the book.

"Lily, where is this place?"

"Hawaii," she said. "Big Island."

Houston looked at the picture and then back at her. "That's impossible."

"I know what you're thinking."

"Hawaii has been a nuclear wasteland for the past ten years. There's no way you're from there."

In the aftermath of Sixkills's execution of the Buffalo Six, with the Specials and humans at each other's throats, President Mathias, in coordination with Patriot Gold, had granted the Specials a homeland on the Hawaiian Islands. Military ships ferried Specials by the thousands across the Pacific toward their new destiny.

But it was a trap.

Four million Specials had reached the islands when three thermonuclear warheads detonated. Historians agreed that the bombs were supposed to explode the next day, when Patriot Gold and twelve million other Specials arrived on the islands, but something went wrong—a breakdown in communication, a rogue military faction—no one knew what. What was clear when the smoke cleared was that there were no survivors.

And no chance of peace.

The Immortal War began that day.

Ever since, Hawaii had been a radioactive wasteland—the Black Isles, they called it. Something in the nuclear blast mixed with the energy of the doomed Specials and created an impenetrable shield of hundred-foot waves and aerial firestorms called Furies that swirled endlessly in the blackened skies. No one survived Hawaii—especially not a girl who wasn't even born when the bombs went off.

"You want to know how old I am?" Lily asked, putting her book down, guessing his question. "I was born on the Big Island. I lived there with my dad. I was eight years old when the Specials started moving in. One day . . ." she paused and disappeared again for a moment, her body there, her attention in another world. "One day, my father was gone and I was by myself. These people from the government found me and put me on a plane to get off the island. I was scared and excited because it was my first time on a plane, and I was watching the clouds, and then . . . that's the last thing I remember."

"Your plane never landed."

She shook her head. Her arms clenched around her knees, and she hugged them tightly to her body, guarded against an old nightmare. "After that, I dreamed a dream that went on and on . . ." Her eyes went wide, and she fell into a dark memory for an awful moment. She blinked hard and shook off whatever darkness clung to her. "And then, four years ago, I woke up—a prisoner of the Frontier. Of the Snake Mother."

Houston sat quietly with that information. There was no guile in Lily's voice. Her story had the clear, terrifying ring of truth.

"If you were there when the bombs went off, does that mean . . . did you . . . ?"

"Die?"

He nodded.

"I think so."

"That's impossible."

"It's not. The king died and came back."

"But that's why he's the king—because he's the Firstborn. The only one who *can* come back."

She smiled mischievously. "Why do you think he's so eager to meet me?"

Houston was about to say something when an alarm sounded. He jumped to his feet and reached for his weapon. Except he had no weapon. He looked at the clock. Twenty-six minutes left. The alarm was for something else.

"They're here," Lily said.

Before he could ask who, he heard heavy blades whipping the air. Together they ran to the window overlooking the rear of the estate. A large group of people had gathered on the lawn, a safe distance away from the helipad. A dozen Redbloods in suits stood in neat rows, flanked by two lines of Redguns wearing crisp uniforms. At the head of the receiving party, Houston saw a woman he recognized. He could only see her from the back, and her long black hair was streaked with white, but he remembered that posture, that grounded power.

Carmen.

She wore a black peacoat and leather boots. Her head was turned slightly upward, watching as the helicopters traced the tops of the trees and swiveled around for a landing. The two Black Hawks lowered simultaneously, grass rippling under the assault of their combined rotor wash. The waiting dignitaries tried frantically to control their billowing suits and blowing hair, but not Carmen. She and the Redguns stood at attention like statues.

The helicopters touched down. The rotors slowed, and their occupants stepped out.

"They're so big," Lily marveled, looking at the newcomers.

Big was an understatement. The first eight men off the helicopters were brutal giants, as densely muscled as oxen and clad in black combat uniforms that stole the light as they spread across the lawn, forming a thick perimeter around the choppers. On their chests, the men wore an altered version of the king's gold phoenix sigil. Houston recognized it immediately, marking the men as spec Marines from the Phoenix Expeditionary Unit.

Houston hadn't encountered the Phoenix Marines during the war, as the unit had been unleashed only for classified missions, but he had heard stories about them—ugly stories. Looking at the twelve pitiless faces down there on the lawn, he believed every one.

Behind the spec soldiers, four officials stepped out of the choppers—two men and two women, all wearing long dark coats and smug expressions. The man in the lead, tall and bald with a cropped white beard, stepped forward to shake Carmen's hand.

"Who are they?" Lily asked.

"The king's people."

"I don't like the look of them."

"Me neither, kid."

*

When the clock hit zero, the door opened and a duo of Redguns grabbed Houston and marched him downstairs. Lily followed at his heels, tripping over her own feet half the time. Just as Houston passed underneath another pebble eye, a rumble of distant thunder sounded above.

Downstairs, the Redguns brought Houston into a large vestibule. The circular room was lined with uniformed Redguns on one side and Phoenix Marines on the other. The two units glared at each other, the Redguns tracing the trigger guards of their rifles, the Marines flexing their mighty fists.

The Reds pushed open the lone set of doors on the opposite end and ushered Houston forward. Before Houston stepped inside, Lily grabbed his hand from behind. He turned to see her looking up at him, worried.

"Remember," she said, "you have something left to do."

"I hope so."

She let go of his hand, and one of the Redguns pushed him through the door and shut it behind him. Houston stood at the head of a table large enough to support a shipping container. The long room was lit by lamps, its arched windows covered in blackout shades.

The eight people at the table were looking at him with pointed expressions. There were four on each side, the Redblood contingent with Carmen on one side and the four grim Sovereign diplomats on the other. Two huskies sat behind Carmen. They all studied him silently, as if he were a slave on display at the market.

A bespectacled Redblood next to Carmen broke the silence. "If you will all please turn to page 134, section 4.5, of your agenda books, we now come to the case of Houston Holt."

All eight people simultaneously turned a page in the heavy black binders in front of them.

Houston felt a strange sensation as he watched them. Something about the room felt off. It took him a moment to realize what it was:

Midnight was not here. There was no pebble eye in the room, no watchful presence or agitated humming.

The lead Sovereign diplomat ran his thumb along his white beard and glared at Houston, as if he were a particularly problematic morsel stuck in his teeth.

"You were a United States Marine during the war," the bearded diplomat said.

"Yes."

"Which battalion?"

"Ambassador Trevayne," Carmen said, "I believe all of this information is in your agenda book."

Houston noted that Carmen was older than she had been in the construct. The young woman from the dream was gone, replaced by someone harder, who had less hope but more wisdom.

"With all due respect, Miss Vega," Ambassador Trevayne said, "there are things about a man's character that cannot be ascertained from a book. I will be brief with this line of questioning, I assure you." Trevayne turned back to Houston. "Which battalion did you fight with?"

"The First Mechanized Raiders."

"Ah. The Iron Vikings. Quite the esteemed unit, if I remember correctly. You must have fought in a number of pivotal battles, yes?"

Houston suspected he was being led to the slaughter. "Yes, sir."

"You must have had an illustrious career, I'm sure. Tell me something, young man." Trevayne leaned forward. "How much did you enjoy massacring Specials?"

The room froze. Carmen glared at Trevayne. Houston met the man's gaze and held it.

The diplomat continued, "I'm sure it was just a sport to you. I can understand all the resentment you must have felt, being so ordinary—especially compared to your brother. Putting on a uniform and shooting Specials? Why, that must have been an incredibly effective therapy for you."

"Ambassador Trevayne." Carmen's voice took on an ominous register. "Nothing can be gained from rehashing a man's actions from over a decade ago. We are here to discuss the future."

Trevayne raised an eyebrow and smiled. It was the smile of a man who was used to being catered to. Houston wanted to slap that smile off his face.

"Of course, Miss Vega." Trevayne said her name as if he were addressing an incompetent house slave. "His Majesty has deemed it prudent to pursue peace with you, and who am I to question his Royal Highness? Let's get back to business, shall we?"

Carmen was too experienced to take the bait. She nodded to her bespectacled subordinate.

"If we turn back to our agenda," the subordinate announced to the room, "you will see that despite having taken unlawful possession of the Sun Angel last night, Houston Holt was instrumental in its return to us today."

"That does not change the fact that he stole it," Trevayne grumbled.

"No," the subordinate agreed. "We are not disputing that. However, Houston Holt is the biological brother of Robert Holt, whom we all now know as Augustus Sky."

"We are aware of this," Trevayne said.

"So you are aware," Carmen said, "that executing the brother of Augustus Sky could present some problems—especially given your king's fondness for Sky."

"He is *your* king as well," Trevayne snapped.

"If you say so, Ambassador."

The veins bulged violently in Trevayne's neck. He took a moment to compose himself before turning to Houston. "It says here you were part of the Ohana."

"Not part of it. Forced into it."

"The Ohana are friends of the Crown. Your brother is still quite active in their ranks. It amazes me how different the two of you are.

He, one of the Kingdom's most celebrated talents, and . . . *you*, a war criminal."

"Now, now," Carmen interjected. "The past is dead."

"So are a lot of our people," Trevayne retorted. His subordinates all nodded in unison. "Let it be said that if it were up to me, you would be hanging from a beam by your neck. But your brother has personally vouched for you."

It took a moment for that to land. Houston blinked. "My brother knows I'm here?"

"We informed him earlier today, when Miss Vega briefed us about you. It is quite normal for Specials to distance themselves from their human families—especially during the war, when many families outright butchered their own Gifted kin. And yet, not your brother. He was quite insistent that we let you go. And Augustus Sky is very much favored by His Majesty, so—" Trevayne clasped his hands and settled them on the table. "Houston Holt, today you are the luckiest man on the king's great Earth. Today we are going to make a deal."

"I don't need my brother's help," Houston said.

"Don't you? The other option is the rope."

"What kind of deal, Ambassador?" Carmen asked.

Trevayne removed a sheaf of papers from a blue envelope and signed each one. He then stamped each form and slotted them back into the envelope. He slid it across the long table to Houston.

"What is this?" Houston asked.

"Temporary citizenship status."

Houston stared at the envelope.

"They are valid as papers of passage," Trevayne continued. "You will have to present them at your local Border Patrol Processing Center to obtain the Gold Stamp. However, their validity is contingent upon you reporting to Augustus Sky immediately upon your arrival in Sovereign City. You will be under his sponsorship and required to check in monthly."

Houston's fingers drifted across the top of the envelope. He knew there was a catch. "And what do *you* want out of this deal?"

"That's what I'd like to know too," Carmen said.

Trevayne smiled at Houston. "You were privy to classified information, Mister Holt. You attempted to steal the Sun Angel on behalf of what we believe was a terrorist cell—who, along with the help of Redblood agents—"

"*Traitorous* Redblood agents," Carmen corrected him.

"Regardless, agents intent on causing havoc in Sovereign City. You were hired by this cell and therefore possess valuable information about their means and motives." One of the Specials put a blank piece of paper on the table in front of Houston and a pen. "You will write, sign, and date a written confession telling us everything—who was involved and what you know about them. *Everything.*"

"What happens to her?" Houston asked.

"Excuse me?"

"The girl. What happens to her when the king has her?"

The room shifted. The Specials bristled, and the Reds looked embarrassed.

"That is not your concern." Trevayne's mouth turned into an ugly leer.

"Houston." Carmen sat forward, her voice calming the room. "Lily will not be hurt. The king wants to learn from her, not exploit her."

She stood up and approached him, putting a gentle hand on his shoulder. "Put your guns down, soldier. Your fight's over."

Houston turned to her. It was an order but delivered in a tone fluid with hard-earned wisdom and compassion. Looking into Carmen's eyes, hearing her voice, he understood now why only she could have led the rebellion.

He sat down at the table and wrote his confession. He wrote for ten minutes, and when he was done, he signed and dated the document. He slid the paper back to Trevayne, who read the confession carefully before slipping it to his associate.

The doors opened behind Houston. He picked up the blue envelope, and Carmen led him out. He suddenly felt very lost, his mind unable to comprehend what had just happened to him. Outside the room, he turned to Carmen.

"So what do I do now?" He asked.

"Anything you want, Mister Holt," she said with a smile. "You're free."

She went back into the conference room and shut the door, leaving him in the vestibule.

33

The Silverback driver dropped Veena off on the side of a wooded mountain. The sky was darkening, and the storm had followed her out here from Sovereign, the clouds sweeping toward the peaks, heavy with rain.

Veena looked around at the mountains. "Where are we?"

"Adirondacks," the driver replied. "Leave that here." He pointed to the garment bag in her hands.

"Not a chance," Veena said.

"They won't let you in with it. It'll be here when I pick you up after."

"After what?"

The driver came around the Jeep and pointed a hefty finger at a narrow hiking path leading up to a ridge. "Head up that way. There's a shelter there."

He snatched the garment bag from her, jumped back into the Jeep and drove down the fire road to level ground, leaving her alone. She looked up at the short climb with its loose rocks and earth, then at her four-inch heels.

She wanted to call Caspar to get her out of here—maybe even that ditz Shanti, or Kormedia. Anyone who could save her from this ominous meeting with her father. But they had taken her phone, and here she was, alone in the wild.

Dark clouds slid quickly overhead. Veena shivered as she struggled up the slope, breaking the heels of both shoes and twisting her ankles. This was typical of her father. Why make it easy when you can make it excruciatingly hard?

The shelter sat on a flat stretch of mountain overlooking a deep valley shrouded in trees. It was nothing more than a wooden bench covered by a corrugated tin roof—what a Silverback might call "luxury accommodations."

There was no one waiting for her. She sat on the bench just as the first drops of rain drummed on the tin roof. The quiet out here unnerved her. It was a wild hush that seemed to have eyes. After a few minutes of yoga breathing, she relaxed. A quiet mind was the best weapon against whatever her father was about to throw at her.

Something flashed in the distance. The distant roar of an aftershock followed a few seconds later.

It was then Veena realized that whatever she had done to prepare for this moment, it was not nearly enough.

The second blast nearly shook her out of her skin. Blinding light reflected in the raindrops like a million teeth. The third blast rocked her bones and flung her to the mud.

A silver cloud rose above the trees. Veena tried to get up, slipping on the mud, squaring herself to the valley just as the concussion wave rattled inside her chest. Clambering back into the shelter, she saw shapes moving above her in the dark.

The Silverbacks dipped low over the trees, unleashing silver bolts onto some hidden enemy. Crackling black bolts flew back at them in response. Veena smelled burnt flesh.

The battle moved up the valley, toward her. Fingers of silver lightning reached across the treetops. Shards of broken trees and exploded earth arced through the sky and fell on her, battering the shelter roof. The heat of the blasts scorched her skin.

The trees shook, and the battle echoed off the hard face of the mountains. The men dove into the darkness and back up. Some of them fell, hit by black tracers.

And then came the howling—a primal scream that rose from the valley's dark heart, a cry so severe and anguished that it could only be the call of death.

Veena screamed and screamed. The howl became a living thing with talons that swept through the rain and pierced her heart.

He had brought her here to die.

The thought was a cancer, growing in her mind until all she could do was close her eyes and wait for the end.

When the silence came, she refused to open her eyes, for she was dead, and she was not ready for what she might see.

The wind picked up and swept cool rain across her face. She smelled pine and dirt and felt the wetness of the earth. She blinked her eyes open.

Six rough men marched out of the trees, carrying the wounded on their shoulders. Ten in total, metallic hulks in their black power armor, battered and burned from their ordeal. Some wore visored helmets that reflected the night. Her father did not.

General Sixkills's face was covered in sweat and blood as he led his men out of the woods, the rain *thunking* off his armored bulk.

Fire. Blood. Fury. These were the words that came to Veena's mind as she watched her father rise like a scarred god from the shadow of the forest and onto the ridge. When he saw Veena, he holstered his massive greatmace along his right thigh and frowned at her.

"Are you dead?" he demanded.

Veena pushed herself up to a sitting position. She shook her head. "No."

The general turned away. "Then walk."

He continued along the ridge, his men behind him as they trudged into the dark mountains.

*

Their base was a twenty-minute walk uphill. Veena's calves screamed with exertion as the group approached a collection of squat gray buildings jutting out of the side of a mountain, bordered by a heavy wall.

A uniformed Silverback stood outside the restroom door while Veena splashed water on her face and clothes. She dried herself with rough paper towels. It made no difference; she was still a muddy mess.

The Silverback led her up a flight of stairs to her father's office. He told her the general would be in shortly and left, shutting the door.

The first thing she saw in Sixkills's office was the picture. It hung behind the giant desk on the opposite wall, forcing visitors to grapple with its dark meaning.

The woman in the picture was on her knees, holding her young son. Their faces were dirty and streaked with tears, and the mother pleaded with the man standing above them—a muscled youth wearing the heavy boots and black denim uniform of the Native Sons Militia. He held a gun to the woman's head. He was smiling.

To never be ruled again, the primary duty of the Silverbacks, was encapsulated in that one image with all its life-and-death gravity.

Buzzing with nervous energy, Veena paced around the room. The entire right side was a window facing the dark valley. On her left was a large conference table next to a wall covered in maps and aerial spy shots of mountains and rocky deserts. A small library held the kind of books her father devoured: *Rise of our People*, *The Human Devil*, and *The Integrationists' Fallacy*.

Something on the table caught her eye. It was a short sword mounted on a display stand, its curved blade engraved with snakes and its dyed bone hilt wrapped in black leather. As she stepped closer to inspect the sword, the blade's color shifted like oil in water, from black to indigo. Now, standing above it, Veena realized the blade was *vibrating*.

She reached out to touch it.

Bang. Veena jumped, snapping her hand away as the doors swung open and General Sixkills strode into the room.

As always in his presence, Veena felt like a six-year-old girl again, cowering against the fearsome mass of her father. He didn't look at her as he walked behind his desk. He had showered and changed into forest camo pants and a matching combat shirt that wrapped around his mountainous shoulders and chest like a second skin. In his right hand he carried his greatmace, Crossbreaker. He cleared out a space on his desk, unrolled a square of stained leather, and laid the fearsome weapon on it.

The room was silent. It wasn't clear if he realized Veena was there.

Oh, he knows I'm here.

Sixkills began dismantling the weapon. Walking slowly, as if trying to soothe a wild animal, Veena approached the visitor chair and sat down. She watched her father's hands fluidly unscrew the mace.

He still made no sign that he had noticed her.

"Who were you fighting outside?" she asked.

Click. His hands swept across steel. *Click.*

"Training exercise," he replied.

"Training? But your men were wounded."

He unscrewed a flap and laid it on the cloth. "Bleed in training, win in war."

Veena struggled to fill the silence. She looked out into the darkness and remembered the howling from the battle. It was a sound she knew would haunt her nightmares.

"What was that sound?" she asked. "That howling?"

"Our enemies have developed new weapons. If we want to beat them, we have to train against those weapons."

"Frontier?" Veena glanced over her shoulder at the black sword on the conference table.

He ignored her, his eyes never leaving his work. Veena swallowed down fear and reacted the only way she knew how—by going on the offensive. "What was the point of dropping me out in the woods? I nearly died! Why couldn't you just bring me here if you wanted to see me?"

"You arrived earlier than expected. We don't allow civilians into this facility unescorted."

Sixkills now had the mace dismantled into six parts, all laid out in a precise grid on the leather—the spiked finial, the flanged steel head, the shaft divided in two to reveal the hidden silver core, the grip wrapped in corded leather, and the sphere pommel at the base.

Behind her father was a bank of phones, next to which Veena noticed a framed picture she had missed before. It was of her mother, Mable, standing in a field, carrying a shotgun and wearing a bird hunting vest. She looked rugged and chic. No easy feat, Veena knew.

"You are clean, correct?" Sixkills asked.

"What?"

"You are off the drugs?"

She sputtered. "Yes, of course."

"You're lying."

"Want to give me a blood test?"

He looked at her as if he were considering it. Veena changed the subject just to escape his arctic gaze. She pointed to the picture of Mable.

"I've never seen that picture of mother before. I didn't know she hunted."

Her father returned to his work, using a small brush to clean Crossbreaker's flanged head.

Veena swallowed. "So . . . peace with the lowbloods?"

Sixkills eyebrow twitched.

"It makes me sick," she said, hoping to find common ground.

As she said the words, the vision blossomed again—her father, hanging from his neck. Her own bloody steps toward the noose as the hangman—

"What are you doing?" Sixkills's voice snapped her back to reality.

"Sorry. I was . . . thinking."

"Daydreamers die first."

"I'm sorry. The whole ceasefire just makes me so *angry*. The lowbloods don't deserve a piece of our land."

"The king believes they do."

Soon, you will be king.

"I know," Veena said. "I should just trust his wisdom."

"People don't get what they deserve. They get what they fight for." He put down his brush and turned to the bank of phones behind him. He lifted a receiver and simply said, "Stand by," before hanging up.

"What people really don't understand," he continued, turning back to Veena, "is that there are worse things than lowbloods out there." He looked at her now, his eyes narrow. "Do you understand?"

"What do you mean?"

"Do you understand that this is not a world to play games in?" Something like a smile crept onto his face—a cold, curved line that turned Veena's stomach.

"I . . . I don't understand."

The weight of his gaze buried her like an avalanche, and Veena suddenly understood that her father had arrived at his reason for bringing her here. This was the moment before the reveal, and just by looking into his eyes, by seeing the violence waiting there, she knew that whatever his reason may be, it was *far* worse than she could have ever imagined.

He flipped a switch under his desk. Veena jumped as a large projection screen slid down from the ceiling behind her. The lights dimmed, and the projector flickered on.

The image on the screen shook. It wasn't immediately clear to Veena what she was looking at except that it had been shot on a camera phone. She heard laughter and the ominous boom of a distant bass line echoing in a cavernous space. The image stabilized, and Veena's heart stopped when she recognized a face:

Her own.

At some party after she had left the Tangle nightclub two nights ago. Veena always cringed when she saw herself on camera. Being her own biggest critic, she was unable to tolerate even the tiniest of imperfections in her face, hair, or outfits. But now she recoiled for a different reason. It was clear, looking at her face on the screen— the glazed eyes, the sweaty brow, the drooping lips—that she was as high as fuck on Moxi.

"Fuck the queen!" she yelled onscreen. "Fuck the king!"

Oh, god.

She heard the man behind the camera laugh. "Holy shit, this is amazing."

"I'm serious," Veena slurred onscreen. "I'm serious, okay? My father will be king. You'll see. He'll take the throne the second we kill those royal cunts. He'll sweep the fucking lowbloods into the sea!" She swayed on her heels and stuck her tongue out, blinking rapidly, suddenly overwhelmed by her surroundings. "Long live King Sixkills!"

No . . .

Onscreen, Veena tapped her chest proudly. "Me. I'm the one. I'm the savior. You'll see."

The image paused on her gruesome face. Veena did not dare move. She was still facing the screen. Behind her, waiting like a hungry wolf, she could feel her father's eyes land on her.

"Look," she stammered, turning around, "I can explain—"

Her father lifted a finger.

Concrete pylons smashed into her chest. She flew halfway across the room and skidded hard on the ground. She gasped in pain, twinkling silver motes spinning around her like bees.

Across the room, Sixkills turned up his palm.

The silver motes hardened around her neck and wrenched her into the air. Her toes scrabbled at the ground, but the ground was gone.

The general watched her from behind his desk.

"Please . . ." Veena managed with the last of her air.

The silver noose evaporated, and she crashed onto the floor. Sixkills arrived above her. "Explain," he said.

"Somebody . . . somebody tricked me . . . into taking Moxi. I didn't know—"

The noose yanked her up with so much force that her stomach lurched. It lifted her higher now, to the point where her father's face was level with her toes. The noose disappeared, and she fell, cracking on the hard floor.

"Explain better."

Tears streamed down Veena's face. The skin around her throat burned, and her entire body screamed with a hundred different agonies. What could she say to him? The truth would mean death. To stall would mean a slower death.

She saw her father lift his hand.

"No," she pleaded, trying to rise. "No, no, *please*—"

Crash. His giant hand flicked to the left, and the noose ricocheted her against the glass door so hard her back spasmed.

Veena was crying now. "Please, I'm your daughter—"

The noose crackled and jerked her airborne. It dragged her through the air toward her father like a conveyer belt. He stood waiting, an immovable mountain—her final judgment.

"Daughter?" His eyes were pitiless voids. "You are the blood of a whore."

Veena kicked at the air. Her eyes flickered to the picture of Mable.

"Don't ever look at her. She is not your mother."

"*What?*" Veena sputtered for a few seconds before the silver rope unraveled and she fell again. But this time, her father caught her. He grabbed a fistful of her dress and held her up.

"Did you hear me?" he demanded. "She is not your mother."

". . . not true . . ."

"You came from my weakness."

"I'm your daughter."

"You are the daughter of who I was—a lowblood. Your mother was a nobody, a tramp I met in a bar. And when she showed up at my door fifteen months later and Mable answered the bell and saw *you* . . ." Sixkills's hand trembled.

"No . . ."

Sixkills's eyes blazed and he dragged Veena toward his desk. He picked up the picture of Mable and held it up for Veena to see. "You were six months old. I was out of the house when your mother—that filthy *whore*—came to our home looking for a handout. When Mable realized what you were, what I had done—"

"Mable . . . Mable was my mother . . ."

"You think Mable died in a car accident? It was no accident. She *chose* to drive her car into that ravine because every time she saw you, she was reminded of my weakness—that I had betrayed her . . . for *nothing.*"

"*No!*" Veena cried. "That's not true!"

"The only reason you still breathe is because I have allowed it—because you are a reminder to me of the price of weakness."

Veena's throat filled with acid, and she felt an endless darkness sweep in. Everything she thought she was collapsed with the weight of bricks.

She was the blood of weakness. She was the blood of a whore.

And then, like the soft wash of sleep, another sensation fell over her. The pain left her body, and she realized she didn't care if she lived or died.

Veena.

The voice snapped in her head like a whip, clearing away the shock and pain instantaneously.

It was *Him*.

He Who Knows All had not forgotten her. He was here to *save* her.

And then, in words that filled her veins like fresh blood, He Who Knows All spoke to her. He wove a story. And it took Veena a few moments to understand that he was weaving it *for* her. The perfect words and images sewn together to create an alibi—a sliver of hope.

"Father . . ." she croaked. "I'll tell you the truth."

Her father glared at her. "If you lie . . ."

"I won't."

He dropped her into a chair and took his seat behind the desk. Veena cleared her throat and told him the story—not the real story, but the one He Who Knows All fed to her, moving her lips and tongue as if she were in a trance.

She had been blackmailed into helping them. Who *they* were, she did not know. They communicated through packages and phone calls, and all she could glean about them was that they considered themselves patriots who worked for her father, General Sixkills, with the mission of raising him to the throne of a rudderless kingdom. At first she'd resisted, but then they'd turned violent. They'd killed Makini and threatened Veena's life. All they needed was her help getting close to her childhood friend, the queen. They were bringing in a weapon called the Sun Angel, and Veena would have to bring it close to the royal couple. But the weapon was lost, stolen by a lowblood thief named Houston Holt.

Sixkills's eyes never moved from her as she spoke.

Veena never mentioned the dress. She never mentioned Faraz or Caspar or the Lady in the Veil.

"I thought I was helping you become king," she finished. "They said they would kill me if I didn't cooperate. I was so confused.

I wanted to call you and ask you, but they said that would expose you to the Gray Faces." She looked at her father with pleading eyes. "Don't you want to be king?"

A rumble rose up his throat, rolling like a landslide. Veena realized he was laughing. "I could take the throne with ten good men."

He stood and walked to the window. He watched the mountains.

"Was that the truth?" she asked. "What you said about my mother?"

"Yes."

"But all this time, you led me to believe she was . . ." Veena's voice cracked. "You lied about my *mother*. That is wrong—"

He wheeled around on her, and immediately she realized her mistake.

"Wrong?" His fists clenched.

"No. I'm sorry—"

"Did you already forget what I taught you about *wrong*?"

How could she forget the words he had drilled it into her head as a child? She started, "No right, no wrong—"

"*Louder.*"

She yelled, "No right! No wrong! Only the strong!"

"No right. No wrong. Only the strong," his voice boomed.

He returned to Veena, towering above her. His eyes raked over her like icicles. "Do you think you are strong?"

She knew her answer would decide if she lived or died. "Yes."

He pressed a button under his desk, and the doors behind her opened.

"Prove it."

Two uniformed Silverbacks rolled in wheelchairs with two hooded captives strapped to them—a man and a woman, naked, moaning beneath their hoods.

"No one else has seen the video," Sixkills said, "because my men intercepted these two criminals before they had a chance to sell it on the black market."

The Silverbacks whipped off the hoods. Veena choked in horror.

Kormedia and Shanti stared back at her with swollen eyes. The black tape over their mouths stifled their cries. Neither of them made eye contact with Veena.

"These friends of yours took the tape to the press, demanding eight hundred thousand goldmarks for it." Sixkills smirked. "What they didn't count on was the number of people in the press that answer to me."

Sixkills nodded at his men, and they disappeared back out the door.

Veena closed her eyes and sat with the anger for a moment. Her palms grew sweaty, and her face felt hot.

Sixkills spoke. "On the first day of Silverback selection, we prepare our recruits for the ordeal ahead of them by teaching them three simple words: Reborn in blood. What does that mean, Veena?"

Veena looked at her hands, then at her father.

"It means," he continued, "that we are not fixed. We can change ourselves." He picked up Crossbreaker's hilt from his desk and brought it to her. "But first, we must do what the weak cannot."

He thumbed a switch, and an eight-inch blade *shunked* out of the bottom of the hilt. "Show me what kind of blood runs through your veins now."

The blade felt heavy and final in her hands. She found herself studying its cruel lines and the coils of black leather along the handle.

She turned to the two prisoners. Kormedia trembled. Shanti stared back at her with bug eyes, screaming through the tape as if to say, *Please, Veena, don't do this! We're friends, remember?*

When Veena moved, it was without doubt.

Her feet flew over the floor. She was dimly aware of her own voice, a shrieking howl, as she plunged the blade through the owl tattoo on Kormedia's chest. She felt his heart shudder and stop. She laughed as she slashed the blade across Shanti's throat, her friend screaming through the gag. And then, all Veena heard was the deafening drumbeat of her own heart.

Blood pooled on the floor.

Veena was wiped clean, as pure as virgin snow.

Sixkills took the blade from her hands. He laid a giant paw across the back of her neck, gently at first. Then his fingers gripped down and he pulled her close, bending her spine like twig.

"Run," he rasped into her ear.

Never in her life had Veena run as fast as she did out of her father's office. Her body was soaked with mud, sweat, and blood, and she was barefoot and broken, but she ran until her legs gave out and she collapsed in a patch of dirt under the clouded sky.

34

There was some serious voodoo shit up here in these woods.

Lieutenant Whitmer felt it in his spine—the warning that he wasn't welcome here, that he was being watched by something that wanted him dead.

Whitmer held down his unease. They had a job to do and not much time to do it in. The Red Bitch was counting on them.

The wind rustled through the trees, the branches flittering like dead fingers against the night sky. The heavy rains had washed through Ringwood State Park on their way south and left the ground sodden with slick rocks and dead leaves.

Whitmer looked at his three soldiers in the clearing, Sergeants Jeong, Dirk, and Teller. All Redgun veterans. Whitmer had served most of his career with these elite warriors, and if shit went down tonight, he trusted them all with his life.

Trust, he realized as he looked down at the corpses of the traitorous Redguns, was a rare commodity these days.

They had tracked down the bodies to the edge of Shepherd's Lake. Here, their former comrade, Lazlo Koyle, had intended to betray them all and sell the Sun Angel to the highest bidder.

Guess shit went sideways, Whitmer mused, looking down at Lazlo's corpse, which was glistening with rainwater. Behind him, Sergeant Dirk, who was as big as a bison, zipped up another

Redgun traitor in a body bag and strapped it to one of the off-road buggies they'd ridden in on.

Sergeant Teller, the youngest operator in the unit and team medic, was intently waving the Hoover over the ground, sucking up the brass shell casings in the dirt. Whitmer radioed the two snipers he had stationed out on the perimeter.

"Wolf One, report," Whitmer whispered into his bone mike.

"Wolf One, all clear," Keane drawled.

"Wolf Two, report."

"Wolf Two, all clear," Moore replied.

That gave Whitmer some comfort. Not many living things could sneak past both Keane and Moore. And even if something did get past them, the clearing was strapped with enough anti-intrusion tech to protect a platoon, from the Owl-Sight spec sensors in the buggies to the electronic tripwires that could recognize any unauthorized heartbeats inside their perimeter.

A sliver of moon hung above them, slipping in and out of the clouds. The wind picked up and shook the leaves. Once again, Lieutenant Whitmer felt it—that unsettling sensation, like cold fingertips brushing the back of his neck.

Something told him to look up, and when he did, his eyes met the two tiny black orbs glaring at him. Perched on a long branch that stretched out over the lake, a crow sat very still, its feathers tinged silver by the moon.

"You see something, sir?" Sergeant Jeong asked, noticing Whitmer's expression.

"Nothing." Whitmer turned away from the bird. He shook off his nerves and turned back to Lazlo's body. He had one mission here: secure the Leash.

Whitmer knelt down and rummaged around in Lazlo's pockets. As he did so, Dirk came over and stood behind him.

"Damn, Lazlo." Dirk scratched his beard. "You were better than this, brother."

Whitmer found what he was looking for in Lazlo's chest pocket: a sleek black device with a screen—the Leash.

He slotted a keycard into the Leash. A decrypted map blipped to life across its screen. A white circle pulsed above Shenandoah National Park, Virginia. The text read: TARGET ACQUIRED, along with the exact coordinates.

The Leash was keyed into the location of the Sun Angel's Clamp. Right now, Whitmer could tell from the map that the Sun Angel was safe in the Red Bitch's compound.

Whitmer dropped the Leash into his vest. Dirk opened a body bag and rolled Lazlo inside it.

Almost done. Whitmer stretched his neck.

"Boss?" Dirk looked at him.

"What?"

"What the fuck is this?" Dirk pointed at the back of Lazlo's neck.

Whitmer leaned forward.

Shit . . .

At the base of Lazlo's skull, perfectly aligned with his spine, was a neat puncture wound, too big to be made by a needle but too surgical to be from a blade. Whitmer called over their medic, Teller.

"You know what that is?"

Teller squinted at the wound. "Huh."

"What?" Whitmer asked.

"No blood." Teller ran a gloved finger over the wound.

"Spec weapons?"

Teller didn't reply. He knelt down and put his face very close to the hole.

"Damn," he finally said. "This is clean through to the spine. Not a kill wound, but . . . something else. Parasitic, maybe."

Whitmer felt the crow's eyes on him. "Wrap him up and haul ass."

Dirk zipped up Lazlo, threw him over his shoulder, and headed toward his buggie. Teller swept up the last of the casings before breaking down the Hoover and packing it away. Jeong was waiting behind the wheel of the second buggie.

Whitmer radioed Moore and Keane and ordered them back. He lifted up one of the abandoned bikes in the clearing next to him and straddled it. The electric engine purred to life.

Tires whipped up dead leaves as Jeong wheeled the vehicle around. Whitmer turned to Dirk's buggie.

Where the hell was Dirk?

The second vehicle sat empty in the shadows. Whitmer pinged Dirk on the radio but heard only dead air.

Shit. Whitmer was about to get off the bike when his wrist computer vibrated, tracking a burst of spec activity on the Owl-Sight feed for a second before going silent.

And then an unrecognized heartbeat entered their perimeter.

The signal blipped faintly and vanished.

Whitmer watched the woods. There was still no sign of Dirk. He keyed in his computer to the big man's vitals.

There were none. The screen that was supposed to display Dirk's biometric data was blank.

The lake glistened as the moon reappeared. Whitmer gave the signal to Teller and Jeong. Both men hit the ground and scoped the woods with their guns.

Whitmer unslung his rifle and crept over to Dirk's vehicle. He came around the back of the buggie and stopped short.

Dirk lay dead on the leaves, the whites of his eyes shining at Whitmer. His rifle was missing.

Whitmer was about to raise the alarm when he saw Lazlo's body bag.

It was empty—torn through *from the inside.*

Whitmer scrabbled backwards to his men. "Weapons free. We've got contact!" The three Redguns formed a tight circle, searching the darkness through their scopes.

"Anyone got eyes on target?" Whitmer whispered.

"Negative," Jeong and Teller replied.

Whitmer radioed his snipers. "Wolf One, Wolf Two, you see anything?"

The radio was silent. Whitmer tried again. Dead air. Whitmer felt his stomach twist. Dirk dead. Now, Keane and Moore.

A scream erupted from their right. Whitmer whipped around to see a man burst out of the woods holding Dirk's rifle, an earsplitting cry tearing out of his throat. The man fired two shots through Teller's chest, killing him instantly.

Whitmer and Jeong fired as one. The attacker moved inhumanly fast, shooting wildly across the clearing. Whitmer buried three shots into the attacker's chest.

The man shuddered but did not fall. He grunted and turned, and in that instant, Whitmer glimpsed the shooter's face through the night vision.

"Lazlo," Whitmer muttered, dumbfounded.

The once-dead Redgun came whirling toward them, demented.

Whitmer and Jeong's bullets tore stone-sized chunks out of Lazlo's torso and legs, but Lazlo kept running, firing a burst into Jeong's face.

Lazlo came for Whitmer, his mouth hanging open in a bloody yawn, his legs churning the mud and leaves. Whitmer fired.

Click.

Whitmer's gun jammed.

Lazlo's shadow fell on him. The dead Redgun lined up his barrel with Whitmer's head.

Thwack!

Lazlo's skull blew out of his right eye.

Thwack!

Another round blasted off his jaw. Lazlo grunted and toppled hard onto the leaves.

Whitmer staggered to his feet, staring at Lazlo's corpse as if it were a live grenade. He unholstered his Glock and fired two rounds into Lazlo's face.

"Incoming," a voice buzzed over his radio. From the tree line, Whitmer saw the tall form of Sergeant Keane melt out of the darkness, running toward him with his sniper rifle in his hands.

"Son of a bitch," Keane muttered, looking down at Lazlo.

Lazlo's skull was a ruined mess, but it was his neck that both men stared at with dumb fascination. The puncture wound was moving. It pulsed and discharged a thick black liquid onto the ground that sizzled like hot oil when it touched the damp leaves.

"You ever seen shit like this?" Whitmer asked Keane. The sniper shook his head.

Whitmer checked his computer. He and Keane were the only living heartbeats inside the perimeter.

"Where's Moore?" Whitmer asked.

"Lost contact," Keane drawled, still alert. "'Bout a minute before I heard the shootin' out here."

Whitmer took a deep, pained breath. Losing one of your men in battle was a brutal blow, an eventuality that every commanding officer dreaded to his core. But losing *four* . . .

He would have to worry about that later. It was clear that Lazlo had been under someone—or *something's*—control. Which meant—

"They're still out there," Whitmer said, bringing his rifle up, covering the field of fire behind Keane.

"Who?"

"Specs. Some kind of kinetic."

"Aw, fuck," Keane said. "Well, they picked the wrong posse to fuck with."

"Get on the horn. Get us backup."

As Keane keyed in his mic, Whitmer checked his computer. It was only then that he noticed that the Owl-Sight feed was dead.

He turned toward the two buggies where the Owl-Sights were strapped to the dashboards. His stomach dropped when he saw them.

All that remained of the spec sensors were two shredded black boxes, their wires splayed out like entrails over the ruined bullet-ridden carapaces.

Their stalker's plot came together with sickening *click* in Whitmer's mind.

Lazlo had been controlled by a kinetic and sent in to destroy the Owl-Sights. He was just a decoy to take out their early warning system, leaving them blind to the *real* attack.

Whitmer caught a flash of movement out the corner of his eye. Keane grunted, then fell facedown in the dirt.

Whitmer dove to the ground. Keane's blank eyes stared back at him. The moonlight washed over the dark steel of the tomahawk blade embedded deep in his skull.

Whitmer gritted his teeth. There was no time left for fear. All his brothers were dead, but there was still one gun left in this fight.

Whitmer grabbed the sniper rifle and fired into the trees where the tomahawk had spun in from. He didn't know how many hostiles he was dealing with. All he knew was that they were going to bleed.

Staying low, he hustled backward, firing and moving, firing and moving, until he was through the tree line and behind cover. He reloaded and eyed the scope but saw nothing. Just a green-tinged wilderness.

Maybe he had scared them off.

Maybe they were waiting for him to run out of ammo.

Whitmer hit the EXTRACT button on his computer. It was the equivalent of firing a thousand flares into the night sky. Reinforcements would be on their way—fast.

Zing. Metal flashed, and Whitmer felt a burning pain explode in his right arm.

"Get back in the fight," he hissed to himself. He tried to aim the rifle, but it wasn't there anymore. Neither was his hand.

Whitmer stared at the bloody stump of his right wrist, the pink flesh glistening around the white stub of bone.

That's weird . . .

Longhorn melted out of the shadows and loped toward him without making a sound.

Whitmer fumbled for his pistol with his left hand. Longhorn smacked the pistol away, then plunged a dagger through Whitmer's palm, pinning it to the tree behind him. Whitmer screamed.

Longhorn retrieved his tomahawk and stood above Whitmer, the weapon held loosely in his scarred hand, his face dark beneath the Stetson. His fur collar ruffled in the breeze.

Longhorn reached into Whitmer's harness and pulled out the Leash and decoder chip. He plugged in the chip and read the Leash display, studying the location of the Sun Angel. In the dim light of the screen, Whitmer saw a hard mouth set in a sun-baked face. He couldn't see the eyes.

This was no Silverback, no Phoenix Marine or Gray Face horror. This was something else.

Satisfied, Longhorn crushed the tracker underfoot.

"Fucking spec," Whitmer slurred, realizing what the man was after. "You think you can take it from us? Good luck, asshole. It's protected by the best soldiers on the planet—men who have killed a hundred specs like you."

The man's lip twitched. "No," he said in a voice like splintering bone. "None like me."

Longhorn raised the tomahawk. Whitmer watched the moonlight ripple across its blade with serene fascination as the weapon swung down toward his throat.

35

The Ford Bronco trundled up the rocky path and entered the mountain base through a discreet side gate. The Silverback guards waved the truck through without checking the driver's identification, under strict orders from the general to forgo their usual security checks for this one visitor. A highly unusual order, they thought, especially given the top-secret nature of this training facility. But they followed their orders resolutely and said nothing as the Bronco passed the blast-proof gates and rumbled into the compound.

The Bronco circled around the outer road of the base and parked next to a chain-link fence with a sign that read: DANGER. LIVE FIRE EXERCISES.

The man who stepped out of the truck was not notable by Silverback standards. Five foot ten and leanly muscled, most observers would guess that the newcomer was a support engineer or mechanic, his size disqualifying him immediately from the ranks of the colossal warriors who prowled the base.

They would be wrong.

Master Chief Eric Magnusson was no stranger to these grounds. He had trained here. More recently, he had been an instructor here, imparting the bloody lessons he had learned during his combat tours in Frontier territory. Now he had returned at the call of his supreme leader.

Magnusson noticed a group of young Silverbacks walking toward him from the opposite direction. He kept his pace even and evaded them. The general's instructions to him were very clear: Do not be seen under any circumstances.

He headed toward the designated meeting point, his ears picking up the yelled commands of the marksmanship instructors followed by the distinctive sizzle of Silverback bolts tearing up the firing range. It had been years since he had served in a regular Silverback battalion, but the sound of bolts fired in battle never failed to rouse him. Often he missed the camaraderie of the teams, of being side by side with your brothers against a massed enemy on the open battlefield.

But he was no longer that kind of soldier. His war had changed, shifting from the accepted theaters into the shadows. His war was hidden, ugly, and excruciatingly brutal, and Magnusson, along with a small cadre of exceptional men, were the only ones trained to fight it.

The Silverback Battalion was divided into four operational squadrons: Red Team, Blue Team, Green Team, and White Team. Each squadron was comprised of the most elite soldiers in the Kingdom—shooters and strategists who were trained to do the bloody counterinsurgency work vital to the Kingdom's survival.

But there was, off the books, a secret fifth squadron. They had no official name. Unlike the regular squadrons, who had become celebrities in the wake of their extraordinary conduct during the Immortal War, this squadron's existence was hidden from the public eye. On budget reports sent to the King's Council, they were simply referred to as the Tactical Applications Group, or TAG. But the men within this secret brotherhood referred to themselves by another name.

The Spearhead.

Magnusson made his way to the kill house complex beneath a large rock spur. He had been one of Spearhead's founding officers.

Back then, in the aftermath of the war, Sixkills had needed a specialized force, one drawn from the elite of the Silverback ranks, that could perform a vital mission: hunt down and kill those who had escaped justice—the war criminals, the former lowblood generals, money men, concentration camp officers, and scientists from the Pentagon's Unholy programs. No matter where they hid or how protected they thought they were, Spearhead would find them, and Spearhead would make them pay.

From Mumbai to Buenos Aires, Magnusson had tracked down and killed many of them himself, often at close range.

But in the past four years, Spearhead was forced to pivot from its core mission to fight a new enemy, a *real* threat—the Snake Mother and her army of barbarians amassing out in the west.

The Frontier were tougher, deadlier, and more fearsome in battle than any opponent he had ever faced. They were exactly what Magnusson had been waiting for his whole life. He lived to fight a true adversary, a Gifted warrior who could truly test him in the arena. The Frontier Nation was that adversary. And when the war—the big war—finally came, Magnusson would not hesitate to wade into the bloody fray.

He reached the kill house complex and slinked along the shadows as he made his way to Kill House B, preparing himself for whatever mission the general had in store for him.

He entered the darkness of the kill house. Every wall was cratered with blast marks, and the house smelled of smoke, sweat, and the acrid animal odor of Frontier weapons. To Magnusson, it smelled like home.

Sixkills was waiting for him on the shadowy upper walkway, from where the instructor cadre would watch their students hone their hostage rescue skills in the narrow warren of rooms below. Magnusson greeted Sixkills the Silverback way, clashing his right forearm with the general's in a strong *X*.

"Excellent work in Argentina," Sixkills said.

"Thank you, sir," Magnusson replied, allowing himself some pride in a job well done. The Argentina op had been flawless. Only three days had passed from the moment Magnusson and his hit team had landed in Ministro Pistarini International Airport in Buenos Aires to the second that their target was confirmed dead—three days to track down and neutralize Thiago Zabaleta, a man known in his local community as a doting grandfather and successful proprietor of a small liquor store empire.

The Spearhead intelligence analysts, however, saw through that ruse.

It was the culmination of a grueling ten-year manhunt that brought Magnusson to Zabaleta's hideout, where he confirmed with his own eyes that Zabaleta was none other than Miguel Herrera.

Herrera, former legal counsel to the CIA's Orchid Program, had promoted the Extraordinary Detainment Doctrine—the legal framework that had given President Mathias cover to launch the extermination camps during the war.

Herrera was number five on the Spearhead's kill list.

And there he was, growing fat and rich out in the trendy Las Cañitas neighborhood while a thousand graves sat heavy with the corpses of murdered Specials.

It had taken two days of dodging the Argentine Federal Police and painstakingly tracking Herrera's every movement before they were ready to strike. When they finally caught up to Herrera on a chilly Thursday night as he left his favorite social club on Azcuénaga, Magnusson had taken the shot.

Herrera didn't notice Magnusson step out of the black sedan until it was too late. The team had brainstormed simpler, faster ways they could have neutralized Herrera, but Magnusson wanted him to *feel* it. He wanted Herrera to know in his last moments that the Specials had killed him.

Herrera, drunk and smiling, nodded Magnusson's way.

Magnusson raised his right hand in a stopping motion. Herrera paused, uncertain but not yet afraid.

The bolts that flew out of Magnusson's palm were invisible and as slim as sharpened wood slivers. Thousands of them crossed the space between the two men in milliseconds and then slowed down abruptly to pierce Herrera's skin, muscles, and organs at the pace of vaccination syringes. It took six excruciating seconds for the bolts to pass through Herrera's body and out his back. His face contorted in a silent gasp of agony the entire time.

Magnusson had calmly stepped back into the sedan. Herrera had bled to death on the street as the hit team raced away.

Magnusson smiled now, thinking about the look on the lowblood's face as he'd died.

"Any UN trouble?" Sixkills asked.

"No. We were over the border before their people got our scent."

Sixkills turned to him. "You'll be going back into the field."

"When?"

"Tonight."

"Understood."

Sixkills's eyes shone in the dark. "Two days ago, I received word of a potential situation developing, and I put you on standby as a precaution. Tonight I received confirmation of my suspicions. There will be two targets, potentially more."

"Crown territory or denied areas?"

"Crown territory. Targets are on the run and minimally armed. I don't expect this to be difficult for you."

"I can assemble a team within the hour."

"No. You'll be going total dark on this one."

"Total dark?"

Sixkills nodded.

Total dark. Wherever Magnusson was going, he would be going alone, off the grid, with no oversight. You didn't go total dark unless what you were about to do was both illegal and of the utmost personal importance to your commander.

Magnusson couldn't wait to get started.

"ROE?" he asked.

"Zero margin."

"Yes, sir," Magnusson replied. Rules of engagement: zero margin—leave no witnesses; kill all who oppose you.

Sixkills handed him a red USB drive, which Magnusson pocketed.

Magnusson stood at ease. Sixkills looked troubled, as if he were grappling with a problem that had no easy solution. He gripped the rail with his massive hands and shook his head, at a loss for words. He cleared his throat. "How are the girls?" he asked.

The girls? Was Sixkills really asking him about his daughters? It threw Magnusson off balance for a moment. Ever since their first days together in the Army's Detachment Delta, he had never known Sixkills to tolerate personal conversations.

"The girls are fine, sir."

"Do you speak to them often?"

"No, sir. They live in Raleigh now, with their mother." Magnusson stopped there, but Sixkills looked at him like he wanted him to continue. Magnusson plowed on. "We talk on the phone sometimes, but we're speaking different languages."

"Our children." Sixkills shook his head. "They are not like us, are they?"

"No, sir."

Even though Magnusson felt lost and obsolete around his two teenage girls, he knew the gulf between the general and Veena Sixkills was uncrossable. For the longest time, he'd believed Sixkills preferred it that way. Now, looking at the expression on his face in the darkened kill house, he wasn't so sure.

"It is our duty to take responsibility for them," Sixkills said. "Even when they fail."

"We are the guardians of our race, sir. For me, that duty has always come first."

"As it has for me." Sixkills looked down onto the killing floor. "And yet, the gravest threats come from those closest to us." He fixed Magnusson with his eyes, his face changing. He now spoke not as his superior officer, but as one seasoned professional to another. "Know that I would have gone myself, but I am known— and the consequences of discovery are as severe as those of failure. I trust you above all others to fix this."

"I will not fail, sir."

"I know."

They crossed forearms again, proud and bracing.

"Only the strong," Sixkills said.

"Only the strong."

*

The safe house was an isolated cabin far away from the main road and accessible only by an off-road vehicle. Magnusson returned to it twenty minutes after his meeting with Sixkills and went straight to work. He slotted the red USB drive into his laptop and scanned the contents of the file.

This would not be difficult, Magnusson realized as he read. Not difficult at all.

Target name: Houston Holt.

Classification: Human

Primary objective: Immediate neutralization of Target and Target's associates.

Magnusson scrolled down to the detailed briefing paragraphs below. The lowblood's last confirmed sighting had been this morning in Seekers Port, spotted by an SSD undercover asset. The lowblood was a River Town criminal with Redblood connections who had supplied weapons that had killed Specials in terrorist attacks. Standard stuff.

But the last paragraph grabbed Magnusson's attention.

Target is traveling with an eight-year-old female. Intelligence assets confirm with 90% probability that Female is an Unholy weapons system. Female is to be neutralized immediately under the guidelines of Zero Margin ROE.

A child.

It turned Magnusson's stomach. He read the paragraph again. The targeting of children had no place in the sacred warrior code engraved in the soul of every Silverback.

But if the spooks were right, this child was an Unholy.

The Unholies were what scared the Kingdom most of all. Those weapons small enough to be smuggled across borders in the back of a car yet powerful enough to kill millions of Specials. Unholies ranged from the horrific plasma bombs developed in the bowels of the Pentagon's weapons labs to—and this was the possibility that kept most Specials up at night—*one of their own*, an extraordinarily Gifted Special weaponized to kill on a genocidal scale.

Magnusson shut the laptop and removed the USB. He crushed it underfoot and went downstairs to his equipment cage. His operational gear was arranged in color-coded duffels. The red duffel held his desert kit, the blue duffel his dive kit, and the green one, which he opened now, held his undercover aviation kit. He stacked the gear onto one of the metal shelves and opened his safe. He rifled through the stack of Gold Stamp ID cards and settled on the identity of Dominic Foyle, senior attaché of the Royal Diplomatic Corps.

Magnusson changed into dark jeans, a flight jacket, and trekking boots. He zipped open his flight ruck and filled it with everything he would need in the field: clothes, pistol, goldmarks. He strapped on his wristwatch and checked its connection to the Spearhead satellites. The watch streamed weather and target data into the heads-up digital display on his sunglasses.

When he was dressed and packed, he turned, finally, to the weapons rack.

Magnusson gripped the cool shaft of his spear. He shifted his wrist, and the staff telescoped out on both ends, powerful springs shooting the NightAlloy blade forward. Over six feet in length, the spear had been the primary weapon of the Silverbacks when the Immortal War began. The greatmaces only became a necessity when the mechs appeared on the battlefields and a blunt-force weapon was needed.

The spear had been Magnusson's closest ally ever since the day he'd earned his Silver Stripe.

You never forget your first.

Magnusson slipped the retracted spear into a hidden holster along the left thigh of his jeans. He was about to leave the cage when he realized he had forgotten the letter. He went back to the safe and slipped out the thin white envelope.

It was the letter that every soldier had to write—the one that he had struggled with for weeks, unable to find the right sentiment to convey to his family upon his death. The letter was short, and given the fractured nature of his relationship with his ex-wife and daughters, he figured the less said, the better.

Upstairs, he slipped the letter into the secure documents box by the staircase and turned off all the lights in the house. He activated the security system and trekked a half mile into the woods until he got to higher ground.

The earth was still wet, scoured and clean after the terrible storm. The air was fresh, and Magnusson felt alive and happy to be hunting again.

He reached a narrow ridge that gave him a clear view of the night sky. His first stop would be Seekers Port, the last place Houston Holt had been seen. He had an informant there, one with feelers inside the Redblood system.

He plugged the location of Seekers Port into his wristwatch and watched the computer design a covert flight plan south.

The moon slipped behind a cloud. The night was dark, cool, and had low wind—perfect conditions for a stealth flight.

Magnusson slipped on his glasses and studied the data streaming into the heads-up display: route, magnetic compass, airspeed, flight time, and altitude.

Then, inhaling deeply, he took two steps forward and focused his Gift in his core. Exhaling, he allowed it to uncoil like a spring and launch him upward. His feet left the ground, and then the wind was on his face as he rocketed toward the gray clouds, the call of war sounding through his blood again.

36

"The Gift was our salvation and our cross. We were almost crushed by its weight, by the patriarchal oppression it invited. But our king, our savior, came forth to bear the burden for all of us . . ."

The young writer droned on from the lectern, reading from his latest work. Caspar had stopped listening to his drivel five minutes ago. All he wanted to do was clamp his hands over his ears and yell, "Make it stop!"

Around him, the faces in the audience smiled and nodded appreciatively. They pretended to pay attention to the words while their eyes constantly drifted, like moths to a flame, to the true center of power here: Queen Callista.

She sat demurely in the place of honor to the right of the lectern, on a gilded Bergère chair, hand on her chin, leaning forward, nodding gently. Around the large room, Caspar saw at least five other audience members in the same pose.

Callista didn't make eye contact, but Caspar knew his sister was aware of his uninvited presence at her Grand Salon the way a mongoose is aware of an uncoiling cobra.

The feeling was mutual. He would rather be anywhere but here, in the gaudy confines of the Lady's Eye, surrounded by vapid socialites and equine art, but he was desperate. Veena had called earlier with the disastrous news: Callista would no longer be wearing the Peacock Gown tomorrow night. Their carefully crafted revolution, two years in the making, was hanging by a thread. Somehow, some way, Caspar had to convince Callista, chilly toward him at the best of times, to reconsider.

Caspar glanced over at his sister. He had to admit, having heard the sordid details from Veena, he now saw her in a whole new light.

Saucy little minx! He'd always suspected she had a sexual wildness hidden behind all those years of repression. Caspar wondered what other naughty little secrets his sister was hiding.

The interminable writer finally finished, stepping off the lectern to a hearty round of applause.

Oh, thank heaven. Caspar didn't know if it was medically possible to die from exposure to kitsch, but he was sure he was coming dangerously close.

Callista clapped and beamed like a proud mother. Heart pounding, Caspar began the agonizing walk over to her. He hoped his assumptions had been correct. He knew the controlling creature that lived under Callista's perfect exterior would leave nothing to chance, no detail left unmanaged. It had only been a few hours since her fallout with Veena at the House of Azaleas, but he was certain his sister already had another dress lined up.

All Caspar needed to do tonight was find out where that dress was. After that, more plans would have to be made—messier plans.

With each step closer to the queen, he became acutely aware of the burly Phoenix Guards stationed around the room, eyes roving, earpieces curling down into their dark suits. Callista stood in the center of a circle of nodding couples. As Caspar approached, her eyes raked over him like an arctic squall. She turned back to her guests, the charming smile returning to her face like the sun from behind the clouds.

But the message to Caspar was clear: *Do not embarrass me.*

His plan formed then—a desperate ploy with little hope for success. God help him.

Correction: He Who Knows All help him.

"Your Majesty." Caspar bowed as he jostled into her circle. He ignored the miffed looks of her companions and focused on his sister, stifling a gag when he saw her.

My lord, she looks awful.

From across the room she could cover it up, but up close, beneath mounds of makeup, Callista was in bad shape. Her eyes had the sheen of dull street puddles, and her fragile frame sagged beneath the weight of shame and nausea. Caspar was no stranger to horrific hangovers, and he spotted hers immediately.

"Dear brother!" She smiled and hugged him. "I'm so happy you could come. What did you think of Thaddeus?"

"Who?"

"The writer, silly." She rolled her eyes playfully at her companions. They laughed nervously.

"Oh, he was wonderful," Caspar replied. "I've always admired your taste in—"

An older couple broke into the circle and stole Callista's attention. She greeted them warmly, turning away from Caspar.

Fuck it.

He reached out and touched Callista's arm.

The guests reacted first, faces freezing in shock. Callista turned to him in midsentence, her expression unchanged but a frantic energy burning behind her eyes—shocked at this breach of etiquette but savvy enough not to draw more attention to it.

One does not touch the queen.

One *never* touches the queen.

But Caspar was not done yet.

She deftly slid her arm away and held up a finger. "One moment, brother," she said, her eyes conveying a more pointed rebuke. "I'm in the middle of a fascinating discussion with Dame Shuzuki here."

"Oh, take your time," Caspar said. "When you have a moment, I would love to discuss an incredible experience I recently had in Miami."

The bomb detonated as expected. Shock bristled across her face, bubbling above the surface for an instant before diving back down into the depths.

"Miami!" she laughed. "I have been on pins and needles waiting to hear about that! Everyone, please excuse us. My brother and I have some catching up to do. Enjoy the food. I won't be long!"

The pained smile remained on her face as she quickly guided Caspar through the crowd and into a private antechamber. She shut the door and switched on the lamps. Her face burned with anger. "Are you out of your fucking mind?" she hissed. "Do you enjoy humiliating me in public?"

"Heavens, no. Do you enjoy humiliating me in private?"

She waved her finger in his face. "No, no, no. You will not bring this up here. Not *here* and not *now!*"

"It's been two years, Callista. When *should* I bring it up?"

She threw up her hands in exasperation. "You do this on purpose. I always thought you were feckless, but you aren't, are you? You're a determined little man with infinite capacity to embarrass this family. What did you even come here for, an apology?"

"You signed off on it. You sat back and watched as . . ."— Caspar's face grew hot—". . . they did things to me. They *hurt* me!"

The door opened, and a Phoenix Guard maneuvered his bulk inside. "Your Highness, is there a problem?"

Callista looked from the guard to Caspar.

"I'm fine, Jerome," she said. "Just give us a minute."

The guard glared at Caspar for a few terrifying moments before disappearing back out the door.

She slapped him on the shoulder. "Lower your voice! And do you really think I sign off on anything around here? Do you even understand how little of a say I have in these matters?"

"You could have warned me."

"If you had even a shred of awareness, you would realize that you brought—" She stopped herself, clenching her fists and inhaling deeply.

"That I what?" Caspar asked.

She shook her head, turning away.

"That I brought it on myself," he said quietly.

Callista sat down on a bench, shaking. "I tried to help you, Caspar. I tried many times. But you refused to grow up, and this is the life you have sowed. You can't keep blaming me for it."

"You've always seen me as a stupid child, haven't you?"

"I saw you as my big brother." Callista's voice fell to a whisper, her eyes suddenly losing all traces of hardness. Her lips quivered. "I adored you."

Caspar opened his mouth and then closed it, his words stolen. Her words punctured him like bullets, killing the rage that had been swelling inside his chest for two years. He stood awkwardly, stripped of his armor and suddenly feeling very guilty.

"You look lovely in that dress," he said finally.

"Oh, shut up."

"You do. You wear far too much blue and gold these days, though. Pinks and yellows were always your colors."

She made a sound between a laugh and a sob. Caspar sat down next to her, careful not to spook her. With the slow, clumsy movements of someone unaccustomed to physical affection, he laid his arm gently around her shoulders.

"I should go," Callista said, standing up and straightening her dress and hair. Caspar could see her putting the mask back on, and he realized it wasn't as easy for her as it once was. What a wretched, lonely creature.

She turned to leave, taking with her any chance Caspar had of completing his mission.

Caspar considered letting her go.

He felt as if the ground had shifted under his feet and that necessary edge he needed to go through with murder—mass murder—had blunted unexpectedly.

But then, like flash of distant lightning, he remembered Guillermo.

He had been humiliated, manipulated . . . and *betrayed*.

Caspar shot off the bench and caught up to his sister. He turned her around and, before she could protest, hugged her hard.

Callista stood stiff as a board, arms trapped to her side in his embrace. And then, unsurely at first, she wrapped her arms around him and buried her head in his chest. For a moment, just a moment, Caspar felt terrible that tomorrow night she would be dead. But being back in Paris would do wonders for his conscience.

The embrace ended, both gently pulling away, both a little confused.

"That was strange," Caspar said.

Callista giggled, her mascara running.

"You need to get your face fixed up," he said.

She swatted his shoulder. "Look at what you've done to me. Oh, god, can you go outside and get Lana for me? Tell her to bring her makeup kit. Discreetly, of course."

"Of course." He turned toward the door and gripped the handle. "Oh, by the way," he said, turning back to her, "what will you be wearing at the parade?"

"Don't get me started on that whole fiasco."

"Oh, really? Spill the gossip, sister."

"It's too long a story. I had a dress, then I didn't have a dress. But it's fine; it's all fixed now. I arranged for another gown." Her eyes misted over dreamily. "A truly stunning design."

"What does it look like?"

"Oh, that's a state secret, Caspar." She smiled mischievously.

"Don't be coy, little sister. I ask for my sake. I think it would be marvelous if the two most stylish people in the Kingdom were matching tomorrow night."

She looked unsure, but Caspar knew that if there was one thing his sister loved, it was sharing a secret.

"Out with it," Caspar pushed.

"You're going to laugh, but it's a blue and gold gown."

"Of course." He rolled his eyes. "What else? Silk? Lace? Leather?"

She chewed it over, studying him. "Can you keep a secret?"

"Only a style secret."

"It's *so* lovely. The finest metallic silk laced with daisies, and the *sleeve*—oh my, that is the show stopper, Caspar—a gold filigree Phoenix wrapping around my entire arm!" She hopped up and down on her toes. "I wish I could show it to you, but Deb's still making some final adjustments."

Caspar's ears perked up. "Deb?"

"Debashish. The designer."

"Oh? I've never heard of him."

"Debashish Kumar. He's my little secret. I discovered him at his senior show at the Royal Design Institute. He designs exclusively for me now." She smiled devilishly, her eyes trained on the door and the crowd beyond. "They will be *so* jealous."

Caspar smiled. "Oh, I can just imagine their faces when they see you up there. They have no idea what they're in store for. No idea at all."

37

Peace was here, and this was the after-party.

Houston felt the five bourbons in his system take root. He knocked back his sixth in the ballroom bar. Around him, Reds packed the dance floor, music blasting from huge speakers.

Carmen and Ambassador Trevayne had signed a draft ceasefire agreement. It still had to be ratified by Patriot Gold, but the Reds saw no point in delaying the celebration.

Katya twirled Lily around in the center of the dance floor. Lily's Clamp glittered in the strobe lights. Houston ducked out of the room before they could see him.

He stumbled through the crowded hallways, jostling past soldiers and workers. A pressure valve had been released inside him, and he needed to move, to unclench something that had been wrapped tight in his chest.

The Reds glared at him as he passed, muttering "traitor" just loud enough for him to hear.

Houston couldn't care less what they thought. The signed papers from Ambassador Trevayne were still in his jacket pocket.

He was a citizen now. He was free—free to work legally in any of the Four Provinces, to own property, to start a business. Free to be *somebody*.

Upon their return to the capital, the king's envoy would act on Houston's confession. They would systematically dismantle Ibrahim & Sons for Faraz's role in the Sun Angel theft. Houston wouldn't have time to feel bad—he would be too busy trying to fill the power vacuum.

This was the break he had been waiting for.

If he moved fast—and he fully intended to—he could corner the market. He would be the new Mehmet Ibrahim—a two-bit thug transformed into the most powerful human in the Kingdom.

The hallway swirled, and Houston had to grip a doorframe to stay upright. He heard his brother's voice calling his name. He saw his face smiling at him from the crowd. Houston screwed his eyes shut, and when he opened them again, Bobby was gone.

For fifteen years he hadn't seen or heard from his brother, and now he had risen like a ghost, reaching out to save Houston. Bobby was the only reason he was now a citizen and not a prisoner. And all Houston had done for his brother was abandon him in the Ohana's Last Shelter.

He'd wondered if Bobby would ever understand why he left, if his brother could remember what it felt like to be human and mortal, chased by time and hounded by an ambition that shimmered over the horizon. Maybe Bobby would understand what it was like for Houston back then, desperate to live his own life after years of being dragged along in someone else's.

More likely, Bobby wouldn't understand, and Houston had one hell of an awkward reunion in his near future.

In the ballroom, he heard the DJ switch tracks on his laptop. The crowd cheered. Houston careened through the house, and in the first quiet room he found, he crashed on a stack of pallets and closed his eyes.

*

He opened his eyes to the sound of rain and wind crashing against glass. He blinked in the darkness and saw a shape looming above him.

"Jesus!" Houston jumped back, banging his head against the wall. It took him a moment to realize the shape was Lily.

"You snore," she said.

Houston rubbed his brow, a hangover blooming.

"Take this." She dropped a pile of pilfered goods on his lap. "Water, aspirin, and this—" She pulled out two pouches of military MREs and handed them to Houston. "It's the only greasy food I could find."

Houston looked at the MREs. The bourbon sloshed in his stomach. "Thanks, kid."

Lily watched him as he gurgled down a bottle of water and inhaled the MRE. "Are you an angry drunk?" she asked.

"Haven't been a drunk for a long time." He offered her an MRE.

"You need it more than me," she said.

"You know your way around drunk people."

"Experience," she said. "The same kind you have."

He looked at her. Her eyes held his, sparkling with hidden worlds. In that moment, Houston saw the watchfulness behind her gaze—the kind you develop when you grow up around an unpredictable animal, an addict who knows only how to hurt.

"Shucks, kid," he said. "I'm sorry."

She sat next to him. "We survived."

Lightning lit up the room. For the first time, Houston noticed his surroundings. Pallets and empty storage cubes filled the space, but Houston could tell it had once been a sunroom, its windows curving out of the flank of the house, overlooking the lake. A spray of howling, wet wind blew through the trees in the rear lawn where the two Black Hawks sat under heavy tarps.

"I like storms," Lily said, watching the water streak down the glass.

"A lot of storms in Hawaii," Houston said.

"Short storms. They came and went fast. None of them stayed like this one. My dad used to say they came to wipe away all the bad stuff people did. Like once the sun came back, you could start from the beginning."

"Your dad sounds like a crazy person."

Lily laughed. "All parents are crazy."

They watched the monsoon howl across the night. Lily remained quiet, but Houston could feel her energy warping around them, absorbing the storm's power, communicating with it in an ancient language. Finally, she yawned and stretched. Within minutes, Lily was asleep, her head resting gently on his arm.

She slept against him as if she trusted him completely. It was a weight Houston couldn't bear.

In the morning, when the storm had cleared, the king's delegation would whisk her away to Sovereign City. Houston would leave tonight, before she woke. It would be easier that way—though for him or her, he didn't know.

She had saved his life, and, yes, he had kept her away from Faraz's goons, but he still felt like he had failed her. Every time she looked at him, Houston could tell she expected more from him, as if she saw facets of him that were strong and yet undiscovered. And in light of that belief, whatever he had done to repay his debt wasn't nearly enough.

Behind him, Katya entered the room. "Hey, have you seen—"

Houston put a finger to his lips, then pointed to Lily sleeping.

Katya smiled. "You make a fine pillow, Houston Holt," she whispered as she sat down next to him. Lily mumbled in her sleep.

"Sovereign, huh?" Katya whispered.

"You heard."

Katya watched the rain rush down the curved glass. "I guess I should say congratulations."

"That's what a normal person would do."

"Congratulations, then."

He looked at her. "What's next for you?"

"Heading home. I spoke to Carmen. She's sending advisors with me to River Town to help the Badges organize and build up our tech."

"Look at you, running a legit operation now."

She shrugged. "Looks like we both got what we wanted."

Lily shifted against Houston's shoulder and let out a light snore. Both Houston and Katya watched her for a moment.

"Did she tell you?" Houston asked.

"About Hawaii? Yes."

"Do you believe her?"

"I don't know." Katya paused. "She's a thief, but she's not a liar."

"There's a difference?"

"A big difference."

"If she's telling the truth, that means she was once dead."

"I don't know what to tell you, Holt. All I see is a little girl trying to get home."

"I couldn't help her with that."

"No, but she'll be safe with the king. Carmen assured me, and I believe her." Katya lifted Lily into her arms. "You got her as far as you could."

"Yeah."

"We're leaving early tomorrow," she said. "We're catching a ride with the king's people."

When Houston didn't say anything, she pressed, "What are your plans?"

"Don't know yet."

"Come with us."

"I'll catch my own ride." He glanced at Lily, sleeping against Katya. "It's better to cut the cord now."

Katya took a deep breath. When she spoke, her voice was frigid. "The cord?"

"You know what I mean."

"So that's it?" Katya's neck strained with the effort of holding her anger down. "You're done with River Town?"

He held her gaze silently.

"Look at you, Mister Holt," Katya said. "You have everything now, don't you?"

She turned and left the room with Lily. Outside, the clouds lit up with lightning. A few moments later, a rumble of thunder rolled across the sky.

*

Tommy cursed and smacked the dead computer. As if he didn't have enough shit to deal with.

The storm had been shaking Crow Nest Four like a rattle all night, the cold rain drenching Tommy despite his poncho.

And then the computer went and died.

He smacked the monitor again, but nothing—a black screen. He plugged and unplugged the battery, but no dice. The storm must have blown the relay tower and their network along with it. He was in the dark here, with no Reaper drone feed, no motion sensors, and no missile control.

And worst of all, no radio.

He tried radioing the other three crow nests and heard only static. Same thing when he tried the control tower. The only thing working was the battery-powered Owl-Sight spec sensor. It wasn't much, but it gave him *some* solace. He watched the rain pelt the empty road, and for the twentieth time, he checked his watch.

This had to happen right now, didn't it? Twenty minutes before the end of his shift.

He was the last of his unit to be relieved. The other three crow nest sentries had ended their shifts in thirty-minute intervals as fresh Redbloods came in from the compound to relieve their tree-bound comrades.

Everyone else, except him, was already at the party.

Control definitely knew about the blackout already. His relief was probably on his way now, trudging through the rain with a backup generator.

Just a few more minutes . . .

Tommy sat tight, wishing he was inside the compound. Sometimes he felt like he was on the moon in this platform.

And it was getting harder and harder to shake this *feeling.* It had crept up on him as the sun had set—a prickling sensation along his back that he knew well.

His father had put a .22 rifle in his hand before his sixth birthday, and every season they would hike out into the Nushagak Peninsula, hunting for caribou. Out in the wild, Tommy had learned how to keep his heart rate flat, his movements silent. He had learned to become the predator. But sometimes, out there in bear country, he would feel another way—like the roles had been switched and he was the prey.

Tommy felt that now—the arrival of something bigger and meaner than him out there in the dark, nose up in the air, tracking his scent.

He wrapped his hand around the SAW's grip, its lethal weight reassuring.

Easy, Tommy. Ain't no bears out there.

*

You have everything now, don't you?

Katya's words rung in Houston's head. Even the booming music couldn't jostle them out of there.

Taking great pains to avoid the booming dance hall and raucous drinking games, Houston finally found a room with a lower-key clientele. In here, Redguns and techs shot pool and chatted quietly on leather chairs. In the far corner, Houston spotted Ambassador Trevayne smoking a pungent cigar, deep in conversation with a colleague.

Stationing himself at the dartboard, Houston played a few rounds solo. Back in the corps, he and his platoon would string up pictures of their anointed douchebag of the day, whether it was a spec terrorist they were hunting or their officious lieutenant, and toss homemade darts at the face. The points system was looser, but it was generally accepted among the grunts that anywhere on the eyes counted as fifty. Houston had been platoon champion, a title he remembered proudly as his darts clustered around the bull's-eye.

Someone tapped him on the shoulder. He turned.

Carmen smiled at him. "A table just opened up," she said. "Join me."

"Are you any good?" Houston asked.

"I'm decent. I don't get to play much."

"That's what all hustlers say."

She squeezed his arm. "I know."

She walked toward the table, her two huskies at her feet. Houston watched her rack the balls, fascinated by the way she moved, her efficiency and controlled grace. It was like he was meeting the third version of her—not the young, striking socialite from the construct nor the hard-edged statesman at the negotiating table. This version of Carmen was softer, her hair was down, and she was dressed in a short leather jacket over black jeans. Where she usually wore a watch, she wore a silver bracelet held together with gold and turquoise medallions.

"I'd offer you a drink," she said as she handed Houston a cue, "but Midnight Rider says you've had enough for one night."

Houston glanced up at the pebble eye watching the room from the crown molding. "Tell Midnight Rider to mind his own business."

Carmen took the break shot, scattering the balls and pocketing a solid. "Midnight Rider is not your enemy," she said.

"Not yet."

"It's not like us," she said as she pocketed another solid. "It's present in the moment in a way that we can no longer be. In that way, I believe it has evolved past us."

"That's what worries me." Houston took his shot after Carmen missed hers. He slid by her, and her perfume was in his nose now. "Ask your AI something for me," he said.

"What's that?"

"What are the chances for a guy like me and a girl like you?"

"Close to zero," she said, smiling.

"I stand by what I said before. I would ask you out."

"I'm not a dinner and drinks kind of girl."

"Dinner and drinks?" Houston shook his head and missed the nine in the side pocket. "I was thinking a day at the gun range and a home-cooked steak."

"Ah." She nailed the six in the left corner. "Unfortunately, I'm vegan."

"No wonder you're single."

"Who said I was single? In any case, I thought you were spoken for."

"Me?"

"The redhead?" she asked.

"Katya? You're out of your mind."

"Why not? She's beautiful. And smart."

"She's an idealist."

"So that makes her oil and you water?"

"Exactly."

Carmen waited for him to shoot, watching him intently. "She likes you."

"No, she just wants to rescue me."

"Not Katya. I meant Lily."

Houston shanked the ball. It bounced on the floor loudly until a Redgun caught it and tossed it back.

"Lily doesn't trust most people. I don't blame her. But she sees something in you."

"That kid is weird."

"She's much more than a kid, Houston." Carmen slid up beside him. That perfume again. "Aren't you even a little bit curious as to what she is?"

"Too much knowledge is risky in my line of work."

"She's one of the Five Totems."

Houston frowned. "The Five Totems?"

"Ah. Now you're interested." Carmen popped the three in the corner and glided next to Houston, her voice low. "We found her out in Arizona."

"You guys took her from Frontier."

"*Rescued* her. She was being used by the Snake Mother, along with four other extraordinary Specials."

"The Five Totems."

Carmen nodded. "All five from the Black Isles. As impossible as it sounds, Lily and the other four were brought through the Furies and onto the mainland in cryogenic fugue."

"Who brought them out?"

"People you know well." When Houston looked confused, Carmen elaborated. "People who have a very special—almost religious—interest in the Black Isles."

Houston's throat went dry. "The Ohana."

"Correct. Their agents penetrated the islands four years ago and brought back five Specials unlike any other. But . . ." Carmen clucked her tongue. "The Ohana never made it home. Somewhere along the coast of California, after making landfall, the entire expedition disappeared. And then do you know what happened?"

"What?"

"Think. What happened around that time?"

Houston did the math in his head as the huskies trotted around his feet. When it came to him, he simply said, "Frontier."

"Within a year of the Ohana and their five specimens disappearing in California, the Snake Mother had risen and overthrown the Western Province. Somehow a nameless revolutionary on nobody's radar overthrows the Crown? That is a world-changing Gift, and it doesn't take Midnight Rider to determine where she found it."

Houston stood quietly as Carmen cleared the solids off the table. When she came back, Houston asked, "Did I fuck up her life?"

"Lily's?"

Houston nodded.

"No. She'll be safe with Patriot Gold. He isn't looking for a weapon."

"How do you know?"

Carmen looked into distance in a way that made Houston think she was remembering something bittersweet. "The Specials weren't built by us. They originated from something *beyond* us—something that I have seen but that I still cannot fathom." She pierced Houston with her eyes, alive with the memory of an old wonder. "At some point, all living beings want to find their way back to their creator. Patriot Gold isn't a monster; he's just lost. And Lily is how he finds his way back."

"Sounds like you know the king well," Houston remarked.

Carmen cracked the eight ball into the right corner, clearing the table. She put her cue away and squeezed Houston's arm. "Eight delta charlie fourteen sixty zero zero."

"Is that a code?"

"Third floor, first door on your right. Meet me there in ten." She smiled and swept out of the room.

*

Tommy heard the hooting of a swallow below—four quick, rhythmic whistles, a pause, then two more.

Tommy glanced at the swallow bird whistle by his arm. The Reds used them to identify themselves when the radio was not an option. Tommy crawled over to the periscope in the floor and peeked through the leaves at the ground thirty feet below.

A man stood at the base of the oak, wearing a Redblood-issue black poncho. He carried a heavy rucksack, bulging with the mass of the portable generator.

"About fucking time," Tommy grumbled.

Tommy lowered the ladder and watched as the sentry struggled up the rungs under the weight of the generator. The sentry clambered into the platform through the floor hatch and dropped the pack on the ground with a *thud*.

Water dripped off the sentry onto the floor and he stood eerily still, studying the platform from under his hood.

"That the generator?" Tommy pointed to the ruck.

The sentry nodded. He slid his hood back, revealing a flat nose and a shaved head. Tommy recognized him as another newbie the others called Deeks, short for Declan.

"I'm Tommy. I've seen you around."

Deeks nodded slowly, his eyes still roving.

"What are you looking for?" Tommy asked, struggling to keep his voice level.

Deeks said nothing, but his eyes stopped on something in the corner. Tommy followed his gaze toward the Owl-Sight sensor.

Before Tommy could react, Deeks took two quick strides over to the sensor and flipped the power off.

"What are you doing?" Tommy stood up, alarmed.

Deeks turned toward Tommy.

His eyes pulsed, black and horrifying.

Tommy lunged for his SAW. His palm wrapped around the grip and his finger found the trigger—

Deeks tore across the platform and grabbed a handful of Tommy's shirt. Tommy twisted and threw a punch toward the bigger man, but Deeks was too fast.

So fucking fast.

Tommy felt the gun rip out of his hands, and before he could blink, his feet left the floor as Deeks tossed him across the nest.

He spun over and crashed on his back. His head was still spinning when he heard Deeks's boots thump toward him. Tommy rose onto his knees and went for the bowie knife in his boot.

Deeks gripped him by the collar and threw him through the open hatch in the floor.

Branches swatted Tommy's back and scratched his face as he bounced off the heavy trunk and hit the ground with a painful crack.

Oh, fuck . . .

Rain hit him squarely in the face. When he gasped, the rain sloshed into his throat.

Get up, Tommy!

He rolled onto his front. With aching joints, he pushed himself up to his feet, nearly collapsing from the pain.

He had to warn the others.

He cried out into the darkness, but the storm drowned him out. He took a few stumbling steps toward the compound when a body hit the ground.

Tommy leapt back as Deeks fell headfirst at his feet, a trail of leaves and broken twigs following him down. Lightning laced the sky, and Tommy saw the sentry's dead face staring back at him.

What the fuck? Tommy looked back up at the crow nest. Had Deeks just thrown himself off the platform?

Tommy limped around the body, studying it from a safe distance. From the way he had landed, it was obvious that Deeks's neck was broken.

His neck.

Tommy squinted at what he saw on the back of Deeks's neck. It looked like a cigarette burn, a perfectly round circle above the spine.

In his gut, Tommy knew that this was just the beginning of something real bad. Deeks had been some sort of traitor—tasked with turning the Owl-Sight off to open the way for a spec attack.

He had to get to the compound. *Now.*

He heard movement behind him. He spun around.

The man was tall and sleek, his face hidden under a black Stetson and ringed with a fur collar. He stood on the edge of shadow, and whatever hope remained in Tommy died at the sight of the man, for reasons he couldn't understand. The man stepped forward, reaching out of the dark like a clawed hand.

Tommy grasped for the knife in his boot, but he had no chance. The man was on him in a blink. Tommy screamed as the man pinned him facedown on the ground. His throat and nose filled with mud.

The man's knee drove into his spine, heavy as a car. The man's palm wrapped around the back of Tommy's neck, and Tommy felt rough skin scrape over his flesh like sandpaper.

And then the palm *opened.*

It was a sensation that made Tommy want to puke. Across the back of his neck, Tommy felt a wet mouth suction to his skin. Then something sharp touched his flesh—a probing stinger that traced the vertebrae of his spine.

Tommy screamed into the mud as the stinger drove into his neck. Cold entered his body, harsher and more painful than any Alaskan winter. Vipers entered his bloodstream, wriggling around and spreading through his arms and legs, swimming up toward his skull.

So fucking cold.

Tommy's body turned to lead. He heard his heartbeat slow down. When he closed his eyes, he knew he was somewhere between life and death—a dark valley crawling with snakes.

38

Houston climbed to the third floor, past the watchful eyes of the Redgun security guards, and punched in the door code Carmen had given him. He stepped into a pitch-dark room and felt the temperature drop twenty degrees.

"Close the door." Carmen's voice came from deep in the shadow.

Houston shut the door. He stood there in the frigid dark for a few moments, waiting for something to happen.

A city appeared, floating in the air.

Houston blinked. The spires of the city glowed pink and amber, the colors of a mountain sunset. The magnificent skyline swept forty feet across the chamber, a metropolis of victory rising out of the ashes of a dark past.

Carmen stood on the other side of the city, her face illuminated with its hues. Houston ran his hand through the tall buildings. The entire cityscape was made of lights—a hologram with a texture and precision he had never seen before. Between the skyscrapers he saw smaller brownstones, parks, even little families walking down the streets.

"How is this possible?" Houston asked.

Carmen didn't move, still observing the hologram. Then, very slowly, she pointed upwards. Houston craned his neck to look at the ceiling. At first, all he saw was blackness. But then the city lights glimmered across a lustrous surface. It took him a moment to realize that the surface was *moving*. He could only see fragments of it—something large and sentient shifting in the darkness above him, forming and deconstructing like an Escher maze, reconstituting into alien shapes.

"Shit," Houston said.

"If Midnight Rider can be said to have a physical form," Carmen said, "then *that* is its nervous system. Unsettling at first, I know, but you get used to it." She looked at Houston. "Do you remember the construct?"

"It's hard to forget."

"You told me something in there—that I was responsible for unleashing the Specials into this world."

"That doesn't sound like me."

Carmen walked through the hologram, bisecting a large park. "You were right. And that mistake can't be my legacy."

Houston looked at the city. "But this will be."

"If all goes well, yes. We're still finalizing the details, but our homeland will most likely be in Michigan or Illinois."

"You couldn't have negotiated for someplace warmer?"

She sighed. "I'm a California girl. Trust me, I tried." She stood next to Houston and took in the vision. "This will be our capital."

"Maybe I'll visit."

"You and I are lucky, Houston. We get to choose our legacies."

"I don't think about that."

"Of course you do—becoming a citizen, starting over in Sovereign—you're building something that wipes away what you believe you once were."

"When you invited me up here . . ."

"You thought it was a different type of invitation?"

Houston shrugged. Carmen laughed. "If only we had time for such things. But for me, time seems to run faster than it should. Whatever little of it I have left will be gone before my work is done."

He looked into her eyes. He knew she was telling him something—something she didn't want to say out loud. Her eyes were glistening, and the fading pinks and golds of the shimmering city lit her like a fleeting apparition.

Houston had seen that look before, in the camps and the forward base hospitals during the war. It was the look of a person who knew, and accepted, that death was very close.

"I'm sorry." It was all Houston could say, feeling an inexplicable loss in the pit of his stomach.

"Don't be," Carmen said. "We've lost many good people—people who would have loved to see this." She waved her hand through the hologram. "At least I get to see the beginning of something hopeful. And," she said, her eyes turning serious, "I get to set the foundation for the real prize."

Houston raised an eyebrow. "The real prize?"

"A homeland is just the beginning, Houston. We want it *all* back—from sea to shining sea."

Houston already knew the moves to this dance. "And you want me to work for you."

"Not for me—*with* me. With us."

She came close to him. "Your legacy will be whatever you want it to be in Sovereign City. But you can't build it alone. You will need friends who can get you in the right circles, who can fund your early ventures."

"And what's the price of this friendship?"

"Simply keep your eyes and ears open. When you move among the Specials and you come across something that affects us, pass it along. We may have a ceasefire now, but neither side has any illusions. We still want our country back, and they still want us dead. We've just kicked that ball down the road a few years."

"And I thought we were in peacetime now."

She laughed the clean, pure laugh of someone with no patience for falsehood. "War brings peace. Vigilance maintains it. If it helps," Carmen continued, "we ran the stats on Midnight Rider. Eighty-seven percent chance of financial success if you take our offer."

Houston looked at her. "I want to ask the computer about you."

"Not a chance."

"How much time do you have?"

"Long enough that maybe you and I can sit right here." She pointed to a small bar in the hologram. "Sit with the shades drawn, an oldie on the jukebox, and share a drink while the world carries on outside. How does that sound?" She held out her hand.

He took it. "I look forward to that."

"Likewise, Mister Holt. Likewise."

*

Katya stood in the darkened second-floor bedroom and watched Lily sleep. She envied the ability of children to just forget the day and drift off into slumber with a simple closing of the eyes. It was never that easy for adults. Katya adjusted the covers over Lily's arms and crept out of the room.

In the hallway, as Katya closed the door, she realized how much it would break her heart to see Lily go. She had spent all of one day with her, and yet it felt like so much more. Carmen had reassured her that Lily would be safe with the king. When it came to most people, Katya didn't take them at their word, but Carmen? Carmen she believed unquestioningly. Katya tried not to be too starstruck around her, but she had to admit, Carmen was one impressive human being—strong, brilliant, driven, and idealistic, the Redblood leader was everything Katya aspired to be.

On the opposite end of the character spectrum, however, was Houston Holt.

She shook her head, remembering Houston's last words to her: *It's better to cut the cord now.* The bastard could be so infuriating. But she was done—really done this time. After tonight, after helping him return Lily here, her debt to him was repaid.

Katya nodded at the Redgun guards posted along the hallway. They watched her pass, expressionless. She had just reached the top of the stairs when she heard a door open behind her.

She turned to see Lily rushing out of the bedroom. Before Katya could say anything, Lily ran over to the hallway window and gripped the bars. She stood on her toes and craned her neck to peer out into the darkness.

"Lily?" Katya called to her. Lily didn't respond. Katya walked back down the hallway and knelt next to Lily. The girl was wide awake, and her eyes searched the darkened woods of the estate.

"Lily, what's wrong?"

Lily kept looking out into the woods. Katya touched her shoulder and Lily turned, her eyes alive with fear.

"Something's coming."

"Lily, what are you talking about?"

Lily's aura appeared, dancing with dark lights. "Something's here. I'm telling you—something bad is here for me. I can feel it."

"Specials?" Katya asked, alarmed. "How many?"

"Just one."

Katya hugged Lily, holding her tight. "Hey, listen to me." She looked into Lily's eyes. "I believe you. But look around you. You're surrounded by the best soldiers in the world—hundreds of them. You're safe from one Special."

Lily scrutinized the guards one by one. "They can't stop him."

"Lily, you're safe. Do you believe me?"

Lily studied Katya for a long time. She nodded. But Katya could see she was unconvinced.

"Let's do this," Katya said. "I'm going to go talk to Carmen and have her send her best soldiers outside to take a look around, just to be extra careful. Would that help?"

Lily scratched her nose and shrugged.

"We're going to deal with this one Special. Don't you worry." She lifted Lily into her arms. "Now, I think the safest place for you is back in bed, little lady."

After putting Lily back to bed, it took Katya twenty minutes to convince the stocky Redgun in the hallway to send an extra patrol out onto the grounds. Midnight Rider hadn't detected any suspicious activity, and if Midnight Rider said they were safe, the Reds didn't argue.

But even Redguns had their limits. After enduring a particularly grueling version of Katya's patented verbal onslaught, spiked with endless questions and naked threats, the soldier finally agreed to notify Control of a possible intruder on the grounds.

"The patrols will run two extra rounds," the Redgun said after radioing back and forth with Control. "That's all I can do."

Katya nodded. She still felt like it might not be enough, but there was nothing else she could do. "Okay. Let me know if you find anything."

The Redgun looked visibly relieved when she turned toward the stairs and headed downstairs. She grabbed a Modelo at the bar and watched the people on the dance floor, her mind still latched onto Lily's warning. All kids believed in monsters under the bed, but Lily was different. The Snake Mother herself had tattooed her arm. Lily had seen real monsters, and if *she* was afraid . . .

Katya finished her beer and ordered another. She watched a towering Phoenix Marine patrol through the hall. Eight of the elite Special soldiers had arrived with the envoy, and more than their numbers, it was their reputation that soothed Katya's anxiety. The Marines were hellish warriors, nearly on par with the Silverbacks in their destructive capacity. If there was a Special out there hunting Lily, he would have to go through these Marines first.

Katya inhaled her Modelo down to the bottom. There was nothing to be afraid of.

So why was her stomach churning?

Her hand traced the grip of the Hammer in its holster. Its deadly presence didn't reassure her like it once had.

A loud swell of cheers rose up on the dance floor. The banquet hall was packed with revelers, and yet, for a reason she couldn't explain, Katya's eyes fell on the young man standing in the doorway.

He wore a black poncho dripping with rain. He stood unnaturally still as he watched the dancers, his rifle strapped behind his back.

Katya felt a twinge in her throat. Years on the street as a River Town Badge had sharpened her instinct for trouble, and that man in the poncho looked like trouble.

Katya stopped a passing female Redgun and pointed to the watching man. "Who is that?"

The Redgun squinted at the man. "Him? That's Tommy."

"Who is he?"

"One of our guards. Why, you like him? I can introduce you."

"You trust him?"

"Him?" The Redgun looked confused. "He's a baby Red. I could break him with a look." Her face turned suspicious. "Why?"

Katya watched Tommy for a few seconds. Lily had warned her about a Special, not some strange kid in a poncho.

"It's nothing," Katya said, raising her empty bottle. "Too many of these."

The woman disappeared into the party. Katya turned back just in time to see Tommy leave the room.

Katya rubbed her tired eyes. Thoughts of sleep beckoned her as she walked past the dancers and headed toward her room upstairs.

She saw it from the corner of her eye. At first, she thought someone had rolled a ball onto the dance floor. The sphere wobbled past her leisurely and into the center of the cheering crowd.

Katya scrabbled backward the moment she recognized the object.

"*Grenade!*" she screamed at the top of her lungs.

A few people turned to look at her. Most of the crowd was still dancing when the grenade exploded.

39

Houston felt the blast shake the floor beneath his feet. He locked eyes with Carmen, both their faces frozen in shock.

Carmen moved fast, sweeping a pistol out of her jacket and barking orders into her lapel radio. Houston unholstered his pistol and followed her out into the hallway.

Below them, Houston heard the first screams. He felt sick.

Katya. Lily. "I'm going down," he said, racing for the stairs.

"Go." Carmen said, joining the Redguns in the hall. "And watch your back, Marine."

*

The music and laughter were gone. Katya could only hear the ringing in her ears, could only see the bloodshed around her. She blinked in the smoky room, the strobe lights still spinning sickeningly over the carnage. Somewhere in her mind, she noticed a funny fact—she had survived two bombings in less than two days.

No. She hadn't survived this one yet.

She limped through the dusty banquet hall, studying its remnants as if she were far away, as if the torn, lifeless bodies lying around her were stills from some gruesome silent film. Her foot slipped on a pool of blood.

Men with guns poured into the room. Katya fell to the floor and threw up. The smoke burned her nose as she pushed her way through a jumble of overturned tables and chairs, gasping for clean air. A team of medics raced past her, carrying gurneys. She wanted to help the survivors, but there was only one instinct left now: get to Lily.

Katya lurched toward the stairs, the memory of Tommy boiling inside her. It was him. It had to be him.

She had just reached the stairway when the gunfire started. It was behind her, deeper in the house—the concussive barks of an M6 rifle firing in three-round bursts, followed by the sounds of breaking glass and screams.

Katya raced up the stairs as fast as she could, bumping like a pinball between columns of Redguns running the opposite way.

Somebody grabbed her by the arm.

"Houston?" Katya blinked tears out of her eyes.

He was saying something, but Katya could only watch his mouth move. "WHAT?" she yelled.

"*Are you okay?*" Houston yelled back.

She nodded and coughed up something black from her lungs.

Houston was yelling in her ear. "What happened?"

"One of the Redbloods. He threw a grenade into the ballroom."

"A *Redblood?*"

"Skinny guy. I saw him. Black poncho." She spun as the stairs shook with the reverberation of another grenade blast somewhere in the house. The foyer chandelier rattled, and a bulbous mass of black air crept down the halls toward them.

"Lily's upstairs," Katya said. "Come with me."

They waded through the crowd onto the upstairs landing. The stocky Redgun she had spoken to earlier shoved his rifle in their faces.

"Get the fuck back!" He yelled.

"It's me!" Katya raised her hands. "Remember? It's me!"

The Redgun's barrel swiveled between them.

"We need to get Lily," Katya said. "She's not safe in here."

The Redgun's eyes shifted to the stairs as another burst of automatic gunfire echoed below them. He turned back to Katya, obviously itching to get into the fight downstairs. "Get out of this hallway. Nobody moves the girl without authorization."

"For Christ's sake!" Houston bellowed. "Whoever's shooting downstairs is here for Lily!"

As if on cue, another grenade detonated at the foot of the stairway. Katya and Houston hit the floor as shrapnel shot up onto the landing. Fire climbed the curving steps, and a plume of black smoke rose toward them, a choking wall that blocked out all light.

Katya looked at Houston, and he nodded. They both pulled their sidearms. The Redgun lined up his sights with Katya's head—

"Katya!"

Katya gasped with relief as Lily came running out of the darkness, straight past the Redgun, and hugged her leg. The Redgun lunged forward to grab Lily's shirt, but Houston shoved his pistol in his face.

"Back up," Houston growled.

"Shoot us," Katya dared, covering Lily with her body. "But we're not leaving without her."

With a small prayer, Katya backed away from the Redgun, Houston edging back with her, his gun still trained on the soldier. Behind them, Katya felt the heat of the flames climbing up the stairs, blocking their exit.

Houston smashed the glass of the fire extinguisher case on the wall and pulled out two extinguishers.

"Make yourself useful," Houston said, tossing one to the Redgun. Houston turned the second extinguisher toward the blaze.

"Get her out," he said to Katya. "Don't wait for me."

Within seconds, he was enveloped in darkness. In the thickening fog, Katya glimpsed the Redgun rushing past her and down the stairs, spraying the encroaching flames. Katya picked up Lily and covered both their faces with their shirts.

"The bad man is here," Lily whispered in her ear.

"I know, little lady. I should have listened to you."

Katya ran away from the stairs with Lily, knowing that she had to find another exit before the smoke killed them. The heat was now unbearable. As she ran back down the hall, Katya could feel Lily's little hands dig into her shoulders, her little body shaking with heavy coughs.

Each door she opened led only to a room with barricaded windows. At the far end of the hall they found a brick wall with another barred window. Outside the window, Katya spotted teams of heavily armed Reds racing across the lawn toward the house. But there was no way to get down there.

Lily coughed harder now, shaking against Katya.

"Stay strong, little lady. We're going to find a way out." Katya turned back toward the stairs—

Fuck. An impenetrable mass of smoke advanced toward them like a primordial beast, filling the hallway.

"Cover your ears," Katya said to Lily as she brought the Hammer up. She stepped back from the window and fired two rounds into the glass. The glass shook and spiderwebbed but did not break. Katya fired again, but the glass held.

The thick black air was on them now, so dense that she could barely see her own shooting hand. Lily coughed and spit up on the floor. Katya kicked at the window as hard as she could. She kicked until her legs ached. The window did not budge.

The smoke closed in around them, filling their world. Katya hacked up something bitter from her lungs. Lily's eyes watered, her body spasming for oxygen.

"Close your eyes," Katya croaked as she wrapped Lily in her arms. "I'm so sorry . . ."

Katya held Lily close, protecting her as best she could. Katya felt like she was on fire, the heat incinerating the last of her strength. Smoke filled her lungs.

Two massive shapes strode out of the blackness. Katya felt a large hand lift her up, and in the rush of movement she glimpsed a gold phoenix burning across a broad chest.

Phoenix Marines, Katya realized, her heart suddenly alive with hope. The marine wrapped his giant arm around both her and Lily and lifted them up as if they were firewood.

"You're coming with us," he said. He turned to the second marine and nodded, taking five steps away from the wall as he did so. He ordered Katya and Lily, "Cover your ears."

The second marine turned toward the brick wall and punched both fists simultaneously through the air. Katya felt the hallway vibrate at a feverish pitch, and all her hairs stood on end as the atoms holding the world together broke apart and everything turned to pure energy. She clamped her hands over her ears but kept watching as golden rods burst from the marine's arms and hit the wall with a deafening roar, ripping a hole straight through the reinforced bricks. A gust of fresh, wet air hit Katya in the face, scouring her lungs clean.

The first marine carried them toward the hole.

"Wait!" Katya yelled. "We need to get Houston!" She twisted around to see Houston's silhouette, still deep in the smoke, battling the blaze.

"Houston!" Lily cried out as the marine ran up to the breach.

"We have to wait for him!" Katya beat her fist against the marine's thick chest. "We have to—" But the marine launched himself, and a powerful force buoyed them up into the air. Wind rushed beneath Katya's feet as they sailed out into the rain. Within seconds, the screams of the house fell away behind them, and all she saw was sky.

*

Houston wiped the sweat out of his eyes and blasted the last flames on the stairway with foam, watching with relief as the fire drowned. Houston followed the stocky Redgun down the stairs to the foyer. He had seen the Phoenix Marines swoop past him onto the landing, and he knew Lily and Katya were with them. Right now, that was the safest place to be.

Downstairs, a gray haze hung in the air, reducing visibility to fifteen feet. A mass of shocked survivors snarled the entryway in a traffic jam as teams of Redguns herded them out the front door while other Redgun fire teams simultaneously raced into the house, looking for a fight.

Houston spotted a face he recognized. Pixie ran toward him with a crew-cut Redgun, both wearing flak vests and carrying rifles. Four combat medics followed behind them, carrying leather cases.

"Murphy!" Pixie called out to the stocky Redgun. "Stack up. We're getting these docs inside."

"Where's the shooter?" Murphy asked.

"Somewhere in the east wing. Last we heard, we have twenty-plus fatalities. Even more wounded trapped inside."

"The fuck we waiting for?" Murphy spat on the ground and lined up in the column behind the medics. The crew-cut Redgun took point and pushed his way through the tide of evacuees.

"Hey!" Houston called out to them. The line kept moving, but Pixie turned around.

"What?"

"I can help. Get me in the fight."

"Get out of here," she said. "We don't need you."

"You need one more gun to make a full fire team."

Pixie glared at him. Then she tapped the point man on the shoulder. He turned and studied Houston with dark eyes. Houston noticed the chest patch on his flak vest read *Ruiz*.

"Can you shoot?" Ruiz asked.

"Marine Corps," Houston said. "Raider Battalion."

"Well, fuck me." Ruiz grinned. He unslung an extra M6 rifle from his pack and tossed it to Houston. "*Semper fi*, motherfucker."

Houston racked the slide on the rifle and joined the column as they moved out, slotting behind Pixie and ahead of the medics. Ruiz led them through the crowd with Murphy covering the back of the train. After much elbowing and shouldering, they broke free of the logjam and snaked into the blackened east wing.

They entered a wide hallway and stacked up by the first open doorway, glass cracking softly under their boots. Pixie strapped a chemlight to Houston's shirt with an elastic band. The small glowsticks shed no light under normal circumstances but would glow green through the scope of night-vision goggles. She and all the other Reds wore them.

"Just so we don't shoot you," she said. "As much as I want to."

"Appreciate it. Now, how about a flak vest?"

She shrugged and turned back toward the doorway. Ruiz counted down on his hand from three and then burst into the room. Ruiz broke right and up to the far corner, Pixie left, and Houston took the near right corner. Murphy rolled in behind Houston and took the opposite corner.

A poker table lay overturned in the center of the room, which was pockmarked with bullet holes. Shell casings lay scattered around their feet, and cold rain blew in from the shattered windows, turning the ground slick. They found a cluster of wounded survivors in the third room, hiding in the storage closet. After the medics had checked their wounds, the fire team escorted them back into the hallway to join the exodus.

Ruiz led the team back into the east wing. They made it only a few steps before Houston saw Ruiz and Pixie touch their earpieces. Pixie's eyes widened.

"Fuck!" she hissed.

"What is it?" Houston asked.

"Fire team Bravo just got hit in the library. Major casualties."

"Move!" Murphy yelled from the back, even though he didn't have to. The entire line was already running full-tilt behind Ruiz. At the end of a lightless passageway, Ruiz lined them up next to a thick oak door carved with an ornate crest.

"This is the library," Ruiz whispered back to his shooters as he unslung a sledgehammer. "It has two levels, so keep your eyes up. Bravo's not responding, but the call came from in here. Medics hang back. Shooters might still be in there."

Bang! The sledgehammer smashed the double doors inward. Pixie flung in a flash bang and barreled into the room after the detonation. Houston was on her heels, the entire world narrowed down to the narrow tunnel of his gun sight.

Houston scoped four Redguns sprawled on the thick rug in pools of blood. He arced his rifle up, checking the walkway above for movement. The only light came from a fallen lamp.

"Clear!" He heard Ruiz call out, followed by Pixie and Murphy.

"Clear!" He called back.

Pixie called in the medics. They knelt over the fallen soldiers, checking for signs of life.

Of the four fallen soldiers, it was clear that at least two of them were beyond help. Pixie bit her inner cheek as she watched the medics work, her hands clenched so tightly around her gun that they trembled. Houston knew there was nothing he could say to help.

"Got a live one," one of the medics said as his hands pressed into the neck of one of the soldiers. "Need to move him. *Now.*"

The medics unrolled a portable gurney and an IV bag. The medics turned the soldier onto the gurney and lifted him up.

"Jesus," Pixie said when she saw the soldier's young face. "What the hell was Tommy doing in here?"

"Who?" Houston asked.

"Stupid rookie," Murphy growled as he watched the medics carry Tommy toward the door.

Houston was about to ask another question when Tommy opened his eyes and plunged a shard of glass through the medic's throat. The medic screamed, and Houston watched in horror as Tommy spun off the gurney, unholstered a pistol, and blew three ragged holes in the second medic.

Gunfire erupted, muzzle flashes strobing like lightning. The boy was moving at impossible speeds, leaping onto the upper platform and firing before spinning away into the darkness. The other Reds ducked behind cover, bullets snapping past their heads and disintegrating the furniture into shrapnel.

Houston caught the spec in his sights as he leapt off the platform and fired off three rounds that punched fleshy chunks out of Tommy's torso.

But Tommy shook off the hits like they were ant bites. He spun around and, still in midair, slammed two bullets into Ruiz's neck.

Pixie's rounds tore into the boy's legs as he ran across the room. The boy fell into a forward flip, rolled across broken glass, and then kept running. As he raced by Murphy, the stocky Redgun tackled him head-on. The spec saw it coming and twisted away at the last second, firing two shots into Murphy's chest.

Tommy bolted out the heavy doors, Houston and Pixie's bullets splintering the wood behind him.

Houston ran to the door and edged into the hallway. He saw a trail of blood leading to his right and around a corner, but no Tommy.

"*Medic!*" Pixie called out as she knelt over Murphy. Houston stood guard by the doors, ears still rattling from the gunfire. Pixie watched as the medics cut open Murphy's shirt. She walked over and looked at Ruiz's corpse. She stood over him quietly, her head lowered. After a few moments she unstrapped Ruiz's night vision goggles and marched over to Houston, her eyes blazing. "Whatever that thing is, we need to kill it. *Now.*"

Houston glanced over at Murphy, who was gasping as the medics tried to clear his airways. He looked at Pixie. "I need ammo."

She tossed him two 30-round magazines from her vest and then slammed a fresh one into her own rifle.

"Don't get dead, Houston," she said as she slipped out into the hallway.

40

The Phoenix Marine touched down like a bird on the wet grass and carried Katya and Lily toward the waiting Black Hawks. A circle of marines surrounded the choppers in a defensive formation, a wall of black.

The pilots pulled down the protective tarps and jumped into the cockpits. Within seconds the rotors were spinning, blasting Katya with a wave of wet air. She covered Lily's eyes against the rotor gusts.

The marine dropped them inside the helicopter. "Strap in," he barked. Katya quickly snapped Lily into the canvas seat before latching her own belt. Sitting across from them was the king's envoy, the white-bearded man she had heard the others call Ambassador Trevayne.

He looks in worse shape than me, she thought as she watched the once-imposing man rock back and forth in his seat, a manic fear pulsing behind his eyes. A marine yelled at him to buckle up, but Trevayne made no indication that he could hear the man inches from his face. Finally, the marine reached over and buckled Trevayne's seatbelt himself. Trevayne looked up at Katya and Lily, his eyes passing over them like glazed moons.

Lily tugged at Katya's jacket. "What about Houston?"

Katya looked through the rain at the house. Four plumes of smoke rose high above it. Behind the windows, she saw muzzle flashes light up the darkness all along the bottom floor.

"Is he okay?" Lily asked again, watching the house with worry.

"I don't know," Katya said quietly.

The choppers powered up and lifted off the ground. Lily grasped Katya's hand and held it tight as the helicopter swayed in the wind and spun around, nosing forward into the storm.

*

Houston followed Pixie as she tracked the trail of bloody corpses down to the end of the passageway. They were deep inside the house. It was quiet here, away from the fires and evacuees. Pixie stopped and pointed her gun forward. Houston saw bloody handprints streaked across a set of double-wide swinging doors.

"What's in here?" Houston whispered.

"Hold up." She scanned her wrist computer, her face pensive in the blue glow. She tapped the screen a few times, then smiled.

"What?"

"It's the catering kitchen." On Pixie's wrist computer, Houston saw a schematic of a large L-shaped room with a deep walk-in freezer. "This is the only entry or exit," Pixie continued, nodding her head at the door. "If he's in there, he's trapped."

"We go in, and *we're* trapped."

Pixie unclipped a flash bang from her harness. "So we smoke him out."

She crept toward the door and braced herself on the right side. Houston stacked up against the left of the doorframe.

"By the way, what's your name?" Houston asked.

"Does it really matter now?"

"In my head, I just call you Pixie."

"Good enough."

Inside the kitchen, something metal clattered against the floor.

Pixie nodded, and Houston pushed the door open a crack. Pixie tossed in the flash bang. The explosion swung the doors outward, and blinding light shot through the opening.

The two of them swept into opposite sides of the room. Through the shimmering green of night vision, Houston's gun sight swept over tight corners and shining metal surfaces—a nightmare space for a firefight. At the end of the center island, he found the trail of blood again. Big drops splotched on the floor, careening in shallow zigzags, marking the trail of a wounded animal. Step by step he followed it along, past the dry storage shelves, until it abruptly stopped in front of the heavy metal door of the walk-in freezer.

Houston pointed his gun toward the far end of the kitchen where Pixie was and flashed his gun's LED light three times. Her LED light flashed back at him once. Within seconds she was standing next to him.

Houston pointed toward the bloodstains and the freezer door. *He's inside.*

She ran a finger across her throat and unlatched a frag grenade from her vest. In the confined space of the freezer, it would turn a human body into confetti.

Houston gripped the door handle. Pixie wrapped a finger around the grenade pin. Houston set his feet and was just about to pull the door when they heard the scream.

Houston froze. It was the scream of a man in terrible pain, and it was coming from inside the freezer.

The man screamed again, but this time his voice broke down into a soft whimper. Houston heard two words at the end before the voice crumbled into a wet sob.

"Help me . . ."

He looked at Pixie. It could be a trap—a hook designed to lure them into the narrow killzone of the freezer.

"Help me . . . please . . . somebody help me," the man pleaded before unfurling another high-pitched wail.

Pixie pocketed the grenade and nodded at the door handle. Houston swung the door open, and a gust of frozen air blew out into the kitchen.

Pixie and Houston edged their rifles around the doorframe.

In the wash of the white lights they saw Tommy, propped up against the far wall, sitting in a pool of his own blood. Houston eyed the M6 rifle laid across his waist.

"Drop your weapon!" Houston ordered.

Tommy didn't respond. He sucked in air through his teeth, shaking in pain.

"Drop your weapon or we shoot!" Pixie yelled.

"Help me . . ." Tommy groaned, his teeth bloody.

"I have the shot," Houston said, his sights lined up with Tommy's forehead. "It's your call."

Pixie studied Tommy for a long moment. Then, when Houston was convinced she was going to give the order to shoot, she lowered her own gun and stepped inside the freezer. Houston followed her inside.

Pixie pulled away Tommy's weapon. His body was soaked in blood from multiple gunshot wounds. He stank of urine.

"Who do you work for?" Pixie demanded, shining the LED in his eyes.

Tommy blinked rapidly. "Oh, God . . . I can feel it."

"Who do you work for?"

"Please . . ." Tommy sobbed. "I can feel it inside me . . ."

Houston stepped forward. "What are you talking about?"

Tommy turned to face him, and Houston felt a crawling horror when he saw the boy's eyes. They were inhuman, as black and dead as space.

He was about to say something when the boy arched violently and screamed louder than he ever had before, "*Get him out of me! Get him out!*"

"Who?" Pixie demanded again. "Who are you talking about—"

"KILL ME!"

"Tommy, you need to—"

Tommy lunged for Pixie's gun. Pixie pulled the trigger. Two slugs snapped Tommy's head back, bouncing it against the wall. The gunshots echoed in the freezer as Tommy's body sagged forward, pulling his ruined head along with it. He looked like he was bowing.

"Motherfucker," Pixie cursed.

For a moment, they just stared at the body. It wasn't until Houston's adrenaline faded that he noticed the hole in the back of the boy's neck. He shone his light on it.

"What the hell?"

The puncture wound lay right above the spine. And it was *moving*, pulsing like a small maw, oozing a black viscous liquid that smoked in the icy air.

"Fuck me," Pixie gasped.

Houston dropped to the floor and sat, his stomach tying itself up in knots.

"What is it?" Pixie asked.

"He's a Stringer. That's what he meant when he said—"

"Someone was inside him."

They looked at each other in the dark freezer.

"If he was being controlled . . ." Pixie started. But she didn't want to finish.

Then where was the controller?

"He was a diversion." Houston jumped to his feet. "The real attack hasn't started yet."

They both heard it at the same time—rotors thundering overhead. The Black Hawks were leaving the compound, flying straight into a trap.

*

The Black Hawks rose high into the slashing rain. Katya strained against her seat belt as the pilot banked hard left, then right—evasive maneuvers to throw off any possible shooters below. The pilot nosed the bird down and swung it around the right flank of the ruined house.

Below, through the open doors of the Black Hawk, Katya watched the house burn. Columns of smoke poured out of windows and into the sky like blackened trees. She could see people still running in and out of the building, and before the helicopter banked again, she glimpsed the mass of dead and wounded, spread out in a ghastly triage across the huge lawn. Lily saw it too, and she squeezed Katya's hand hard.

The chopper nosed up and climbed. On either side of them, perched in the open doors, were four Phoenix Marines, two on each side, facing the brunt of the rain that blew into the cabin. When the choppers were high enough, the marines dropped out of the cabin and fell into the emptiness below. Lily gasped.

But they were gone only for a moment. They reappeared alongside the chopper, their bodies straight and strong in flight. They flew two to a side, in a staggered formation like fighter jet escorts. Ahead of them, Katya glimpsed the other Black Hawk chopper cutting sharply to the right, flanked by four more cruising marines.

The towers of smoke passed beneath them, replaced by a moon-tinged carpet of trees, endless and strangely serene. Katya closed her eyes, her mind lost in chaos. The world had darkened so suddenly. Men, women, fathers, brothers, and mothers, all dead. For what? It was so random, so . . . *senseless*. She thought of Houston, still somewhere back there, and a bubble of guilt swelled in her chest. She could have done more to save him.

She felt Lily rub her nose against her arm. She turned and saw herself reflected in the bright pools of Lily's eyes.

"He'll be all right," Lily said over the rotors.

"You think so?"

Lily nodded. "He has something left to do."

Lily leaned into her, and Katya felt a soft warmth spread across her body—a sensation of peace that brought her back to solid ground.

Across from them, Trevayne stared at his hands, his mouth moving silently.

A road appeared below, snaking through the wooded mountainside. Katya was shocked to see how close they were to the ground. The pilots maneuvered the choppers low and fast, and the marines seemed to be skimming only inches above the bed of trees underneath. Katya was watching the marines when she saw the flash of light.

Lightning was her first thought. But that was impossible, she realized—the light had come from the trees *below*.

The streak of light arced into the sky and hit the first chopper right below the rotors.

"Tango!" The pilot yelled as the chopper ahead of them grew a crown of fire. Katya gasped as the pilot cut a hard left. She reached out and held Lily.

"Incoming!"

Another white streak shot past them, sizzling in the rainy air. Trevayne screamed as the chopper dropped suddenly and then nosed back up, pinning them all to their seats.

All Katya could see now was the blur of sky and trees. Around her she heard the *thwoom, thwoom* of the marines returning fire, and she caught a dizzying glimpse of golden bolts pouring out of the sky.

In the chaos, she heard a new sound—the unmistakable bellow of a heavy machine gun. Bullets pinged off metal, and the Black Hawk jolted and shuddered like it had hit a speed bump.

"We're hit!" The pilot called out.

The chopper began to spin. It tumbled down, around and around, spinning faster than Katya could comprehend. All detail was stripped away from her vision. The rain slashed her face and she was lifted from her seat, floating in midair as the bird plummeted out of the sky.

41

Houston and Pixie clambered onto the motorbikes inside the transport shed and raced out over the hilly property toward the front gates, weaving through the traffic jam of evacuation trucks. They had just cleared the gates when the first chopper went down.

The missile caught it right under the rotors on the left side. The fireball sparked in the night sky and then, almost gracefully, the Black Hawk spun down below the trees.

Something cold plunged into Houston's chest.

Lily and Katya were in one of those choppers.

"That's one of ours," Pixie said over the radio as she swerved past a truck.

"What?"

"One of our own missile batteries took out the chopper—from the crow's nest. Whoever strung up Tommy must have taken over his nest."

They redlined the bikes down the hill.

"Lily's in the second chopper," Pixie said over the radio.

"How do you know?" Houston asked.

"I synced up Lily's Clamp signal to my computer. It's still moving, which means she's in the second chopper."

Machine gun fire roared in the trees ahead, and Houston watched in horror as tracers raked the Black Hawk. The chopper belched smoke and spiraled downward. It struggled valiantly for a few seconds before plummeting below the tree line.

Pixie revved her bike and rocketed down the dark mountain road, spewing a wall of rainwater behind her. Houston jammed the accelerator.

Lily and Katya *might* have survived the crash. But even if they had, the worst was still to come: whatever had shot them down—whatever monster had hijacked Tommy—would now come looking for them.

*

Lily brought Katya back.

Through layers of black smoke tinged with fire, Katya rose out of the darkness. Sounds returned first—voices shouting, the wind howling—and then came the pain lancing up her spine, running in volcanic rivers across her body. But above it all, like a frequency that resonated across all time, she heard Lily:

"Wake up. Katya, wake up!"

Katya blinked in the rain.

"Katya!" Lily's voice flooded with relief.

Katya tried to raise her head, but a stab of pain made her groan. "Where are we?" she asked.

"The helicopter crashed. We're in the woods."

Katya looked around, her eyes adapting to the darkness. She was still strapped into her seat. The forest pressed in on them from either side of the open Black Hawk doors, and the cold wind carried heavy diesel fumes into the cabin.

The crash came back to her—a series of distorted images and sounds aligning into a shaky narrative. She remembered the warmth of Lily's hand in hers, a sharp intake of breath as she braced for the crash, and then a jarring impact as the helicopter was stopped mid spin by the four marines. Together, they had braced the Black Hawk and stopped its tremendous centrifugal force above the trees. They had managed to slow it down just enough to straighten the bird out for a bone-rattling, but survivable, landing.

With shaking fingers, Katya unlatched her harness and pulled herself forward, onto her knees. "Are you okay?" she asked Lily.

"My hand is a little sore," Lily said, raising her left hand. Katya saw that Lily's arm was bruised black from her wrist to the back of her thumb. The black Clamp she wore, once smooth and shiny, was now rippled and dented with damage.

"How bad does it hurt?" Katya asked.

"I'll be okay," Lily said, not quite convincingly.

"We need to get out of here," Katya said. "Can you walk?"

Lily nodded. "Giddyup."

Katya took Lily's hand and turned to the open door just as a large shadow filled the opening. Katya grasped for the Hammer—

"Ma'am, we need to move. Now."

It was the Phoenix Marine that had taken them from the house. He reached in and pulled them out of the chopper and onto the muddy ground. His three comrades stood in a security perimeter around the aircraft, their black uniforms slick with rain. Ambassador Trevayne and the two pilots were already outside, dazed and on weak legs.

Within seconds they were moving away from the crash, the civilians in the center, two marines out front and two behind. The lead marine led them uphill, all of them clawing with their hands and feet on the sodden earth.

"Where are we going?" Katya whispered to the marine next to her.

"Don't talk," he replied gruffly. "We don't know how many of them are out here."

Katya held Lily's hand as they crossed a narrow stream. The marines communicated with hand signals, moving in and out of different formations, slowing and speeding up the train with silent gestures.

They were being hunted—that much Katya could gather from the soldiers' body language. She felt a vast and open vulnerability heightened by their wild, storm-swept surroundings. She pulled Lily closer and unholstered the Hammer. She clicked the safety off, but she knew bullets alone wouldn't be enough for whatever waited for them out in the dark.

*

"Get off the road," Pixie ordered.

"Why?"

"There's a minefield at the bottom of this drop. Control doesn't know whether it's offline."

"Shit."

Houston's bike sprayed a plume of rain as he angled it left, following Pixie off the road and into the tree line. Immediately, a barbed line of branches whipped at his face and shoulders, the dark masses of heavy trunks flashing past him at breakneck speed.

Pixie cut a sharp left, speeding them down a stomach-dropping decline before slingshotting up a steep rise.

"We're close," she said over the radio. "Half mile."

Houston ripped the accelerator hard. Then, up ahead, he heard the unmistakable roar of the Hammer.

*

The shot came out of the darkness above. It was so black and formless that Katya didn't see it until it hit the lead marine and slammed him into an oak trunk with a sickening *crack*.

"Contact!" a marine yelled, grabbing Katya and Lily while a second marine pulled Trevayne behind cover. Together, they sped off to the right as the third marine swiveled behind them, firing gold bolts into the trees. The two helicopter pilots fired their pistols blindly into the night.

Katya lifted Lily and ran, the marine pushing her. Behind them, she felt the air burning, heard the thudding bolts splinter tree trunks. She tripped and fell, banging her toe against a boulder and dropping Lily.

The marine shoved her forward. "Move!" he yelled.

No matter how fast they tried to run, the terrain held them back. Mud pulled them down; branches swatted at their faces. Trevayne wailed as he tumbled into a muddy pond.

A man's scream detonated behind them like a bomb. Lily gripped Katya tight as the scream died out in a long, agonized pitch. Silence remained. The fight behind them was over. But who had won?

The convoy did not pause. The marines drove them forward, skirting around the edge of a wet gully.

"Why don't you just fly us out of here?" Katya yelled at the marine beside her.

"Airspace is compromised," he said, scanning the woods.

Lily tugged at Katya's shirt and pointed behind them. "Katya, look."

Katya saw the movement on their left flank—a rustle of leaves and a fleeting shadow running parallel to them.

"Katya . . ." Lily's voice was a warning.

"I know." Katya put Lily down behind her.

"What are you doing?" The marine next to her barked.

"On our left!" Katya was already bringing up the Hammer as the shadow raced toward them. The gun kicked like a mule in her hands as she ripped off three roaring shots. Both marines spun around and lit up the dark with a hellish fusillade.

A crackling black bolt answered from the treetops, slicing Trevayne's screaming head clean off his neck.

Katya fired into the trees as Trevayne's head rolled down the mud toward her feet. One of the marines stepped back and grabbed a fistful of Katya's jacket. "Get down and cover up!" He growled before tossing her to the ground. Katya shielded Lily with her body.

One of the marines went airborne, ten feet up, as the other slid directly below him on the ground. A gust of wind threw a wall of leaves in the air, and Katya watched in awe as gold lights danced around them, growing with violent force. An incendiary energy flowed through the bodies of both marines as they combined their Gifts into an infernal mass of potential energy.

The two marines smashed their fists together simultaneously.

The circle of gold contracted for a second, sucking the air out of Katya's lungs before a new sensation arrived: a tremble as the forest froze in place, holding its breath. And then, every ounce of trapped energy exploded outward at once.

Katya held on to Lily with all her strength as the cataclysmic force threatened to rip them into the sky. Leaves spun in a cyclone, and rainwater sizzled and twisted upward in towering columns through the canopies. The concussive blast thundered like a herd of stampeding elephants through the fabric of the world, reverberating apocalyptically in Katya's chest.

The silence that followed was deafening. The air cooled rapidly, and Katya opened her eyes to see misty rain swinging on charged currents, moving like a golden veil in hypnotic loops. The earth had been torched into an alien landscape glowing with small fires.

The marines scoured the clearing, searching for any unlikely survivors. When they were done, they came back for Katya and Lily and pulled them to their feet. Katya tried to catch her breath. Lily blinked, studying the destruction with a strange serenity.

"We're safe," was all Katya could manage. She shivered in the rapidly cooling air and put a hand on Lily's shoulder. "We're—"

Thunk! The marine closest to them exhaled sharply and fell forward.

Thunk! The last marine exhaled and crumpled to the mud.

Katya stared dumbly at the axes embedded in the two dead men's scalps.

"Run!" Katya screamed. She pushed Lily across the clearing. "Go!"

The Hammer swung up, its iron sights searching for targets. Lily looked around and took a step back toward Katya. "I'm not going," she said.

"Lily." Katya's steadied her voice, her eyes still locked on her sights. "You run as far and as fast as you can. Do you understand?"

"I'm not leaving you alone."

"Lily, go. Now!"

With one last defiant look, Lily raced into the trees. Katya let her finger rest on the trigger and took a deep, steadying breath.

She waited, aware that she was being watched—that something in the darkness was looking back at her.

The rain was now a mist, almost peaceful.

When he showed himself, he did so slowly.

He swung down from the trees and landed soundlessly. Katya took a step back, pure terror coursing through her body. The man rose to his full height, dappled with shadow. He stalked toward her, fur bristling across his shoulders.

Boom, boom, boom! Every one of her shots hit air. He advanced relentlessly. All she saw were the wisps of his trail, the shimmer of his speed.

Click. The Hammer came up empty.

He was right on her, five steps away. She plunged a hand into her jacket for ammo.

He kicked her hard in the stomach. Pain lit up her body, and she went tumbling to the dirt. Another blow cracked across her cheekbone.

Katya groaned. Her attacker strode over to the dead marines and retrieved his axes from their skulls with a wet *chunk*. The axes dripped blood as he returned for her.

His aura reached her before he did—a starless dark so severe it burned her from the inside and stole her breath.

A wind rustled Katya's hair, cool and gentle and alien. The wind picked up, moved around her in shallow circles, and then *through* her. She felt her hair, then her body, defy gravity and *rise*.

She opened her eyes and saw Lily standing at the edge of the clearing. She was glaring at the tall man.

"Get away from her!" Lily yelled.

The man crooked his head and studied Lily. His face was a black pool under the Stetson, but Katya thought she saw his upper lip curl.

Lily took a step forward, the space around her body luminescent. Her aura shimmered and twinkled, pink, purple, white lights darting, blazing, and dying like fireflies.

One look at Lily's pained face, and Katya saw the brutal effort it took to sustain her Gift with the Clamp around her wrist. Her small fists were clenched against the force of the Clamp, its crystal latticework buzzing with a harsh halogen light that ate away at Lily's spectral aura.

"Get away from her!" Lily yelled again, her voice breaking.

The man held his tomahawks inches from Katya's face, caked with brain and flecks of bone. He moved without hurry, his long legs unfurling and his steps soundless as he walked down to Lily.

The ground shook. The air bubbled hotly. Lily's aura overwhelmed the Clamp, amplifying into an incandescent globe that hardened and funneled sharply into a thrusting battering ram that pummeled the man head-on, blasting him back across the clearing.

The light receded as if a door had been closed on the sun. Lily collapsed to her hands and knees, the Clamp glowing like a branding iron.

Katya stumbled to her feet and ran to Lily. She felt intense heat rising off Lily's skin.

The man stood in the center of the clearing. The Stetson had blown off his head, and what Katya could see of his face horrified her. He picked up his hat and dusted it off, placing it firmly back on his head. When he came this time, he ran.

Lily screamed—a primal yell that burst forth with a thousand points of jagged light. Katya felt a burst of heat and had to close her eyes against the brightness of the blast. As Lily's Gift passed over her, Katya felt things move and speak inside it—an ocean of memories and heartbeats, thunder and fire, and above all, pain.

The man dug his feet deep into the wet ground and pushed himself forward, his shoulder set against Lily's Gift. Step by step he advanced, pushing back the blazing wall. The barrier shook unsteadily, then cracked and splintered until webs of black spread across its face. Lily cried out, and the light flittered away and died.

Lily's body was shaking hard now. Katya put an arm around her and shielded her body with her own. She held Lily until the shaking had slowed. She didn't even look up at the man. She could feel his aura approaching, but there was nothing more to do.

Light filled the clearing again—but this time it came with gunfire.

Katya swiveled around to see two headlights bathing the man in white light, pinning him down as a volley of bullets spun him around. The motorbikes were near silent as they bounced into the clearing, their riders' rifles spitting death. The man fell back, twisting to avoid the onslaught until he tumbled backward off the hill and disappeared down the slope.

The two bikes circled. Katya recognized the first rider as the short-haired Redgun she had met at the compound. The second rider was—

"Houston," Katya whispered.

Houston dropped his bike and came to them. He lifted Katya and Lily up together and handed Lily to the Redgun, who sat her down behind the handlebars.

"Move faster," the Redgun urged. "He's still out there."

Katya climbed up behind Houston, and they roared out of the clearing together, bumping up and down on the jagged terrain of slope. The whole way down, Katya felt eyes on her back.

*

Houston followed Pixie to the foot of the mountain and toward a shed hidden in a copse. They parked their bikes, and Pixie punched a code into a keypad and led them inside the shed.

Inside were two black Jeep Wranglers standing tall on all-terrain run-flat tires. Pixie threw Houston a set of keys.

"Get your asses out of here," she ordered.

"You're coming with us," Houston said.

"I have to get back to my people." She looked at Lily. "Get her safe. We'll find you when things settle down."

Houston nodded.

"It's Archie," she said.

"What's that?"

"My name. You wanted to know—it's Archie."

"Is that short for something?"

"Archana."

"Beautiful name."

"Yeah, yeah. C'mon, go."

Lily ran up to Archie and hugged her. "Bye, Archie."

"Stay strong, little one."

"Thank you," Katya said from the passenger side, her voice still hoarse.

Houston strapped Lily into the back seat and started up the Jeep. The engine woke with a muscular growl. Archie stood by the doors and watched as they drove out of the shed. Houston glanced in the rearview mirror as they trundled off the dirt and onto the road, but by then, Archie was gone.

42

Through the windshield, the mountain road curved downward, colored a crisp electronic blue and overlaid with white data. *Cool trick*, Houston thought.

The Wrangler was outfitted with a night vision windshield that allowed him to see the road clearly even with the headlights off. Unfortunately, as far as Houston could tell, it had no tech designed to keep the driver awake.

Houston rubbed his eyes. The adrenaline was seeping away, exhaustion creeping up behind it. Next to him, Katya slumped in her seat, flexing the tension out of her jaw. Behind them, Lily sat quietly, huddled underneath Katya's jacket.

"Where are we going?" Katya asked.

"Don't know. We need to put some distance between us and here."

"River Town?"

Houston shook his head. "No."

Katya flexed her jaw again. She looked out the window for some time. "I've never seen anything like that," she said.

"Like what?" Houston asked.

"A Special like that, who . . . who made me feel so hopeless."

"The man in the black hat?" Houston had seen a glimpse of the man in the woods as he and Archana had raced up to him.

Katya straightened up and gathered her thoughts, her mind still in the wooded clearing. "When he appeared, all the light went out of the world. Everything I've ever thought was important and good was stolen. Have you ever felt like that, like all you wanted to do was die?"

Houston shrugged. "You're alive. That's all that's important now."

Katya bit her lip. "I never thought something like that could exist in this world."

"Maybe he's a Gray Face," Houston said. "One of their kinetics."

"No," Lily said from the back, her voice startling them with its certainty. "He's one of *them*."

Katya turned around in her seat. "One of whom?"

Lily's eyes locked with hers for a long moment. When she finally spoke, her voice was flat and hard. "Frontier."

A cold silence fell over the car. Beneath them, the tires trundled over asphalt, and the dark faces of the mountains pressed in closer from both sides.

Houston met Lily's eyes in the rearview mirror. "The Snake Mother sent him?"

"No," she said, her voice trembling. "I know the Snake Mother. I know her Gift. He wasn't one of hers—not anymore."

"I don't understand," Houston said.

"Lily," Katya interjected, sensing Lily's unease, "you don't have to talk about this if you don't want to."

Lily sat up in her seat and took a deep breath, steadying herself. "I've seen how the Frontier live. There's so many of them, but they're all part of one body—the Snake Mother's body. They are her children, and they would burn down *everything* for her. But the man in the hat—" Lily looked at her hands. "He's different. He is alone."

"What does that mean?" Katya asked. "Alone?"

"A Gift like his . . ." Lily drifted off into her other world before returning with a sharp blink of the eyes. "He was once one of the Warborn."

"Fuck," Houston cursed under his breath.

"The Warborn," Lily continued, "are the Snake Mother's guardians—the strongest of all her warriors. This man was once part of them, but now he walks alone. His Gifts came from the body of the Mother, but she is not his master anymore. He has no master now."

"Someone hired him," Houston said.

Katya looked at Houston. "Faraz."

Houston gripped the steering wheel, feeling the cords tighten along the back of his neck. Faraz's warning returned, a tumor swelling in his memory: *They will reach into the darkness and bring back the nightmares.*

That they had done.

Soon they would arrive at the bottom of this mountain, and . . . then what? Where in the Kingdom could they safely hide from a Warborn?

"Do you think Carmen is still alive?" Katya asked.

"I hope so," Houston said.

"Me too," Lily chimed in from the back.

A thought struck Houston. "The Reds are tracking us."

"What?" Katya asked.

"The Reds install tracking devices in all their vehicles. All we need to do is lie low for a few hours, and Carmen will find us." Houston pointed to the glove compartment. "See if there's a map in there. We need to find the closest town."

Katya reached into the back of the glove compartment and pulled out a rectangular device. "What's this?"

"That's an Owl-Sight," Houston said. Katya just stared at him blankly. "It's a spec sensor," he explained.

"Don't use that word," Lily warned.

"*Special* sensor. Happy?" Houston smiled in the rearview.

He saw Lily holding her left arm, the mangled Clamp around her wrist. "What happened to your arm?"

"Bruised it in the helicopter."

"Does it still hurt?" Katya asked.

Lily shrugged. "Eh."

"Brave girl," Houston said.

Katya switched on the Owl-Sight. Immediately, a line of red lights blinked across its side and it emitted a series of sharp, insistent *beeps.* Katya turned the device around in her hands, frowning. "How do you stop it from beeping?"

Houston took the sensor and held it back toward Lily. "Lily, place your thumb on that black square on the back. Yeah, that one. Now press your thumb down. Keep pressing." The beeping stopped, and the line of lights extinguished. Houston took the sensor back and placed it on the dash.

"What did you just do?" Katya asked.

"Keyed it into Lily's spectrum. It won't see her as a threat anymore."

"So it just beeps when it detects other Specials?"

"Exactly."

The road curved up again, the mountain's face thick and wide ahead of them. Houston pressed the gas and pushed the truck up the slope as Katya continued searching for a map.

Beep.

Houston's eyes darted toward the Owl-Sight. A single red light burned along its side before dying abruptly.

"What was that?" Lily asked.

Houston kept watching the Owl-Sight. "Nothing," he finally said. "These things act up sometimes."

Beep.

The red light flashed again. Houston caught Katya's eye.

Beep. Beep.

Two red lights flashed along the line. Houston's jaw tightened.

The lights were a proximity warning, which meant that if there was a Special out there, that Special was getting closer.

Houston drew his rifle onto his lap. Katya slapped a fresh cylinder into the Hammer. Houston stared at the two red lights.

For a moment, the lights hung in there stubbornly. Then the second light disappeared, leaving only one.

Houston exhaled. Katya lowered the Hammer.

And then all the lights lit up like a Christmas tree.

Beep, beep, beep, beep!

A dark shape bloomed in Houston's rearview mirror, launching high off the road and into the air.

Crash! The roof bent inward. Houston spun the wheel, throwing the jeep into a violent turn. A tomahawk slashed through the ceiling, passing inches from Houston's scalp.

The Star-Spangled Hammer boomed in the confined space, Katya blasting rounds through the ceiling. The blue expanse beyond the windshield turned black as the attacker leapt off the roof and onto the hood. Houston yanked the wheel harshly to the right.

Katya's shots smashed uselessly against the bulletproof glass in frosted spiderwebs. The night vision optics pixelated and died in the onslaught.

Shards of glass scraped across Houston's neck as the tomahawk tore chunks out of the windshield. He spun the wheel hard to the left. He heard himself grunt as the truck ricocheted off the guardrail with a shuddering blow and then spiraled back toward the mountain wall.

They hit side-on with a loud *crunch*. The truck boomeranged off the wall with a dull rattle, jerking Houston's head violently. The truck's spin stalled in the middle of the road, a cloud of smoke curling around its battered frame.

Houston's face burned where the airbag had hit him. With great pain, he turned his head. Katya was pressed against her seat by the airbag. Her eyes were closed but she moaned softly.

Houston unlatched his seat belt and felt the muscles strain along his war wound as he checked on Lily. She was in the gap between the seats, curled up in a ball. She squinted at Houston and picked herself up.

Somewhere in the car, the Owl-Sight was still beeping.

"Houston." Lily pointed toward the windshield.

The Warborn rose to his feet twenty feet ahead of them, where the impact had thrown him. In the space between him and the truck, the moonlight winked across the blades of the twin tomahawks lying on the asphalt. Through the cracked glass, Houston could feel the Warborn's eyes fall on him, sharp as cut stone.

"Get down," Houston growled at Lily. He threw open his door and dropped onto the road. Using the door as cover he brought up his rifle and locked the Special in its sights.

He realized at that moment how badly the crash had hurt him. His eyes watered, and his body swayed unsteadily. His grip on the gun was shaky as his brain reeled desperately to realign its axis.

Longhorn took a step forward. Houston fired a burst that went wide, skimming past the Warborn's shifting body. Houston bit down and unleashed another salvo, but his target moved again, a time-lapse horror untethered to the laws of reality.

The man ducked and rolled into a crouch, the harsh glint of metal in his hands.

"Houston!" He heard Lily's scream too late. His ears popped as the warped air arrived, followed by the spinning tomahawk. The blade cleaved his rifle in two and continued right through the top of his left shoulder. He fell, screaming. Pain tore through him, slithering, spiked coils squeezing his insides. Houston felt the man's black aura fall over him, perching on his carcass and spreading its skeletal wings.

The car door opened behind him. He heard feet hit the ground, and then Lily was by his side. He looked up at her as she knelt next to him and touched his shoulder. The pain of the wound dissipated like steam. "Stay with me," she whispered in his ear.

She lifted the bloody tomahawk off the ground. For a moment, she struggled with its weight in her small hands. But then she braced her feet and swung it down with surprising strength. Houston heard the tomahawk crack against metal. Lily dropped the tomahawk onto the road and then, a second later, dropped something else on top of it with a clanking sound. Two black rinds rolled on the asphalt and tipped over.

The Clamp. Houston stared at the cloven bracelet lying five feet away, abandoned in Lily's wake as she kept walking, her eyes focused on the man in the hat, who waited for her with a predatory patience.

Houston tried to reach for her, but she was gone.

The man squatted down on the balls of his feet and held out his hand. Lily stopped ten feet away from him.

And then Houston felt it—that same electricity from that night in Ringwood, when Lily had reached out from the truck and saved him.

Except this was more powerful—*much* more powerful.

White light poured off her skin, brighter than the sun. Steam rose from the earth, and a powerful wind blew down the mountain, carrying with it whispers of an ancient language. The white light grew, encapsulating Lily and spinning the air around her in a swirling torrent, gathering mass and energy, growing larger and larger until it towered fifteen feet over Lily's head and stretched across the width of the road. Houston saw the truck rise off the ground and then felt his own body leave the earth and hover on a bed of stars.

Lily rose into the air and raised her arms out to her sides.

The white storm shook the world.

In the turbulence, Houston watched the man in the hat brace himself, trying to crawl forward as rocks, wind, and sky tore at him. Monstrous bolts of lightning shot down from the sky and scorched the Warborn, thunder rippling across the mountain with hurricane force. Houston gripped the truck's doorframe with white knuckles as the howling gale threatened to toss him down the mountain, whipping his body like a flag.

The wind died suddenly. Houston and the truck dropped to the ground. The white light dimmed and returned to its source.

Boulders lay across the road. The man in the hat was gone, a blackened blast crater warping the asphalt where he had once been.

Lily lay on her side, her ribcage rising and falling with labored breaths. Distant stars faded in and out of her aura. Houston tried to crawl toward her, but the pain in his left shoulder exploded. His cheek hit the rough asphalt, and his eyelids dropped like steel shutters.

He sank slowly into warm water, down to a depth where the pain was gone and all he could feel was Lily's heartbeat—a vibration that sounded like the voice of his mother, the songs of Bobby, and the music of the ocean against black cliffs.

43

The first light of the morning wedged its way past the tattered blinds and grazed the walls of the disheveled bedroom. Magnusson sat up on the bed and stretched, breathing deep into his core and settling his Gift across his limbs like warm water. He went to the windows and peered behind the blinds. Four floors below, the first hawkers were setting up their stalls across Seekers Port, the village slowly rising out of its slumber in the early sunlight.

"Mmm."

Magnusson watched Izzy moan and turn over in bed. She stretched her naked body and collapsed back into sleep with liquid ecstasy, her blue hair catching the light. Magnusson marveled at her beauty; she was blessed with the taut, limber energy of the young and desired, but like all beautiful young women, she was cursed with a fundamental misunderstanding of time: she thought she had more than she really did.

The moment General Sixkills had sent Magnusson to hunt down the Sun Angel, he knew Izzy would be his first stop. She had been his reliable asset in Seekers Port for three years, but this morning, on the verge of a clear, bright day, Magnusson knew her time had run out.

In Izzy's mind he was Dominic Foyle, a rakish, high-flying attaché of the Royal Diplomatic Corps, stationed out of Sovereign City and traveling the country on top secret Crown business. He knew the moment he scouted her in the Crosswinds bar three years ago that all she wanted was excitement and escape. Girls like Izzy desired more out of life—*expected* more from life than a shitty apartment and a sales job at the Wonder Emporium. Magnusson, as Attaché Foyle, could provide her that excitement, and she could provide him with a direct line to the Redblood underground through her employer—and part-time lover—the Mad Fox himself.

Last night, Izzy had told Magnusson many things.

She had been in the Mad Fox's apartment yesterday morning when Houston had come to visit. Otis had kicked her out, but then, just as Magnusson had trained her to do, she had waited outside the door and listened.

If Izzy's recollection was accurate, Houston had tried to barter the Sun Angel—the Unholy girl—back to the Red Bitch, using Otis as a fence.

For a few minutes, Magnusson just stared at the peeling wall across the bed. A chill formed at the base of his spine. If Houston had succeeded, that meant the Redbloods were in possession of an Unholy weapon system—a doomsday scenario.

"Come back to bed," Izzy purred, peeking at him from under the covers. "My shift doesn't start till noon."

Tempting, but Magnusson already had what he needed. He got dressed.

"Is this about what happened down south?" Izzy asked.

"What?"

"You know, that attack down south. I figured that's why you're here."

"Down south . . ." he said to himself.

She was looking at him strangely. "Why *are* you here, Royal Attaché Dominic Foyle?"

He turned away from the window. "You know not to ask that question."

"I like to pretend you're here for me."

"Sometimes I am."

"You think I'm dumb, don't you?"

"I think we help each other."

"And how exactly are you helping me?" She pursed her lips.

"I told you, when I—"

She cut him off with a raised hand and a roll of her eyes. "Yeah, yeah. When you can, you'll bring me to Sovereign. You'll buy me an apartment in the Flower District." She pushed herself up on her elbow, eyes flashing. "So is Sovereign even happening, or was everything you said bullshit?"

"It's happening," he said. "Sooner than you think."

Her eyes didn't leave him, glowering with suspicion. Her body tensed, ready to blow if he fed her one more stalling tactic, one more false promise.

"Tonight," he said. "Pack your things."

"Tonight?" She looked confused.

"Be ready to leave by five this afternoon. Take only what you need. You can buy the rest there."

Her anger bled off instantly. She unleashed a megawatt smile and hugged Magnusson so hard he couldn't breathe. She ran around the room squealing like an escaped convict.

"Coffee?" Magnusson asked.

"Yes, please!" Izzy came over and kissed him. "Thank you," she said.

Before stepping out into the living room, Magnusson paused. "What was it you were saying? About something happening down south?"

"Oh, that?" Izzy called out, hidden inside her closet, flinging dresses onto the bed. "I was partying with Otis last night—before you called, of course—and he started getting all these calls. I heard small bits and pieces—some sort of attack on Redblood camp down south. Virginia or something. Sounded like a lot of people were hurt. Anyway, he skipped town fast. Probably down there now." She popped her head out from the closet. "Shouldn't your people know about this? I thought the Diplomatic Corps knew everything that went on in the Kingdom."

"We do," he said. "We just like to play dumb."

Magnusson closed the door behind him and walked through the long, bohemian living room, his mind working over what he had just heard. The apartment was a squat, U-shaped design, and he had to cross the thin Moroccan rug and turn the corner to reach the surprisingly large kitchen at the end of the narrow hallway. As he emptied a bag of Arabica beans into the grinder, he was already charting flight paths to Virginia in his head.

But first, a cup of coffee. Then, eliminate Izzy. It would be a shame for the clock to run out on her blue-haired splendor, but Magnusson knew there was no other way.

No right. No wrong. Only the strong.

44

Houston bubbled back above the surface for an instant, breaking through a membrane of dark water. Pressure built in his ears, and a mechanical rumble vibrated up his spine and the back of his legs.

Airplane.

Above the drone of the plane's engines, he heard voices. Faces swam into focus above him. Had he seen them before?

Two faces: a young woman and a man. They prodded him, spoke to him. He didn't understand their words, but he recognized their tone, their demeanor. They were battlefield medics, and his prognosis was grim.

A pain chewed on his left shoulder—*that* pain, where the tomahawk had carved him and left a trail of lava.

He saw two more people watching him from their seats. The first was a man with brown eyes beneath blue spectacles. A yellow hibiscus shone on his field jacket. Houston recognized him from some faraway place. Next to the man, he saw Katya.

Don't worry, Kat, he wanted to say when he saw her stricken face. *It's only a flesh wound.*

By his side, he felt Lily before he saw her. Her aura drifted over him, pinks melting into the violets, drifting across a backdrop of starlit lapis. Her hand was in his, and he felt a reviving warmth creep up his arm and mist across his body. *Like a good Scotch.*

Then pain again, excruciating. What had the man in the hat taken from him? Something integral—a part of his soul he didn't know he needed so desperately. The tomahawk blade had taken his flesh, blood, and *hope*.

Warmth pumped into him from Lily's hand, returning to him what the man had taken, reconstituting him cell by cell with each beat of her heart.

The medics leaned over him and spoke urgently. A needle bit into the black furnace of his wound, and he screamed.

He sank back below the surface.

He wanted to take Katya and Lily with him so he wouldn't have to face the darkness alone again, but the black waters closed over him and he was gone from them.

No.

Pink and violet and white comets followed him down, breaking the darkness, surrounding him. He was not alone when he fell back into the dark.

*

Houston couldn't see the ocean yet, but he could hear it crashing against the shore. He moved downhill toward the sound, through a jungle unlike any he had seen before.

It glowed. Thick with trees and undergrowth, there were things here—living things—that burned with turquoise and white lights. They flitted and sang through the treetops, glittering like stars in the salted air. Houston didn't stop to study them. He knew he had to keep walking. He had to get to the ocean.

Halfway down the mountain, after he had slipped and stumbled for what felt like hours through the luminescent jungle, Houston saw the sea.

The ground leveled beneath him. Palm trees formed arches like church entrances, a black sand beach beyond them. The jungle behind him rustled and shimmered, announcing his arrival.

Houston heard a woman's laughter, warm and inviting, and he knew that when he found her, he would be home. He took one step onto the black sand.

"Not yet."

The voice snapped his eyes open. It came from behind him—Lily's voice.

He looked into the jungle. All the living lights had extinguished, leaving a heavy darkness. Then a constellation of violet, pink, and white lights drifted between the trees like a fog.

"Not yet."

"Why?" he asked.

She didn't answer. The woman on the beach laughed again.

Staring into the trees, watching the lights shift, Houston was certain Lily wouldn't speak again. He took a step back toward the ocean.

"You have something left to do."

This time, the voice was his own. It was in his head now, repeating the mantra—*something left to do.*

The beat of his own heart drowned out the crashing waves. He walked back into the jungle and touched the colored fog. His body lifted, then went instantly limp. A force beyond his control carried him upward, away from the black sand and away from the laughter that still rang in his ears. The surface rushed toward him, a flat, crystalline sheet of water, blue and black.

He hit the surface.

Voices.

Fire in his shoulder, dryness in his throat, a clammy sweat across his skin. The plane shook in the turbulence, the engines whining. In the cool, artificial air of the cabin, Houston took his first deep breaths.

Her hand was in his. Instinctively, he knew he was not going back down.

When he opened his eyes, all he saw was sunlight.

45

Magnusson brewed the coffee and let his gaze fall out the kitchen windows and onto the bodegas and electronics stores peddling stolen wares along Valley Road. He watched them quietly, letting the grisly mechanics of his imminent task lock into shape. He would make Izzy's death look like an accident—a single time-release bolt through the throat, a bolus of pure energy that would travel through her blood and bloom like a toxic rose in her brain arteries. When the authorities—if there even were such a thing in Seekers Port—found Izzy's corpse, they would chalk the cause of death up to a stroke and dump her in a shallow grave.

By then Magnusson would be in the wind, following the Sun Angel's trail to Virginia.

He was about to turn away from the window when he did a double take. He didn't understand why, but a face down on the street jarred him back to the present. At first glance, there was nothing extraordinary about the man standing across Valley Road, smoking a cigarette—dark jacket, blue jeans, lightweight boots, midthirties, maybe. He did not stand out; he didn't act strange; he was unremarkable in every way.

And yet . . .

Magnusson sidled to the window, careful not to create a silhouette.

The man's eyes scanned Izzy's building, rising up with considered nonchalance to the windows of her fourth-floor apartment.

Forgetting the coffee, Magnusson walked back to the bedroom. Izzy said something to him as he went to the window, but he wasn't listening.

There, just as he had expected, was another man on the street—dark haired and wiry, with sunbaked skin, a military-style green jacket, and lightweight boots.

But this man was moving. He strolled calmly, watchfully, toward the front entrance of Izzy's apartment building.

Magnusson turned away from the window. Izzy was trying on dresses and smiling at him. Had she set him up?

Magnusson smiled back and said, "Coffee's nearly ready."

In the living room, he opened the cheap curtains and found the third man in the crowd: taller, with long hair in a samurai knot, the mountainous muscles of his shoulders nearly breaching the fabric of his black windbreaker. He bore down on the building with the same catlike grace of the second man.

Quickly returning to the kitchen, Magnusson watched the cigarette man cross Valley Road and enter the building through the back door.

Three men. SSD? Redguns? Whoever they were, they had not come to talk. These three men were not the talking type—they were the type sent to make things bloody.

Magnusson *moved*. He grabbed his rucksack from its secure location in the hallway closet and extracted his spear.

"Coffee's in the kitchen," he called out to Izzy. "I'm going for a shower."

"Have fun!"

Magnusson locked himself inside the narrow bathroom and turned the shower on. The showerhead spat and sputtered, finally releasing a steady stream of hot water. He had a minute at most.

Magnusson twisted the spear's shaft, releasing the twelve-inch NightAlloy blade. It glistened in the steamy air. He kept the shaft retracted, adapting the long spear into a short sword for close-quarters combat. If there was a fight coming his way, the blade would be his only weapon.

He had two things working against him: first, the apartment with its U-shape, sharp corners, and narrow spaces was a perfect death funnel. In here, Magnusson's Gift of flight was neutralized, which meant his ability to evade and escape was gone. If the three men were Specials—as he was beginning to suspect—the confines of Izzy's apartment would dictate the terms of the coming fight: face to face, eye to eye, bolt for bloody bolt.

Second, at full capacity, the spear would *magnify* his Gift. The resulting destruction would turn this covert mission into a public nightmare.

Pressed against the wall next to the door, Magnusson controlled his breathing and melted into his own senses. He smelled the strong Arabica coffee cooling on the kitchen countertop. He heard Izzy singing to herself somewhere in the bedroom. And there, underneath the pitch of her voice, he heard the shuffling of feet outside the front door as the men primed themselves for their gruesome task.

He was outnumbered, but Magnusson had one thing going for him: the element of surprise.

The three men would think they had surprise on *their* side, but they had been woefully misinformed. No one, not even the Frontier Scouts, attacked a Spearhead Silverback with only three men. It would be the last mistake of their lives.

The steam moistened the room. Water sprayed on the shower tiles in a rhythmic patter.

The men made very little sound when they entered the apartment. The door swung open and their boots slid over the wooden floor in faint, rapid whispers.

He heard the impact of skin on skin and Izzy's half scream before she went silent. The hushed footsteps left the bedroom and moved across the living room, toward him.

Magnusson stretched his fingers and let his Gift ride along the tide of his adrenaline, priming his limbs for the terrible violence that was to come.

A killing blow with the Gift was immensely difficult to master, especially a blow powerful enough to eliminate another Special. But to kill silently, like a Spearhead Silverback, required a level of virtuosity that only a devoted few could ever attain.

What Magnusson was about to do, outnumbered and undercover, was an art—a fusion of focus, timing, and complete awareness of one's environment.

The footsteps grew louder along the hallway—only one set.

Perfect. Magnusson gripped the brass doorknob and clenched his core. Waves of his Gift raced from his solar plexus up his spine and through his arm. He felt the energy pass through his clenched fingers and amass inside the doorknob like a rapidly brightening bulb, traveling into the knob on the hallway side. His palm grew hot. He willed his heart rate steady.

The intruder reached the bathroom door.

Magnusson sensed his presence like heat through the wood, felt the roughness of the man's palm as he gripped the doorknob and turned it open.

Now.

Magnusson unclenched his fist. All the energy trapped in the doorknob released in one violent rush and exploded on the other side with a muffled *crack*. Magnusson threw the door open and rolled into the hall.

A line of concentrated heat brushed over his shoulder blades. The bolt lanced overhead and hit the falling water behind him, instantly boiling it into a cloud of steam.

Magnusson rolled upright, his bare feet unsteady on a slick pool of blood. Cigarette Man was up against the wall, cradling the bloody stump of his right arm and hissing in pain.

Movement on his periphery. The two other intruders barked at each other, racing down the hall toward him. Green Jacket in the lead, and the big boy with the samurai knot sprinting up behind.

Magnusson fired two slicer bolts down the hall. The two men somersaulted in perfect unison over the spinning discs and landed like cats.

Magnusson lifted the stunned cigarette man off the ground and whipped him around as a shield. The two attackers stood staggered, trying to get a bead on Magnusson as he swung their comrade in front of him from side to side.

A flash of metal swiped by Magnusson's head, blindingly fast. The blade crackled by his ear with dark energy before retreating. The two men wielded short swords, poking and prodding, aiming for Magnusson's exposed flesh behind their partner. The hallway was too narrow for both men to stand shoulder to shoulder, but they maneuvered themselves expertly, feinting and stutter-stepping, their blades stabbing.

Cigarette Man shook off the stun bolt and fought back. He writhed like an animal, wrenching his own shoulder nearly out of its socket to break free from Magnusson.

A sword nicked Magnusson's ribs, and another one traced the top of his left knee. Magnusson had to act fast. As long as their comrade was blocking their way, the other two attackers could not fire their bolts.

Magnusson, however, had no such restrictions.

Cigarette Man wrenched violently. Magnusson timed him, waited until his movement had passed its peak, then let go of his jacket collar and pressed his open palm against the center of his back.

Thoompf! The man's body muffled the power bolt—a rippling silver torpedo blew a hole clean through the man's torso and exploded out of his sternum with enough residual force to blast his companions back down the hallway.

The two men hit the floor, rolled, and leapt back onto their feet.

Magnusson let the body fall, focusing now on the two men. With his bare feet, he tried to get a solid foothold on the warped parquet, now wet with blood.

It was only then that he got a good look at the short swords the two men wielded. Two feet long, made of curved black metal engraved with snakes, their surfaces flickered between black and purple, pulsing with the lights of a dark, seething Gift—*Viper blades.*

Magnusson set his feet and unsheathed his short spear, the NightAlloy blade pressed out in front him.

"What are you snakefuckers waiting for?" he growled.

The two Frontier Scouts tore toward him.

The spear clashed against the first Viper blade with a satisfying *clang.* The second sword followed immediately after, parried away at the last second. Magnusson knew he was fighting two men who acted as one organism. Frontier Scouts always trained and fought in pairs. In battle, the pair was connected by a primal link like the tether that connects the wolf pack on the hunt, their attacks coordinated subconsciously. The blades came at him like pincers, chomping at his head, stomach, and legs. The Scouts danced between each other, moving so fast that Magnusson thought he was battling four men. His hands grew slick with sweat on the spear's shaft.

A Viper blade bit the outside of his right thigh. Another one carved a burning gash across his ribs. The fury of their attack pushed him against the wall, toppling shelves. He was being herded into a kill box.

Magnusson dropped to the floor. Every ounce of his weight plummeted down on his spear as he drove its blade through the small bones of Green Jacket's foot with an ugly *crunch*. Magnusson, both hands now free, grabbed Green Jacket's shins and unloaded a double shatter bolt.

Green Jacket screamed as the bolts disintegrated his shin bones. He collapsed onto his useless legs, the spear pinning his foot to the floor. Samurai Knot leapt over his partner, sword swinging.

Magnusson spun into the kitchen. Samurai Knot scraped his massive shoulders through the doorway and charged.

Magnusson ducked under his swing and uppercutted with his right fist, driving enough of his Gift into the punch to snap the Scout's head back. As the big man stumbled, Magnusson coiled his fingers around the still-steaming pot of coffee and swung. The pot exploded against the Scout's cheek in an explosion of glass and steam.

Samurai Knot howled and crashed backward into a bar cart. Magnusson lined up the kill shot, the Gift burning through his fists.

Pain shot up Magnusson's calf. He twisted around to see Green Jacket on the floor, his teeth clamped into Magnusson's leg.

It was a surreal sight, but one Magnusson had come to expect from years of battling the Frontier Nation. Green Jacket had crawled with two shattered legs into the kitchen to get back into the fight. These snakefuckers had no quit in them. He respected that.

He tossed Green Jacket off his leg and gathered a mass of energy into his right foot before *stomping* it down on Green Jacket's skull with a wet *crack*. He spun back to Samurai Knot.

The kick glanced off Magnusson's temple with enough force to lift him off his feet. He toppled sideways into the hallway, his elbows smacking on the floor. His vision turned to water, and blood flooded his teeth.

Samurai Knot, breathing like a bear, followed him out. He reached Magnusson in one step and swung the Viper blade down toward his skull. But Magnusson had started his counterattack a split second before the Scout. He was launching upward as the blade came down, moving inside the bigger man's reach and thrusting his palm into the soft flesh beneath his jaw. Magnusson clasped his fingers around the hard edges of bone and fired.

Whoompf! The silenced bolt tore through the man's head like a javelin, cracking his skull open at the crown and painting the ceiling red. The big man gurgled and fell forward with a heavy thud.

Blood pounded in Magnusson's ears as he steadied himself against a wall.

He had been here many times before, in the aftermath of bloodshed—a lonely, unsettling place as forlorn and as dark as the space between planets. He closed his eyes and forced himself to breathe slowly.

And then it hit him. His eyes snapped open.

This attack wasn't over yet.

The Cigarette Man, Green Jacket, and Samurai Knot—three broken corpses. He lifted his spear off the ground, slick with crimson, and braced himself.

Frontier Scouts always hunted in pairs. The fourth Scout was still out there.

Magnusson listened, finding the sounds in his environment that did not belong. The shower was still running. Outside, he heard the voices of hawkers and buyers as they haggled and crowed. He crept forward, his feet soundless on the hallway floor as he edged into the living room.

The fourth Scout stood on the edge of the bedroom door. Her face was sharp and bony, her dark brown eyes following Magnusson intently. The lean muscles of her right arm were crooked around Izzy's neck, a black dagger biting into the girl's pale throat.

Izzy's mouth was covered in black tape, and her cheeks were wet with streaming tears.

But Magnusson was focused on the Scout's other arm, which was pointed toward him and crackling with a virulent purple Gift from elbow to wrist.

Magnusson stood very still. He had seen what a Scout power bolt like that could do to a man.

"You're good, for a goldspawn," the Scout rasped, "but are you fast enough to kill me before I kill you?"

"I was fast enough to kill your partner." Magnusson took a step forward.

She hardened the muscles of her arm, the purple cloud sizzling. "Make your move, goldspawn."

"You Scouts are a long way from home."

The woman bared her teeth and dug the dagger into Izzy's flesh. "Where is the girl?"

"What girl?"

Izzy screamed into the tape as the dagger pierced her skin and drew blood. The Scout took a step forward, the purple cloud bristling with sparks. "Lie to me one more time."

"You want the Unholy," Magnusson said.

"Where is she?"

"She was here. I don't know where she is now." Magnusson flexed his feet, feeling the rough wool of the Moroccan rug beneath him. "But I suggest you give up your search."

The Scout growled. "She is ours. She belongs to *us*."

Magnusson kept his eyes on her while he focused a sliver of his Gift into his feet. When he felt his soles heating up, he softly exhaled the Gift into the rug. Invisible cords of destruction seeped into the cheap fibers. "Forget about this and walk out of here," he said. "You don't want to die this far away from your Snake Mother."

"Don't *ever* take her name, infidel!" she hissed, taking another angry step forward—onto the rug. "You and your false god king will bow before her power. Every last one—"

But she never finished her thought. Magnusson, having lured her onto the rug, unleashed the coiled Gift right then. With one sharp exhalation, he shot it violently through the atoms of the wool and ignited it in a burst of silver flame beneath the Scout's boots. The flame flashed and shot up the Scout's legs, forcing her to drop Izzy as she fell backwards, gasping.

Magnusson flicked out a fusillade of stun bolts, hitting the Scout square in the chest. She tumbled to the floor, the purple nimbus around her weapon arm evaporating. Two quick steps, and Magnusson had her pinned down, one fist clamping her wrists above her head, the other crackling with silver lightning inches from her face.

"Now you're going to talk." He brought his fist closer, silver energy tracing her skin. "What do you want with the Unholy?"

The woman spat in his face. Her legs were covered in third-degree burns, but she refused to show pain.

"What do you want with her?" Magnusson demanded.

The woman's grimace turned into a hellish grin. "The false gods will fall," she said serenely. "The Snake Mother rises."

Before Magnusson could react, she stuck out her tongue and gnashed her yellowed teeth down on it *hard*. Her eyes never left him, bulging with fanatic zeal as she swallowed the severed tip of her tongue and began to choke on it. She writhed furiously under Magnusson, spitting up bloody saliva and still grinning, still defying him despite her agony.

He ended her suffering with a kill bolt to the head.

Izzy was curled up against the wall. The sound of her muffled cries grated on Magnusson's nerves. He lifted her up and sat her down in an armchair. He put a finger to his lips.

"Not a sound when I take this off," he said, touching the tape. "Do you understand?"

But she was beyond understanding. Her eyes bulged with fear, incapable of reason.

Magnusson looked into those once-beautiful green eyes. He ran a hand through her long blue hair, enjoying it one last time before placing his palm over the crown of her head.

The shudder bolt overloaded the circuits in her brain as every nerve in her body swelled and burst. The bolt had gotten its name because of the way its victims shuddered once before they died.

Izzy was no exception.

*

Total dark.

The words were a joke to Magnusson now. Five corpses, a shattered apartment, and blood everywhere.

He stood for a few moments, absorbing the carnage. He had checked the pockets of all the Frontier agents. They all carried perfectly forged New Hampshire ID cards. He didn't have the tech to confirm it, but he was certain they were all implanted with illegal Gold Stamps under their skin too.

He crinkled his nose. The stench of the female Scout's burned flesh clung to the walls.

This mess needed to disappear—fast.

He went into the bedroom and dialed a number on his phone. He let it ring three times and then hung up. He waited a total of thirty seconds before his contact called back.

"I'm in town," he said into the phone. "Need help with the local customs. Fast."

The woman on the other end laughed, a hard, shaking bark that Magnusson had never grown accustomed to. "Well, sod all Mags," she said. "You stop by my neighborhood without so much as a hello, and now you need my help? Oh, in that case, let me just drop absolutely all my plans for today and come scooting over. It's not like I do anything important for a living."

46

Oh, heavens, no. She's dead.

Caspar was struck with the thought the moment he saw Veena slumped along an elegant chaise in her Starlet Manor studio. Her jade romper was crumpled, her lipstick smeared, and her bare right foot hung over the chair arm. The whites of her eyes shone through half-closed lids.

She looked, Caspar thought, like a beautiful sea nymph grounded on dry land.

"She's alive," Militiaman Abel said. "Her breathing is shallow, but we didn't see any immediate need to intervene before you arrived, Master Caspar."

Caspar exhaled. *Thank god.*

The Lady in the Veil hovered behind him, unnerving him. She put her ear very close to Veena's mouth and ran an alabaster hand along the top of Veena's chest.

"Her heartbeat is slow," the Lady said.

Caspar had spent the whole night searching for Veena after leaving his sister's Grand Salon. The last time he had heard from Veena was after her disastrous visit to the House of Azaleas. He had sent a car to pick her up from Williamsburg, but she was nowhere to be found. His Militiamen had covertly scoured Sovereign City looking for her.

But it wasn't until Militiaman Abel had returned to check Starlet Manor for the fourth time that he had stumbled upon Veena in her studio. As Caspar, Militiaman Karl, and the Lady had entered the home, the sun was already in the sky, but it didn't seem to touch the insides of Starlet Manor.

Now Caspar watched Veena's chest rise and fall with each short breath. He stepped back from the chaise, and it was only then that he noticed the studio around them.

It looked like Veena had set off a grenade in here. A giant picture frame leaned against the wall. Whatever picture had once been inside was now cut up and glued to the tailor's dummy in a macabre collage. General Sixkills's face glared at Caspar from the dummy's bust. He saw Veena's mother, Mable, stapled onto a sheath of black lace along the dummy's midriff. A pair of scissors lay by Veena's outstretched arm.

"Give me a flashlight," Caspar said, kneeling down next to Veena. Karl handed him one, and in the small circle of light, Caspar immediately found the sprinkles of dried white powder around Veena's left nostril. "Moxi."

The Lady pierced him with a look. "This is supposed to be a clean house. Where did she get it?"

"Well, our dear Veena Sixkills here is nothing if not an enterprising young woman." Caspar stood and turned to Karl, suddenly in his element. "Karl, give me the spray."

Within Caspar's rarefied social circle, Moxi was a party favor—an expected appetizer served at get-togethers. Caspar had fought his own hellish battles against Moxi for most of his life, but it wasn't until He Who Knows All had shown him a higher path that he'd left his addiction behind for good. He thought Veena had undergone a similar awakening. But he couldn't blame her for relapsing—the drug never really left you.

Moxi had first appeared during the war in the Specials' military field hospitals as a super painkiller. Special soldiers became the first addicts, and their addictions carried on into the aftermath, serviced by the drug cartels that rose like weeds in Texas, Arizona, and California.

Moxi, angel hair, silver sugar, YOLO powder, jet fuel. Call it what you wanted, but the high was euphoric, the comedown vicious. It had flooded the party circuits of Los Angeles, Miami, and Sovereign City like a silver-tinged typhoon. Even after the cartels fell to Frontier, the spigot never ran dry. Except now, every time you bought a gram of Moxi, you were funding the Snake Mother and her army of savages. Not that the addicts really gave a shit.

Caspar had watched friends and lovers overdose and die right in front of him. He had been clean for two years now, but he still never left home without the Feloxin spray.

Karl handed him the Feloxin, a clear syringe with a white pyramidal tip. He inserted the thick tip into Veena's left nostril and pressed the plunger all the way down with his thumb. A fine mist blew into her nose.

She didn't move a muscle. Caspar stepped back.

"What happens now?" The Lady asked.

"Nothing. Or something." Caspar rubbed his eyes. "We just have to wait."

The Feloxin was the best opioid receptor antagonist on the market. Right now it was working rapidly in Veena's brain, binding to her opioid receptors before the Moxi could hijack them. At least, Caspar hoped so. Sometimes, even with the Feloxin, they didn't come back.

Veena coughed. A sputter heaved out of her chest. Her eyes fluttered for a moment, and she tried to form words. Then she closed her eyes again and sank into a heavy sleep.

Caspar checked his watch. They didn't have time for this.

"Abel." He called over the bodyguard. "Sting her."

Caspar moved away as the big Militiaman stood over Veena. He rubbed his coarse palms together, and with the firm movements of an expert, gripped the back of Veena's neck with his broad fingers.

"What is he doing?" The Lady asked.

"Watch."

Abel tightened his grip, and his Gift flooded Veena's body from hair to toenails. She gasped in shock and arched her back violently, her arms and legs thrashing.

Veena sat up on the chaise, blinking rapidly. Her eyes passed over the others but saw none of them. She swayed, pushed herself off the chaise, tottered on unwilling legs, and then threw up into a potted fern.

"Abel, find some water and food downstairs." Caspar turned to his other bodyguard. "Karl, gather your men here. *All* of them."

He met the Lady's gray eyes. "As for us,"—he paused as Veena retched loudly next to him—"we need to get our little Cinderella ready for the ball. Come. I'll start the shower."

*

Veena Sixkills came back to life slowly, a sad, sodden creature. She sat at the end of her bed, her hair wet, shivering in a black robe. Caspar and the Lady had scrubbed her hard under the cold shower, and she smelled of vanilla. Her eyes stared out at something invisible and terrifying in the distance.

Caspar had drawn all the curtains, keeping the sun out so as not to startle her. The primary symptoms of a Moxi comedown included confusion, nodding off, dry mouth, and aversion to bright lights. Veena displayed them all.

"Veena, did you hear me?" Caspar asked again.

Her eyes flickered over him.

"Veena, do you know Debashish Kumar?"

She mouthed something silently and looked away.

Caspar's face grew hot. Time was running out, and he had a dozen other questions he wanted to ask her. Why did you relapse? Where did you get the Moxi? And, having seen her naked in the shower, where did those awful bruises across your chest and throat come from? She looked like she had wrestled a jackhammer.

He paced, growing angrier and angrier. They had to do something about the new designer of Callista's dress—find him, sabotage him, do *something*. And for that, he needed Veena.

"Blood of a whore," Veena said, the words escaping her lips like a curse.

Caspar frowned. "What does that mean, darling? Blood of a whore?"

"Who am I?" She pinned him with desperate eyes. "Who am I? The blood of a whore." She spat it out, her voice louder, shriller. "The blood of a whore."

She was crying now, crumpling into herself. "That's all I am: a mistake." She hid her face behind her hands.

Caspar watched her cry for a few moments, her sobs swallowed by the cavernous bedroom. He knelt down and gently removed her hands from her face. He looked in her eyes and smiled.

And then he slapped her so hard it snapped her head sideways. She gaped at him, his handprint burning red on her cheek. Caspar clamped her by the neck and pulled her close. He backhanded the other side of her face.

"Do I have your attention now, you sordid little cunt? Because we are hours away from the biggest moment of our lives, and this damaged princess act of yours needs to end *now*."

Veena's face coiled into an ugly mask, and she pushed herself up off the bed. Caspar pushed her back down and slapped her again. The mask flew away, replaced by the face of a little girl, shocked and in pain.

"Everything is on the line, dear Vee. The Parade starts in less than sixteen hours, and we have no Sun Angel and no dress. You need to snap out of it and help me fix this. Otherwise, it's all over."

"I know," she said, tears streaming. "We're in so much danger. He knows."

Caspar's eyes narrowed. "What do you mean, 'he knows'?"

Veena's eyes fell on him for a brief terrified moment before darting away. "Nothing," she stammered. "It's just . . . Him." She glanced upward. "I let *Him* down."

Caspar watched her for a few seconds, a knot in his belly. She got up and paced the room.

"What do we do now, Caspar?" she asked, still not meeting his eyes.

"There is a way we can still salvage this."

"How?"

He told her about his meeting with Callista, and when he mentioned the designer of the new dress, Veena's eyes lit up with recognition.

"Deb? You're sure it's Deb Kumar?"

"Without question."

"Little Deb," she said to herself.

"Do you know him personally?" Caspar asked.

"Of course I know him. He used to be my assistant."

Hope swelled in Caspar's chest. "That's fabulous!"

Veena bit her lip. "Little Deb designing for the queen."

"Now, here's the important part, dear—the crux of the whole thing. First, do you know where to find him? And second, can you get him alone?"

"Yes and yes." Her hands pulled at each other. "What do you plan to do to him?"

He noticed the tension in her voice. "Are you *friends* with this man?"

She waved him off. "No. It's just . . . I mean . . . we can't kill him."

"Veena, we have no friends anymore. What we do, we do for He Who Knows All. For the future."

"You don't understand, Caspar—this is the fashion world. Dying dramatically only *raises* your stature. If you kill Deb, all his work doubles in value. Triples. They'll be clawing each other's eyes out to get a hold of his designs."

"Ah. So if he dies—"

"Callista would wear a tampon covered in tinsel if it was the last work of a tragic young talent."

"So what do we do?"

Veena circled the room, her strength returning. "Callista is working against the clock. She recruited him last night for the dress, which you say is already designed but not fitted to her yet. Deb will be racing to finish before the Parade at midnight tonight."

"We could damage the dress? Leave her no choice but to revert back to the Peacock Gown?"

"Caspar," she fixed him now with her eyes, shaking her head. "Do you even know your own sister?"

"Based on her attempted pass at you yesterday, apparently not."

She ignored that. "Damage the dress, and you raise suspicions. We can't sabotage the dress without going through Deb, which instantly puts the spotlight on us as the number-one suspects. No, Caspar. *Think.* What is it that your precious little sister fears most of all?"

It dawned on him immediately. "Looking imperfect."

"Smart boy. The dress isn't our target—it's Deb's reputation. Create enough of a stench around him, and Queen Callista will run back to the Peacock Gown so fast her thighs will chafe."

"And I'm confident that you know exactly how to muddy up our dear little Deb?"

Veena walked up to Caspar proudly and slapped him full force across the face.

He floundered backward, cheek stinging. Veena's eyes flashed with rage. "Just in case you forgot who you were dealing with, you little faggot. Of course I know how to do it. I'm Veena fucking

Sixkills, and if you put your hands on me again, I will castrate you myself and throw your shriveled little prunes into the Emerald Ring. Now get your prancing ass out of my bedroom. I need to get dressed. We leave for Sovereign City in fifteen."

As Caspar Von Arx, stunned and humiliated, closed the bedroom doors behind him, he knew without a shadow of a doubt that once Veena Sixkills had outlived her usefulness, there was only one thing left for him to do—he would coil his fingers around her frail white throat and pull the life out of her slowly, joyful in the knowledge that she was feeling every second of it.

47

The storm had left the mountains before dawn, but the wind was still strong and the ground was heavy with rainwater. Longhorn's feet found the dry rocks, and he moved through the forest without leaving a trail. The air was crisp and cold, carrying the good, clean scent of blood.

The Redblood compound was four miles behind him, a shattered, abandoned ruin—but not for much longer. The Gray Faces would descend on the wreckage within the hour. They would scatter like cockroaches across the rubble, reading the energy waves and piecing together an Emotional Spectrum File to determine the mindset and motives of the attacker.

Longhorn did not fear the Gray Faces. Their ESF would lead them to Tommy, and they would never know Longhorn existed.

A branch cracked to his right. A shiver of leaves. Longhorn stood very still, reading the air. A small animal, nothing more. He continued across a narrow stream and stayed on the scent—the scent of a survivor.

The Reds had left behind one of their wounded.

His bird had found the survivor first, when the sun was still hidden behind the mountains. Now the crow hovered a mile ahead of him, gliding in an ominous ring above the treetops, marking the body's location. Longhorn tracked the survivor over shallow ridges and thick walls of oaks and poplars, the smell of distress intensifying with each step.

Pain burned across Longhorn's back and shoulders again. He welcomed it, forcing his body to feel every inch of it.

After the girl had torn him off the mountainside with a bolt of lightning, he had awoken at dawn in a bramble patch, feeling pain like he had never felt before. He had boiled acorns and the inner bark of an oak tree in water and then soaked rags in the brown solution. When the rags cooled, he had placed them on the ugly slash of crisped skin along his back, gritting his teeth as the wound renewed its fire.

Longhorn had listened to what the wound was telling him.

Every Special he had faced carried the potential for death in their Gift. But the girl—she had carried something very different. He had underestimated her. He would not make that mistake again.

He dropped down a shallow slope and entered the radius of the bird's flight. She squawked and dipped down below the canopies, landing on a rock in the crystal waters of a stream.

The survivor watched Longhorn approach with icy blue eyes. Wounded and afraid, he had crawled toward the stream and dug a shallow hole for himself under the shade of an elm tree.

The survivor whimpered. Longhorn knelt next to the husky. He ran a hand across its fur until he found the wetness—a shrapnel wound along the left flank, deep in the meaty muscle of the left hind leg. Blood pooled in the dirt below.

They watched the water together for a while. The dog's heart was slowing. It lay its head between its paws and closed its eyes. Longhorn gripped the meat of the Husky's muscular neck and focused his Gift. The muscle of his palm parted, and the stinger stabbed into the dog's spine.

He corkscrewed through the husky's memory, riding giant double helixes of scent and sensation. There was no past or future, simply one extended moment, the bristling, bright clarity of the now.

Running over grass, chasing squirrels, wet earth beneath the paws, a woman's voice resonating with love, harsher voices triggering subconscious alarms and raising the hackles. Smells bloomed like orchids, a sensory tapestry woven into threads large and small—auras vibrating around every living thing.

Longhorn slipped through the memories, absorbing information in blinks, narrowing down his focus to the last forty-eight hours.

He saw the girl, her aura the brightest white he'd ever seen.

He skipped through time again, speeding up and slowing down the husky's life like a tape.

Stop. There. The thief, Houston Holt. Longhorn watched through the husky's eyes as Houston entered a large conference room. A bearded man spoke to him.

"These are valid as papers of passage," the bearded man said to Houston. "You will have to present them at your local Border Patrol Processing Center to obtain the Gold Stamp. However, their validity is contingent upon you reporting to Augustus Sky immediately."

Longhorn detached himself from the dog's memory and floated back to the present. He opened his eyes and retracted his stinger. The dog shuddered and turned to him expectantly. The wind had grown colder.

Longhorn unsheathed his dagger. He scratched the husky between the ears, his other hand tracing the blade along its fur, below its heart.

"No more pain," he said. The dog turned to the stream.

He plunged the dagger in.

*

The black Cessna waited under a forest camouflage net on the southern edge of the hidden airfield. Longhorn pulled off the netting and settled inside the cockpit.

He slid the onboard computer out of its compartment and tapped in Augustus Sky's name. He searched Sky's known residences. He narrowed the search down to local residences and neighboring states. Houston Holt had been wounded, and his companions would need to get him to the closest ally possible.

The computer calculated silently, bouncing its signal off a half dozen illegal satellites, including a United Nations spy orbital cruising over the Mexican border.

The computer listed its results. Longhorn needed only a glance to know where Houston was headed.

He unstrapped his tomahawk holsters and placed them on the passenger seat. He rehydrated, finishing a liter of water, before starting up the Cessna's engines and keying his destination into the computer. It produced a flight path to an airfield four miles away from Houston's presumed location.

The control tower, little more than a shed with an antenna array, cleared him for takeoff. He was airborne in minutes.

48

Magnusson waited by the door as footsteps came up the stairs toward Izzy's apartment. The door was unlocked, and the woman showed herself inside.

"Mags." She nodded in his general direction before her attention fell on the corpses of Izzy and the female Scout on the living room floor.

"There's three more in the hallway," Magnusson said.

"Well, of course there are," she said, her English accent crisp and unfettered by the two decades she had spent out of her homeland. "There's always more sodding corpses when you're around."

She shook her head in exasperation, but Magnusson knew better than anyone how much she enjoyed her work. She took off her heavy woolen overcoat, the one she wore year-round regardless of the weather, and tossed it to Magnusson.

"I suppose I'll take a stroll around," she said as she turned into the hallway, her sensible black flats soundless on the parquet, her wedding band glinting on a hand strong enough to crush a larynx.

With her outdated hairstyle and frumpy pantsuit, it was easy to mistake the Englishwoman for a harried civil servant—which, Magnusson knew, was the point. Officially, she was a Senior Project Manager for the understaffed and underutilized Public Works Office, tasked with surveying the Kingdom's crumbling infrastructure and allocating construction funds. The deception allowed her to do her real work: assimilate, observe, and vanish—the creed of her true employers. When the Kingdom's enemies came knocking, Magnusson knew there were few Gray Faces better suited to facing them down than SSD Special Agent Fenicia Farrows.

He heard her humming in the hallway, making small remarks to herself as she absorbed every detail of the carnage. Magnusson moved to the bedroom and waited on the bed, the shades blocking out the sun.

Fenicia returned to the living room, deftly navigating the bloodstained floor. She knelt next to the dead female Scout and studied her from head to toe. Next, she scanned Izzy's corpse and stood with a heavy sigh.

"God, I remember when I had a waistline like that. Now just looking at these skinny twats gives me a tumor." She stepped over the bodies into the bedroom and leaned against the doorframe, looking at Magnusson. "Before I give you the righteous bollocking you deserve, are you all right?"

"Yes."

She pointed her thumb behind her. "Quite a little squabble you had back there, eh?"

"They dropped in unannounced," he said.

"Don't you hate it when people do that?" She pulled a tangle of fluff out of her hair, her words pointed.

"I can't always tell you when I'm in your backyard."

"No. Not until you have to."

"Can you handle this?"

She looked at her watch. "Well, despite the fact that you've been an absolute sod about all of this . . . yes. Hand me my coat."

She dialed a number.

"Oh, poor dear," Fenicia said, looking down at Izzy while she held the phone to her ear. "Such a tragedy. I would kill my own husband to have an arse like yours."

*

The SSD safe house was nestled in the wooded fringes of Seekers Port, hidden from view. The interior was simply decorated with far more color coordination and warmth than Magnusson thought the SSD were capable of.

After Fenicia led him inside, he showered and changed into fresh clothes. He put salve on his wounds and bandaged them. When he stepped out of the bathroom, Fenicia had tea ready.

"I know, I know," Fenicia said. "An Englishwoman drinking tea? I'm such a unique snowflake. Sit." She offered him a seat at the small table.

Magnusson sipped the fragrant tea. "Darjeeling?" he asked.

"Only the best." She opened a tin of Rich Tea biscuits and offered the tin to Magnusson. "Have one. I had them smuggled in from London."

Magnusson dipped the biscuit in the tea and bit off a chunk. He said nothing for a while, knowing that questions were on their way.

Fenicia did not disappoint. "Mags, usually I wouldn't ask what you're doing out here, but right now an SSD crew is scraping five carcasses off the walls of your girlfriend's house. I cashed in some rather large chips for you. I think, in the spirit of friendship and teatime, that a little sharing is in order."

"I have to fly solo on this one."

"Ah. So will you kill me once we're done here to maintain your cover?"

He met her wise brown eyes. "Never."

She raised her cup. "Good to know."

"How's the husband?" Magnusson asked.

"Don't change the subject."

"This is what friends talk about."

She rolled her eyes. "Mister Harold Farrows of the Royal Revenue Service is as titillating to my nether regions as ever.

You must stop by one of these days to meet him. He'll talk your ear off about the new inherited estate tax." She sipped her tea. "And how are the girls?"

"Oblivious to my existence."

"Ah, marriage and family—these are the good things, at least according to someone."

Magnusson smiled. Ever since they had first worked together seven years ago on a joint task force to stop the Redbloods from smuggling foreign fighters in through Mexican border tunnels, he had come to respect—and like—the indomitable Agent Farrows. Despite her best efforts at cynicism, he recognized her as one of his tribe—practical, smart, and dogged in her duty to her people.

But her bosses saw her differently. Her performance reviews often described her as "overly aggressive" and "insubordinate by default." They stalled her promotions, shifted her from the foreign desk to the now—in light of the ceasefire—middling role on the Redblood desk. Fenicia, disillusioned by the intractable bureaucracy and political knife fights at headquarters, literally jumped with glee at the chance to freelance—in violation of SSD protocol—for Spearhead.

Magnusson looked at her now. His experience told him that she already knew everything about the Unholy girl—possibly more than he did.

Her phone rang. She moved to the kitchen, where Magnusson heard her murmuring for a few seconds before hanging up. She returned to the table and sat down.

"That was my mop-up crew. They're wheeling your five dead chums out as we speak. Oh, and one more thing." Her eyes glinted like blades. "According to them, four of the bodies were Frontier agents. Shocking, eh?"

"Shocking indeed."

"Act thick all you want, Mags, but it's no coincidence that you ran into those Frontier Scouts." Fenicia plopped another sugar cube into her mug. "Scouts don't penetrate this deep into Crown territory for trinkets. As a matter of fact, neither do Spearhead Silverbacks. At least, not without informing their friends."

Before Magnusson could respond, he felt a crawling sensation behind his eyes. Velvet fingers traced the inside of his skull, pulling open the drawers of his mind—the opening salvo of a telepathic interrogation. Magnusson sat up and glared at Fenicia. "Don't do that, Fenicia."

The fingers pulled away as if on a string. "Sorry. Investigator's habit."

Magnusson rose. "I have to go."

"Finish your tea first." She smiled. "And at least hear me out."

Magnusson settled back into his seat.

She ran a hand through her hair, catching it on a tangle of knots. After much struggling, she freed her hand and tapped the table. "I'm not thick, Mags. I have an inkling of what you were all after. And if I'm right, which I obviously am, then I am more convinced than ever that you are one hare-brained wanker."

"Do you know where it is?"

"That is the question, isn't it? The one everyone is asking."

"Everyone?"

Fenicia nodded. "So it seems. We've intercepted enough chatter from the Frontier to know that they seem quite miffed these days. Apparently, something was stolen from them—something they are now determined to retrieve."

The female Scout's face, teeth bared, returned to Magnusson's mind. *She is ours. She belongs to us.*

Fenicia continued, "But it gets better. Half the knobs at SSD are down in Virginia right now, crawling through the remains of a once-top secret military compound. According to my sources, the Red Bitch was there last night."

Magnusson kept a straight face. "How are the two connected?"

She smiled. "We run surveillance drones constantly over the mainland. Eight nights ago, our drone boys were ordered—discreetly, of course—to remove all surveillance assets from a small patch of Shenandoah, Virginia. As it happens, the exact place where the Red Bitch's compound was located. Are you putting all of this together?"

"An order like that had to come from high up."

"How high up is the question."

Magnusson sat back, a dark picture forming.

Fenicia spoke. "Whatever you and our Frontier friends are looking for was in that compound, which means that someone with a lot of juice in the Golden Fort has their eyes on the same prize."

"What's your theory?"

"I believe this ceasefire of ours is wholly based on the Redbloods exchanging their stolen Frontier goodies for peace."

"That's impossible," Magnusson said. "That would mean . . ." he stopped himself, the possibility too absurd.

"That His Majesty himself is involved." She finished her tea and put her cup down with a loud exhale.

Magnusson remembered the briefing file's description of the Unholy—a girl, eight or nine years of age. A child that left chaos in her wake.

"I won't impede your mission, Mags. I trust the General's judgement without question. But," Fenicia said, her eyes growing worried, "if you're after what I think you're after, then as your friend, I would be remiss if I didn't deliver a warning."

Magnusson knocked back what remained of his cold tea. He looked at her and waited.

"There is something else out there, hunting for the same thing you are."

"Something worse than four Frontier Scouts?"

She wasn't smiling. She put her cup down and looked out the window at the sun falling through the leaves. When she looked back at Magnusson, her eyes had changed. "We don't know what he is, exactly. We've seen his work—his victims. Whatever he leaves behind for us to find."

"An assassin," Magnusson said.

"A hunter. A highly gifted one. Over the years I've come across at least a dozen of his victims, and they all follow the same pattern: a high-value target protected behind impenetrable walls, killed by someone close to them. Murder-suicides, according to the official reports."

"But you believe differently," Magnusson said.

"In all these cases, after killing their victims, the supposed perpetrators always killed themselves in exceedingly gruesome ways, causing catastrophic damage above the neck. Shotgun blast at close range, self-immolation—you get the idea."

"They were Stringers."

"And their kinetic left a mark on them somewhere above the neck—evidence that had to be destroyed."

"And you think he's after the same thing I am?"

"This is a man who can create Stringers at will and control them with a precision we have never seen before. He's been off my radar for over a year now. I thought he was gone. But it seems like last night someone walked into a Redblood fortification bristling to the teeth with Redgun commandos and burned it all down to the ground. All to cover his true intent."

Magnusson finished her thought. "Retrieve the prize."

"I would bet Mister Farrows's piddling pension that the investigation will conclude it was an inside job—an attack by a disgruntled Redblood, who, I am sure, will have suffered catastrophic damage above the neck."

"If you're right—"

"I am."

"*If* you're right, then someone hired him to take out that compound. And that someone may now be in possession of what I'm looking for."

Fenicia watched him for some time, and it seemed like she was on the verge of something close to fear, tiptoeing on the edge of asking a Silverback to do the one thing they never could: back down. But in the end, she simply said, "The underworld has their own myths about this man. Stories you wouldn't believe—that you don't *want* to believe. In these stories, this man has a name." She paused and let the name uncoil off her tongue, bristling and barbed. "They call him Longhorn. And if he has what you are looking for, then you don't have much time, Mags." She checked her phone and typed out a quick message. "Have you heard of the outlaw airfields?"

"Unregulated airports. The wild west for short-hop smugglers."

"Smugglers, traffickers, thrill-seekers—a haven for literally anyone with a small plane and big secrets." She leaned forward, elbows on the table. "But as it happens, every single one of the killings I could trace back to Longhorn had one thing in common."

"What? "

"They were all ground attacks. Now, as you know very well, any Special that can attack from the air will do so. It is the safest, most efficient way to neutralize a target."

Magnusson scratched his jaw. "So Longhorn can't fly."

"Precisely. And each of the killings I suspect him of are not isolated to one part of the Kingdom. They range from coast to coast."

"He could be a speeder," Magnusson said.

"Or he could be using the outlaw airfields." Fenicia cracked her fingers, getting into it now. "Last year, on a hunch, I started looking into the outlaw airfields in the areas where the attacks had taken place. A real barmy crowd in those places, I tell you. Closed down like vaults, but you know how I am—I batted my eyelashes and flashed some leg, and I was able to crack a few of the locals open. All of those airfields had records for a black Cessna arriving and leaving within twenty-four hours of the killings. Including," she said as she held up her phone, "an airfield within six miles of the Redblood compound in Virginia. According to my source, a black Cessna just left the airfield a half hour ago."

Magnusson smiled. "Solid work, Special Agent Farrows."

She stood and curtsied. "I serve at the King's pleasure."

Magnusson rose and shouldered his rucksack. "You have my number."

"As soon as our friend lands, I'll let you know where."

They shook hands. Fenicia held on to his. "You're good, Mags, but you'll have to be at your best to face this man."

"Don't worry about me."

"I never worry about you. I worry about Harold's prostate and why, even though I'm immortal, my bum seems to sag a few more inches with each passing year. But you I don't worry about."

"If I meet this Longhorn, I'll bring him your regards."

"Do so, Master Chief Magnusson."

She followed him out the door. When he was halfway down the garden pathway, she called out to him, "Oh, one other thing."

He turned, waiting.

"When this is over, do you think you'll be making any trips out to London in the near future?"

"It's possible."

"I only ask," she continued, "because I'm running dreadfully low on Rich Tea biscuits."

"I'll pick up a case."

"Good lad. Only if it's not too much trouble. Also, maybe some real cheese and perhaps some marmalade." She closed her eyes and shook her head. "Oh God, how I miss the civilized world."

"Careful. Anyone listening might think you're a UN spy."

"Oh, Mags, at least let me have my nostalgia." She laughed that big, barreling peal of laughter that Magnusson could still hear even after she had shut the door.

49

The sound of waves had always soothed Katya as a child, and under normal circumstances, she would have welcomed a chance to be back by the ocean under the morning sun. But right now, she didn't know if they had been saved or imprisoned.

If it was a prison, it was the most luxurious one she had ever seen. She leaned against the railing of the home's second-floor terrace, overlooking the empty beach. The house was a massive hacienda with a pink roof, dark wood floors, and miles of windows. The rooms were cavernous but minimally furnished, and the only people here were the guards patrolling the home's perimeter below.

She'd counted at least fifteen of them since arriving. They wore simple clothes and moved like professionals. Katya couldn't spot any weapons on them, but she was certain they were packing.

Katya rubbed the sleep from her eyes. The horrors of last night were still fresh in her mind.

Their rescuers—or captors—had descended on their wrecked SUV out of the darkness of the mountains. Katya had still been in shock from the crash, her head swimming with feverish visions of the man in the hat attacking them, of Houston falling, of Lily . . . of Lily raining down fire and lightning, tearing the world apart.

Katya had a vague recollection of being moved to another car, followed by a stomach-churning race down the mountain. They had then been loaded onto a private jet, where the medics had given her hot tea and her strength returned slowly.

There was another man with the medics—the man in charge, who wore a yellow hibiscus, his eyes sharp behind blue-rimmed glasses. Katya had wanted to ask a hundred questions, but as the plane took off, everyone's focus had been on Houston.

The medics had worked on him the entire flight. Lily had held his hand, not saying one word. By the time the plane had landed and a van with darkened windows had brought them to the beach house, Houston had stabilized. The worst, it seemed, was over.

Houston was in the hacienda's master bedroom, sleeping under the watch of the medics. His face was pale. A thick gauze was wrapped around his left shoulder, held in place with medical tape. The medics told Katya he was over the hump, that he just needed rest and rehydration, but they refused to answer any of her queries about their location or identities.

"Ask the man in charge," the female medic had said before shooing her out of the room.

It seemed the reticence of their hosts had rubbed off on Lily as well. She had been quiet and distracted when Katya had found her on the patio, off in one of her parallel worlds. Eventually, Lily left the patio and walked out toward the sea. Katya was about to follow but realized that Lily needed to be alone. She watched Lily, free of the Clamp, pick up seashells along the shoreline, studying each one intently.

Maybe she could sense Katya's fear of her.

Katya saw what Lily had done to the Warborn on that mountainside, how she had rained down lightning and fire. The image was seared in Katya's memory—the terrible *cry* of the world ripping apart still in her ears. It was a power that couldn't—*shouldn't*—exist in a child.

Lily slid a stack of shells in her pocket and looked out at the sea. Watching her, Katya realized that Lily was proof of something beyond—something *larger*. She had opened Katya's eyes to mysteries—and horrors—hidden in the depths of the universe, and Katya didn't know if she had the strength left to face them. She turned away from the glass and walked back into the house, her focus turning to more pressing matters—chief among them, figuring out who the hell had brought them here.

Somewhere in this house was a clue as to who their captor was and why they were here. She was going to find it.

*

As it turned out, the owner had hidden his identity very well. Katya explored both floors of the home; all the cabinets and drawers were locked. There were no books in the home, no magazines with mailing addresses, and—most unsettling—no personal photographs. She was beginning to think there were no pictures of real people anywhere when she found the picture of the woman. It was in a room hidden off to the side of the first floor, with a glass wall overlooking the ocean. Except for the picture, the room was completely bare.

Katya studied the woman in the portrait. She was in her late thirties; long, dark hair in an elegant updo, slim shoulders bared in a black evening gown. She sat at a table in the middle of an elegant party, catching sight of something off frame.

Katya stepped forward, fascinated by the woman. Even though she was surrounded by wealth, this was not some society dame—not a woman who had risen on a cloud of inherited wealth. There was a survival instinct there, finely honed, sheathed beneath the glamor.

"There you are."

Katya spun around, ready to block a blow. The man with the blue eyeglasses was standing in the room.

"I was looking for you," he said, smiling.

"Who are you?" Katya asked, maintaining her defensive posture.

"I'm Baxter Lee," he said matter-of-factly.

"Is that name supposed to mean something?"

"I wouldn't be very good at my job if it did." He looked at the picture and then turned back to Katya. Katya shifted, uncomfortable under his placid gaze. He was wholly present in the moment, unaffected by any tics, nervousness, or distractions. He wore dark jeans and a trim green field jacket with a yellow hibiscus in the lapel.

Katya knew that if he left, everything about him would be forgotten, his entire presence reduced to a few slivers of smoke. She wondered if that was part of his job, to be interesting but instantly forgettable at once. She didn't like the idea of the kind of job that would require that skill set.

"I have a lot of questions," Katya warned.

"Of course. Do you want something to eat? You—"

"No. I want answers first."

"Okay, fire away."

"Where are we?"

"Beach Haven, New Jersey."

"Who do you work for?"

"I am here on behalf of the Ohana."

"The Ohana," Katya repeated.

"Yes. You helped us in the past."

"I know," Katya said, still off balance. "Five years ago—the boy."

It had been a freelance assignment, off the books—not that the Badges kept any sort of official records (a continuing sore spot for Katya). Five years ago, the Ohana had asked for her help in tracking down one of their own, a young boy taken from his mother by his estranged Blade Boy father. The Ohana had offered to pay Katya, but she'd waved them off.

"I mess up Blade Boys for free," she had said.

Twenty-four hours later, mother and son were reunited, and the Blade Boy was in a back-alley clinic, wheezing through three broken ribs.

"We haven't forgotten what you did for us," Baxter said.

"You brought me here to say thank you?"

"Among other things."

"The Ohana live in the Last Shelter," Katya said. "You live in the mountains and hug trees. When did you guys start flying private jets and buying beachfront mansions?"

"The plane and the house belong to one of our own—someone who has exposed himself to great risk to harbor you."

Katya pointed at the woman in the picture. "Her?"

"No. Close, though. Her son." Baxter stepped closer to the portrait, his eyes thoughtful. "She sought refuge in the Last Shelter with her two boys before the war." He turned to the window and the Atlantic beyond. "Her son had this room built in her memory. She loved to watch the ocean."

"Who is her son?"

He looked at her like the answer was obvious. "Robert Holt."

"Holt?" She gaped at Baxter. "Wait, is Robert—?"

"Houston's younger brother."

Katya shook her head, stunned. "Houston has a *brother*?"

"A brother he hasn't seen in over sixteen years. They were separated before the war. In any case, it was probably best they didn't reunite."

"Why?"

"Robert is a Special," Baxter said. "When one member of the family is Gifted and the other isn't, it can make things complicated."

"You're telling me that Houston used to be part of the Ohana?"

"Reluctantly. When he and Robert arrived with their mother, Jessalyn, they were only teenagers." Baxter straightened his glasses. "Robert fit in with us immediately. Houston . . . not so much."

"Not surprising," Katya said.

Baxter shrugged. "We are not a cult. We don't hold on to people. Those who need us, find us. Others find their own way. Houston needed to find his own way."

"Walk alone, stay alive," Katya repeated

"What was that?"

"Nothing."

The breeze picked up outside. "You must have been following us since Seekers Port, if not longer." Katya went to the glass wall and watched Lily chase seagulls off the beach. "This is about her."

"Yes."

"Son of a bitch. You're just like all the others, trying to *use* her—"

"No, Katya. We are trying to get her home."

Baxter's eyes were sincere. Katya saw her own harried face reflected for a moment in his lenses. She looked like a stranger.

"We don't involve ourselves in the affairs of the Kingdom," Baxter continued. "We do not seek power or influence. But we do intervene when it matters, and Lily matters more to all of us— human *and* Special—than anyone can fathom."

Lily sat on the sand and watched the waves.

"Have you heard of the Wanderer?" Baxter asked.

"Vaguely. He's your messiah—your founder."

"Yes. He predicted the arrival of the Specials long before the world knew they existed. He was killed on the eve of war by a mob of Native Sons. His views on human-Special equality are quite blasphemous to some ears, even to this day. Those of us that survived the war carried on his message—his one true message that terrified so many: the Specials are here to *help* us."

"That's a hard sell."

"At one point, the discovery that the Earth revolved around the Sun was a hard sell." Baxter watched Lily. "The Specials have forgotten what they are—their true purpose. But Lily has not. If we can get her home, the place she belongs . . ." He smiled at Katya. "*Everything* changes."

"I don't—"

Baxter's phone rang. "Excuse me, Katya. I have to take this."

"I'm not done with you," Katya grumbled.

"Make yourself at home," he said. "Robert will be here shortly. He'll have more answers for you."

"He's coming *here*?" Katya asked, shocked. But Baxter was already slipping into the hallway, the phone to his ear.

*

The sand was warm between Katya's toes, the sun high and bright. Lily looked up as Katya reached the water and showed her the collection of shells she had excavated—white, pearlescent beauties. Katya handed her a bottle of water, and Lily downed it with four big gulps.

They sat just beyond the reach of the water, watching it rise up the sand and pull back into the depths. They watched it for a long time. Lily was placing her shells in a neat pile by her feet when suddenly she keeled over and gulped loudly. Tears streamed down her cheeks and her shoulders heaved, every breath ragged and struggling to escape.

Katya wrapped her arms around her, feeling Lily's body vibrate with deep pain. She felt the darkness burn off Lily's skin, edged memories of fire and bloody axes and lightning.

"He's not here anymore," Katya said. "You're safe. He's gone."

"I didn't want any of this," Lily said, sobbing. "All these people dying for me. I didn't want this power."

"This isn't your fault, Lily."

"I didn't want this . . ."

She cried into Katya's chest, her words gone. The fear, the terrible memory of Lily's power on the mountainside, slipped from Katya's mind. Whatever else she was, Lily was still a child, and Katya knew that sometimes just holding a child when they were afraid was the greatest power of all.

The sun slipped behind a cloud and the bright blue waters waxed metallic, an ominous sheet rippled by the breeze. Katya heard footsteps behind her. The female medic trudged toward them.

The medic said, "Your friend is awake."

Katya's heart leapt. Lily jumped to her feet.

"Can we go see him?" Katya asked.

"He refuses to stay in his room." The medic frowned. "He's coming out here."

The patio door opened. Houston walked out gingerly, looking like a wet ghoul, squinting in the sunlight. The medic shook her head. "Is he always this difficult?"

"Always," Katya said. Lily nodded her head vigorously in agreement.

"Well, just don't startle him." She handed them a backpack full of water bottles. "Keep him hydrated, and make sure he doesn't move around too much. Maybe he'll listen to you."

"Unlikely," Katya said. The medic walked past them to the water, struggling out of her boots. Katya and Lily climbed the rise toward Houston. He tried to smile when he saw them, but it came out an odd, tight grimace.

"I forgot my beach towel," he said. "Either of you bring one?"

"Shut up," Katya said and hugged him. Lily joined in, both of them holding him so tight that Katya was afraid they'd break him.

*

"Ohana," Katya said when they were all sitting on the sand, watching the patrolling guards.

"I know," Houston said.

"Seems like you have a history with them."

"Ancient history."

"Do you know who owns this house?"

"I figured it out."

"Why didn't you tell me you had a brother?"

Houston shrugged. "We were separated before the war."

"Baxter said you ran away from the Last Shelter. From your family."

Houston was quiet for some time. "Family can feel like a prison," he finally said.

She handed him a water, deciding not to press further. "Baxter Lee—you know him?"

"No, but I remember his face from Seekers Port." He turned to Lily and squeezed her shoulder. "How you doing, kid?"

"Meh."

"Thank you," he said.

Lily nodded and looked away.

"'Thank you' for what?" Katya asked.

"She brought me out," Houston said. When Katya looked confused, he continued, "After the man hit me with the axe, I fell into this . . . place. Far from here. I thought I'd be there forever, but I heard Lily. She came down there with me and led me out."

"You have something left to do," Lily said.

"So you keep telling me."

The patio door opened behind them, and Baxter waved them over. He nodded at Houston when they reached him.

"Welcome back, Houston. I'm Baxter Lee." He held out his hand.

Houston frowned at his hand suspiciously. "You guys have been following us since Seekers Port. Why?"

"If we hadn't been, you would still be bleeding on that mountain." Baxter's voice took on an edge that Katya hadn't noticed before. He held Houston's look and stepped back into the house. "Now, if you'll please follow me, Robert's car has just entered the property. He's anxious to meet all of you."

Baxter led them out the side door and onto the driveway.

Katya watched as a black Acura glided through the gated entrance and rolled to a stop in front of them. Katya involuntarily leaned forward to catch a glimpse of Robert Holt inside, but the windows were opaque. She looked over at Houston. He stood stiffly next to her, his face unreadable.

The driver, a white-haired gentleman, smiled at them as he opened the rear door.

The man who stepped out was alone. He was not large, and like Houston, he had dark hair and sharp features. His suit was a shade of blue that Katya had never seen before. She found herself staring at it, lost in its moody, shifting hues as his boots clopped down on the paving stones. His scent arrived ahead of him, crisp as fall foliage, welcoming as a warm fireplace.

The resemblance with Houston was there, but there was something more—a recognition that went beyond resemblance, as if Katya had seen his face many times before, but never at this distance or this scale.

Robert Holt hugged Baxter first. They spoke quietly for a few seconds.

Robert turned to them and smiled. His eyes shone with a peaceful intelligence, and when he looked at Houston, Houston tried to look everywhere but at him.

"Aren't you going to introduce me to your friends?" Robert asked.

An awkward moment stretched out. Katya watched Houston flex his hands and take a deep breath, as if he had been preparing for this moment his whole life and, now that it was here, he had forgotten all his lines.

"Katya, Lily," he finally said, "this is my brother, Bobby Holt. Better known as Augustus Sky. Or—"

"Augustus Sky!" Katya cried, Robert's face barreling out of her memory with the force of a train.

"Or," Houston continued, "you may know him as the Songbird."

"Please," the Kingdom's most famous and beloved entertainer said with a smile, "that name isn't doing me any favors. Call me Bobby."

50

Kormedia and Shanti stared at Veena through the car windows, the whites of their eyes glowing like full moons from every street corner and every window.

Veena's nerves thrummed on the edge of panic. She could feel her father's blade in her hands, piercing Shanti's and Kormedia's flesh.

Show me what kind of blood runs through your veins now.

She was seeing ghosts, courtesy of her Moxi hangover.

Veena looked behind them. Was that black Suburban following their Honda SUV? It had been behind them for the last three turns. Who was that man on the street corner? Was he looking at her strangely? What if they were her father's men and they saw her out here, in direct violation of her father's orders? The bruises along her chest and throat throbbed in warning.

Get ahold of yourself.

The Lady in the Veil sat silently beside her as they rolled onto Northern Boulevard, her hands crossed on her lap, her face turned away.

Veena could handle Debashish Kumar by herself. She didn't need the Lady. Nor did she need the *two* Von Arx Militiamen, Abel and Luca, that Caspar had sent with her.

Veena had brushed off Caspar's questions at the house the best she could, not daring to reveal that her father was now involved. That her own stupidity—that awful *video*—had exposed them. Caspar she could stall. But the Lady . . . Veena glanced at her. How much did she *really* know?

Had He Who Knows All revealed to the Lady how much peril Veena had sunk them in? Would they, after Veena had neutralized Deb and restored the Peacock Gown to Callista's lineup, cut her throat and watch her bleed out on the rug?

The Moxi called out to her, pinching at her nerves. It wasn't her fault she had relapsed. What else was she supposed to do last night? After the Silverback driver had deposited her back at Starlet Manor, the bruises still burning across her body, she had stumbled from room to room, lost.

Across the street, in his sweeping mansion, the Songbird was throwing a pre-Decennial celebration. She had seen the invite weeks ago and left it on her foyer counter, assuming she would have no time for such things.

She wasn't seeking relief, simply obliteration.

She didn't remember who had brought out the vial of Moxi in the Songbird's den, but she remembered the way it felt when it hit her blood—the good stuff, pure as snow, shipped out from the western shadowlands. Straight out of the Snake Mother's tight little—

"We're here," the Lady said.

Veena blinked. Outside, the grungy colors of Jackson Heights, Queens, swirled around the car. Veena watched as groups of young bohemians strode down the wide stretch of Roosevelt Avenue, past small boutiques, live music bars, and prewar apartments streaked with surrealist murals. This was the home of a certain type of artist—reclusive but politically engaged, fiercely opinionated, and often skirting the line of treason.

Back when he was Veena's assistant, Deb Kumar had often, in his own awkward way, invited her to come visit his home here. She had never taken him up on the offer until today.

"Your friend will be here?" The Lady asked.

"Of course," Veena snapped with a certainty she did not feel. Across the street, the awning of the Tangra Chinese Restaurant was clearly visible.

"He may have changed his habits," the Lady said.

"Trust me," Veena said, "he hasn't. Designers are a superstitious lot—Deb more than most. When he worked for me, he ate the same lunch every day at 3:00 p.m. When he wasn't in Sovereign, he would eat here—every day, 3:00 p.m."

The Lady's gray eyes held her like hooks. Then she turned away.

Veena checked her watch. 2:52 p.m. Her fingers flitted nervously in her coat pocket and grazed the USB stick Abel had given her.

Poor Deb, she thought. He had been her best assistant.

Two fifty-five. A large man slid past the car, startling Veena. He was the size and shape of a Silverback, moving with their arrogant stride. He turned into a liquor store and was gone.

Veena closed her eyes. In the darkness, the hangman watched her.

War criminal!

Fascist!

No peace without justice!

"Is that him?" The Lady's voice snapped Veena's eyes open. Veena followed the Lady's finger, which was pointing to a short, trim man with long black hair hurrying across the avenue toward Tangra Chinese.

"Yes," Veena said. She opened the door and was halfway out when she felt a hand on her arm. It was the Lady, her eyes like flashlights.

"Veena, are you all right?"

Veena scowled at her. "Yes. Why?"

"Your energy is troubled."

"I'm fine."

"Come back inside." It was an order.

Veena watched Deb walk inside the restaurant. Then she slid back into the car and closed the door.

"Tell me the truth," the Lady said.

"I've told you the truth."

"No, not the truth of the situation." The Lady leaned forward. "*Your* truth."

Veena suddenly fell into the gray pools of her eyes. She tumbled deep into their depths, and she felt something hard and calcified dislodge from her chest.

"I'm so afraid," Veena said.

"I know. And the antidote to fear is faith."

Veena snorted. "I *have* faith. But why is everything going so wrong?"

"Faith does not vanquish obstacles. It creates them."

"That makes no sense. Why would it be that way?"

"Because the obstacles teach you how to overcome them—how to become the person strong enough to fulfill your destiny."

"My destiny." Veena felt the dirt in her blood—the blood of a whore. "I'm not who I thought I was."

"He Who Knows All knows your true beauty. He sees *you*."

"And what does he see in me?" Veena asked.

The Lady blinked and reset her hands gently on her lap. "I know this path is difficult, Veena, but He has carried you out of a much greater darkness because he believes that you are special above all others."

The sadness built up inside Veena, hot and terrifying. Veena gulped it down, balling her fists.

"You are more than what you think you are, Veena."

Veena nodded.

"Say it, Veena. Say you are more."

"I am more," Veena sniffled.

"Louder."

"I am more!" Veena yelled with all the strength she could muster. She sat up straight, reinvigorated. "I haven't lost faith in Him."

"And He will never lose faith in you."

"May He protect me."

"Always."

Veena stepped out into the brisk breeze. She slipped on her sunglasses and trotted over to Tangra Chinese, her fingers wrapped tightly around the USB drive.

In the end, it was incredibly easy. Given that Deb was most likely working under a hellish deadline to tailor-fit the queen's new dress before tonight, Veena had expected that it would require all her charm to finagle an invite back to his place. But as it turned out, everyone—especially insecure young designers—crumbled under the onslaught of wine and flattery.

Deb smiled brightly when he saw Veena enter the restaurant. They exchanged gushing pleasantries, Veena making a pointed effort to shower him with compliments. He wore flannels and boots, and his wildlife tattoos shone on his slim forearms. He spoke with a soft voice that made everything he said sound like an apology.

Throughout the dinner, Veena did most of the talking. Deb was, as always, content to listen intently. When she saw him glancing at his watch, she quickly ordered another bottle of wine. She had been sober for over a year, and the Riesling hit her system like a bomb.

Nine hours remained on the clock before Queen Callista would step out onto the Royal Dais next to her husband. Halfway through the second bottle of Riesling, Deb invited Veena up to his loft for a nightcap.

Veena kept her jacket on in Deb's loft apartment, the USB drive a leaden weight in her pocket. The space resembled its owner—slim, with fragile sculptures and elegant glass tables crowded with odd knickknacks, typewriters, and wooden beams slashed with graffiti. Deb's two Persian cats, Haley and Scud, judged her from the sofa.

"Do you still like martinis?" Deb asked.

"Darling, you just *get* me." Veena smiled and walked over to the window. She could see the windows of Deb's studio in the converted apartment building across the street, the shades drawn.

"You must tell me what you have been up to," Veena said.

Deb giggled, his eyes glimmering with mischief. "Oh, this and that."

"Debby." Veena smiled. "I can tell when you're keeping a secret."

He placed two martini glasses on the counter tipsily. "Oh, hush."

"Don't hush me. You know there are no secrets between us."

"Oh, Veena, I want it to be a surprise. Trust me. When you see it . . . oh, how I wish I could show it to you!"

"Show it to me now."

"I can't." He bit his lip. "It's a commission from . . . well, from a very important client. Top secret. Nondisclosure agreements and all that." His shoulders slumped, and he rubbed his eyes. "I've been working on it all day, and I could get in *so* much trouble if I talk about it before . . . before my client can wear it. Please don't be upset with me, Veena."

She walked toward him slowly. He shrank under her gaze. "Well, then," Veena said, popping an olive into her mouth from her glass, "even though you insist on keeping me in the dark . . . I am *very* excited for you."

"You'll be so proud of me when you see it." He puffed out his narrow chest. "And you'll be seeing it very soon." His eyes quickly flitted to the clock on the wall.

Veena was running out of time.

"Darling, point me toward the ladies' room."

"Down the hall, past the bedroom."

Veena turned the corner, around the Japanese room dividers that sectioned the living area and kitchen off from the bedroom space. She had taken her shoes off at the door, so her feet made no sound on the wood floors. The "bedroom" was another sectioned-off space, containing a queen bed and a large window. A small, neat desk stood next to the window. Deb's laptop was on it.

Veena kept her eyes on the computer as she stood outside the bathroom and opened and closed the door loudly. She waited. She heard Deb's voice on the phone in the living room.

Veena crept into the bedroom and opened the laptop. She wedged the USB stick into the slot, her heart banging like a piston in her chest.

"Slot in the stick and let it work," Abel had told her back at Starlet Manor. "The program will bypass his security and give you full access. Once you're in, it's up to you to find the file."

The laptop hummed. She couldn't hear Deb on the phone anymore.

"Come on, come on, come on," she urged the blank screen.

Deb's desktop filled the screen—a Coco Chanel backdrop and a collection of folders aligned perfectly on the right side. She knew the file she was looking for would not be on his desktop. *That* folder he would keep hidden—if it still existed.

Deb had been working for her about a year when, in a fit of lonely grief, he had shown her his secret folder—the one with pictures taken by the hustler, the grand love of Deb's small life.

Deb had thought they would be together forever, his naiveté blinding him to his lover's true colors—a self-promoting narcissist whose charm and handsomeness masked a deep parasitic need to suck the life out of his unwitting string of lovers. When the hustler had skipped town with all of Deb's money, Deb had hit the bottle hard and shown Veena, in a dark moment, the pictures that the hustler had taken.

A sound behind Veena made her gasp. She spun around, expecting to see Deb's glowering face, but it was one of the cats—the black one, staring at her from the edge of the divider.

"Stupid cat."

Veena found the folder stashed deep in his hard drive, labeled Tax Returns.

In the kitchen, Deb hung up his call.

Shit. Veena quickly scanned through the jpeg previews in the folder. There were forty pictures in total—entangled sweaty flesh, crumpled hotel sheets, lines of Moxi. Veena swiped the images onto her USB drive and closed out of the folder.

Something caught her eye—a card taped to the wall by the desk, one she hadn't noticed before in her haste. In a neat cursive, it simply said: *You can be anything you want to be. I believe in you, Deb. —Mom.*

Veena lost it. A big gurgling sob stuck in her throat, threatening to choke her.

Poor Deb. Poor little Deb, who had been the only one to send her letters in rehab. He didn't deserve this. She gripped the drive so hard her knuckles went white. She wanted to fling it into the trash or stomp it under her bare feet.

Her father's words rang in her ears: *Show me what kind of blood runs through your veins now.*

She slipped past the cat and back toward the bathroom. She flushed the toilet and let the faucet run for a few seconds, careful to not look at herself in the mirror.

*

Deb was standing in the kitchen when she returned.

"Not feeling to well, hon," she said, rubbing her temple.

"Oh, no. Was it the food?"

"I think it was a lot of things." She ran a sweaty finger over the drive in her coat pocket. "I should go."

As they hugged and she felt the weight of his fragile body against hers, she wondered how he would survive what came next.

The pictures would be sent from an untraceable account to a dark web file-sharing site. Then an anonymous call would be placed to a certain amoral reporter at the online society scandal rag *ChatterBox*, along with a wire transfer of five thousand goldmarks. Deb would be on the *ChatterBox* front page by 5:00 p.m.

Nobody admitted to reading *ChatterBox*, especially not high-society ladies, but Veena knew they all did. They tuned in daily to see who was sleeping with whom, which celebrity was back in rehab, and whose divorce had gotten nasty. As fast as a wildfire, the queen's people would get wind of the pictures. It would take less than two hours for Deb's life to come crumbling down.

"It was so good to see you, Veena," Deb said. "I'm not just saying that." He looked to the floor, suddenly bashful. "I don't really . . . *have* a lot of people in my life outside of my work."

Veena's smiled tightly, her back soaked in sweat.

Deb continued, "I wish I had more time to spend with you. But next Wednesday, come over. We'll open a bottle of Prosecco. It'll be our night." He looked at her, hopeful.

Veena squeezed his shoulder and smiled. "I would love that, hon."

The cats watched her as she left. The black one had returned from the hallway, its eyes never wavering from her as she took the stairs and Deb closed the door behind her.

*

Once back in the car, she gave the drive to Abel. Veena sat in silence as Luca drove them home, content to watch the grim landscape roll by. The Lady must have sensed her mood, for she opted to stay silent. As they cruised down the Grand Central Parkway, Abel slotted the drive into his laptop and typed loudly.

The sun fell lower in the sky, tracing the top of the skyline. The Kingspire ignited above the city. The Grand Decennial began tonight, and the single white beam had been transformed into a tube of sparkling azure embedded with stars.

Tonight, it would mark the center of the earth.

It was a tombstone, Veena knew—a monument to a dead king. Tomorrow night, rising from the ashes, the Kingspire would mark the site of a coronation—the ascension of the War Monarch, King Sixkills.

"File is sent," Abel informed them from the front.

Veena nodded dully, only half listening.

After suffering through an hour and a half of interminable Decennial traffic, their car was just turning into Starlet Manor when the Queen's Style Secretary, Gwendolyn Pierce, called Veena.

"Her Majesty has . . . *evolved* on her style choices for tonight," Gwendolyn cooed. "And she has decided to wear your gown at the Decennial Parade. Congratulations, Miss Sixkills. You must be *so* thrilled."

51

The cumulus clouds were a white mountain range below Magnusson. The heads-up display on his visor relayed his altitude as 8,178 feet, his flight time, 42 minutes.

Agent Farrows had called him twenty minutes earlier. "Guess who just landed at Manahawkin Airfield?" She had sent him Longhorn's coordinates, and Magnusson was cruising within minutes.

A hundred feet ahead, the cloud cover broke apart, exposing a wide gulf before the next range of low-hanging cumulus. Magnusson shot up higher into the sky, distancing himself from any prying eyes below. His altimeter read 11,342 feet.

His teeth chattered, and the wind howled through his earplugs. He felt like he was crawling through a block of ice. An easy day for a Silverback.

The map on his visor beeped with a preprogrammed alert. Magnusson spotted the metallic stretch of the Delaware River below.

He dropped down below six thousand feet, underneath the clouds. From here he could see the river stretch out to the horizon until it reached the bend around Philadelphia. Follow it south for a few hundred miles, and you'd reach a small rust-bucket town, a place Magnusson had once called home before the war—a forgotten place of steely winters and seething locals scrounging for their lives in the shadow of the shuttered plant. It had surprised no one how rapidly the town had fallen into the clutches of Native Son extremists.

Magnusson had been on the run with Sixkills when he'd heard the first reports of the purges back home. The Sons and their supporters had gone door to door before dawn and torn the Specials out of their beds, herding the terrified men, women, and children out into the cold streets, where—even though they were armed with guns—the Native Sons had chosen to use knives. When the slaughter ended in the gray morning light, Magnusson's seventy-year-old father and twenty-six-year-old sister had been among the dead.

Magnusson stared out at the stretch of shapeless land to the west. After the war, he had hunted down and killed dozens of former Native Sons. But their leaders—the small despots who had fomented and incited the hateful violence—had escaped.

For now.

Their time would come. It was inevitable. The long hand of Spearhead was sleepless, pitiless, and—ultimately—deathless.

Magnusson arched his back and shot back up to eight thousand feet, leaving the old world beneath the clouds.

*

Magnusson landed in a dense patch of forest two miles away from the target and hiked the rest of the way. The Manahawkin Airfield was no more than a quarter mile across and bordered on all sides by trees. It had one working runway, eight hundred feet long and studded with potholes. A long red barn with battered radar dishes stood on the far left of the field.

Magnusson spied pilots stumbling out of the building, music following them when they opened the doors. Magnusson smiled. An air control tower and a bar in the same building—real high-caliber operation they were running here.

A small garage stood on the opposite end of the runway, housing a large fuel truck. There was no sign of the driver, but a pack of stray dogs scrounged for food outside the garage door. The planes were parked on a patch of flattened grass by the tree line—four of them, covered by a ceiling of camouflage netting.

One of them was a black Cessna.

Magnusson crept around the airfield, hidden in the trees, until he was behind the planes. Two brick security walls blocked his line of sight from the trees to the plane.

After a quick scan of his surroundings, Magnusson broke cover and raced toward the walls. He pushed his back up against the first one and then skirted around it, toward the next wall.

A brown dog with a white patch around his left eye sat by the planes. It jumped up when it saw Magnusson and trotted over to sniff his boots. Vaguely disappointed, the dog blinked and ambled back to his shaded spot.

The Cessna was just ahead of Magnusson. It was polished and smooth, clashing against the other parked planes, which looked like they had just been flown through a mud storm.

Longhorn takes pride in his tools, Magnusson noted. *Good.* It confirmed his working theory about the man: meticulous, professional, and worthy. Magnusson was looking forward to meeting him.

The plane was ten steps away, and Magnusson considered investigating it further, but the Cessna was most likely armed with anti-personnel tech or worse.

The dog swiveled its head as a group of four men roared out of the barn, arguing. Magnusson backed away from the Cessna and returned to his hiding place amid the trees.

He crouched in the shade and scanned a map of the local area on his smartwatch. Longhorn had at least an hour's head start, so tracking him—if Longhorn even left a trail—would be inefficient.

There were two scenarios, as Magnusson saw them: either Longhorn had stolen the Unholy from the Redblood compound in Virginia and had brought it here for delivery, or, the Unholy had slipped away and Longhorn had tracked it down to this area.

Either way, he would have to return to his plane eventually.

In scenario one, Longhorn would return alone. Magnusson's job would be to incapacitate him quickly and interrogate him for the Unholy's location. He wouldn't have much time. Longhorn's employers were a mystery, but their intentions were becoming very clear to Magnusson—detonate the Unholy in Sovereign City.

Scenario two was simpler. If Longhorn found the Unholy out here, he would bring it back to his plane for transport. All Magnusson needed to do was shoot from cover and claim possession of the girl.

This was the place. No matter how it went down, he would face Longhorn here.

Magnusson circled the airfield two more times, memorizing all the lines of fire, all the paths Longhorn could take to approach his plane. From the cover of forest, to the right of the security walls, Magnusson found a spot with a perfect line of sight to the Cessna.

Magnusson slowed his breathing and let himself sink into the soft dirt. His eyes never left the Cessna as he settled in to the long, deep quiet of the hunt.

5 2

The dinner table had been set on the patio, overlooking the beach. Houston didn't touch his food. Baxter and Katya continued some old conversation, and Bobby sat at the head of the table, creating daisies in a flying circle around Lily's head. She laughed heartily at his conjuring tricks, the two of them already best friends.

Houston had barely spoken to Bobby since his arrival. He was no longer the shy, fidgety little brother he remembered. This was Augustus Sky, the Songbird, the most beloved singer in all the Kingdom. Houston searched his brother's lean face but found no trace of the plain fifteen-year-old he had abandoned all those years ago.

"Houston, aren't you going to eat?" Bobby asked. "You've barely touched your food."

"Not hungry."

"Houston, you're being rude," Katya admonished, her plate piled high.

"It's all right," Bobby said, sipping from a steaming mug. "Honestly, I usually just subsist on Oolong tea. Better for my vocal cords."

"That's right," Katya said. "Aren't you performing tonight?"

"In about eight hours, actually. I'm closing out the Decennial Parade."

"Shouldn't you be in Sovereign City right now?" Katya asked.

"Family is more important."

Houston felt all of their eyes shift onto him expectantly. He drank his water and looked away.

Katya broke the awkward silence. "I saw the picture of your mother," she said to Bobby. "She was beautiful."

"Thank you. It's my favorite picture of her. Taken in the Ivory Room, in New York. Remember that place, Houston?"

"Vaguely."

"I used to perform there—illegally, of course. This was during the Emergency. But it was a wonderful venue. Mom's favorite."

"Tell me more about her," Katya said. "Houston tells me nothing."

Before Bobby could speak, Houston interrupted. "What do you want to know about—the drinking, or that she once murdered a man?"

Katya and Baxter stared at Houston, aghast. Even Lily stopped eating and looked up. Bobby was the only one unmoved. "That's all true," he said, "but it was also more complicated than that."

Bobby glanced at Baxter, who took the cue immediately. He rose from the table. "There's dessert in the kitchen," Baxter said. "Fudge gelato."

Baxter guided Lily and Katya back into the house. Before she went inside, Katya glared daggers at Houston.

Bobby sipped his tea. On the beach, an Ohana guard paced by the water, the sky darkening above. Bobby reached into his jacket and pulled out an envelope. He slid it over to Houston. The envelope was wrinkled and discolored, and Houston's name was written on the front.

"What is this?" Houston asked.

"Mom made me promise that if I ever found you, I'd give it to you."

"What does it say?"

"That's for your eyes only." Bobby brought his fingers together.

"But I'm guessing she wanted to explain some things."

Houston turned the letter around in his hands. "Big Don?"

"Among other things. By the end, I think she realized that she could have done things differently. She was human, Houston. She did her best."

Houston studied his mother's handwriting on the envelope. He put the letter down and slid it back. "When I left the Last Shelter, I wanted that part of my life to be over. I'm done with her."

Bobby looked at the letter, then back at Houston, disappointed. "Family can be a burden. You and I know that more than anyone. But I've come to believe—and trust me, it took me a while to arrive here—that family can be the last, best thing we have when everything else is gone." Bobby left the letter where it was. "She wasn't perfect, Houston, but she deserves a chance to explain herself."

"She had many chances."

Bobby sighed. "And you've never killed anyone?"

"When necessary."

"What mom did was necessary."

"Why are *you* defending her?" Houston leaned forward. "After how she treated us? She was a criminal, a low-life. We were happy in New York. We could have had a home there, with Big Don. She ruined it for—"

"Big Don liked boys."

Houston stopped short.

Bobby clasped his hands together and laid them on the table. "Big Don wasn't in love with mom. He was using her to acquire what he really wanted." He paused. "*Who* he really wanted."

Houston looked at Bobby for a long time. He felt sick. "You."

Bobby nodded.

"Did he . . . ?" Houston's shock boiled into a black anger. "Were you—"

"No. Mom found out before he could try. That bastard came straight out and told her. Threatened to turn her over to the government if she refused to turn a blind eye." Bobby's eyes fell, and he stared at the steam rising off his tea. "And so she acted in the only way she could."

Houston remembered his mother, rushing into their room at night, her white nightie stained in blood.

If we don't leave now, we're all dead.

He stood and walked to the edge of the patio. After a moment, Bobby joined him there, and they watched the sun fall toward the sea.

Bobby spoke. "Four years ago, the Ohana notified me that they had found you in River Town. I had been searching for you after the war. I wanted to reach out, but in the end, I decided against it."

"Why?"

"Because I understood why you left."

"I didn't want to . . . I wasn't angry at you."

Bobby looked at him. "You were a good brother. You protected me as much as you could. And I won't lie—I was hurt when you left without telling me. But I was being selfish. I see that now. If you had stayed with me, with mom, you would always be . . . you had dreams, and they would have died with us. You had to find your own way."

Houston tilted his head toward the massive house. "Looks like you found your way before I did."

They both laughed. As the tension eased from Houston's shoulders, a thought occurred to him. "Four years ago, I got set up on a bad deal. The SSD were after me. Did you know about that?"

"The Songbird has many fans, even in the SSD." Bobby smiled when he saw the shock on Houston's face.

"You sent Faraz."

"Not specifically. I made a few calls to Ibrahim & Sons, but I didn't know they'd send the Sultan himself. Nor did I have any idea that your association with him would lead you here."

The glass door opened behind them and Lily stepped out, her mouth covered in gelato. "Houston, come get some fudge before Katya finishes it all."

"On my way," Houston said.

Lily went back inside. Houston watched her walk back into the kitchen and dig her spoon into the ice cream tub. Something heavy knotted itself inside his chest.

"How do I stop what's coming for her?" he asked.

Bobby squeezed Houston's shoulder. "First, you have to understand who she really is." Bobby looked at his watch. "Come. The show's about to begin."

53

―――――――

"The first thing you have to realize, my friends, is that we have all been lied to." Bobby's voice was low, burnished with an ominous register that reverberated in the darkened library like a dangerous secret. "We have been misled by myth. For if we were to truly understand the origin of the Specials and what that means for *all* of life on the planet, well, . . . we would never be the same.

"So before we start, I would ask you to keep in mind two important questions: Where did the Specials come from? And second, why is the king himself ready to sacrifice everything for a girl with a Frontier tattoo on her arm? These two questions are inextricably linked." Bobby rubbed his palms together in the dark. "Let's begin."

A miniature military cargo plane flew across the room, engines rumbling as a squadron of fighter jets flanked its massive fuselage. Houston watched in wonder as the miniature, but shockingly lifelike, planes flew over his head. He heard Katya gasp next to him. The only other person in the room, Baxter, sat very still.

Bobby narrated along, his voice expanding to fill every available nook of the library. "The Immortal War—the fall of the United States. When the historians look back at these cataclysmic events, they will find the blame lies with a single culprit: the Orchid Program."

"The Orcs," Houston said, remembering Otis and Carmen.

"Correct. An elite CIA paramilitary unit that, twenty-six years before the Emergency, brought something back from over the Atlantic—an energetic anomaly the likes of which the world had never seen."

The planes passed overhead and then quickly dissipated into sparkling dust. The dust sprinkled across the floor, and a giant, ridged mountain range rose up, streaming with cobalt waterfalls and lush vegetation.

Bobby continued. "They brought it to the Big Island of Hawaii, where they experimented on it in secret. The military called the anomaly Jupiter Sky. For our purposes, we shall call it by the Ohana name: the Source. After twenty years of experimenting on the Source . . ."

The Big Island disappeared in a crackling cloud of blue and gold that rose up to their shins.

"Whoa," Katya whispered. Houston followed her gaze to the center of the cloud.

Patriot Gold rose from the lightning, arms outstretched in flight.

"The Firstborn," Bobby said. "The first and only Special to be created by the Orchid Program—a living weapon imbued with the energy of the Source. Who the king was before the program, we don't know. But who the CIA turned him into—well, the entire world would soon come to know his name."

Bobby tilted his head, and the scene broke into dust and a new world formed before their eyes. "Fast forward a few years." Salt Lake City, Utah, the streets streaming with armored military carriers and hundreds of Army infantrymen in biohazard armor. Helicopters hovered above the dome of the Utah State Capitol like hornets. Houston blinked rapidly, shaking off the creeping disorientation.

"You all know as much about the Incident as I do—which is to say, not much. The Orchids were running a secret facility outside of Salt Lake City—one that, even though the Source was still on the Big Island, most likely housed samples of its energy. The facts are unclear, but what is certain is that the Orcs lost control of the installation, resulting in a catastrophic energy outbreak that led to one hundred and twenty-seven million Americans on the western half of America being imbued with the Gift. Fast forward again, past the Emergency and all that followed, right to Annihilation Day."

The room plunged into blackness. Houston felt the floor vibrate, and the darkness grew barbs laced with a monstrous heat. The first mushroom cloud ignited in the center of the rug. It rose ten feet up in the air, followed by six more explosions around the room. Houston gripped his armrests as his seat heaved with the force.

Baxter spoke this time. "The official version of events states that President Mathias ordered the nuclear strike on Hawaii to assassinate Patriot Gold. But the real reason . . ." He paused and waited for the nuclear towers to dissipate. ". . . was to destroy the Source."

"Kill the Source, and the Specials lose their Gift," Katya said.

"Yes," Bobby said. "But their plan failed."

The Hawaiian Islands at their feet shook with earthquakes, battered by the ferocious storms known as the Furies. The sharp tinge of sulfur filled Houston's nose as the Big Island's volcanoes spewed lava across the dark lands and into the steaming sea.

"The nuclear blasts only served to wound the Source and, in the process, make it very angry."

"Bobby," Houston said, "Lily was on those islands when it happened. She told me."

"Ah." Bobby smiled. "And now we come to Lily. When the bombs detonated, Lily was right about . . ."

He flicked his hand, and the Pacific slid beneath their feet, crossing over hundreds of miles until Bobby stopped the scene abruptly. "Here."

Houston leaned forward to see what Bobby was pointing at and then immediately wished he hadn't. Bobby plunged them below the surface of the Pacific, enveloping the entire room in green water.

"Easy," Bobby said when he saw the expressions on Houston and Katya's faces. "Breathe. We're all safe."

Houston inhaled clear air, a bewildering sensation because his eyes were telling him he was underwater. They sank deeper and deeper, past schools of fish. Gargantuan shadows glided in the distance.

Bobby spoke. "Many of the humans from Hawaii were forced to leave the islands to make way for the Special refugees. But not all the humans made it to safety before the bombs fell. One plane, in particular, left an hour too late."

A small passenger jet appeared on the ocean floor, broken in half. Electricity bubbled in the water, and Houston watched in awe as the whales and the fish around the wreck ballooned in size, mutating into new, terrifying species.

"The Source's power, now unleashed by the nuclear blasts, changed the world around it. Everything it touched evolved in ways we had never seen—including a young girl who had been on that last plane out."

Baxter spoke. "We found her entirely by accident." He turned to Katya. "As I told you before, Katya, our founder, the Wanderer, was from the Big Island. He spoke of a powerful energy, the Source energy, before the world knew about Specials. He sensed the Source's power, and he knew that it was here to help us—that the Gift, before the CIA turned it into a weapon, was an energy that could heal the world. For the Ohana, finding and freeing the Source has always been priority number one. And ever since the war ended, we've been sending expeditions out to the Black Isles in hopes of finding it."

"How many expeditions?" Katya asked.

"Six." Baxter's expression darkened. "None of them made it back. The Furies are impenetrable."

"We lost many good people," Bobby said, "but it was not in vain. Out of the six, one expedition, the last one we sent, discovered something before they entered the Furies."

Heavy chains dropped down into the ocean. Magnetic clamps on the chains gripped the plane's fuselage and lifted it off the sea floor.

"That was four years ago," Bobby continued. "The expedition was able to recover Lily and four other bodies from the wreckage. They were transported to the California coast, where our people were supposed to rendezvous with a plane and bring them back to the Last Shelter—an incredibly risky operation, right under the nose of the Western Province, but these were seasoned operatives. We thought they had a chance."

"Our last communication with them was right before they crossed into Chula Vista," Baxter said.

"What happened to them?" Katya asked.

"The Five Totems," Houston said, remembering Carmen's story. Before Houston could explain, the room went black again—but this time, something reptilian moved in the darkness.

Chanting voices echoed off the walls—thousands of them, crying out in a guttural tongue, savagery in every syllable.

The light of an unseen fire flickered. Shadows fell across the wall, shifting, writhing, wielding blades. The ground shook as the shadows marched, an army of demons moving unstoppably across the world.

And above them all, Houston saw *her*—the silhouette of the dancing Snake Mother, bristling with spikes and horns, overcome by a fervent ecstasy as she willed her soldiers into battle.

Houston realized he was pushing back on his armrests, trying to move away from the demonic shadow. Mercifully, the shadows disappeared, and light returned to the room. Houston's hands were shaking.

Bobby faced Katya. "The Five Totems," he said, "are Lily and the four others we took from the plane. Having been exposed to the Source's raw power for eleven years by that point, they were neither living nor dead, human nor Special. Before we could bring them back, they were intercepted and stolen. Less than a year later, the Frontier Nation ruled the west."

Katya put it together. "The Frontier's power comes from the Five Totems." She looked at everyone in the room, her face troubled. "That's why the king wants her. She's a power source."

"Perhaps," Bobby said, holding up a cautionary hand. "We once knew the king well. We sheltered him in the dark days of the war, but now we can only guess at his motives."

"What's your best guess?" Houston asked.

"The Specials are connected to the Source like an umbilical cord," Baxter said. "It is the mother of all their Gifts, and with each passing day, the Source grows weaker."

"It is dying," Bobby said.

Baxter straightened his glasses, grim. "The Wanderer told us that out of many, we are one. There is no separation between humans and Specials. If the Source dies, and the Specials along with it, we lose our only chance."

"Only chance at what?" Katya asked.

Baxter's lenses glimmered in the dim light. "Peace."

He picked up a book, *The Wandering Words*, from the table next to him and turned to a bookmarked page. "This is the book that guides all Ohana. It is the Wanderer's philosophy, written by him forty years ago." Baxter read a passage. "'From the womb of the Source, all life will flourish. The Source is the mother, the creative force, and our only light that leads back home.'"

Houston waited for the words to settle over the room. "You think Lily can help you find the Source."

"She is our only hope of freeing it," Bobby said.

"You're putting a lot of faith in a book."

"Faith is a form of strength, Houston," Baxter said. "Not weakness."

"So Lily leads you back to the Source. You free it somehow. And then . . . what? We all just cross our fingers?"

Baxter leaned forward, his voice edged. "The people who are hunting Lily now, the ones you worked for? They want to use her as a weapon—a weapon powerful enough to do the impossible."

Houston frowned. "The impossible?"

"To kill that which cannot die."

Katya realized it first. "The king."

"An assassination . . ." Houston's voice trailed off.

"And then the dominos fall," Baxter said. "Whatever comes next, however it plays out, will always lead to the same inevitable end."

Katya inhaled sharply. "War."

A forbidding silence fell, thick as fog. Bobby cleared his throat. "You may not agree with the Ohana's plans for her, but everyone else's plans result in her death."

Before Houston could respond, Katya chimed in, "Look, I usually don't agree with Houston on much, but on this, I'm just as skeptical. I know Lily is different. I've seen what she can do. But this whole business about a Wanderer and a Source that can save us all? It's a huge leap for me. Because from what I can tell, the Source has only brought us war."

"Fair enough," Bobby said. "What if we could show you?"

"What do you mean?"

Bobby took *The Wandering Words* and read, "'When the Source opens its wings upon the world, we shall see the impossible: the end of fear and the true resurrection of all life, freed from time and death.'" Bobby put down the book, checked his watch, and stood.

"You should see the Source's true power for yourselves before you make up your minds."

Baxter opened the door. As they were leaving, he stopped Houston. "Just so you know, that this wasn't our idea—it was Lily's."

*

A cool breeze blew in off the ocean as they made their way across the beach. They walked for nearly five minutes across the pristine sand without seeing another house. When they reached Lily, she was painted in the soft glow of the setting sun. She stood by a large black tarp at the water's edge. The tarp had been nailed down with wooden stakes into the soft sand, and something large lay hidden beneath it.

Lily turned and smiled at them. When she looked at Houston, he could tell she was already slipping the bonds of this reality, one foot in the secret world she kept to herself. The tide rushed in and soaked her ankles.

Baxter nodded to the four Ohana guards, and together they yanked out the wooden stakes and pulled the tarp away.

Houston saw a row of bladed teeth, a thickly muscled torso of mottled gray flesh, and a strange oblong head.

"Whoa," Katya said beside him.

It was a dead hammerhead shark—a juvenile that had washed up recently, Houston guessed, judging from its black eyes, which were not yet dried out.

Lily faced the shark. The guards stepped back to a respectful distance and clasped their hands, bowing their heads like monks. Lily took a deep breath. With her exhale, her body relaxed, and Houston felt the air around them loosen, as if the world was settling down for the night.

Lily closed her eyes and knelt next to the shark. When she opened them, it was clear she had crossed an invisible boundary.

She melted into the rhythm of the ocean, hearing, listening, *being*. She carried something back over the boundary with her.

She stood tall and filled her lungs with the salty air. Her body vibrated, and a sheen of sweat covered her face. The tide picked up, pulling back from the shore and then rolling in fast, soaking her jeans to the knee. The entire Earth rearranged itself to her call. She released her breath.

The light couldn't have lasted for more than a second, but Houston felt it as much longer—a timeless journey. A doorway opened in a dark room, and the sensation was so serene, so fluid, that Houston didn't even notice that he was no longer standing on the beach.

He had stepped into her world. Through a veil of fog, he glimpsed a vista of such breathtaking beauty that it opened his mind like a box and poured into him like a waterfall. He was beyond all cares here, in this deathless space filled with stars. Great unknowable things drifted and shimmered in the far reaches of a vibrant cosmos, benevolent and wise, reaching out to him with endless compassion. It was a world that should not have existed so far away as it was from the cares of mortal men, so much higher and nobler was its majestic call.

The stars fell away, and Houston landed back on the sand. The people around him came back into focus, all of them awakening from the same dream.

He heard splashing.

A sharp pain stung his right arm. It was Katya, digging her nails into him. Her jaw was open as she looked toward the shoreline.

The hammerhead writhed on the sand, its tail slapping at the incoming waves. Its head jerked back and forth, its eyes burning with a terrified surge of new life.

Lily stepped away from the shark, but her aura remained around it, blazing with pinks and blues and whites. The guards moved swiftly to the beached animal and looped a rope around its tail fin.

They dragged it into deeper water and released it.

Houston watched the hammerhead swim away, the dorsal fin carving through the dark surface. The cloud of colors kept glittering underwater for a few seconds before it dove into the depths and disappeared.

Lily waded into the shallows up to her knees, watching the shark go. Then, as if a switch had been flipped, her body went limp, and she fell into the water with a soft splash.

Houston rushed into the ocean. The waves had risen in height, and he had to fight his way through them. He dove under a six footer and came up next to Lily's body, saltwater burning his eyes and nose. He lifted her out of the water and carried her back. The sky was dark now, the sun dipping below the far horizon. He shivered in his soaked clothes, his feet sinking into the sand.

Bobby threw a thick blanket over his shoulders. Katya came up on his other side and held his arm, her body warm against his. He could feel Lily breathing against his chest, her shoulders trembling against the cold.

Bobby and Katya stayed by his side the entire walk back to the house. None of them said a word. They simply walked, their shadows stretching long and narrow across the twilight sand.

54

The crow glided above South Bay Avenue at a brisk clip before turning left onto Ocean Street. The crow had been cruising above the long strip of Long Beach Island for the last thirty minutes, drinking up every detail of the town and transmitting a detailed operational map back to its master.

The house with the pink roof was located on the southern tip of the island in a town called Beach Haven. Lights burned in its windows, and the bird spied people moving around inside.

The crow felt a psychic tug at the base of its skull. It pulled up, rising higher above the pink roof before dropping down fast to circle the second floor of the house.

The crow glimpsed the targets through the windows. The red-haired woman stood in a doorway, her arms crossed as she spoke to Houston Holt. Holt had his back to the window, sitting next to the bed where the girl was drinking thirstily from a bottle of water. A weak aura burned around the girl.

Houston Holt said a few words to the girl, and she smiled and pulled the covers over herself. Holt stood and dimmed the lights, but he remained in the room with the red-haired woman.

The girl's protectors.

The sound of a car engine caught the crow's attention, and it watched as a black sedan pulled up to the side of the house, the driver waiting behind the wheel.

The psychic tug called the crow home. It swept back around, and on a patch of sand a mile from the house, it settled down next to its master.

Longhorn rose out of his cocoon, sand streaming off his roped muscles like waterfalls. His lizard eyes opened slowly, an intelligence nefarious and vast locking back into place. The crow shuddered, feathers rustling with an icy jolt as its master shifted his consciousness out of its body and back into his own.

Longhorn watched the pink-roofed house.

It was a process of elimination that had led him to this beach home. His plane's computer had listed all of Augustus Sky's known residences, and he had ruled out the ones that were in Sovereign City or too far away for the injured Houston Holt to reach in time. This was the closest and most isolated shelter possible.

Longhorn's hunch had paid off. He was within striking distance.

Getting in was not a problem. He could slice through the guards without a sound and leave with the Sun Angel before they were dead, but there were risks. This wasn't a backwoods Redblood compound. These were the homes of the Kingdom's wealthiest titans—friends of the Royal Court. A frontal attack in this neighborhood would be met with a swift response from Sovereign City.

Longhorn shifted his eyes away from the house and studied the Kingspire in the distance.

There was another way.

Longhorn lay back down in his narrow trench and covered himself with cool sand. He flipped his consciousness back into the bird, sliding smoothly into its nervous system like glacial water. He felt the brisk air under its wings as it speared high into the air and cruised along the shore, returning to the home with the pink roof.

55

The picture was immense, spreading from wall to wall, its proportions designed to intimidate the viewer. Houston felt like he could walk into its boiling seas and touch the pillars of volcanic smoke.

The dark majesty of hell.

He has been staring at it for a long time. After Lily had fallen asleep, he had wandered around the house and found Katya in this den, sitting on a bench and gazing at the picture. He sat next to her. They didn't say anything to each other.

Over and over, his eyes traced the arc of the ruined islands: Kauai, Oahu, Molokai, Lanai, Maui, Big Island. The picture was taken from high in the atmosphere and blown up to such massive proportions that a small child could curl up comfortably inside the smallest island of Lanai. The Big Island volcanoes spewed smoke into the air, and angry streams of bright lava flowed across the landscape into the Pacific. The boiling storm clouds of the Furies ringed the islands. A plaque at the bottom of the frame read, Image recorded by Hobart Geospatial Satellite.

"Did you see it?" Katya asked, surprising Houston. She was looking at him with a strange expression on her face, beyond tiredness—a simple clarity.

"Yes," Houston replied, knowing what she was talking about. It was what he had been thinking about ever since Lily had brought the hammerhead back to life—that glimpse into another world, the veil swept away for an instant, revealing something neither of them had the words to describe.

"You're taking her home," Katya said. It wasn't a question or an order; she simply knew.

He didn't argue. Two days ago, he would have scoffed at the idea of Sources and Wanderers and prophecies of peace. Two days ago, he was a guy with a gun and a dream, on his way to a Gold Stamp.

But that was two days ago. Now his eyes fell upon the dark islands and contemplated madness.

Katya spoke. "I'm coming with you."

"No."

"I wasn't asking."

"I dragged you into this. You're not going to die because of me."

"Die?" She shook her head, incredulous. Death was a strange concept now, free from what either one of them thought they knew about it. "When the Specials first arrived, my father would always watch the news and say, 'If they can't die, how are they supposed to appreciate life?'"

She massaged her hands, remembering. "I thought about that for a long time. I never really understood what he meant, but I think I get it now." She looked at Houston. "If life lasts forever, it has no value. Whatever little time we humans have, we have to choose how we spend it—what we want to fight for. Wherever that place was that Lily took us to, if that is what the Source is, then it is worth fighting for. Worth dying for."

The room was silent for some time. Katya's hand lay on the bench. Houston squeezed it. "Walk alone, stay alive," he said.

"Not anymore, Houston. That part of your life is over."

Houston turned back to the picture. He wondered again what monsters lay beneath that dark foliage. What beasts waited below the surface of the endless ocean?

He jumped when he realized Lily was sitting next to him.

"Stop doing that!" he yelled, startled. "How long have you been there?"

Lily shrugged. "Not long." She wore the flight cap she had picked up in Seekers Port, the goggles perched above her brows.

"Did you sleep?" Katya asked.

"A little."

"Are you hydrating?" Houston asked.

Lily held up her bottle of water and nodded, the goggles falling over her eyes. She pushed them back up and scratched her nose.

She's a kid, Houston reminded himself, almost shocked by the realization. Despite everything he had seen her do, he felt that surge within him to protect her, to shelter her from the ugliness of the world. It was a ridiculous impulse, but it wasn't one that would ever go away. He knew that now.

She saw him staring and raised an eyebrow. He asked her the question that had been on his mind since the beach. "Does it hurt?"

"Does what hurt?"

"What you did out there."

"No." Lily said softly. "Not like *hurt* hurt. But it . . . it's like I'm giving up something. Like I lose a part of my life to give back life."

"What happens to you," Katya asked, "if you try to bring back something bigger?"

"Like a person?"

Katya nodded.

Lily thought about it, her brow furrowing. "I'd have to give everything. There would be nothing left." She pulled off her cap and twisted it in her hands. "Exactly like the Source."

"What do you mean?" Houston asked.

"The Source gives. That's what she's here for. She will give everything to stop us from destroying ourselves. But if we don't get to her in time . . ." Lily turned to the map, and something hopeless passed across her eyes.

They all sat silently for a few moments, absorbed by the islands and the impossibility of the task ahead of them. Houston cracked a smile and shook his head. "So that's home, huh?"

"It was much nicer when I was there," Lily replied.

Houston shrugged. "Send me a postcard when you get back."

Lily giggled. "You're coming with me."

"Who says?"

"I do."

"I don't know. Looks like the weather sucks."

"Bring an umbrella."

Houston looked at Katya and shook his head. "You believe this kid?"

"We'll have to pack rain boots," Katya said.

"Sunscreen too," Houston said. "What you think, kid? SPF 100 should do the trick, right?"

"More like SPF 300." Lily laughed so hard she hiccuped.

Katya snorted. "I think I have a can of industrial strength bug spray I can bring."

"Does that work on sea serpents?" Houston asked.

"That's what the Hammer is for."

Before long they were all laughing so hard it hurt. The sound of footsteps interrupted them, and Baxter appeared in the doorway. "Bobby is heading back. He wants to see you all before he leaves." He studied the giant photo and adjusted his glasses. "Stunning, isn't it?"

Houston stood up and stretched his neck. "That's one word for it."

They found Bobby waiting for them in the driveway, the black Acura idling behind him. His cell phone rang, but he silenced it.

"My people are having ulcers trying to find me," Bobby said. "You would think I have a big show tonight or something."

"Do we get tickets?" Houston asked.

"Of course. I'll have them reserve you seats on the Royal Dais." Bobby's phone rang again. "Unfortunately, I do have to run."

Katya and Lily hugged him tight, surprising him. "Thank you," Lily said.

Bobby held on to them, smiling. When they let go, Bobby knelt down and produced a beautiful white lily out of the air for Lily. It floated and bloomed brightly, producing its own celestial light before disappearing. "Take care, little one," he said. "You're in good hands."

Bobby stood and motioned his head toward the car. "Houston, walk with me."

Houston followed Bobby out of earshot of the others.

"Not every day you find out you're responsible for the fate of the planet," Bobby joked.

"It's been a weird day."

"Thank you," Bobby said. "It's a lot to ask."

"Don't thank me yet. It's a long way to Hawaii."

"I know. But I feel bad. I wish we had more time." Bobby paused. "I know all of this—" he indicated the house. "—makes it seem like I have everything. And I shouldn't complain, but despite it all, despite all the fans and glamor, I always felt alone. For the longest time, I thought my family was gone. And now that you're here, all I want to do is just sit down and catch up on everything I missed in your life."

"One day," Houston said, "we'll grab a drink at this bar I know back in River Town. Great whiskey."

"That would be nice."

They shook hands. Bobby's brows furrowed. "I should say, Houston, that my offer still stands. If you do want the Gold Stamp, I can sponsor you. We can find another way to get her home."

Houston thought about it for a moment. He watched Lily in her ridiculous hat, shadowboxing the way he had taught her.

"Hold on to that Gold Stamp. I might need it when I get back."

Bobby nodded. "I had no doubt that would be your answer," he said as he turned back to the car. He slipped into the backseat. "Godspeed."

Houston chuckled.

"What?" Bobby asked.

"Someone else said that to me two nights ago. I think it's an omen."

"I hope it's a good one." Bobby shut the door, and the Acura pulled away and disappeared out of the gates.

*

The Acura rolled onto South Bay Avenue and wove its way through the island toward the bridge. High above it, the crow followed, its wings taut against the cool sea wind.

56

The Militiamen waited patiently for the Songbird's Acura to enter the killzone.

On a lonely wooded road, ten minutes away from the Songbird's Victory Island mansion, four Von Arx Militiamen hid under cover of darkness at a sharp bend in the road where they knew the target vehicle would have to slow down. The soldiers were set up in an L-shaped ambush formation, Luca and Abel hidden along the right side of the road while Willem and Karl waited in the Acura's path.

Willem waited until the Acura's headlights had curved around the bend and nosed into the killzone before giving the signal: *Weapons free.*

Immediately, Luca and Abel fired dual bolts four inches above the asphalt, slicing off the bottoms of the speeding car's wheels.

The Acura plummeted onto its severed hubcaps and skidded in a shower of sparks toward the trees, the headlights sweeping across the empty road as the driver struggled to regain control.

The militiamen broke cover simultaneously as the Acura whirled past them and *crunched* against a tree. They descended on the wreck.

The front door opened, and the white-haired driver stumbled out, his bloody hand clenched around an automatic pistol.

Willem closed the gap in a blink and drilled a bolt through the driver's left temple. The man collapsed, dead.

They pulled Augustus Sky out of the broken rear window. He was unconscious and bleeding, but a biological scan by Luca confirmed that he had sustained no life-threatening injuries.

They wrapped him in a black windproof tarp, and Willem hoisted him onto his thick shoulders. Then, with Karl behind him, Willem went airborne, streaking toward Starlet Manor as the other two Militiamen remained behind to dispose of the car and the driver.

The entire operation had taken forty-eight seconds.

High above the treetops, the crow circled over the violent scene. It had followed the Acura all the way from Beach Haven, and the moment its master was certain that Augustus Sky was returning to his Victory Island mansion, the plan had been set in motion.

*

As soon as the car had taken the exit for the Verrazano Bridge, Longhorn had called the Lady in the Veil. Caspar had been sitting next to her in Starlet Manor when her phone had rung. He watched her glide away soundlessly to the lightless parlor, the phone to her ear.

It had been hours since Veena and the Lady had returned from neutralizing Deb, and even though the Peacock Gown was back in play, the missing Sun Angel had kept Caspar's nerves on edge—that and Veena's troubling behavior all day.

"Caspar," the Lady said when she returned to the room.

"Who was that?" Caspar asked.

The Lady in the Veil pocketed the phone, her eyes shining victoriously. "Gather your men. Gather them fast. We have work to do."

*

Caspar was watching the breathless on-scene coverage of the parade preparations on the Crown News Network when Willem and Karl hauled the Songbird into the Manor. Three Militiamen met them at the back door and took possession of the tarp-wrapped body.

Not wanting to get too close, Caspar stood off to the side with the Lady and watched his bodyguards carry their captive along the hall and down the basement steps. It was hard for Caspar to fathom that the Songbird himself was their prisoner. They had crossed a line by kidnapping the king's favorite singer.

Paris, he whispered. *Remember Paris.*

He turned to the Lady. "Will this work?"

She adjusted her shawl. "Of course."

Behind them on the TV, the crowds cheered. Millions of people had gathered along Phoenix Avenue, thronging behind the barricades, many of them having waited there since the early morning hours for the best viewing spots. Caspar pulled on his jacket lapel as the camera panned to the empty Royal Dais.

He closed his eyes and saw the sidewalk cafés of the Fourth Arrondissement.

The Lady spoke. "I'm going to inform Veena that our guest is here."

Caspar opened his eyes, Paris disappearing. His thoughts darkened as he focused on his next problem: Veena Sixkills.

She had hidden herself away since returning from her mission, appearing only briefly, glum faced and distracted, as the Lady had explained Longhorn's plan. Veena had listened quietly until the Lady mentioned that the Songbird would be held hostage here.

"Here?" Veena had exclaimed, eyes wide. "You can't bring him here. He's performing tonight. He lives right across the street, for God's sake. What if someone sees him here?" Veena had then paused. "What if someone's watching us?"

"Who would be watching us, dear?" Caspar had interjected.

"We have all been *so* careful. Haven't we?"

Veena had fixed him with a long, strange look—part guilt, part hostility. Then she'd waved him away dismissively. "Do what you want," she had huffed before leaving the room under a dark cloud. A few seconds later, they'd heard the door to the back garden open and slam shut.

If Caspar had any reservations about killing her when this was over, they were lessening by the minute.

He hadn't mentioned his plans to the Lady. He trusted her a fraction more than he did Veena, but that wasn't saying much. Their strange family arrangement was coming to an end, and for Caspar, surviving the aftermath meant removing Veena from the equation.

Now he took a step forward and blocked the Lady's path. The Lady peered at him curiously from under her shawl.

"Allow me to inform Veena," he said. "I need the fresh air anyway."

*

Veena's back was to Caspar as he approached her. A soft breeze blew off the dark waters of the Sound and through her hair

He joined her by the water's edge, on her private pier. She was looking toward Sovereign City, which was hazy beneath the stunning light of the Kingspire. She ignored his presence.

Caspar broke the silence. "Our guest has arrived."

Veena didn't move. Her eyes stayed on the Kingspire.

"Veena," he started again, "our guest—"

"I heard you the first time."

Caspar waited. When it became clear he wasn't going to get anything else from her, he sighed and turned to leave.

She said something he didn't catch.

"What was that?" he asked.

"Reborn in blood."

Caspar frowned. "What does that mean, dear?"

"It's one of my father's creeds," Veena said, her eyes finding him. "It means that we can change ourselves and become who we were meant to be—but only if we make the choice everyone else is afraid to make."

"Which is what we've done—what *you* have done. Your father would be proud."

"You've obviously never met my father."

"Well, if it's any consolation, my parents won't have a chance to be proud of me because they'll be dead."

"Along with that cunt sister of yours."

"My toes just tingle at the thought."

Just then, the Kingspire burst open like a fountain and reformed in ropes of brilliant blue.

"It really is stunning," Caspar marveled.

"My father's first order as king will be to destroy it."

Caspar chuckled. "Oh, well. Just one of the ways the world will look different tomorrow."

"Reborn," Veena said.

"Yes. Reborn."

Caspar looked at his watch. "Let's head back, darling. It's time we chatted with the Songbird."

They walked back together through the dark lawn. Lights had been strung up from the trees, and the pool glowed turquoise. It was a lovely place for get-togethers, family reunions, good friends, and big laughs—not that this place had seen any of those things, Caspar mused. This was a lonely place, like its owner—bereft of something vital.

Veena strode a few feet ahead of him. He glimpsed her pale neck in the dimness.

He had already provided instructions to his militiamen on how to deal with Veena Sixkills.

As soon as the Sun Angel had been repossessed and dispatched to Sovereign, the Von Arx Militiamen would hold Veena down while Caspar wrapped his fingers around that beautiful throat.

It wasn't even about the slap, although he could still feel the sting of her hand across his cheek. That insult to his pride he could get over. There was something far more important that Veena had put at risk. Right at this moment, a young drifter with a remarkable resemblance to Caspar was checked in at the penthouse suite of the palatial Marrakech Hotel on Phoenix Avenue. He was wearing the finest clothes and marveling at his good fortune as he wandered around his opulent apartment with its sweeping views of the Decennial Parade below.

Only Caspar's own family would be able to spot the man as an impostor—a clueless body double with a very short life expectancy.

When the Sun Angel—locked in a vehicle in the hotel's basement garage—detonated, the body double would be obliterated.

To the outside world, Caspar Von Arx would be just one of the countless casualties of the Redblood terror attack, a sidebar in the *Sovereign Times* overshadowed by the deaths of his parents and the Royal Couple.

And that suited Caspar just fine.

By then he would be across the border in Mexico, courtesy of a well-compensated bush pilot who would never know the true identity of his disguised passenger. Then another smuggler would fly him to Jamaica before his long-haul flight to Johannesburg. In Cape Town he would go under the knife, plastic surgeons reconstructing his face and sucking out the stubborn fat around his midriff.

Next, after a ludicrously short recovery time, he would fly to Dublin, where fresh identity papers and stacks of crisp Euros would be waiting for him in a rented loft on Exchequer Street.

And finally, a stealthy boat ride across the channel to Paris.

It had been planned months in advance. The mechanics of his escape were intricate, meticulous, and dangerously fragile.

And Veena could bring it all crashing down with a single word.

Her Moxi relapse had been the final nail in her coffin. Caspar didn't know what had triggered the relapse or what she had revealed under the influence, but he did know one thing: she would relapse again.

And again.

And all it took was one slip, one indiscrete word in front of the wrong people, and the dream would end.

Between the trees, he saw his Von Arx Militiamen patrolling the grounds. His entire contingent of eighteen bodyguards was here. He had called them all up earlier in the day, and now, in the shadowy garden, he was glad that he had. In these final hours, he felt a shift—a heightening of the stakes, as if he were dancing on the edge of a blade.

*

Willem and the Lady were waiting in the kitchen when Caspar returned with Veena. Willem held up a cell phone, dwarfed in his massive paw.

"Is that the Songbird's phone?" Caspar asked.

"Yes. Abel bypassed his phone's security. This is the number for his house in Beach Haven."

"Excellent," Caspar said. "Make the call."

"What call?" Veena asked from the doorway.

"To Houston Holt," the Lady explained.

"What will you say?" Veena asked Willem.

The big guard glared at her, stone-faced. Veena threw up her hands and turned to Caspar, exasperated.

"Don't worry yourself, darling," Caspar said. "Willem has done this before."

Veena looked at the mounted TV, at the parade crowds thrumming with wild energy. "No, Caspar, he hasn't—not like this. We have less than three hours before the biggest coup in history. Your brute here needs to communicate a sense of urgency."

She pulled a heavy chef's knife off the counter and tossed it to Willem. The blade spun and then shuddered to a halt in midair. Using his Gift, Willem guided the blade into his fist.

"If you're going to send those lowbloods a message," she said, looking between the knife and Willem's stone eyes, "send them one they won't forget."

57

Baxter picked up the call on the landline. "It's Bobby," he said, glancing at the screen. He excused himself and left the room.

Houston dug his spoon into the tub of cookie dough ice cream and unearthed a giant chunk. Lily followed suit, digging out an even larger ball.

"You're an animal," Houston said, incredulous.

"Animals don't eat that much," she said. "They only eat what they need."

"Not hippos."

"I like hippos," she said, slurping the ice cream off her spoon. "They remind me of grumpy old men. Like you."

Houston pulled the tub away from her. "You've lost dessert privileges for the rest of the day."

In the living room, Katya watched the Crown News Network. It had been three hours since Bobby had left, and the crowds along the parade route had multiplied, their cheers ringing through the speakers.

Earlier in the newscast, the correspondents had brought on military analysts to discuss the meaning of this day. They spoke in grave tones about the sacrifices the young Kingdom had to endure to reach this momentous occasion. But now, the focus of the discussion had shifted to a more pressing matter: the gown

Queen Callista would wear on the Royal Dais. No less than six style analysts batted around their predictions.

"Who is this?"

Houston looked up. Baxter's voice came from two rooms over, loud and hostile. "How did you get this phone?" Baxter demanded.

Houston and Lily looked at each other. They went to the living room, where Katya was already on alert. Baxter entered, phone to his ear.

"I'm going to ask you again," Baxter said. "How—"

He stopped and listened. His jaw tightened. He mouthed *pen* to the others and held out his hand, hurrying them. Lily found one on a side table. Baxter snatched it and scribbled on an envelope.

"Slow down," he said. "Let me make sure I have this right. Wait . . . *wait!*" Baxter yelled. He glared at the phone before hanging up.

"Who was that?" Houston asked.

"Somebody has Bobby's phone."

"What do you mean, someone has Bobby's phone?"

"Where's Bobby?" Lily asked.

"I don't know." Baxter carried the envelope with him to his laptop on the dining table. They leaned over his shoulder while he typed in the web address he had scrawled on the envelope. "Whoever took Bobby's phone said we have to log on to this site right now. If we don't . . ."

A password prompt appeared on his screen. Baxter typed in the string of digits written below the web address. The prompt disappeared, and a single video file floated in white space.

Baxter clicked on the file. The video screen opened, a rectangle of black.

For a few seconds, nothing happened. The black rectangle remained inert and silent.

"This is bullshit," Katya said.

"Wait," Baxter said.

The rectangle moved. Someone exhaled loudly behind the frame, and the first trickles of light entered the darkness. Then they saw Bobby.

"No." Houston heard the words come from outside him, but he knew they were his own.

His brother sat under a single lightbulb, ringed by shadow. He was shackled, wrist and ankle, to a wooden chair, and his mouth was covered in duct tape. A sheen of sweat layered his skin, but if Bobby was afraid, his eyes did not show it. They glared at someone offscreen.

The voice, when it spoke, caused Lily to flinch against Houston. It was a man's voice run through a digital distorter so that nothing human remained.

"Augustus Sky," the voice drawled, "is ours now."

Katya hissed between her teeth. Baxter never took his eyes off the screen, but his hands reached for his phone and typed a number from memory.

"The girl," the voice said. "Give us the girl."

Houston put his hand on Lily's shoulder. "Lily, go upstairs."

"No," she snapped. "Don't treat me like I'm a kid."

Houston glared at her and she glared back, solid as a boulder.

The man spoke again. "Give us the girl, and the Songbird lives. If you refuse—"

Bobby's eyes widened for an instant as something sharp entered the frame. A chef's knife cruised through the dark toward Bobby's throat.

Katya gripped Lily's shoulder. "Turn away."

Lily ignored her, but Houston noticed something in Lily's eyes he hadn't seen before—an energy beyond anger, darker and more ancient.

Onscreen, the hovering blade circled Bobby, tracing the contours of his exposed neck, caressing the line of his jaw.

"Bring the girl to the jade fire pit outside your house at 9:45 p.m. If you are even one minute late—" The blade sliced open Bobby's cheek, drawing a line of blood. Bobby barely flinched, his eyes fixed on his offscreen tormentor.

"Bring the girl at 9:45 p.m., or the next video will be bloodier."

The rectangle went black.

They all looked up at the clock on the wall.

9:35 p.m.

Baxter stood and faced Houston and Katya, simmering. Lily's dark energy filled the room like a storm cloud, vibrating rebelliously. They didn't have to say anything. They had come to a silent agreement, a circling of the wagons.

"We're not giving her up," Katya said.

"No, we're not," Houston agreed.

"But what about Bobby?" Lily asked.

Baxter's phone rang. He went to the kitchen and picked up the call.

"What about Bobby?" Lily asked again.

It was now 9:36 p.m.

"I can't leave him," Houston said finally.

"No, you can't," Lily agreed.

Katya crossed her arms. "We can't just hand over Lily."

Houston paced. "If we knew where they were . . ."

"But we don't," Katya said. "And even if we did, how do we fight people like this?"

"I thought that was what your life was about," Houston said coldly. "Fighting power."

"You want to wrap Lily up in a box and hand her over?"

Houston rubbed his brow. They didn't have many options, and the ones they did have were hopeless.

Baxter returned from the kitchen, pocketing his phone. He glanced at the clock and then at the others in the room.

"We're not abandoning Bobby," he said.

"You can't—" Katya began, but Baxter held up a hand.

"And we're not abandoning Lily either."

Houston and Katya looked at each other. Baxter continued, "I've lost a lot of good people over the years. I've had to live with the fact that there are members of the Ohana rotting away in unmarked graves hundreds of miles from home. But we have learned our lesson. The Ohana always bring back our own—at any cost." He straightened his glasses, strangely calm. "Every Ohana member is now surgically implanted with a GPS locator linked to our private satellite network."

It was like an electric current had rippled through the room. "You know where Bobby is?" Houston asked, hope rising.

"Not yet. I just got off the phone with my people. They're tracking him. The technology can be spotty, but—"

"But you *can* find him?" Katya pressed.

"Eventually, yes."

"We have to buy time," Houston said. "Get his location and find a way to get him out."

"For once, I agree with you, Houston," Baxter said. "Katya, what are you thinking?"

Katya worked her jaw, one hand on her holster. "How do we buy time—by handing Lily over and then hoping we track Bobby down before it's too late?"

When Houston and Baxter didn't respond, Katya continued, "I won't accept that. I can't."

"I'm going," Lily said.

They all turned. Lily had a way of disappearing in a room and then reappearing when she wanted to. She was looking at all of them, her body very still, but there was no mistaking the fear in her eyes, the tremble in her voice.

"No." Katya shook her head. "No. There must be another way."

"I'm going," Lily said again, louder this time. She turned to the windows, and it was as if her eyes glimpsed terrible shapes out there in the darkness. They all felt the night pushing in on them, a malevolent, suffocating fate none of them could escape. Lily struggled to say something else, but her voice betrayed her, refusing to form the words. She broke her gaze away from the dark and clenched her fists. When she spoke, she spoke from a deeper place, a reservoir of courage that only children seemed to find. She forced the words out, quieting the quiver in her voice. "You can't let Bobby die. You need time. It's the only way."

It was 9:38 p.m.

"We're not letting them take you," Houston said, adamant. "I'll find a way—"

"This *is* the way," Lily interrupted, the strength in her voice piercing Houston. She turned her face up to him, all eyes and hope. Her hand slipped into his and squeezed. "You'll come for me. You'll get me back home."

The moment she said those words, something died inside of Houston. Something vital and human dissipated into ash, and a barbaric shadow emerged, born of blood and violence and rage, clawing at his insides, clamoring for war. He wrapped his calloused fingers around her tiny hand. His body trembled. She believed he could do the impossible, and—in that moment—he believed it too. He knelt down. "I'll come for you."

"You better," Lily said.

Katya covered her mouth, stricken. Lily ran over and hugged her. Baxter checked his phone again.

"It's almost 9:40," he said. "The jade pit is a few minutes down the beach."

Lily shouldered her backpack. Houston and Katya stuffed it with bottles of water.

"Anything else you need?" Houston asked.

"Maybe a tub of cookie dough."

"How about something with some nutrients? You might like it."

Lily rolled her eyes. "Fine."

Houston went to the kitchen and pulled out a handful of energy bars from the cabinet. He stopped and looked at them. They were the same energy bars he'd carried to Ringwood on the night of the exchange—the same bars a strange little girl had munched on next to him while they drove through the darkness together.

When he returned, Katya was helping Lily into her jacket. "What are you thinking?" Katya asked her.

"Nothing," Lily replied.

"It's okay to be afraid," Katya said.

Lily tugged on her backpack. "Get there fast."

"Fast as we can."

Houston took Lily's hand.

"You ready?" he asked.

"Giddyup."

He led her out the back door to the beach. Katya and Baxter stood at the door and watched them as they made their way down the cool sand toward the jade fire pit in the distance.

The walk was the longest Houston had taken in his life. Every step of the way, he felt like he was sinking into despair. He held Lily's hand tight.

Up ahead, he saw the low outline of the fire pit. He didn't see anyone waiting for them there.

The water rushed up the beach, soft and soothing.

Houston felt a certainty in Lily's grip, a message she was passing along to him. He wanted to embed it deep into his marrow, because once he let go—once she was gone—he was afraid he would forget it.

A crow cawed overhead when they arrived at the fire pit. Houston's watch flipped to 9:45.

Burning pain returned to Houston's left shoulder. He gritted his teeth and braced himself.

The man in the hat had arrived. He slid out of the night and stood on the other side of the fire pit, watching them.

It took the last of Houston's strength to release Lily's hand. She turned to him and held his gaze.

"See you later," she said.

Houston held up his palm. "In case I'm a little late, remember what I taught you."

She popped a quick jab against his palm.

"And if that doesn't work?"

"*Bam!* Punch 'em in the noodles." Lily smiled and turned to the waiting man. Before leaving, she reached into her backpack, pulled out a folded piece of paper, and handed it to Houston.

She walked across the sand. Longhorn reached out and grabbed her roughly. He locked a Clamp around her right wrist and pulled her into the shadows.

They were gone.

Houston opened the folded paper. It was her drawing of the Big Island. Her home.

Houston took a moment, just one moment that he needed for himself, before the hunt began. The shadow inside him rustled and unfurled its claws as he watched the ocean and thought about the breed of people who would do this, who would take Lily and hurt her for a crown. In that moment, he made a promise:

I'm going to kill every last one of you.

58

Houston raced back into the house and found it teeming with the Ohana guards. They stood around Baxter, nodding silently as he gave them orders. Katya raced down the stairs, throwing on her jacket.

"We found Bobby," Katya said, tossing Houston his SIG Sauer and holster.

"Where?"

"I'll tell you in the car."

Baxter broke away from the Ohana guards and made a call. "Yes, prepare it for immediate takeoff," Baxter said into the phone. "Victory Island. Yes, I am aware. But this is the Songbird's aircraft. They'll let us through."

Houston followed Katya to the garage. At the door, she turned and pulled him aside.

"Was it him?" she asked. "The man in the hat?"

Houston nodded.

Katya shuddered. "What about Lily? Was she afraid?"

"Don't think about that," Houston said as Baxter joined them at the door. "Just keep moving."

"Let's go. The plane's refueling," Baxter said, stepping into the garage.

"Where's Bobby?" Houston asked.

Katya shook her head as they rushed to the waiting Land Rover. "You're not going to freaking believe this."

*

Even if anyone had been paying attention to Melody House, the Songbird's Victory Island mansion, they wouldn't have noticed the two Ohana operatives slip through a side gate as stealthy as thieves. The two men were in their forties, and they carried rucksacks loaded out with the tools of their trade. They crept through the shadows of the garden and hoisted themselves up the mansion walls much too quickly for men of their years.

On the roof, the two Ohana opened their rucksacks and assembled their gear. Each man, from time to time, glanced at the glowing beauty of Starlet Manor across a half mile of garden and asphalt. The first man assembled and programmed his spy drone in less than two minutes. Small enough to be launched by hand, it carried three cameras: a navigation camera on the nose and two lenses mounted on the undercarriage capable of recording thermal and night vision images. The second man checked the drone's camera transmissions on his laptop.

"Eyes one and two both open," he said.

The pilot nodded and tossed the drone in the air. The drone swept up high, black against the night as it cruised over the Songbird's property and crossed behind enemy lines, over the high red walls of Starlet Manor.

*

"Veena fucking Sixkills."

Houston muttered the name like a curse. The drone circled three thousand feet above Veena's mansion, streaming a night vision image back to Baxter's laptop.

Houston was crammed into the back seat of the Land Rover, alongside Baxter and Katya, as an Ohana guard drove them through the empty streets of Beach Haven. The ride to the airport was only supposed to take ten minutes, but the driver kept his foot on the brake, keeping his eye out for cruising security patrols.

Baxter communicated back and forth with the Ohana drone team, typing out commands on his laptop. They scanned the immense property using the night vision camera first, Houston memorizing all the entry and exit points. Next to him, Katya multitasked, sketching the layout on her notepad while cradling Baxter's cell phone between her shoulder and ear. The voice on the other end sounded flustered to Houston. Obviously, one of her Badge subordinates was wilting under her barrage of questions as she dug for any intel the Badges had on Veena Sixkills.

Houston noticed movement on Veena's estate—people slipping in and out of the trees. It wasn't until they switched to infrared that they realized how dire their situation was.

"Uh-oh," Katya whispered, glaring at the screen.

The guards burned brightly in the blackness. Their heat signatures spread out along the gardens and the woods, moving purposefully in the manner of soldiers. Houston counted their numbers.

"Twenty-two," Houston said. "Eighteen on the perimeter. Four people inside the house, including one person who isn't moving."

"Bobby," Baxter said, focusing on the immobile heat signature inside the house.

"How can you be sure?" Katya asked, ignoring her chattering subordinate on the phone.

"Look." Baxter pointed to the screen. A thin layer of translucent light shimmered above the prone figure. The other three figures in the home moved freely atop the surface. "These three are on the first level. This layer, that's a floor. Bobby," he said, pointing to the figure again, "is in the basement."

"Imprisoned," Houston grunted, his pulse throbbing in his temple.

"But alive," Baxter said.

Houston leaned over the laptop screen. "Run a bio on everyone."

Baxter began typing out a command. His fingers froze on the keyboard as a patrol car cruised by them going the opposite way. When it was lost in their rearview mirror, he sent the command.

Twelve seconds later, the Ohana drone switched from its infrared lens to its biowave setting. The red-orange heat signatures changed color immediately. A handful glowed yellow, but the vast majority, including all of the men out in the gardens, burned with fierce white lattices of light.

Houston felt the muscles knot in his neck. "Fuck."

He counted the number of burning white figures. When he was done, he leaned back and stared at the ceiling. "Eighteen Alphas."

"Shit," Katya whispered.

"Shit indeed," Baxter concurred.

"Silverbacks?" Katya asked. "Sixkills is next in line to the throne, and that's his daughter's home. He could be using Lily to kill the king."

"Possible," Houston said.

"Possible, but not likely," Baxter interjected. "The general and his daughter have a painful history. The last person he would trust is Veena. And in any case, Houston, does this look like a Silverback operation to you?"

Houston had to admit that it didn't. The Silverbacks only knew one way: overwhelming force. If General Sixkills wanted the throne, he would rip Patriot Gold off it with his bare hands.

In any case, it didn't matter. Going head-to-head with eighteen Alphas, regardless of who they were, was beyond dangerous. It was suicide.

"The Badges can handle this," Katya announced. "I can get thirty men banging down Veena's door within the hour."

Houston looked at Baxter. Baxter looked at Houston. A bubble of silence hung in the car as both men struggled with how to respond. Then Houston's lip curled up ever so slightly at the sight of Baxter's incredulous expression, and that was all it took for both of them to explode in laughter. They cackled like goons, their laughs sweeping through the tension of the car like ocean air.

"Let's be serious," Houston managed between breaths. "Sending thirty knuckleheads in there isn't going to do anything."

"You're right. The three of us going in alone is a *much* better idea," Katya retorted. "Screw you." She returned to her call. "Fine. The second you get more, you call me on this number." She hung up and turned to the others. "Veena Sixkills is one piece of work."

"What do you have?" Houston asked.

"Famous, beautiful celebrity. Beyond that? Rumors she's a Mox-head who's infamous for killing her own slaves. She had a nervous breakdown a year ago and killed her own seamstresses in an arson attack on a warehouse. Probably more dirt on her record than on a farmer's boot, but because of Daddy Sixkills, the press doesn't touch her." Katya punched the seat in front of her. "Fuck them! They get away with everything, don't they?"

"Not tonight," Houston said.

"She sounds unstable," Baxter said coolly. "Dangerous and unpredictable, but not a mastermind." He turned to the drone image and pointed to two non-Alphas in the house. "Which means one of these two is the brains."

The car passed through a chain-link gate that opened automatically. They sat in silence as the car approached a Lear jet with the Songbird logo on the tail. Its door was open and the stairs were down, waiting for them. They jumped out of the Land Rover and rushed onto the plane. As they buckled into their seats, the jet engines whined, and a prim flight attendant sealed the door.

"Eighteen Alphas." Katya closed her eyes. "How do we take on *eighteen* Alphas?"

The plane swiveled and turned onto the runway. Houston stared out his window, searching for an answer. Maybe there was none.

Baxter regarded him, his glasses reflecting the lights. "What would you need to fight them?"

"A Marine platoon," Houston replied. "Anyone have the number for the Iron Vikings?"

"Seriously." He leveled his gaze at Houston. "If you had the resources, how would you do it?"

"I would do the one thing they wouldn't expect."

"Which is what?" Katya asked.

Houston took Baxter's laptop and studied the feed, his eyes scanning the eighteen Alphas, each one powerful enough to fell a jet. "They see us as lowbloods—small-timers unable to compete with them and their Gifts. We could use stealth and try to avoid them, but they're prepared for that." Houston's eyes locked onto Katya first, then Baxter. "What they're not prepared for is overwhelming force."

"But," Houston said as he leaned back, "we don't have the weapons for that kind of an assault."

Baxter tapped his chin. "That's not entirely accurate."

Houston blinked. "What are you saying?"

"I'm saying that the Ohana may have acquired and stockpiled certain items over the years."

"Wait, wait." Katya held up her hand. "What happened to love and harmony and bringing the world back to peace?"

"We believe all of that, and we practice nonviolent engagement whenever possible. But when it is not possible . . ." Baxter's eyes hardened. "When the time comes to protect one of our own, the Ohana can be quite pragmatic."

"Pragmatic, huh?" Houston said as the plane taxied down the runway. "How pragmatic are you willing to be today?"

Baxter smiled while dialing a number on his phone. "For Robert and Lily? *Ruthlessly* pragmatic."

59

It took Longhorn less than an hour to trek back from Long Beach Island to the Manahawkin Airfield. The Sun Angel lay over his shoulder, unconscious.

The moment they had left the beach he had felt her eyes on him, investigating him, shining a light on places best kept hidden.

"I know where you're from," she had said. Longhorn had detected a trace of sadness in her voice. If she really did know where he was from, she would be more afraid. But then, this was no ordinary child.

Even with the Clamp muting her powers, he had still felt the traces of her Gift reach out and touch his wound, alighting on the ridge of scar tissue in bitter pain.

They had just stepped off the beach when he released the stun bolt into her neck. Her Gift had receded first, yanked out of the air like a tablecloth, before her body went limp.

Longhorn feared neither man nor beast. But this girl—this *being*—was better off unconscious.

She'd breathed softly against his shoulder as he'd carried her across the island and over Manahawkin Bay on a stolen dinghy. Back on the mainland, he had moved lightly over the marshlands and woods, his eyes drinking in the spare ambient light from the clouded moon. More than once, the girl had shuddered against him, under assault from some nightmare. He knew the real nightmare would begin when she awoke.

This girl would die tonight.

Why and how were not his concern. It was her turn to die. There was nothing more to it.

In the near distance, he heard music. Less than three minutes later, the border of the airfield came into view.

Longhorn's Cessna waited under the camouflage tarp. The runway lights were off, and the lights from the air control barn extended weakly out onto the tarmac for a few dozen feet, leaving the rest in darkness. Longhorn approached the airfield from the side. He laid the girl down in the grass and felt her pulse. She would be down for a while. He crept to the edge of the airfield, still hidden in the trees and grass.

For a long time, he watched.

Returning to his plane was the most dangerous stage. If anyone wanted to kill him, this was where they would lay their trap.

Hands pressed into the dirt, nose raised to the winds, he read the world around him, searching for a shift in the atmosphere, a disturbance in the terrain—anything that gave him a warning. After a few seconds, he sent out the call. A sliver of energy shot out across a frequency that no man could hear.

The brown mutt trotted over to him from its home behind the shed. It cocked its head and studied him in the dark with its white-patched eye. The dog licked his palm and waited, watching the airfield with Longhorn. Longhorn rose to his knees and ran his hand along the dog's rough fur. He settled his hand over the dog's neck and closed his eyes.

*

Magnusson waited.

Darkness had fallen, and still no sign of his prey. Two planes took off and one landed, but the black Cessna had not moved. No one had even gone close to it, but it was only a matter of time.

Deep in the painful slog of Silverback Sniper School, he had learned the art of patience—the control of his breathing, the reading of distances, the assimilation into the environment. He'd learned to stalk, to move inches at a time, to kill at great distances. But most of all, he had learned how to wait—in bitter cold, in boiling heat, in light, in dark—the passage of time meant nothing to the sniper.

Movement ahead. Magnusson's eyes shifted over to it, slow as a snake's.

The brown dog shambled out of the darkness. Magnusson tracked it from the corner of his eyes, unconcerned. It was just doing its rounds again. This was its territory.

The dog froze a few feet away from Magnusson's hide. It turned, and—Magnusson was certain of this—glared right at him. The dog had probably smelled his hide much earlier in the day, but until now it had shown no interest.

The dog's eyes glinted, black orbs in the pale light. It stood very still, unblinking.

The dog turned and walked away. If the dog's behavior struck Magnusson as strange, he didn't have time to dwell on it, because it was at that moment he saw the man appear.

Magnusson blinked once, twice. He raised his head an inch and focused on the figure across the airfield.

Longhorn.

His target stepped out of the cover of the woods onto the edge of the tarmac. Over his shoulder, he carried a young girl.

Got you, motherfucker.

A black Stetson and fur collar hid Longhorn's face, but Magnusson could make out the ridge of a sharp nose, the sheen of long black hair. Wolflike, he loped toward the black Cessna. Even from a distance of three hundred feet, Magnusson could recognize one of his own tribe—a born warrior.

But there was something more about this man—the wiry, predatory aura, the shadows that claimed him. *More than a warrior*, Magnusson noted with regret. *An exceptional warrior.*

It was a shame. He would have preferred to meet a man like that in single combat, face to face, steel to steel—the honorable way. The Silverback way.

But he would have to go with option B.

Longhorn was about to eat a double kill bolt from long range.

Magnusson gripped his spear with both hands and steadied it against his shoulder. He placed the center of the targeting sights level with Longhorn's chest, leading him by a few hairs. With a swift slide of his thumb against the range calibrator, he primed the weapon for the three-hundred-foot shot.

Longhorn was now halfway to the Cessna. Magnusson channeled his Gift and stored it inside the spear's shaft. The weapon responded, vibrating against his hands and shoulder. Magnusson was about to fire when the attack came.

It arrived from above, a shrieking missile of talons and feathers tearing at Magnusson's eyes.

The shot left the spear high, spearing into the trees across the tarmac in a shower of sparks. Magnusson rolled and thrust his forearm across his face, the razor talons scraping across his cheeks and hands, leathery wings beating against him.

Magnusson swept the spear in an arc, slashing the bird across its wings. It cawed and took flight, flapping above the trees.

Magnusson was on his feet, racing through the trees, collapsing the spear and sheathing it. Already he could see Longhorn ducking behind cover, putting the equipment shed between himself and Magnusson.

Shunk! A black bolt crackled through the trees and set Magnusson's hide aflame. *Shunk, shunk, shunk*—more bolts sheared the trees around him, skimming his skin like scalding irons.

He ran in a wide circle, dodging right, then left, trying to track where the bolts were coming from. He needed to fire back. *Fast.*

A flurry of bolts burned the air above him. His lungs drew in smoky air, and in that choking breath, he read his opponent's Gift. It was a scripture of blood and pain as dark beings writhed in a pit of snakes—a Warborn.

Magnusson grinned. This would be a fight to remember.

When the next bolt arrived, Magnusson had already gauged its source. Longhorn was moving clockwise, using the far tree line as cover.

Now.

Magnusson unleashed a stream of cluster bolts. The far tree line ruptured into flashes of blinding silver light and heat. He fired more clusters and moved—fired and moved, fired and moved. He circled around to Longhorn's position. The crow cawed above him.

The forest ahead of him *sizzled.*

A tsunami bolt, a ten-foot wall of crashing black energy, tore toward him.

Crafty fucker.

Magnusson went airborne. It would break his cover and turn him into an open target, but that was Longhorn's plan.

Magnusson shot up and back at an angle. The tsunami bolt traced the bottom of his boots, sending a violent jolt up his spine. The black bolts found him fast. Magnusson dodged and corkscrewed furiously, skimming the treetops.

There.

Longhorn darted out from behind a tree toward a rusted junk heap.

Magnusson rocketed down. At sixty miles per hour, he caught Longhorn hard on the chest with both feet. Longhorn tumbled backward. Magnusson's heels hit the ground in a skid that tore grass off the earth. But there was no time to catch his breath. Longhorn was already unleashing his next attack.

They fired at the same time, kill bolt for kill bolt streaking past the other—warning shots across the bow.

The bolts ceased as both men came face-to-face across the dark tarmac. Longhorn's hat had fallen off in the skirmish, but Magnusson still couldn't see his eyes.

Longhorn took a step forward. Magnusson fired. Longhorn dodged. His body twisted and bent like rubber as he plowed forward, inexorable. With each step, Longhorn was sending a message: This fight will not take place at long range. I will make you *feel* it.

Magnusson unholstered his spear.

The weapon telescoped out with *chunk* to its full six-foot length—the most satisfying sound in the world to a Silverback. Hefting the reassuring weight of his sidearm, Magnusson strode forward to meet Longhorn. His opponent unsheathed two gleaming tomahawks. Magnusson noticed the textured grips, the NightAlloy blades—the work of a master.

The two blades met in a shower of sparks, spear versus axe. They clashed, parried, retreated, and clashed again.

The first exchange died within seconds. The two fighters took a step back, eyes level. The opening skirmish had given them vital information on the other, minute tactical details unfolding before the warriors' eyes—speed, reflexes, strength, footwork.

They circled each other.

Magnusson held the spear at half guard, the butt braced at his hip, the tip of the blade tracking Longhorn's head. Longhorn threw up a jab with his axe. Magnusson parried. Longhorn threw up another, and Magnusson parried again.

From here Magnusson could fire a bolt through the spear straight into Longhorn's skull. But those were not the rules they had agreed on. They had chosen the hard way.

A blur of motion. Longhorn shot forward. Magnusson spun, tapping the spear hard against his back. Longhorn tumbled forward with his momentum. Longhorn reset his feet and attacked again. Magnusson deftly sidestepped.

Control the distance—the primary rule of spear fighting. With his longer weapon, Magnusson had the advantage. He could dictate the range at which the battle would take place. With his shorter tomahawks, Longhorn would need to get inside the spear's reach to strike.

Magnusson held a high guard, angling the spear down and bouncing forward, attacking Longhorn's unprotected legs. Longhorn retreated, but not before the spear drew spurts of blood below his knees.

Their feet crushed the grass underfoot. Somewhere far away, Magnusson could hear music, but in this circle of combat, it was peaceful.

Magnusson slashed Longhorn across the shoulder. Longhorn swung his right tomahawk. Magnusson expected a short slice, but Longhorn threw the blade.

The spinning axe tore off a chunk of Magnusson's left tricep. The pain burst in his body like a toxic bubble, weakening his limbs. Magnusson tried to refocus and continue his attack, but it was already too late. In that split second, Longhorn closed the distance.

The tomahawk slashed in tight arcs. Magnusson twisted and snapped the spear release switch, separating it into two close-quarters weapons—a clubbed baton and a short sword—and met Longhorn blow for crushing blow.

In the frenzy of the fight, Magnusson fired stun bolts at Longhorn's feet, disrupting his footwork. Longhorn snaked in and out like a cobra, lightning fast.

A stun bolt hammered into Magnusson's shins. His legs turned to stone, and he crashed to the dirt. Longhorn's tomahawk slashed down toward his skull.

Woompf! Magnusson uncorked his own stun bolt, which blasted Longhorn's legs out from under him.

Crawling now, Magnusson inched his way toward his downed foe. Legs still frozen, the men grappled with clubbing fists, forearms, and cutting elbows.

Magnusson locked Longhorn's neck and shoulder in a vise. Only a fraction of strength had returned to his legs, so when he lifted off, Magnusson had to accelerate entirely from his core.

They went airborne.

Longhorn was fast, strong, and vicious, but there was one thing he couldn't do: fly.

Still gripping Longhorn, Magnusson rose above the trees, sweating and struggling to hold on to his captive, who writhed like a mongoose. The ground receded fast, the planes growing smaller, the barn a cluster of tiny lights. At fifty feet, Magnusson released him.

Longhorn windmilled down and thudded against the tarmac. Magnusson dove down on the prone figure, fists searing with bright globes of flaming silver. Struggling to his knees, Longhorn took the full brunt of the dive in his sternum. Magnusson felt the air leave Longhorn's body as both men streaked across the runway and obliterated the equipment shed in a shower of splintered wood.

Magnusson wobbled upright, blinking in the dust. Longhorn was on the floor, unmoving under a heap of debris.

Clawed feet shuffled behind Magnusson. He heard a vicious bark and spun around to see the brown dog racing toward his throat, teeth bared. Magnusson flashed a stun bolt into the mutt's legs. It whipped around in midair and tumbled onto a plank, still barking as it tried to move its frozen limbs.

The alarm would be raised. It was time to end Longhorn *now.* Magnusson turned back to where Longhorn lay.

But Longhorn was gone. Magnusson was cursing himself for taking his eyes of his opponent when the blow smashed into his kidney. Magnusson crumpled over and glimpsed Longhorn rearing back for another blow. Magnusson pivoted away and threw a right cross.

Crack. Bone-on-bone impact. Longhorn's nose flowered with blood. Magnusson went for his throat as Longhorn went for his, both combatants glowing with the force of their weaponized Gift. They tore each other apart. They clawed, bit, and hammered, frenzied and ferocious, the rules of engagement long discarded.

Magnusson felt a lung collapse, two ribs crack, and his jaw shatter. Sweat drenched his neck and chest, his breath jagged and burning. They were on the grass now, outside the ruin of the shed, the bright stars above. As he landed a fiery uppercut, he felt Longhorn stumble.

Now.

Magnusson marshaled his Gift through his fists in a supernova of kinetic energy and swung the killing blow at Longhorn's temple.

But Longhorn was faster. He dodged.

Magnusson's momentum dragged him forward, past Longhorn's twisting body.

Thunk. Longhorn gripped the back of Magnusson's neck in a thudding paw slap. Magnusson felt something ridged and bony stab into his spine.

He wanted to turn around and continue the fight, but his legs wouldn't obey. Snakes crawled in his bloodstream. The world in front of him fractured and shimmered with blurred shapes.

Magnusson fell to his knees.

Longhorn limped around him, his breath escaping in labored rasps as he walked to where his tomahawks lay. He lifted them and turned to face Magnusson.

A good fight. Magnusson grinned to himself even as pain gnashed its teeth inside him. *A worthy opponent.*

Longhorn regarded him with a long, sullen stare that Magnusson understood as grudging respect. Kneeling down, Longhorn picked up the sword half of Magnusson's spear and tossed it over to him. Then, with a slight nod, he marched forward, tomahawks braced.

Die on your feet, soldier. Summoning the last of his strength, Magnusson resisted the poison in his system and stood on wavering legs. At that moment, he should have thought of his girls, of his family and those he had loved through his life.

But he didn't.

His blood thrummed only with the pride of the fight. He remembered the weight and honor of the Silverback skull General Sixkills had pinned to his chest many years ago. The fight was everything. He had always known that.

He raised his spear, arms trembling.

Longhorn lunged. Magnusson tore forward.

No right, no wrong, *only the strong.*

Longhorn met him in the middle, the tomahawks singing in the air.

60

The Songbird's jet banked, then glided down toward the blinking lights of the private runway. Houston closed his eyes and revisited the assault plan they had just hammered out. It took him ten seconds to determine that it wasn't a plan at all; it was suicide.

The entire flight, he, Katya, and Baxter had strategized, restrategized, and argued over the details of how to rescue Bobby and Lily without killing themselves. Houston remembered what he had learned in the Corps about maneuver warfare: move around your enemies' hard edges and attack their soft spots. As they studied the drone feed of Starlet Manor and its eighteen Alpha guardians, they realized that this enemy had *only* hard edges.

This would get bloody.

"Veena Sixkills," Katya muttered for the tenth time as the plane descended. "Veena fucking Sixkills." She turned to Houston. "Why?"

"Why what?"

"She already has everything." Katya's voice was tight with anger. "Why does she need to kill Lily to get more?"

Baxter shut his laptop and steepled his fingers, turning his attention to Katya. He took his time before answering. "I cannot hope to decipher Veena's true motives, but having seen what war does to people, I can arrive at an understanding of the woman herself—an uneasy understanding." They waited for him to continue. When he did, his voice was tinged with pity. "Veena was a child when the war started, a teenager when it ended. Her entire generation was thrust into adulthood in the most terrifying and traumatic circumstance possible. War breaks the strong and weak alike. Imagine what it does to a child."

"I don't have to," Katya said. "I *was* a child during the war."

"Of course. And I don't doubt that you carry scars—ones that you have spent the last ten years grappling with. But I suspect that Veena, numbed by her celebrity for so long, has come to finally understand that her scars cannot be healed by either money or fame, no matter how hard she tries."

"What are you saying?" Katya asked. "That I should feel sorry for her?"

"No," Baxter said. "But understand that she is not evil—simply wounded and afraid."

"So are Lily and Bobby," Houston remarked.

"That is true, but Lily and Bobby have people who love them very much—people who are willing to face impossible odds to help them. My guess is that Veena has no one like that in her life. And that breaks my heart."

The floor rumbled beneath their feet as the jet's wheels dropped from its belly. The lights of the airfield shone through their windows, growing larger as the plane cruised in for touchdown. As Houston strapped on his seat belt, he remembered something else from his jarhead days: *Execute your duties honorably in the midst of chaos.*

Houston closed his eyes as the plane's wheels hit tarmac. There would be no shortage of chaos tonight.

The plane landed on the eastern tip of Victory Island, where it was met by two Ohana men waiting by a black minivan. The men drove them to a private marina twenty minutes away.

The Ohana team that met them at the darkened marina said little. They seemed to respond to invisible signals Baxter sent out, and they greeted each other with hugs and soft words, then went to work. They were part of an invisible network that had melted out of the cover of their daily lives and mobilized to answer Baxter's call. The call that trumped all others: one of our own is in trouble. They were discreet and competent, with the economy of movement and words that marked them as trained operators. Watching them lower the Zodiac boat from a truck, Houston felt reassured, but only for a moment.

Because at the end, he would be going into the lion's den alone.

The Ohana carried the inflatable boat down the pier to the dark waters of the Long Island Sound. It rocked there gently while a young Ohana woman waited by the outboard motor, her eyes moving serenely back and forth from the clouded moon to the glossy waves.

"The roads into the interior are heavily patrolled," Baxter explained. He looked between Houston and Katya as they clambered onto the boat. "I hope neither of you are prone to seasickness."

Once they were all aboard, the young woman guided them in a wide arc out into the central channel of the Sound. The waves were stronger here, agitated by a stiff, chill wind. Despite the bumps, Baxter kept a firm grip on his laptop, still analyzing the drone feeds.

Above them, the clouds obscured most of the stars. Houston watched the few that he could see, twinkling against the blue-black sky. It had become a habit of his to stare up at the sky on the eve of battle, questioning the heavens. He had never gotten an answer from them. He guessed that no one else had either.

The boat bounced beneath him, and he had to grip the lashings, the salt water spraying him, icy rivulets streaming across his face.

The cold water triggered an old memory. He was eighteen again, running through the rain, leaving Bobby and his mother behind on the mountain, running away as fast as he could.

He had been hurtling toward this point his whole life, he realized. Bobby was somewhere out there in the dark, shackled tight with a blade to his neck. Lily was trapped in the cold grip of a monster dragging her toward the void.

He would not run tonight.

I'm going to kill every last one of you.

Fireworks burst above Sovereign City, painting the sky in glittering streaks of gold. Baxter looked up from his laptop. "The king just arrived at the parade." More fireworks exploded, white rain sparkling in the sky.

The boat bounced. The glowing windows of shorefront homes watched them pass, and the lights played tricks on Houston's eyes.

Baxter waved them over and spun his laptop around. "We have newcomers," he said.

The drone's infrared lens tracked an SUV entering through Starlet Manor's front gate. Through the biowave camera, they glimpsed the three burning white figures inside the vehicle: two men and a little girl.

It was good news and bad news. They had bet on the fact that Lily would be brought back to Starlet Manor before her appointment with the king, and there she was. But now that she was in their clutches, her captors no longer needed Bobby as a bargaining chip.

"They'll take her to the city soon," Baxter continued. "They'll place her somewhere close to the King's dais. And then . . ." He didn't finish.

Katya glared at the screen for a few moments. Then she pulled back and leaned against the gunwales. "How much longer?" Katya asked the captain, an impatient edge in her voice.

"We're here," she replied. She steered them quietly toward a dark port where a cargo vessel was lashed to the pier, framed by a skyline of shipping containers. The Zodiac glided into place alongside the pier, where two Ohana women melted out of the darkness and lashed the boat with a thick rope. The captain stayed on the Zodiac while Baxter led Houston and Katya through a maze of towering containers.

"This is a private port," Baxter said as he turned a corner. "Shipments come here from all over the world."

"The world?" Katya said. "That's illegal."

"The rich live very differently," Baxter said. "The goods that come here are strictly for the inhabitants of Victory Island."

"Perks of being rich," Houston said.

"Yes. Perks that Bobby—and by extension, the Ohana— enjoy as well." Baxter turned another corner. "I must warn you, though—this gentleman who . . . *procures* sensitive items for us is quite mercurial. Do not, under any circumstances, say anything to provoke him."

In the shadow of a warehouse, they reached a sixteen-wheeler cargo truck with a Blue Hive Honey Suppliers logo on it. A few men loitered around the truck's cab, smoking. One man struck Houston as looking particularly agitated. He paced and grumbled under his breath. When he saw them approach, he shook his head and jabbed at his watch.

"Late," he reprimanded.

Houston took a step forward and squinted in the darkness.

"Son of a bitch," Houston said, smiling.

The man looked at him and shook his head again, more vigorously this time. "If there is a son of a bitch here, it is *you*, Houston Holt."

Baxter looked between them, startled. "You two have met?"

Amin Patel, owner and proprietor of Patel Brothers Bakery in River Town, sighed with disappointment. "Yes, unfortunately for me."

"We're old friends," Houston said. "Good friends."

"Ack." Amin waved his hand dismissively. "Just take your stuff and go. You should have heard the thrashing my wife gave me when I had to leave. Don't you know the parade is tonight? I was supposed to watch it with her on TV, but now I'm stuck here with you monkeys." He continued grumbling as he opened a stack of crates by the truck.

"Nice," Katya marveled at the gold orbs nestled inside the crates. "Are these what I think they are?"

"They'd better be," Houston said, nudging Amin with a grin. "Otherwise, I want a refund."

"No refunds! You think I sell counterfeit goods? Don't act smart with me. Only the best quality." He opened another set of crates and dug out pistols, M6 rifles, and boxes of ammunition.

"What did I tell you about not provoking him?" Baxter whispered to Houston.

Houston shrugged him off. He turned to Amin. "And the other thing?"

Amin raised an eyebrow. "And what do you plan to do with this 'other thing'?"

"It's better you don't know."

"This was not an easy thing to find, Holt." Amin glowered at him. "And if you get caught, it is my life as well as yours."

Houston met Amin's eyes. "We're going to fuck some people up."

"And why are you going to do that?"

"Because they messed with our family," Katya said, cold as ice.

Amin looked to Baxter for confirmation. Baxter nodded.

"In that case," Amin said, scowling at the dark mass of the sixteen-wheeler as if he were trying to peer through its hold and study the dangerous cargo inside, "let's get going. Chop, chop!"

61

Queen Callista waved to her subjects from the Royal Dais, the gold confetti falling like rain. The crowds greeted her rapturously, their roar shaking the television speakers.

Callista's makeup and hair was flawless. But as Veena watched the queen from her den TV, she only had eyes for the Peacock Gown.

The gown burned like fire under the klieg lights. The intricate embroidery traced Callista's curves, a swirling tapestry of foxes and orchids and vines. She looked timeless, otherworldly, like a queen who would rule for a thousand years.

Enjoy it, bitch. Veena bared her teeth in a joyless smile. *While you still can.*

The king was almost an afterthought by Callista's side. King Patriot Gold put a hand on his wife's back and led her to their seats at the front of the dais. He wore his standard military dress blues, heavy under the weight of his medals and insignia—the same uniform he wore at the signing of the human surrender.

Tall, slim and coiled like a panther, Veena marveled at how the king carried his strength differently than her father. Sixkills was a battleship, designed to intimidate, break, and devastate. Patriot Gold hid his power behind his beauty, a blade sheathed in fine velvet. When he moved, his muscles swam as if through zero gravity, the world conforming around his fluid grace.

But his true power came from his eyes. Crisp blue and vigilant, they could burn with apocalyptic rage and then shift with the light into deep empathy, an ability to peer fearlessly into places flawed and fractured. They were the eyes of a man who had ventured beyond death and returned. There were no eyes like that anywhere else on Earth.

The applause for the royal couple had just died down when the Lady appeared in Veena's doorway.

"Our guest is here," the Lady announced.

"Here?" Veena responded. "The Sun Angel?"

The Lady nodded. "The car just entered the grounds. Come. Let's meet her."

*

Veena stood at the foot of the stairs, behind Caspar and the Lady, trying to grasp the magnitude of the moment.

She wished she could have a photographer here, someone to snap this scene for posterity. When the history books were written they would not know that it was Veena Sixkills, the girl without the Gift, that had saved the young Nation of Specials.

Outside, she heard heavy tires crunch over gravel. Car doors opened and shut. Seconds dragged out like hours.

The front door swung open. Willem and Karl strode in. Behind them, another man, just as tall, slid into the room.

Veena stifled a gasp. Dead fingers brushed over her throat when she realized Longhorn was looking at her. She couldn't look away, remembering the bullet ripping through Makini's skull, the cold asphalt on her palms as she crawled in terror, the stench of blood in her nose. It was only when she noticed the girl behind him that her fear vanished.

My god. Veena grasped the banister. *She's so young.*

The girl stepped inside hesitantly and took in the house, focusing on every shadow, every unfamiliar face, like a wild bird coming to grips with its new cage. She was dwarfed by Longhorn next to her, and she blinked groggily as if she had just awoken from a sleep scarred by nightmares. To Veena, the girl seemed fragile, disoriented, and nowhere could she find the traces of the king-killing Gift she was supposed to wield.

And then the girl turned toward Veena and their eyes met.

It was as if the floor dropped out from under her, so complete was the sensation of falling. Veena spun, tumbled, *into* those eyes, wheeling through a fog of luminescent mysteries that stole her breath. In that moment, Veena felt a doorway open in time beyond which she glimpsed something pure, unmarred, and breathtaking. Something, she realized with a stab of pain in her chest, that she had been waiting her whole life to see.

The girl turned away and the vision faded abruptly. Veena had to hold the banister to steady her suddenly weak legs. She glanced around quickly, but nobody had noticed her small collapse. Deftly, she turned her face and wiped the tears from her eyes with the back of her hand.

The Lady guided Longhorn into the parlor. As he walked, Veena noticed the field bandages crisscrossed his arms and she detected a slight limp in his right leg. She couldn't imagine what creature had managed to wound him, but it wasn't one she wanted to meet any time soon.

Willem brought the girl forward to Caspar.

"And what is your name?" Caspar kneeled down and asked her.

The girl stared at him, in no rush to answer the question. Caspar fidgeted. "Well, it's not important. It's nice to meet you."

"Where's Bobby?"

Veena blinked, startled. The girl's voice was larger than her body, bristling with an unexpected fearlessness.

"Pardon me?" Caspar asked, equally thrown. "Who, might I ask, is Bobby?"

"The Songbird," the girl answered. She looked between Veena and Caspar evenly. "If he's hurt you're all in trouble."

Caspar laughed. "Ah. Well. The Songbird is our guest. As are you. And I assure you that neither of you will be mistreated in any way."

The girl tilted her head, examining Caspar. "I understand why you're doing this," she said. "But even across the ocean, you won't find your freedom."

Caspar stiffened, struck by invisible lightning. For a painful few seconds he struggled over a series of half-formed vowels, his mouth opening and closing incoherently.

"That is not important," he finally managed to say. "What *is* important is that you have a very important event to go to. And you simply cannot go dressed like that. Come." He gestured toward the stairs. "My men will take you to your room."

Willem and Karl stepped forward, but Veena raised her palm, eyes never leaving the Sun Angel.

"No." She took the girl's hand, which the girl did not seem too happy about. "She'll need a woman's help with this."

*

Her name was Lily.

Veena had found it written on the front cover of a sketchbook in her backpack. "You're a talented artist," Veena said, flipping through the book when they were alone in her bedroom together. "I used to draw a lot at your age."

The girl didn't respond. She wandered around the room and poked at Veena's bookshelves, investigated her closet, and from time to time, ran her eyes across Veena in way that made her feel stark naked.

Lily stopped in front of the full-length mirror and studied the strange contraption Veena had strapped across her body.

"It fits you perfectly," Veena said.

Lily didn't seem to think so. Her hands pulled at the metal buckles and fabric straps of the bridle that Veena had clasped over her black T-shirt, the buckles locked in magnetically at her shoulder blades.

Caspar had tried explaining the bridle's technology to Veena but little of it had registered. All Veena remembered was that the Northern Gears had devised it as a transmitter that had been coded into a single receiver: the Peacock Gown. When in range, the controller—in this case Willem—would detonate the bridle with a long-range radio. The bridle would then trigger Lily's Gift, transmit it from under the Marrakech Hotel on Phoenix Avenue, and—in a matter of milliseconds—trigger the engineered fibers of Callista's dress. The queen would then be transformed into a magnifying glass, vaporizing the king, and five square miles of Sovereign City, instantly.

"It matches your Clamp," Veena said as Lily picked at the contraption pinching into her shoulders. "It's all about the accessories, you know."

A loud knock at the door. "We have to go," Willem barked.

"One minute!" Veena yelled back. "Don't let those brutes scare you, Lily."

Lily sat on an ottoman and looked out the window. Veena was struck by the impression that Lily's entire being seemed to leave the room, traveling to a different world.

Lily sighed and turned to Veena. She was smiling.

"What?" Veena asked, disturbed.

Lily shrugged, the soft smile still on her face.

"What are you smiling at?" Veena took a step toward her.

"Your father," Lily said. "He reminds me of my father."

"What did you say?" Veena took another step forward.

"I watched my father die in front of me. Someone shot him over forty-seven dollars. He died on the street." Lily clasped her hands together and looked at the floor. "I understand why you're doing this. You're trying to save your father."

Veena stopped in the middle of the room, frozen in place.

Lily continued. "Our dads closed off all the doors behind them so we couldn't follow. But that is what they had to do. They were trying to keep us at a distance so that their pain didn't become ours."

Veena didn't move. She felt as if Lily had peeled open her body and was now peering inside her.

Willem pounded the door again.

"Fuck off!" Veena yelled. She turned back to Lily. "You don't know anything."

"Most nights you dream of fire," Lily said. "You were so young when they came for you. When they burned you. And afterward there was nobody there to tell you it would be okay. That you didn't deserve it."

Veena stuttered. A peaceful veil fell over her, blinking with astral lights. Something dislodged inside her, and decrepit structures collapsed around her heart. "I am the Savior" was all she managed to say, realizing how hollow the words sounded as she said them.

Lily nodded, as if she had just been told that the sky was blue. "Sure." She looked up, reading the space around Veena. "That's what he told you."

Veena moved within reach of Lily. "What do you know about Him?"

"I don't know much. But I know that he led you here. To a place where you're alone and afraid. And that," Lily said, a deep sadness in her eyes, "is how I know he's a liar."

The *crack* of Veena's hand across Lily's face was so loud it rang in her ears like a gunshot. The force of the blow sent Lily toppling off the ottoman. Veena pounced on top of her.

She was going to kill her.

Willem pulled her off the girl. Veena was screaming, her throat raw, but she couldn't hear her own words. Willem threw Veena onto the bed and lifted Lily off the ground and toward the door.

"We're going," he said flatly. "The parade has started."

"Wait," Lily said, pushing away from Willem. Veena looked at her. Lily's eyes were wet from the sting of the slap, but nothing else had changed. If anything, her serene strength had deepened.

"I'm sorry," Lily said. "You're so alone."

It was then that Veena realized what it was about the girl that had unleashed such a wave of bitter anger.

"Someone really loved you once, didn't they?" Veena said. "But it won't help you now. You're the one who's all alone now."

"I'm not alone."

A laugh escaped Veena's throat. "Look at where you are. Who is coming to save you?"

"You'll see."

A clammy hand gripped Veena's insides and twisted. Lily's last words hung in the air as Willem dragged her out into the hallway.

62

Is this what accomplishment feels like? Caspar marveled. *Perhaps this is why Father constantly prattles on about it.*

Caspar sipped his champagne and smiled at the Songbird. He really shouldn't be drinking. He had been sober two years now but what could one glass hurt? He had earned it.

God, how he had earned it.

He raised a toast. The Songbird watched him, silent behind his gag.

"I really love your work," Caspar said. "I've been to almost all of your performances, and I can't even put into words how they affected me. Your talent is sublime."

The Songbird stared back at him, mute.

Caspar sipped his champagne awkwardly. It was a strange impulse that brought him down here to the basement. He couldn't blame it on the bubbly; he had barely finished one flute. The most likely reason was that he needed someone to share this moment with.

The grand plan had come together at long last. Of course there had been delays and unexpected bumps in the road thanks to that sorry lowblood, Houston Holt. But for the first time in his life, Caspar had actually *finished* something.

He wanted to yell it out from the rooftops. He wanted to fling it in the faces of his parents and sister. But they weren't here. And the people who *were* here were not the listening types. His Militiamen were simultaneously patrolling the property and packing up to leave. The Lady was off somewhere dealing with Longhorn. And Veena . . . well, that was out of the question. That girl was as tightly walled off as the Silver Spear.

All that was left of the plan was for Willem to drive the Sun Angel to a rendezvous point on Victory Island where a crooked Sovereign Border Patrol agent would take possession of the girl. The clueless agent would then use her official status to transport the Sun Angel into the Marrakech Hotel. Once the Sun Angel was in the Marrakech's underground parking lot, the agent would then place a call to Willem.

Willem would then press the detonator.

And then . . .

Fireworks.

The Songbird shifted in his seat, his eyes never leaving Caspar. As if he were reading his thoughts.

Caspar averted his eyes. When the time came, Caspar knew he couldn't kill the Songbird. It was painful just being here, seeing the great performer trussed up like a disobedient slave.

A Militiaman would have to do it.

"I truly am sorry for this shabby treatment," Caspar said. "Alas, it is out of my hands."

The Songbird blinked.

With a tip of his glass, Caspar drained the last of the champagne. Emboldened by the alcohol, he walked over to the singer and ran a hand through his lush hair.

"It's your lowblood brother's fault that you're in this predicament." He leaned down and whispered in his ear, "I know what it's like to love a lowblood. I know how much it can hurt."

With one last squeeze of his neck, Caspar turned away from the Songbird.

"Thank you for listening," he said as he walked toward the stairs. "You deserve much better than this."

*

In the kitchen, Caspar poured himself another glass of bubbly. Somewhere in the mansion he heard Militiaman Luca's voice, directing other Militiamen to continue scrubbing all evidence of their presence. Outside the windows he glimpsed the silhouettes of more Militiamen, patrolling in and out of the woods.

He drank and let the champagne settle softly inside him. He still had a long journey ahead of him. His bags were loaded in the back of the Land Rover waiting in the motor pool. He made a mental note to check if he had packed his motion sickness pills.

The parade bloomed and flashed across the mute TV. The floats were magical creations, rendering the crowds awestruck. The camera cut back to the Royal Dais. His parents' faces glowed like ghouls from behind the king. Callista clapped and smiled, a well-trained house pet.

Footsteps tramped down the hall and, like a storm, Veena swept into the kitchen, her face dark. She grabbed the champagne bottle and chugged down a quarter of it straight.

"Darling," Caspar said. "Perhaps I should get you a glass."

"Fuck off," she growled.

They simmered in silence. Veena poured more champagne down her throat. The Lady appeared in the doorway.

"It is time," she said.

Veena looked out the window, unimpressed. Caspar put his glass down and turned to follow the Lady into the living room. He stopped at the doorway and turned back to Veena.

"What will you do?" he asked.

"Drink," Veena said.

"I mean when it happens. Will you stay here?"

Veena gripped the bottle. "I'm going to watch the blast from my pier." She smiled to herself. "I want to see the beginning of a new world."

"I will be leaving immediately," Caspar said, realizing quickly that Veena couldn't care less. "Maybe we'll see each other again. When your father's armies arrive in Europe."

Veena toasted limply to that. "I'll be counting the days."

*

Truth be told, Caspar was most upset that he would have to say goodbye to his Militiamen.

Around him a handful of them were packing up their gear, moving precisely and quietly. They could not come with him on his exodus. He had officially relieved them all of their duty this afternoon in a small private ceremony by the rose garden. He had grown up with most of them and the bond between Von Arx and Militiaman was a lifelong one, stronger than any bond the Von Arx family forged between themselves.

His bodyguards would no longer be bound to his command. That is, Caspar reminded himself, after they had tied up two loose ends.

First, Veena.

As soon as Willem was off the property with the Sun Angel, Luca and Karl would pin Veena down like a butterfly. Caspar would take a moment to savor the terror in her eyes before wrapping his hands around her throat.

He was going to enjoy it.

Once Veena was dead, Luca would deal with Augustus Sky. Caspar didn't need to be here for that. By then, he would already be racing toward the smuggler's plane waiting for him a few miles away.

Willem brushed by him, guiding the Sun Angel with a firm grip out the front door. The girl was looking at Caspar. Was she smiling?

The Militiaman led her down the steps to the waiting Land Rover.

Like a whisper, the Lady appeared next to Caspar, her veil ruffling in the breeze from the open door.

"And so it is done," she sighed.

"So it is." He looked at her, remembering something. "Where's Longhorn?"

"Patching himself up in one of the guest cabins. He took some damage on the way here." She whispered in his ear, "From a Silverback."

Caspar almost retched. With great effort, he stopped himself from glancing at Veena across the foyer. "A Silverback?" he hissed.

She nodded. "The situation is not compromised yet. But"—her eyes slid to the side, indicating Veena behind her—"whatever it is you are planning for our mutual friend, do it fast."

"You know?" Caspar was stunned. He hadn't even breathed a hint of his plans to her.

"Obviously." She blinked placidly as if knowing everything at all times was the most natural thing in the world for her.

Outside Willem eased the girl into the backseat, put on her seatbelt, and shut the door.

"Thank you," Caspar said to the Lady.

"For what?"

"For setting me free."

She pointed upward, her gray eyes sparkling. "Thank Him."

Behind them, he heard Veena's heels on the hardwood, returning to the kitchen. "Show's over!" she hollered. "Now all of you get the *fuck* out of my house!"

Caspar turned to Luca and Karl.

It was time.

The two guards set off behind Veena. The Lady glanced at Caspar and drifted off into the gloom of the parlor.

Caspar steadied his breath and followed Luca and Karl toward the kitchen. He was through the living room and into the hallway when he heard the terrified shout burst through Luca's earpiece like a bomb.

The ground shook with the impact of something monstrous, sending a small earthquake rattling up Caspar's spine.

The lights went out.

Then, stumbling in the blackness, Caspar heard every gun in the world fire at once.

63

It was Militiaman Johann who first saw the disturbance.

Like the other Militiamen on the grounds of Starlet Manor, he was in the process of finishing his final patrol before leaving the estate.

He was free now, released from his sworn duty to protect Caspar Von Arx. What came next, he didn't know. First, he had to secure the pier, radio in his status, and then circle back to the motor pool where the Land Rovers were waiting to carry them all away from here.

But then, on the edge of the pier, Johann saw something in the black water.

He craned his neck forward.

The surface of the Long Island Sound was *moving*.

It was the bladed wake of a boat, cutting across the waves toward the shore. But there was no boat that Johann could see. Only a dark line slicing forward, like an invisible shark fin.

Before Johann could fire off a warning over the radio the water popped like boiling springs and buzzing hornets slammed into his chest.

Johann stumbled backward, a sickening warmth spreading across his shirt.

"*Intruder!*" It was the only word he managed to broadcast before the beast arrived.

The leviathan burst out of the Sound, soared through the air in a shower of cold water, and smashed down seismically in front of Johann.

Johann gaped in awe. "Can't be . . ." he muttered dumbly.

The beast towered over him, a steel monstrosity twenty feet tall, glistening and bladed. Its eyeless head swiveled, the guns on its shoulders finding him.

Johann lifted his arm to fire but the beast fired first.

*

One down.

Houston released the Gatling gun trigger and stomped the accelerator. *Seventeen more to go.*

Between him and Bobby stood four hundred feet of open ground and seventeen pissed-off Alphas. Even in his Tin Man mech he knew the odds were against him.

The Tin Man leaned into its run, ripping up grass at forty miles per hour. In the cramped cockpit nestled in the mech's belly, Houston watched a three-dimensional virtual rendering of the battlefield outside. His onboard artificial intelligence, MAC, projected a spatial world on the bubble canopy, lit up in infrared oranges, overlaid with a grid of streaming data.

Three hundred eighty feet.

The distance to the house was a gleaming number on the bubble, one of a dozen data variables Houston monitored in his virtual environment—targets, incoming threats, ammunition, fuel, armor integrity.

His eyes swiped across the digital clock in the bottom corner. Counting down from ten minutes.

9:43 remaining.

That was their window. Nine minutes and forty-three seconds to complete the mission before the authorities arrived.

When that clock hit zero, Lily and Bobby would either be safe or they would all be dead.

Scanning the drone feed on his bottom left, Houston identified the heat signatures of Katya and Baxter moving into position. He silently wished them luck. They would need it.

"Threats incoming," MAC's voice bubbled down his spinal link.

The targeting reticle swept over the bubble, beeping urgently as it identified the swarm of angry Alphas bursting out of the house and woods toward him.

The digital threat counter on the bubble burned orange: seventeen Alpha hostiles.

Here they come.

Covering four hundred feet and battling seventeen Alphas in a Tin Man mech should have been a challenging—but not impossible—task for a Marine Raider.

But there was a small problem.

As grateful as Houston was to Amin for procuring a mech out of thin air, he still wished the old bastard could have dug up something better than this piece of shit.

This Tin Man was on its last legs. Battered in the Immortal War, the mech hadn't seen a repair bay in ten years. It carried the minimum amount of fuel to cover the distance. Its store of whipper rounds for the Gatling would last through a handful of firefights. It carried no missiles for the mounted launchers. No link up to orbiting fire platforms to call down smart bombs or aerial gun runs.

Houston had gone to war in a steaming pile of junk.

The bubble flashed with threats. The Alphas converged on him.

"Multiple incoming," MAC announced. "Engage?"

"Not yet," Houston said. "Launch orbs."

"Roger."

MAC launched the contents of the Tin Man's cargo bay. Whistling like bottle rockets, the three golden Orbs shot into the sky and spread out above the battlefield. They hung there, fifty-feet high, waiting.

"Incoming fire," MAC announced.

The first bolts went high and to the left. Random, desperate shots from an enemy caught flat-footed.

"Engage?" MAC asked again.

"Smoke these fuckers."

"Roger."

MAC guided the reticle onto the closest Alpha and locked on.

Houston squeezed the trigger.

The Gatling's six barrels boomed.

*

Veena recognized the sound immediately.

In the darkened kitchen, the thudding footfalls and whine of massive gears tore at her eardrums like a banshee's shriek.

No . . .

Veena turned and ran. She was a child again, racing out of a suffocating bunker, hunted by monsters.

A Militiaman bumped into her. Around her she heard the Militiamen shouting to each other and racing toward the disturbance. When they opened the back door, she recoiled in horror at what she saw outside.

This isn't real.

The Tin Man clawed out of her nightmares and tore across the grass, a savage bird spitting fire. Coming for her.

She backpedaled so fast she tripped over a rug and banged her head against the floor. Ignoring the pain she scrambled to her feet and ran for the front door. Something tore loose inside her head, rattling around mockingly.

She crashed into a Militiaman going the opposite way and fell to her hands and knees. The man ignored her and kept running.

Veena was halfway to her feet when she heard the explosion.

At first, she thought it was the mech, but then she realized it couldn't have been.

The blast had come from the *front* of the house.

*

It took every ounce of Willem's resolve not to turn the Land Rover around and join his brothers in their hour of need. They were under attack and he could hear the Militiamen's voices shouting over the radio as they met the threat.

He was their commander and by all rules of combat he should be there with them, leading his men against this new enemy.

He looked into his mirror at the girl in the backseat.

She was the mission now.

Willem was bound by duty to get her to the rendezvous point, and a Von Arx Militiaman *never* failed his duty.

As the sounds of gunfire tore through the night, Willem punched the Rover's accelerator and rocketed toward the front gate. They were fifty feet away from it when it disappeared in a fireball.

Willem slammed the brakes and spun the wheel as the heat wave blew through the car.

Through a curtain of black smoke a sixteen-wheeler with a *Blue Hives Honey Suppliers* logo drove through the breach. It raced down the driveway and jackknifed, blocking the exit with its long cargo hold.

The back of the truck opened, and Willem watched as two figures dropped to the ground and took up firing positions behind the cargo doors.

Willem threw the jeep in reverse.

The figures raised their automatic rifles and fired.

*

Lily.

That was the only thing running through Katya's mind as she leapt out of the truck and hit the ground.

Get Lily.

Smoke from the bombed gate swirled around her and scraped her throat. Her heart was pounding as she came around the front of the truck, Baxter following behind wearing a backpack identical to hers.

The Land Rover stood thirty feet away from them, blazing headlights askew. Katya could only see flames reflected in its windshield. According to the drone feed, Lily was inside with an Alpha.

Katya and Baxter dropped to their knees just as the Alpha threw the SUV in reverse. Together they shredded the front tires with a short burst. The Rover slumped down, hubcaps scraping stone.

"Launch!" Baxter called out.

They unslung their backpacks simultaneously and heaved out their Orbs. Running through the sequence Amin had drilled into her, Katya set the base down and keyed in the launch code. With a fizzing hiss, the Orb sprung off its base and whooshed into the air. Baxter's Orb followed close behind. Fifty feet up the Orbs zipped along as if on rails, circling the target area.

Air superiority. Katya knew it was their only chance at victory against Alphas. With the airspace guarded, the Alpha could only retreat with Lily over land.

Katya shot out the car's headlights. The vehicle stood stranded on the driveway. She slipped behind the cover of the cargo hold door and waited, Baxter by her side.

"Your move," Katya said softly, eyes trained on the dark windshield.

64

"C'mon you piece of shit." Houston gripped the control stick and yanked it hard, swerving the groaning Tin Man away from the barrage of explosive bolts.

Most of them missed. The ones that didn't pounded the mech armor like boulders. The armor integrity dropped to 60 percent.

More bolts streaked toward him.

Cranking the controls like a captain in a swell, Houston zigzagged the mech across the gauntlet. With each passing second as the Specials found their rhythm, their accuracy improved lethally.

Red bolts scraped the Tin Man's arms in a flurry of sparks. A thudding *boom* detonated above Houston—an Orb shredding an airborne Alpha into ribbons.

The threat counter on the bubble dropped to sixteen.

Explosive tracers streaked through the night, the onslaught so thick Houston felt like he was racing through a fiery tunnel. There was no way he could make it in a straight line to the house.

"Two hundred feet to objective," MAC announced.

The Tin Man's legs groaned in pain. Its fuel was down in the red zone, minutes away from running dry.

Houston skidded the Tin Man under a ceiling of slicer bolts, the razor-sharp projectiles shearing the top off his right missile launcher.

"One hundred and seventy-five feet to objective."

MAC swept the Gatling guns in a tight arc, ripping through a duo of Alphas who had been caught in open ground.

Threat counter: fourteen.

Another Orb exploded overhead in a shower of flame.

Threat counter: thirteen.

A bolt slammed into the mech. Houston's body wrenched painfully against his restraints.

"Direct hit," MAC announced. "Catastrophic damage on left tread. Armor integrity 30 percent."

Houston forced himself to focus, his brain still rattling. He checked the machine's vitals. An explosive bolt had sheared away part of the left leg, dropping his speed to thirty miles per hour.

The Alphas saw their opening. Leap-frogging behind covering fire, they converged on the limping mech.

"Shit." Houston had one option left.

A bad one.

The Alphas pounded him with more thundering fire. Houston took one grim look at his sorry fuel reserves and punched in the jump jets.

He ate g-forces as the thrust of the twin-turbine engines smashed him back into this seat. The Tin Man sailed in an arc above the heads of the Alphas. From up here, Starlet Manor looked close enough to touch.

The Orbs, recognizing the Tin Man's friendly frequency codes, ignored him. Ten, twenty, thirty feet the Tin Man flew before gravity reasserted its grip.

The landing was a spine-rattler. Houston grunted under the impact, and with a hard kick on the accelerator, he plunged the Tin Man in a headlong sprint down the final hundred and forty feet.

He had crossed the enemy's line and now there were threats in front *and* behind him. The Gatlings wheeled on their turrets, laying down crackling circles of fire. Every inch of air around the mech burned like the sun, scalding hot with the crossfire of bolts and bullets.

"Incoming—" MAC's warning was drowned out by a loud crash above.

That's no bolt.

An Alpha had landed on the Tin Man's crown. Houston jerked the machine left to right, but the Alpha held tight.

Houston heard metal tear across the Tin Man's frame. Streams of data went dark across his bubble.

"Catastrophic damage. Sensor array."

Houston fired his brights. The bank of xenon spotlights hidden in the mech's armor lit up in a flash of white so blinding they could burn retinas.

The Alpha on the mech found that out firsthand. He screamed and tumbled off, clutching his useless eyes. The lights stopped the rest of the Alphas in their tracks, frozen like deer.

With a giant stomp on the gas, Houston barreled the Tin Man's one hundred tons through the Alphas caught in his path.

Threat counter: ten.

Starlet Manor was within his reach. A few more seconds.

The Gatlings strafed the pool area, bullets ripping up the water, puncturing two more hostiles.

"Low ammo," MAC said.

The mech lurched up the steps onto the patio, thirty feet away from the manor's brick facade.

Then, on the drone feed, Houston saw something that tied a knot in his stomach.

Bobby's heat signature remained seated in the basement. But there was someone else there now—another heat signature closing in on his brother. Fast.

*

Down in the basement, Veena pulled on a fistful of the Songbird's hair and pressed the gun under his chin. The Songbird's pristine face looked hollowed out in the flashlight's beam.

"Your friends are here," she hissed in his ear.

The barrel dug into his soft flesh. Still strapped to the chair, the Songbird glared back at her. Daring her.

Veena had raced down the basement the moment she realized that Starlet Manor was under attack from both the front and the rear. She hadn't come down here, banging and crashing around in the dark, looking for the Songbird.

She was down here because this was where she kept her secret.

Not the secret custom pistol she had hidden in a cubby by the stairs. Nor the emergency duffel stashed here, bulging with extra flashlights, ammunition, energy bars, and anything else she would need in an emergency escape.

No. It was something that could save her life. Something she had concealed down here before the first stone was laid in the house above.

On her way to it, Veena had passed by the Songbird, trussed up and alone. Her first instinct was to shoot him and be on her way.

Her second instinct was smarter.

Augustus Sky was a close friend of the King. If his bullet-riddled body was found in her basement . . .

She stared into Sky's defiant eyes, still debating the point. There was something in the flecks of gold in his irises, the serene intensity that pulled her in and held her. She had never seen him in concert, but she felt a pull, as if it would be an awful tragedy if the lights went out in those eyes. The shadow of her gun fell on his face briefly, and when it had passed, his features had changed.

It was Shanti's crying face staring back at her, begging her not to do it. The shadow moved again and now it was Kormedia, screaming through his taped mouth. The blade was in Veena's hands, the blood warm across her arms as the naked bodies of her friends bled out onto their wheelchairs.

Veena gulped down the horror, screwing her eyes shut against the memory. She moved before she could stop herself. She untied Sky's restraints and pulled him to his feet, keeping his hands cuffed.

"We're going for a walk," she said. "You slow me down and your brains paint my walls."

Moving in the narrow confines of the flashlight beam, Veena pushed her hostage deeper into the basement, toward her last hope for survival.

*

Baxter yelled something to Katya. She couldn't make out what he was saying because she was too busy eating grass as a bolt hissed inches above her head.

Crawling backward behind the truck, Katya turned to Baxter. "What did you say?"

"Seven minutes left!" he yelled again.

"Tell that to him!" She pointed to the Alpha pounding them with firepower. His bolts slammed into the truck, turning the entire side of the cargo hold into a blackened moonscape.

"Powerful fellow, isn't he?" Baxter observed.

Katya reloaded her rifle. Seven minutes until the Victory Island authorities got here. Three hundred and sixty seconds to pull off a miracle.

The fusillade paused.

"He's moving!" Baxter called out, reloading.

Katya peeked under the truck.

Thirty feet away, the large Alpha was on foot, abandoning his wounded Rover and racing back toward the mansion. In his right arm he carried Lily, her mound of hair as visible as a beacon.

"Move!" Katya yelled, jumping to her feet.

She and Baxter chased after the fleeing Alpha. She ran so hard her lungs burned, but not once did her eyes leave Lily, receding as the Alpha picked up speed.

Hold on, little lady. Hold on.

*

Longhorn watched the bursts of light above the trees.

He listened.

The first bark of gunfire had stopped him in his tracks as he left the cabin. Now, through the trees he watched the crimson aurora climb into the sky above the battlefield, the smoky residue of the Militiamen's bolts. He listened intently to the mech's footfalls, the music of its gears. A Mark Two model.

The tiny cabin stood behind him in the thick woods, a mile away from the mansion. Under the cold water of its shower, he had scrubbed the dirt and dried blood off his body. He had rubbed salve into the deep lacerations where the Silverback's spear had caught him.

The Silverback had been a worthy adversary. He had died with honor.

With the full payment for his services transferred to his account, Longhorn had wasted no time in leaving the cabin. Slaves had been housed there, and he could smell their lingering desperation. It was a stench he remembered well.

Ten paces from the front door, the crow had cawed a warning. The gunfire had followed immediately.

Longhorn did not move to join the fight.

He watched.

He listened.

65

The Tin Man buckled over, keening like a wounded animal. Houston fought the tilt, hands slick with sweat on the control stick. The bubble blinked and fizzled. In the chaos, Houston glimpsed the distance to target:

Thirty-four feet.

Bobby's heat signature was now moving in the basement. A second heat signature—the woman Baxter had identified as Veena Sixkills—bullied him forward, heading west.

Seven Alphas remained.

The targeting reticles darted like sparrows across the bubble, overwhelmed by the onslaught. Houston willed the limping Tin Man forward, nearly tottering into the pool.

A bolt crashed into the bubble, rattling Houston's teeth.

"Catastrophic damage . . . fzzz . . . gokdl . . ." MAC's voice crackled in Houston's ear, the last words of a drowning man.

Houston fired the Gatlings, popping off one more Alpha lunging toward him.

Six left.

Impact on his left. On his right. An Alpha crashed down on top of the mech.

Houston pressed the trigger.

Clickclickclick.

The guns swiveled uselessly on their turrets, empty.

*

Caspar wished he had worn different shoes. His hard-soled monk straps were terribly unsuited for the task of running for one's life.

Stumbling around in the dark, breathing like a decrepit moose, Caspar had made little progress in his escape. Panic, accentuated by the darkness, had sent him toppling headfirst over ottomans, cracking his nose against pillars, sprawling inelegantly down short flights of stairs.

And each rip of the mech's guns turned his bowels to water. He picked up his pace and promptly clipped his knee against a table.

His shirt was soaked through with sweat when he hobbled to the motor pool door. The monk straps bit into his feet as he ran down the stairs to the waiting Land Rover. Not that his choice of shoes would have made much of a difference, he thought. It was his stunning lack of athleticism that was the problem. Other than a deft touch at badminton, he had never been much of an athlete growing up.

"Oh, lord," he panted at the bottom of the stairs, hands on knees. Why hadn't he taken his health more seriously? Maybe taken up running. Brisk walking, even. Anything except fucking badminton.

Caspar threw open the driver's door and slid in behind the wheel. He found the keys in the sun visor, started the truck, and pulled out onto the driveway. His initial plan to drive straight out of the front gate fell apart when he saw the burning truck blocking it.

"Damn it to hell!" Caspar swore. He spun the Rover around for the west gate. It was a mile away through a narrow lane in the woods. Once through the gate he would have to drive along a private road for three miles before linking up to the main road. From there it was ten minutes to the private airfield.

The sky to his right pulsed with a shimmering cloud, red as blood. Caspar wiped the sweat from his face and quietly whispered a mantra that slid off his tongue as the truck bobbled and bounced across the road.

Paris. Paris. Paris.

*

Even while balancing a gun, a flashlight, and a hostage, Veena somehow managed to punch the secret code into the touchscreen hidden behind the sconce.

The touchscreen beeped.

Veena felt the Songbird startle as the wall next to him swung away, revealing a rectangle of darkness.

The entrance to the catacombs.

"Go." Veena shoved the Songbird through the doorway into the cold chamber. She stepped inside behind him and smelled the dusty air, the sudden sensation of freedom.

She had ordered the construction of the catacombs long before the first brick of Starlet Manor had been laid. A discreet security company from North Dakota had designed the secret tunnel system that stretched underneath her entire property, a self-sustaining labyrinth with passages leading to all three gates as well as the boathouse. If the estate ever came under attack—as was the case now—Veena would have a fortified escape route out of the property. Other than the engineers—who all signed nondisclosure agreements—no one else knew about the catacombs. Veena had insisted that all the slave laborers who took part in the construction be swiftly executed after its completion.

A backup generator powered the lamps strung up along the gray walls. Veena's bare feet slapped across the cool cement floor as they ran through the pools of light. If the magnificent home above reflected the public face of Veena Sixkills, these tunnels were the cold reality.

She had never forgotten that terrible night in Millsap.

The night the Native Sons had torn through her family ranch. Their angry cries were lodged in her ears like splinters. The fire that burned her reached out from her nightmares, blackening her soul.

Since then she had never known home. She was always running. Through bunkers, safe houses, dark alleyways.

Running, running, running.

The war had never left her. It would *never* leave her.

Wherever Veena laid her head, the first thing she would look for was a way out.

The Songbird stumbled forward and fell. Veena dragged him up by the collar and whipped him across the neck with the pistol.

"Try to stall again and I shoot off an ear," Veena snarled.

She pushed him forward. They still had over a mile to cover to reach the west gate, where a garage held their getaway car.

Above them, the gunfire had stopped.

*

The Alphas knew their prey was fatally wounded. They closed in, salivating jackals driven mad by the smell of blood.

Houston became a human pinball, ricocheting around the cramped cockpit as the Alphas pummeled the ruined mech.

His fuel tanks were bone dry.

The Gatling guns steamed and swiveled uselessly on their turrets, tracking targets they couldn't engage.

The bubble spiderwebbed under the force of a bolt. His drone feed was dead, and the control panel blinked and fizzled as it died.

Time slowed down suddenly and Houston found himself thinking of Katya and Baxter. They had less than six minutes left on target. He wondered if they had rescued Lily. Or if they were— like him—surrounded and doomed.

A heavy fist sent the mech teetering. Houston hit his head against the canopy.

Houston watched an Alpha rip the Tin Man's right arm off. Another one cut through the head with a flaming fist. Four—five—six Alphas perched like vultures on the machine, pecking, biting, burning.

It was only a matter of seconds before the Alphas breached the cockpit. Before he, Katya, Baxter, Lily, and Bobby were all dead and gone.

I'm going to kill every last one of you.

Houston glared at Starlet Manor, calculating the distance to the house. Less than thirty feet.

It was a long shot. A long, *long* shot.

But not impossible.

And those were the only odds a human could hope for in this kingdom.

The attackers ripped off the titanium ribs protecting the cockpit. Houston saw the whites of their eyes.

Houston's hands found the detonator handle beneath his seat.

A fist punched through the canopy.

Then another one, and another. Crackling with red fire, clawing for Houston's throat—

Houston tore the handle upward.

The entire sequence took less than half a second.

Darkness closed in on Houston instantaneously. Steel-polymer fingers wrapped him in a tight fist, snapping his body into a fetal position. The explosive cartridges under his egg-shaped ejection capsule detonated, sending Houston's heart careening into his throat as the blast punched him through the canopy.

BOOM.

The Tin Man went nova behind him, the ejection sequence discharging the cube of incendiaries embedded in its core and hurtling Houston into space. Fiery heat coated his skin and his body wracked with thunder as the mech died in a crash of drums and screams, its body—and the bodies of the six Alphas—erupting into a tower of fire four stories high.

The capsule punctured through Starlet Manor's brick facade, the impact cracking Houston's knees against his jaw. It hit the ground and rolled, and Houston heard things clatter and break around him before the capsule crashed against a wall and stopped.

Stars blinked before Houston's eyes. Metal dug into his spine. He was certain that he had just gone for a ride in a washing machine.

The capsule rumbled. The stars in front of Houston's eyes were now joined by more lights—*real* lights—as the console lit up.

The capsule moved—coming *alive*—

Here we go.

Metal grips locked into place around Houston's joints. With a snap of hinges and tiny pistons, the capsule stood Houston up like a brace. The steel-polymer shell transformed—hexagonal sections detaching, reforming, and slotting together around Houston's midsection, neck, forearms, thighs, and shins. Metal boots locked into place around his feet, clomping down on the wood floor. A visor curved around his eyes, fields of data awakening across the display.

Houston stood up to his full height and flexed his hands and neck.

He never thought he'd be back in a Ballistic Suit.

They had a saying back in the Corps: *You know you're having a shitty day if you find yourself in a Ballsy.*

Designed to protect mech pilots upon ejection, the Ballistic Suit was designed for short bursts of speed and light skirmishes. Other than the SIG Sauer strapped to his right thigh, Houston had no weapons.

He took a step forward, feeling the spring of the suit's powered limbs. He turned to the gaping hole in the wall. Outside, the mech smoldered, belching thick cords of smoke. He saw bodies on the ground, but he couldn't get an accurate count. The blast *should* have incinerated all six Alphas.

As if responding to his thoughts, a cry of rage bellowed through the hole. A charred monster clambered through the breach, eyes blazing.

The scorched Alpha saw Houston. He raised his fists and fired two searing bolts toward his head.

Houston dodged. The pistol was in his hand immediately—*crackcrack*—a whipper double-tap to the Alpha's chest sent him tumbling back through the breach.

Houston didn't have time to tangle with any other potential survivors. He retreated deeper into the lightless house, using the suit's mounted lamps to navigate. He flipped through the suit's radio frequencies until he found the one Katya and Baxter were using.

"*Piece of shit son of a bitch!*" Katya's gasping curses rang in his ears, strangely comforting.

"Sheriff," Houston said, using the call-sign he had chosen for her. "This is Metal Boy. Need eyes."

"*Hou—*" Katya's shocked voice stopped before she revealed his name over the radio. "Metal Boy, you're in the house?"

"Roger. Need eyes on Brother."

"Heading for the west gate," Katya replied. "About a half-mile from you."

"Where's Big Hair?"

"The Alpha's got her," Katya panted. "Heading west. We can't reach her."

Houston used the visor's compass to turn west. The suit's metal feet clomped on the hardwood. He flipped on the suit's electric motor, and pistons pushed against his heels like springs.

"I'm on it."

Houston took off at a dead sprint.

66

What a wonderful day this turned out to be, Caspar mused darkly as he swung the Rover around the house.

Gunfire.

Mechs popping in for unannounced visits.

Two years of meticulous planning and work, shattered in an instant.

And then on top of all that—Caspar wrinkled his nose—there was that ghastly smell.

It filled his nose and mouth. An acrid, stomach-turning odor that he hadn't smelled in over a decade.

Burning flesh.

Behind the manor, a tower of smoke spiraled upward from an inferno he couldn't see. A fire like that meant his men had managed to bring down the mech. The smell meant that many of them had died in the effort.

Caspar kicked down on the accelerator. He was in no rush to join them.

But his escape was hounded by one inconvenient fact: Caspar was an *awful* driver.

The Rover lurched and skidded across the road, tortured by Caspar's frantic footwork on the pedals. Twenty feet ahead, he saw the turnoff onto the road that would lead him to the west gate.

All he needed to do was try not to crash for the one-mile journey on the narrow, unfinished country road.

He was ten feet from the turnoff when the red blast knocked him sideways. The Rover spun to a stop, tossing Caspar against the door.

Caspar blinked his eyes open. He sat up and squinted at the line of trees in the headlights. Before he could piece it together, a giant shadow flung open his door.

Caspar screamed.

"Control yourself, sir," Willem barked.

"Willem," Caspar gasped. "But—"

Willem tossed Caspar into the backseat of the vehicle. Then, almost gently, the Militiaman deposited Lily next to Caspar and shut the door. In the bustle, her arm pressed against Caspar, and he felt a strange warmth ripple through him, unraveling old knots across his body.

She slid away from him. With a profound sense of loss, Caspar felt the warmth trickle away, leaving him cold again.

Gunfire erupted behind them.

"Heads down!" Willem ordered.

Caspar dove for the floor as Willem started the jeep and zigzagged across the road. Lily remained in her seat, watching Caspar.

"Get down," Caspar hissed. "They'll shoot you."

"No," she said, peering out the rear window. "They're here to take me home."

*

"Metal Boy!" Katya yelled into the radio as the Land Rover carrying Lily swerved around the side of the house at high speed. "Where are you?" She fired a burst at the tires but hit only dirt.

Baxter raced up behind her, the drone feed streaming to the phone strapped on his forearm. "Their lead is too big," he panted, turning the screen toward Katya. The heat signatures for both Bobby and Lily were far ahead of them in the woods.

"Keep moving," Katya growled, pulling Baxter along by the shirt. Her legs were screaming with lactic acid, but she wasn't going to stop.

The countdown clock was down to five minutes.

"Metal Boy, where are you?" Katya yelled again. "We're losing them."

The Rover's red taillights receded ahead of them, disappearing in the trees.

"Metal Boy on the move," Houston's voice crackled over her earpiece. He sounded out of breath like he was running.

"Whatever you're doing, do it faster," Katya huffed.

"Roger," Houston replied. "Stay back from the house."

Katya scowled, looking at the mansion twenty feet ahead of them. "Metal Boy. What do you mean stay back from the house? We—"

The side of the mansion blew out in a spray of bricks and glass. Katya skidded to a stop, Baxter crashing into her as a metal shape flashed through the explosion.

"What the hell?" Katya gasped.

The shape hit the grass and rolled. It rose on two legs and then, with all the grace of a dirt bike, barreled after the escaping Rover.

*

The Ballistic Suit's motor thrust Houston forward, its spiked boots crunching over the treacherous terrain. Up ahead, Houston saw the Rover's lights.

"Metal Boy in pursuit."

Katya said something, but he couldn't hear her over the rattling of his own teeth. The suit had speed but almost no shock absorbers, and Houston felt every inch of the bumpy ground clatter through his joints.

His visor indicated that the Rover was a hundred feet ahead of him moving at forty-three miles per hour. On this twisty, narrow road, he could close that distance in twenty seconds.

*

"Drive faster!" Caspar screamed from the backseat.

Behind them, the metal monster crashed through the woods, closing in.

"Willem, it's gaining!" Caspar yelled. Willem didn't respond. He was a trained combat driver, but the road was too rough to pick up any speed.

Next to Caspar, Lily squealed with laughter, leaning against the back of the chair and egging on the metal monster like she was in a movie theater.

"Shut up!" Caspar pushed her down.

The sound of their pursuer's heavy footfalls grew louder. Caspar closed his eyes and covered his ears with his hands. In the blackness, he saw the disappointed faces of his parents.

He saw Guillermo.

"Hold on!" Willem yelled. He spun the wheel, arcing the Rover into a tight turn. The truck decelerated, skidding—

A shadow flew over the Rover.

A wrecking ball crashed down onto the hood. Caspar's stomach plunged as the Rover lost contact with the ground and spun off the road.

They were *falling*.

The entire time, Caspar heard the girl laughing.

*

Houston's assault was clumsy, but it did the job.

Turning a tight corner, the Rover had decelerated just enough for Houston to cover the distance in one leap. The suit's hydraulics had launched him through the air and deposited him like a girder on the Rover's hood.

The truck's spin tossed Houston onto the road. The Rover careened off the path and jumped down into a ditch, stopping only when its rear fender crunched against a tree.

Moving sideways, Houston took cover behind an elm, eyes never leaving the stricken vehicle. It was parked at a sixty-degree angle on the slope, headlights illuminating the canopies above.

With four shots, Houston took out the front tires.

He waited. Watching the truck's dark windows.

A bolt spat through the windshield, and all hell broke loose. Houston hugged the dirt as more bolts broiled the space around him, setting the woods aflame.

The truck's doors opened; figures moved, shouted. Houston thought about breaking cover, but a barrage of bolts forced his head back into the grass.

"Houston!"

He heard her voice, piercing through the chaos.

Lily.

*

Like he had done all through his life, Caspar fled the scene of a fight.

The moment he heard the gunshots, the void in his soul—where his courage should have been—opened wide. Willem's voice barked commands, but Caspar was beyond listening. He left the girl in the backseat and threw himself onto the grass, his palms slicing open on rocks.

He picked himself up and ran.

*

Willem grabbed Lily. Houston glimpsed the big man from behind his rapidly shrinking cover, his big silhouette gripping Lily's hand and pulling her out of the car. His other hand continued firing.

His razor-sharp shots shredded the elm shielding Houston, cutting it down to the stump. Already scrunched up into a tight ball, Houston knew he had only two options.

Shrink in size.

Or *move.*

Lunging desperately, Houston rolled into the open space between him and the Alpha. Before the big Special could reset and aim, Houston blasted two slugs downrange. The shots skimmed the Alpha's crown, getting his attention and creating enough space and time for Houston to line up his third shot.

Crack. Hiss. The two men fired at the same time. The bolt went low. The whipper slug found its mark, blasting off a meaty chunk of the Alpha's jaw.

Willem stumbled. Lily saw her chance and tore free from his grip. Houston lined up the killing shot, but Willem regained his footing, pulled Lily back with a heavy paw, and held her like a shield.

Houston lined the sights up with the Alpha's skull. The Alpha, bald with iceberg eyes, pointed a wavering fist at Houston's face. His bloody jaw hung on threads, but his eyes were focused, murderous.

Willem moved with Lily in front of him, sliding from side to side, throwing off Houston's aim. Houston circled away from the crackling fist.

Lily caught Houston's eyes and nodded.

She balled her fists.

All Houston could do was crack a small smile.

"Bam!" Lily twisted on the balls of her feet and snapped a ferocious right hook into Willem's groin. He grunted and doubled over as Lily tore free, swan-diving into the dirt.

Crackcrack! Two whippers hit center mass, punching the Alpha back on his heels. The Alpha's arms wheeled, his entire body teetering, falling back—

But then with pure will, Willem found his feet. Houston glimpsed a flash of those frozen eyes and almost squeezed the trigger before the Alpha went airborne.

Even with the Ballistic Suit, Willem's rocketing bulk threw Houston ten feet through the air.

Loose change rattled in Houston's brain. Iron cobwebs pinned his arms and legs to the ground. He wanted to move, to fight back, but his body had other ideas. The suit's visor fizzled sadly, saying its goodbyes.

A great weight landed on Houston's chest. He watched dumbly as the Alpha held him down and smashed fiery red fists into his armor, dismantling it like cardboard.

Houston managed to crack a punch against the Alpha's ruined jaw. The Alpha screamed as metal crunched on broken bone. Houston bucked him off and rolled away as far down the slope as he could, his body moving with the grace of a flour sack.

Wobbling to his feet, Houston watched in horror as the Alpha turned his attention back toward him.

"Lowblood scum," Willem muttered through bloody teeth. Steaming with red fury, he launched across the gap between them.

Houston threw himself up in the air and flung both feet at the onrushing bull.

The spiked three-inch treads on his steel boots caught Willem flush in the face. Houston felt an earthquake travel up his spine before he crashed back to the ground, entangled with the Alpha's limp body.

Houston stared at the stars, winking at him through the trees. All the strength in his body had shut down like a dead power grid. He closed his eyes. This was as good a place as any to get some rest.

Hands grabbed him. Far away, at the other end of a long hallway, voices called his name.

They stood him up and peeled the Ballistic Suit off his limbs. His legs gave out and they held him upright. It started out as a form of support before becoming a strange, desperate embrace. Lily, Katya, himself.

He wrapped his arms around them, felt the hard lines of the holster under Katya's jacket. They held him so tight he wasn't sure if they were happy to see him or punishing him for all the misery he had caused them. If he let go of them he was certain the night would drown him. The dead Alpha lay at his feet, his head ruined.

Baxter cleared his throat. "We have three minutes."

Houston and Katya pulled apart. It was a few more seconds before Lily let go.

"Nice punch," Houston said.

"Bam!" She took a practice swing in the air. Houston had never been prouder of anyone in his life.

"Let's get this off," Katya said, cracking open Lily's Clamp with a pair of pliers. Lily's aura expanded suddenly, burning free.

"Bobby's still moving ahead of us," Baxter said, looking at his wrist-screen. "We have to go."

"There's something else," Lily said. She opened her jacket and pulled off her sweater.

"Jesus," Houston said, seeing the ugly black bridle.

Katya clipped off the buckles with the pliers and held the bridle up between her fingers like a live snake. With a grimace, she tossed it into the woods.

Lily stretched her limbs, happy to be free from the Clamp and bridle. She took a deep breath and focused on each of them, one by one. "Let's go get Bobby."

67

Bloody footprints left a trail behind Veena, a macabre wake. Her feet burned with pain, slashed and bruised from her long run.

Nearly there, she assured herself.

A few feet ahead, the lamps cast a pool of light over a fluorescent yellow marker across the floor. To Veena, it looked very much like the finish line of a marathon.

The yellow line indicated the location of the west wall above their heads, marking the outer bounds of her estate. Veena pushed the Songbird ahead, feeling a thrill in her chest as they crossed the yellow boundary. They were under public land now, a densely wooded two-mile stretch that separated her property from her neighbor's.

Twenty paces past the boundary, at the end of the hall, they arrived at a heavy door. Veena pressed her palm into the fingerprint scanner and the entrance slid open.

Once inside, Veena waved her arms in the darkness. Nothing happened. Frowning, she waved her arms more frantically. Still nothing. The motion sensors that controlled the lights refused to acknowledge her presence.

She went to plan B and clicked on her flashlight. There, in its slim beam, she saw the pale blue haunches of her waiting steed:

a prewar Volkswagen hatchback, so devoid of style or prestige that it was almost comical.

Inside the car, she pinned the Songbird to the passenger seat with the seatbelt. He watched her the entire time, trying to catch her gaze and failing. Veena slid in behind the wheel and fished out the keys from under the seat. She started the engine and switched on the headlights, illuminating the wide ramp leading up to the exit door.

Once out that door, they would find themselves in a small clearing outside the walls. A dirt path would lead them to the country road which would then link up to the main road.

The plan was murky after that.

Escape first. Figure out the rest later.

The Songbird squirmed in his seat next to her, muttering through the duct tape. Veena may not have had a plan, but at least she wasn't in his position.

She found the garage door opener in the armrest. Driving slowly up the ramp, she pressed its single white button.

The door didn't open.

Veena clicked the button again. The steel wall sat in front of them, washed white in the headlights.

Clickclickclickclick.

Her thumb was a jackhammer on the button. Over and over again, a depressing drumbeat.

She pulled out the batteries and reinserted them. When that didn't work, she tried the batteries from her flashlight but they were the wrong type. She scrounged around the glove compartment and found only folded maps and Ziploc bags filled with turkey jerky.

The door watched her. A foot of steel standing between her and freedom.

She pushed down her panic and shot out of the car, searching feverishly for some type of control panel. But even as her hands traced the walls, she knew it was futile. Even if there was a keypad, she didn't have the code.

Fuck.

She glared at the sheet of steel barring her way, wanting to scream.

The thought came to her the way all dangerous ideas did, like a feather floating down behind her eyes.

She plunged back in behind the wheel and threw the hatchback into reverse down the ramp. She strapped on her seatbelt.

"Hold onto your nuts," she quipped to the Songbird.

And then she stomped the gas.

The Songbird yelled into his gag as the car shot up the incline and torpedoed the steel at fifty miles an hour. Veena lurched forward, the seatbelt biting her chest. She heard the groan of buckling metal, but when she looked up the door hadn't budged.

Hit it harder.

Reversing back down the ramp, Veena guided the hatchback all the way down until the rear fender bumped the far wall.

"I'm really never like this," she said to the Songbird. "You caught me on a bad day."

With one last look at her target, Veena hit the accelerator as hard as she could. This time the impact drove the car's hood almost through the body, shattering the headlights and lifting the hatchback's rear tires off the cement. The airbag punched Veena square in the face.

She didn't know how long she sat there, stunned and silent. Her watering eyes traversed the dark, finding the door. In the light of the one remaining headlight, she saw small dents in the steel, etched reminders of her failure.

Maybe she was imagining it, but she saw sympathy in the Songbird's eyes as he watched her. Or maybe it was pity.

Veena left him in the car and slammed the door shut. She wouldn't let anyone see her like this. She held her head in her hands and collapsed against the rear tires. She had danced above the nothingness for so long, unwilling to look down. Now, she let herself peer into the void.

War criminal!

Fascist!

No peace without justice!

Tears stung her eyes, hot and shameful.

She had failed. She had come this far, and she had failed.

Moments like these had come before for Veena. When she let the tether to reality slip out of her hands and where she felt a powerlessness so crushing it stole the oxygen out of her lungs. Here in the void, as her feet kicked at black air, she spun down into the once possible life of Veena Sixkills.

A life where fire had not stained her irrevocably. Where, perhaps, she could have been someone else. What would that life look like? Far away, she saw it. Glimpsed something so wonderful that it cracked her heart in two. She stood on the threshold of their old Millsap ranch, her knuckles knocking on the door while behind her, the Texas sun fell in the sky and cast a blanket of gold over the plains. A man who loved her deeply stood by her side, strong and without scars.

The ranch door opened. Maybe it was her father, smiling and welcoming them inside. Maybe it was her mother, eyes crinkled with laughter as she rushed in to hug her little girl.

Her mother . . . she bit down on the face of Mable and it tasted bitter and bloodlike on her tongue.

She was the blood of a whore.

The pistol grew in size in her hand. She had forgotten it was there, but now the weight pressed against her fingers, the ridges of the grip scratching her palm.

She dug the cold barrel into the wedge between her throat and chin.

The explosion ripped her apart.

She was a loose tangle of splinters, freezing cold, unraveling. Muscles sliding off her bones, skin washing off like sand. The garage, the world, the dark sludge of her failure, fell away.

She was flying.

But only for a moment. All too soon, she felt herself solidify like ice and slide heavily back into her body. When she opened her eyes, she thought she was in heaven.

It was magnificent.

The Eternal Throne Room in the heart of the Golden Fort—a room she had only been in once when, as a child, she watched Patriot Gold assume the crown.

But now she wasn't in the audience. No. Now, she stood next to the throne on the dais, looking out across the hundreds of cheering dignitaries in their finest silks and jewels. The gilded hall rocked with their applause, their adulation for the new king.

Veena's hand rested on her father's shoulder as he commanded the room from the Eternal Throne. He wore no crown, no jewels or trinkets of any kind. He simply *was*. An enormous force, still and watchful, wielding the gravitational pull of a sun.

He turned to Veena and met her eyes. He nodded. The smallest of motions, but it was enough to unlatch a rusted lock in Veena's heart.

The Eternal Throne Room dissipated into a sea of glass and darkened, transforming into the stretch of Long Island Sound behind Veena's home.

Ahead of her, a grassy slope led to the dark waters. She wasn't sure why she was here.

A soft hand turned her head to the right. *Look.*

The object on the water's edge took shape, its outline crystallizing against the night.

Galliano! Veena realized with a lightning bolt of hope.

The boat bobbed in the water, moored to the second pier on her property, close to the west wall. *Galliano* was her plaything, a twenty-two-foot runabout boat with a varnished wood hull and a hundred-twenty-five horsepower outboard motor. She had spent many summers drunkenly tooling around on the Sound in that wave rocket, the exhilarating spray of wind and water on her face.

It was the perfect escape craft, and she had completely forgotten about it.

But *He* hadn't.

Veena landed back in her body with a hard shudder, gasping for air. The gun lay abandoned on the floor between her feet. She blinked, staring at it with mute fascination. A wicked cold blew through her, raising the flesh on her arms, wiping the slate of her soul clean with one exhilarating breath.

Everything had suddenly changed.

He Who Knows All had not abandoned her.

She stood, the strength flowing back into her limbs. Veena retrieved the gun and yanked the Songbird out of the car. Without a word she raced him out of the garage and back down the tunnel.

They wouldn't have far to go. Once they were past the west wall marker, it was just two turns and a short hop to the hatch that opened next to the pier.

The Songbird panted in front of her, battered and exhausted. Unlike her, he hadn't received a second wind and his strength was fading. She motivated him with a crack of the gun butt against his spine. He groaned and stumbled forward.

They passed the marker and turned left, now back under her estate. A sensation in the back of Veena's neck compelled her to turn and look behind her.

Stretching back down the tunnel, as bright as flares in the halogen lights, she saw her bloody footprints. Her father's words returned to her unbidden, snaking around her like a protective shield.

Reborn in blood.

Up ahead, the lights glinted off the rungs of the ladder leading to the surface. If only her father could see her now.

She was the Savior.

She would not fail.

68

It was a strange sight, the caravan of four desperadoes hurtling through the woods. Houston, Katya, Baxter, Lily, chasing after two heat signatures on a screen, tumbling forward like four dice on a crooked table.

It wasn't a chase so much as a series of stumbles and stubbed toes, conducted to the soundtrack of grunts, stringent curses, and promises of retribution toward Houston, the architect of this hopeless plan.

He deserved it, Houston thought as his lungs threatened to shrivel and die. A tree branch slapped him in the face, his ankle twisted in a patch of mud. Struggling to keep up with Baxter ahead, he took a moment to marvel at Lily.

Usually, Lily could barely walk in a straight line without tripping. But now, she had improbably found her grace, leaping and bounding like a baby gazelle springing through the woods.

Katya, on the other hand, was worrying him. She was running a little *too* fast. It seemed that Houston had underestimated the rigorousness of the Badge fitness program back in River Town. If there was one thing Houston couldn't allow, it was for Katya to beat him in a race. He dashed forward like a huffing bear, elbowing past her.

"He's right up ahead!" Baxter yelled back to them. He led them over a shallow stream and up an incline into a clearing.

The moment they broke out into the clearing, Houston saw Veena Sixkills fifty feet ahead of them, her blonde hair shining like a beacon in the dark as she ran for her life. It took Houston less than a second to absorb the terrain—the open hatch in the grass, the speedboat floating on the water's edge, the gun in Veena's hands pointed at the man stumbling ahead of her with his wrists bound.

Bobby.

The sight of his battered brother unleashed a surge of rage through Houston's limbs. Forgetting his exhausted legs, he plunged forward. Veena hadn't noticed she was being pursued yet, her back to them as she made a beeline for the boat.

Houston lined his pistol sights up with Veena's shoulder blades.

It was a treacherous shot, complicated by fatigue and Bobby's erratic movements. He swayed left and right on shaky legs, moving in and out of Houston's sight picture.

Veena's gun's butt pummeled Bobby's neck.

Houston dropped down to a knee and lined up the shot.

The world snapped into a narrow tunnel. A cool, clear line between the barrel of the SIG and Veena's back.

Bobby swayed just enough to the right. For a moment, Veena was exposed.

Houston squeezed the trigger.

The recoil jarred him backward with shocking force. Houston blinked, confused.

He heard Lily scream behind him. It sounded miles away, and he wondered why she was screaming. And then, in a moment of alarming clarity, Houston realized he hadn't heard a gunshot.

He heard the flapping of wings above.

The pain arrived. Piercing through his chest and spreading toxic roots around his heart. The pistol dropped to the ground.

Houston grunted, remembering this pain—this *blackness*—

Trembling, he managed to stand. He stared silently at the tomahawk lodged in his chest.

Lily screamed again, calling his name. Now he heard Katya screaming, too. Ahead of him, Veena and Bobby stopped in their tracks, staring at him with horror.

It's okay, little brother, Houston wanted to say. *I'm not going anywhere.*

But he couldn't form the words. He stumbled backward, his body defying his orders. A pitiless cold settled across his soul as the man in the hat emerged from the trees.

Leathery wings beat the air like drums, swooping down from the sky toward him. The talons of a monstrous crow gripped his spine and pulled. At first it felt like he was flying. But then the ground opened its jaws, and Houston plummeted.

The crow carried him into the endless nothingness. He tried to call out to the others, but his voice was gone and there was no light to see by.

6 9

Katya felt the axe's blade as if it had torn through her own chest.

She felt what it was like to die, to lose everything in the space between heartbeats.

Houston was dead the moment he hit the ground, that much Katya knew. But she wouldn't let herself believe it. All she saw was the reel of horror looping in her mind: the axe flung out of the darkness like a crackling disc, Houston gasping, falling—

Dying.

It was the snap of skeletal fingers, the blink of a jaundiced eye and then . . . it was over. Houston was gone forever. The world tilted like a capsizing boat, and Katya reeled.

Like an idiot she tried to remember her emergency medical training. She thought about staunching the blood flow, opening Houston's airways, checking his pulse. But Houston was beyond help, embalmed by an awful stillness.

Lily's screams rang in her ears. Katya reached out to hold her, but Lily was gone, bolting toward Houston's body.

Katya chased after her. She had a vague sense that the man in the hat was prowling close by and that Veena Sixkills was glaring at them, a gun in her hand. But these were far-off concerns, things that she couldn't deal with now.

Lily fell upon Houston's body and held it, sobbing. Katya gripped her shoulder and tried to pull her away.

"No!" Lily tore herself free. It was a roar of pain, an animal anguish that wracked her body. Her hands clenched the fabric of Houston's shirt, and she pressed her face into the back of his head. Katya saw her whisper into his ear, and with each word her aura heaved with despair.

Longhorn took a step toward them. Katya shielded Lily with her own body, unable to look at Houston. The Hammer felt inert in her hands, a dumb, useless thing. She could fire it until it was empty, rip the world apart with its roar, but it wouldn't matter. The gun could only bring more death, and what she had already tasted of death tonight choked her.

Katya spoke softly into Lily's ear. "Lily, please." Her voice trembled. "He's gone."

Lily turned to her, the fear in her eyes breaking Katya. "I'm so scared," she mumbled.

"Come with me," Katya said, hearing the heavy footsteps of Longhorn's approach, feeling the probing stingers of his Gift dance across the back of her neck. Katya didn't know where they would go, but she had the instinct to move, to not die here like this.

Lily sniffled. She put her hand on Houston's cheek.

"I didn't want anyone to die for me," she said, her lips quivering. She closed her eyes, and Katya felt the wind pick up.

It was then that Katya realized her mistake.

Battered by shock, Katya had misread Lily's fear. Lily was not afraid of Veena. She wasn't afraid of the Warborn anymore.

Because Lily was going beyond them all now.

Lily closed her eyes and inhaled deeply.

"*NO!*" Katya screamed, but she had no voice. She grasped for Lily's shoulders, but it was too late. Katya could not stop her when she released the breath, and all the stars in the night sky exploded.

70

Halfway down the mountain, after he had slipped and stumbled for what felt like hours through the luminescent jungle, Houston saw the ocean.

His pace slowed as the ground leveled beneath him. Palm trees formed arches like church entrances to the black sand beach. The jungle behind him rustled and shimmered with the presence of living things, things he could not see. But the beach was a sanctuary, lapped with soft waves, draped in a hushed serenity.

The black sand was like a cloud beneath his bare feet. Black cliffs walled in the shore, streaked with plunging waterfalls. On the horizon, Houston marveled at the raw power of the Furies. Snapping like vipers, the long arms of lightning lashed the sea and giant breaths of fire bellowed across the surface, unleashing plumes of smoke into the sky.

Houston gasped when he saw the sky.

The cosmos spread out above him, a map of the universe painted in diamonds and celestial gold. Ancient worlds glided around vivid suns, against a backdrop of sparkling purple nebulae. The sky seemed to span millions of miles, yet it was so vibrant that Houston felt he could reach out and touch the stars.

And above it all, beyond the celestial realm, he felt *them*.

Their presence was textured, primal, unquestionable. They were somewhere up there, connecting all the mighty planets, reaching down here, brushing along Houston's cheek like a warm breeze. He could not name them or picture them. He simply *knew* them, intelligences vast and peaceful that guided all things, worlds and broken men, through their orbits.

Houston's gaze was pulled away from the sky when he heard a woman's laughter. Further down the beach, he caught a glimpse of amber lights.

A bungalow. Nestled in the trees, overlooking the ocean. The woman's laughter was coming from inside, now joined by the excited giggle of children.

Houston walked toward the cabin. He knew they were waiting for him. That there would be smiles to greet him when he came through the door and no one would ever tell him he didn't belong.

He saw someone move by the shore. She traipsed across the rocks, climbing down into the remnants of a beached outrigger. Her feet slipped on the slick wood and she fell. For a moment, all Houston could see was the electric-shock puff of her hair above the hull. Gamely, she stood back up and dug around the boat, searching.

Houston ran his hand along his chest, fingers tracing the flesh where the axe had lodged. He remembered the pain like a dream, its tendrils slipping off him, leaving only traces of unease.

Looking at Lily, he knew what she had done, why she was here, but he didn't want to believe it. He couldn't bear it.

He approached. She continued digging around across the bottom of the boat until she found what she was looking for. Between her fingers, she lifted up a wriggling rock crab and studied it for a few moments before placing it gently back down in the boat. The wind blew down the cliffs, a haunting wail.

"I'm sorry." It was all Houston could manage to say, his shoulders heavy with grief.

Lily took a moment before she looked at him, her eyes glistening in the moonlight. A sharp pang of memory flooded Houston, and he was flung back to that bloody night that started it all, when he opened the back of a truck and saw those eyes look at him in the same way. With fear and weariness, with courage and curiosity, and above all else with *hope.*

Lily blinked away tears and clambered off the outrigger. She stood next to him, slipping her small hand into his. They watched the Furies tear apart the horizon.

"You did everything you could," she said. "Thank you."

"I promised to get you home. And I didn't."

She squeezed his hand. He understood then what it meant to give *everything* for someone else, and the sheer pain of the epiphany buckled his knees. He had gone through his life shipwrecked, angry, hurtling through his own loneliness, and it wasn't until this moment that he deciphered what that *everything* meant—how far he had fallen from it and how ruthlessly he had cleaved it out of his own life.

"Home . . ." Lily began. She listened to the sound of singing coming from the bungalow. "I think it might not always be a place. Sometimes I think it's just people. The way we feel about them."

"You should have left me," Houston said, anger in his voice. "You shouldn't have done that."

"But I did."

"Why? The world needs you. It doesn't need *me.*"

She thought about it for a moment, the way she did, with her whole body and soul searching for an answer. "Because that night, when you found me in the truck, you had a choice. You could have closed the doors and forgotten me. But you chose to help. You chose your better self that night, Houston. And when the bad times come, it won't be Specials or gods who save this world. It will be people like you. Standing in the dark, choosing their better self."

A breeze blew off the ocean, braced with salt and fire. From behind them, in the maw of the mountains and jungles, something responded to the wind. A serene vibration that soothed Houston's very bones.

"Did you feel that?" Lily asked.

Houston nodded, the vibration still echoing through him.

"That's her," Lily said. "The Source. She's waiting for me." A cool air shifted around Lily, like the embrace of an old friend. "She's waiting for all of us."

Houston knelt down and gripped a handful of black sand, watching it waterfall through his fingers. "How do we get back here?" he asked. "Without you?"

She took his hand and turned him around to face the beach and the jungle. "There are others like me. Find them. And then find this place."

Her childlike words returned to Houston. "Something left to do before I die."

She rubbed her nose against his arm and looked up at him. "Find your way home, Houston. And lead the rest of us here."

She leaned against him, her warmth seeping through his shirt. He held her and looked out at the ocean for what felt like a very long time.

"You have to go now," she said, wiping a tear from her cheek.

"Yeah," he said, his voice hollow.

"But hurry back here."

"As fast as I can."

She hugged him with every ounce of strength her little body could muster. He felt her tears dampen his shirt, and when he let her go some vital chamber of his heart ripped through his chest and left his body. He watched her walk toward the bungalow, her eyes turned upward, drinking in the stars.

"Oh, I almost forgot," Lily said, turning around. "She says hello."

"Who says hello?"

"She said she's sorry. But she tried her best to take care of you and Bobby. And she hopes you can forgive her."

Houston said nothing. He stared at the black sand between his toes.

"Do you want me to tell her anything?" Lily asked.

Houston shook his head.

"Are you sure?"

Houston studied the Furies. "Tell her," he finally said, "that I understand now. What it takes to look after others. How hard it is. Just tell her that."

Lily smiled. "I will."

She turned back to the bungalow. She crossed through a patch of moonlight and opened the door. A gale of happy voices rose up to greet her. Houston caught one last glimpse of her, brushed with the glittering pink and white of her aura, before the door closed.

He stood alone for a few breaths, listening to the ocean.

"As fast as I can," he whispered before the stars draped around him and his feet left the ground.

71

Houston's eyes opened onto a world of white and pink comets. Thick bands of them wrapped around him, thrumming with power. Beneath him he saw the jade terrain of treetops, the midnight ribbon of the Long Island Sound. Below his heels was fifteen feet of air.

I'm flying, he realized.

From here, he could see the people below him, knocked off their feet by the blast. He saw Baxter and Katya, staring slack-jawed up at him. Veena and Bobby both blinked up at him, awestruck. Even Longhorn stood frozen, not comprehending what he was seeing.

The tomahawk was no longer in his chest. The blackness embedded in him by its blade was gone, and something else had taken its place.

Something he had brought back from the Black Isles.

His eyes fell upon Veena Sixkills.

It was time to finish this.

*

"No freaking way . . ." Katya stared up at what could only be a hallucination.

It had all happened in seconds.

Lily had turned the world into a white hurricane that had blasted Katya off her feet. She had landed hard on the grass, and when she had opened her eyes it took her a few moments to understand what she was seeing.

Houston.

He was floating above them, encased in ribbons of white and pink. His eyes were open, his arms and legs moving.

He was *alive*.

*

Veena choked back her horror as the dead man floated down to the ground in a veil of white and pink lights.

If she hadn't been so shocked, she might have found the entire spectacle beautiful.

She tried to sit up and fell back down. The blast had left her woozy, her limbs as soft as string. Ten feet to her left, the Songbird lay on the grass, transfixed on the resurrected man. Veena's hands felt empty, and she realized that her gun was missing.

The man touched down on the grass. He stood there, crystallizing into focus as the lights fled, dissipating upward. The entire clearing fell back into darkness. But even though the lights were gone, Veena could still feel their essence, their ghosts vibrating around the lowblood.

The man stood very still.

He raised his eyes toward her.

Spurred on by terror, Veena clambered onto her hands and knees.

Her gun.

She had to find her gun.

*

Houston's feet pressed onto grass, and as his eyes adjusted to the darkness, he saw her.

Lily lay on her back, her arms drawn into her body and her eyes closed to the world. There was no sign of pain or struggle on her face, only a quiet serenity, as if she had finally glimpsed home.

The wound in Houston's chest was gone, but another one opened up in the world around him—the loss of Lily was a physical pain, an absence so acute it clung to every living thing. He felt no Gift sieve through his system, he felt no new powers pump through his bloodstream. He was still flesh and blood; still achingly mortal.

But he was alive.

And Lily wasn't.

His work here wasn't done.

He looked up and met Veena's startled gaze. He saw her jolt into action, scrounging around on the grass, looking for something.

Her gun.

Houston's eyes were drawn to the object a few feet away in the grass.

The tomahawk. Its blade painted with his blood.

Lifting the tomahawk with one swoop of his arm, Houston tore toward Veena.

Veena found the gun and arced the barrel up toward Houston's head. Houston dove forward a split-second before she fired. The bullet went high as Houston rolled across the grass and snapped up next to Veena with the swinging tomahawk.

Veena's shriek split the night as the tomahawk carved through her forearm.

Returning to his feet, Houston barely had a moment to recover before he sensed Longhorn's arrival behind him.

The man made no sound, he simply appeared, five steps away from Houston, tomahawk in hand.

"Kill him!" Veena screamed, clutching the bloody stump of her arm, her face bone white. "Kill him now!"

Longhorn didn't move. Somewhere under the shadow of his hat, his eyes were probing, dissecting Houston inch by inch.

Behind Longhorn, Katya and Baxter approached, guns raised. Houston stopped them with a raised hand.

"Fucking end him!" Veena shouted again.

Longhorn took a step forward. Houston stood very still, drowning in the Warborn's energy, an insatiable matter that fed on oxygen and flesh. Houston gripped his tomahawk, waiting for Longhorn's strike.

Longhorn held out his hand.

He tipped his head toward the second tomahawk in Houston's grip.

For a moment, Houston looked between the axe and Longhorn, confused. His heart was pounding, his body still primed for a fight. He tried to decipher the expression on the Warborn's shadowed face.

Moving as slowly as possible, Houston handed over the tomahawk. Longhorn took it and studied its blade blankly. He then sheathed the two weapons.

"What are you doing?" Veena cried, incredulous. "Kill him!"

With the slow, lethal patience of a viper, Longhorn slid his gaze onto Veena. "I did. Death does not want him. Not yet."

Without another word, Longhorn turned his back on them and melted into the woods, his crow gliding above him.

The moment he was gone, Houston started to breathe again. Katya raced up to him while Baxter went to Bobby and cut the straps around his wrists. The first wail of sirens sounded in the distance.

"Let's go," Baxter said, pulling Bobby to his feet.

Veena spat at Houston and Katya. "You're all so *fucked*. You think you can come into *my* home and get away with this? Do you know who I am? You fucking lowbloods are dead. Fucking *dead*!"

Katya stepped forward. "You killed her," she said in a voice so cold it made Houston shiver. "You have everything, and you killed her. For what?"

Veena glared up at her, coiled like a hissing cobra. Houston saw traces of her fabled beauty beneath the snarling mask, something that was once pure but was now so poisoned that she barely resembled a person.

"My father," Veena whispered between her teeth. "My father will tear you limb from limb. He'll feed your flesh to the dogs."

"A child." There was a catch in Katya's voice, a tremor of rage. "Her name was Lily, and she's dead because of you."

"Katya," Baxter called, insistent, as the sirens grew louder. "We need to leave. *Now.*"

But Katya didn't move. She just held Veena's gaze, the space between them thick with venom.

"That child?" Veena smiled. "Who the fuck cares about that child? I am the Savior. I was destined to save this world, and I would kill a hundred fucking children to do that. Does that make sense to you, little miss lowblood?" Veena grinned dementedly, a laugh crackling in her throat. "I would kill a hundred—"

It was the sound of the earth ripping apart. A shockwave that rattled Houston's spine and tore Veena's face in half. That famous face, the one that had graced magazine covers and billboards, exploded into chunks of flesh and splintered bone.

Houston stared at Veena's ruined skull. Then his gaze moved upward, traveling past the smoking barrel of the Hammer, past Katya's shaking grip, and onto the icy wasteland of her eyes. It was a look that Houston had seen in the eyes of many others before but not one he ever expected to see in hers.

She looked at him as he pushed the barrel of the gun down.

"Kat," Houston said. "We're done here."

Baxter and Bobby stared at her. The sirens filled the night, right outside the estate walls. Houston saw a black shape move across the Sound toward them. It was their Zodiac, their captain guiding it in fast and quiet.

Houston lifted Lily's body into his arms and joined Katya, Bobby, and Baxter. Together they ran, supporting each other silently as they struggled across the clearing. No one spoke, but they all felt it, the weight of their loss bearing down on them, crushing them.

They waited together by the shore as the Zodiac pulled in. Bobby put a hand on Houston's shoulder.

"I knew you would come," he said.

"Only took me fifteen years," Houston replied.

They climbed onboard the Zodiac, and the captain sped them out into the black waters. Houston held onto Lily, unable to look at her, the warmth gone from her forever. Katya leaned against him and took Lily's hand in hers.

From a distance, they could see the flames rise above the estate, the towers of smoke painted with the lights of the emergency response vehicles pulling up to the gates. No one said anything on the boat. They just listened to the slap of the water against the hull.

Katya gripped Houston's arm. "Look," she said, pointing to the sky.

Everyone turned to the small cluster of colors floating above them. Vivid pinks and whites, floral purples and azures—a small aurora borealis watching over the Zodiac.

It followed them for a few minutes. Once they were clear of danger, it burned bright and then melted behind them, all of its beautiful colors slowly fading into the starlight.

72

The sky was still dark and the air cool. The sun lay hidden behind the towers of Sovereign, the first arrays of pink blossoming across the city.

Houston stood and watched the black Suburban pull into the private airfield and approach the open hangar where they all waited. Bobby's jet was parked behind them.

Katya pressed up against Houston's arm, her breath fogging in the dawn chill. Neither of them had spoken much in the last two days. Neither of them knew what to say.

The Suburban parked in front of the hangar, and a team of Ohana opened the truck's back door. Houston, Katya, Bobby, and Baxter walked out as one to receive the casket inside.

It was a small casket, dark mahogany and engraved with lilies across its face. It felt unbearably light on Houston's shoulders, the weight of a child, the fragile burden that could break all men.

Houston, Katya, Bobby, and Baxter carried the casket toward the waiting jet. A breeze ruffled their hair and chilled their hands. Houston felt like they were on the moon, the last survivors of a terrible storm. A contingent of Ohana stood guard along their passage, silent and respectful.

They carried Lily into the plane and set her down. They took a step back and let the Ohana strap the casket to the floor. Katya gently placed Lily's Amelia Earhart cap on the polished wood.

"Take care, little lady," she whispered.

Houston stood guard over Lily for a few moments while the others left. Only Baxter remained behind. He would be Lily's companion as she traveled to the Ohana's Last Shelter in West Virginia. There, in a field of flowers by a mountain stream, she would be laid to rest.

Houston nodded at Baxter and exited the plane. On the tarmac, Houston enjoyed the warmth of the dawn's sun on his face as it peaked through the skyline. He closed his eyes and thought of nothing as the jet raced down the runway and went airborne. Silently, they all watched as it disappeared in the distance.

Houston saw Bobby wipe his eyes. He smiled at Houston and then turned away to talk to the Ohana guards.

Katya remained stoic by Houston's side. She was still staring up at the sky, her hand wrapped around the five-pointed star badge she usually wore on her jacket. She turned it over in her hands, as if it were an alien artifact. She looked at Houston and tossed it to him.

"You win," she said. "I'm not cut out to be a Badge."

He looked at the star in his hands. At the dullness in Katya's eyes, raw from two days of crying. Everything she believed she was had died along with Veena Sixkills in the concussive roar of the Hammer. She was lost, and Houston needed her to find her way. He needed her light, because if there were no more people like Katya in the world, if they all became broken and jaded, then there was no hope for the world at all.

He took her hand and pressed the badge into it. "Keep it," he said. "You'll need it one day. We all will."

"Stop trying to save me," she said.

"I will. When you stop trying to save me."

Katya smiled. "I'm officially stopping today." She held his arm. "I'll never repeat this, and I'll deny it forever but . . . I'm proud of you, Holt."

"Can I get that in writing?"

She laughed and turned to enjoy the rising sun, its rays coloring the massive dome of the Golden Fort like honey. For a long moment they felt it together, her absence, all the blank spaces in the world where Lily should have been.

"Did we do everything we could?" Katya asked. "Did we do enough for her?"

It was some time before Houston could answer. "I don't know."

*

An hour later, they were back at Bobby's penthouse hideaway in the lower east side of Sovereign. The secret apartment where Houston and Katya had been lying low after their assault on Starlet Manor three nights ago.

Ever since then, the murder of Veena Sixkills had dominated the news.

Her death threw a pall over the Grand Decennial celebrations. Outpourings of shock and sorrow arrived from all corners of the Kingdom followed by statements from the Crown and SSD, promising swift retribution for the perpetrators.

The news made no mention of the ceasefire, but Houston knew there would be none. Without Lily to trade, the Redbloods had no leverage, and the king had no reason to pursue peace. Houston often wondered about Carmen, about where she was and what she would do now that her dream of a homeland was lost.

Today, Houston chose not to turn on the news. He went to his room and lay down. His old war wound creaked along his side and his new one, the tomahawk cleave across his left shoulder, burned and robbed him of rest. By his bedside table, Lily's drawing of the Big Island sat folded. He opened his bedside drawer, dropped the drawing inside, and shut it.

*

A ribbon of clouds passed across the noontime sun as Houston stood on the penthouse rooftop and studied the city, drinking a Scotch. Behind him, Bobby and Katya were talking at a table laid out with lunch.

Houston studied the Risen King banners fluttering from the buildings, shining from every facade.

He toasted it.

"Look at us two. The resurrected." He tossed back his drink. "Maybe I should be the fucking king."

He rubbed his eyes, anger welling, wondering if the king would ever know that a bunch of lowbloods had sacrificed everything to save his life.

Bobby arrived beside him, drinking a cup of steaming tea. He pointed out over the rooftops. "Remember what used to be there?"

"Big Don's apartment."

"And the Ivory Room was over there." Bobby's finger traced to the right. "The Calabasas Lounge a few blocks east. Your favorite restaurant was on that corner."

"Marzano's," Houston remembered.

"May it, and its heavenly calzones, rest in peace."

They laughed. Bobby blew on his tea for a few seconds before speaking again. "Did you read the letter?"

"I did," Houston said. His mother's letter had been buried at the bottom of his ruck since Bobby had given it to him. Last night, when sleep was as far away as the Black Isles, he had unearthed it from his pack and read it in the moonlight.

It was short, only one page. His mother was not one to emote, and her words were plain and unvarnished. When Houston had finished reading it he had folded the letter into its envelope and entombed it back in his pack.

"Good," Bobby said.

"There was one thing she wrote," Houston said. "One line that keeps coming back to me."

"What did it say?"

"The pain of knowing you failed your children is the worst pain of all."

Bobby sipped his tea and gazed at the Golden Fort. "You didn't fail her, Houston."

"That's not—"

"I mean Lily."

"Oh."

"You didn't fail her. You gave her everything." Bobby raised his hand to the sky, toward a flock of Specials gliding above them. "Look at them. Gifted beyond imagination and yet lost. They've forgotten what the true Gift is."

Houston turned to him. "The true Gift?"

Bobby thought about what he was going to say next, as if it were something beyond the scope of mere words. "When you died, Lily brought you back. Lily sacrificed herself to give you another chance because she believed so strongly in you. Her last measure of love, she gave to you. That is the true Gift. And that is what she needs you to carry back to the Isles. To her home."

Houston stared at his empty glass. The grief perched on his heart, deep and heavy and endless.

Bobby held his shoulder. "You loved her, Houston. More than you realized you ever could. That is the only gift in this world. The only one that matters."

Houston met Bobby's gaze, saw the prisms of light dance in his eyes. "What happens now?" Houston asked. "How do we get to the Black Isles without her?"

"We'll find a way. No matter how long it takes or how steep the climb gets, I have faith that we'll find a way."

They turned and walked over to the table and joined Katya. Together they ate in silence.

"Sovereign City," Katya finally said, looking around. "Never thought I would be here."

"I did," Houston said.

"Is it how you imagined it?" Katya asked.

"I don't remember."

"You're free to stay here, Houston," Bobby said. "You have done more than we could ask. Just say the word, and this can be your home."

"With a Gold Stamp?" Houston asked.

Bobby nodded. "Yes."

Houston studied the domes and glamor and wealth around him. He felt the others looking at him, waiting on his answer. When he spoke, he realized he had made the decision three nights ago, next to the waters of Starlet Manor.

"I promised a little girl I would get her home," he said. "I intend to keep that promise."

Katya and Bobby shared a smile. Then Katya met Houston's gaze, and Houston saw something like hope in her eyes. "Well, Holt," she said. "That's not a promise you'll ever have to keep alone."

———————

73

Caspar hadn't slept in three days.

How could he? He was in hell.

Lightning lashed the sky outside and heavy sheets of rain clattered against his walls. Caspar trembled on his lumpy cot, watching the doorway and waiting for the SSD spider monkeys to knock it down and crawl inside his cell, their eyeless heads swiveling, searching for him.

After escaping Starlet Manor, he had managed to link up with his bush pilot and make the short hop into Ciudad Juárez. The entire flight he had been sick with worry. There were too many loose ends left behind him, a trail of blood that the SSD would follow like jackals.

He had been scheduled to make the second leg onto Jamaica immediately after landing in Juarez, but instead, the stormy weather had grounded him in Mexico indefinitely.

Caspar had little money, and he had to beg the pilot for a place to stay until the next flight. Imagine that. Caspar Von Arx, heir to hundreds of billions of goldmarks, begging some lowblood bush pilot for a bed and a roof in a low-rent border town.

The pilot had driven him in a car filled with strange men to this flophouse, where some exchange had taken place between the pilot and the obese woman behind the desk, after which Caspar found himself in a room with a cot, one slit of a window, and a bathroom shared with the rest of the hall.

He was so far from Paris it made him retch.

He barely left his room. He held in his bodily functions for as long as he could before he was forced to use that disaster of a bathroom. The people here were savages, arguing loudly in the halls and stinking of liquor and weed.

On rare occasions, Caspar would go downstairs to the bodega for bottles of purified water and plain tortillas, the only thing that looked edible there. On the TV behind the counter, he would catch glimpses of the news, the Mexican network beaming images straight from Sovereign City.

The Grand Decennial was going off without a hitch. The king and queen were alive and well, and the entire Golden Kingdom celebrated, bursting with bright lights, music, and fireworks.

Caspar would take his meal back to his room and cry.

Most days, he would lay on his cot, staring at the ceiling, feeling his body shrink away. He alternately prayed to He Who Knows All for salvation and cursed him for his betrayal.

He was such a fool to have believed.

Salvation arrived on the fourth night. A knock on the door. It was the pilot, his eyes bloodshot, tequila on his breath.

"Weather's clearing," he said. "We fly tonight."

*

Caspar wedged himself into the tiny plane and strapped into the seat behind the pilot's. It was a five-hour flight to Jamaica with no air-conditioning and no meal service. He wished he had bought a bottle of tequila from the bodega before leaving.

By his feet, the pilot had placed a cardboard box filled with bottled water and granola bars. Caspar emptied a bottle down his parched throat and sat back, closing his eyes.

Up ahead, the pilot pulled his headset on over his shaggy hair and spoke back and forth with the tower. After a few minutes, he gave Caspar the thumbs up, and they cruised onto the runway. When the plane went airborne, Caspar felt the dark coils around him slip away, and he allowed himself a small smile.

*

When Caspar woke up, the plane wasn't moving.

He felt like he had slept for days. He tried to look out the window, hoping to see palm trees and the mountains of Montego Bay, but he realized he couldn't move.

The empty bottle of water rolled around the cabin by his feet. Caspar tasted something bitter on the back of his tongue.

He tried to sit up, but his body was a sack of wet sand. He blinked dumbly and tried to speak, but only drool escaped his lips. Up ahead he could see the pilot grinning at him with yellowed teeth.

"Morning, sweetheart. Time for you to meet your new family."

A blast of hot air blew into the cockpit, smelling of gasoline, rust, and rotting fruit. Large men entered the aircraft. They grabbed Caspar by the arms.

"How much did you give him?" one of the men asked.

"I didn't know he'd drink the whole bottle," the pilot replied.

Caspar was whisked out of the plane and deposited in the back of a car. He thought he was screaming, but he couldn't hear anything and his mouth wasn't moving. The scream was inside his head, trapped in the confines of his leaden skull.

A scratchy black hood went over his head. As the car took off, Caspar tasted the bitter poison again on his tongue, helpless as it pulled him back down to sleep.

*

The sound woke him.

Unearthly, alien, *virulent*.

Caspar blinked his eyes open. The darkness was a fog, thick and physical, vibrating with the sound. He sat on a metal chair, hands bound behind him, ankles strapped to the chair legs.

He trembled in the frigid air, although not only from the cold. His vision adjusted to the gloom, and he could sense the cavernous dimensions of the space by the way the sound traveled through it.

And there was something in here with him.

Breathing, watching from the curtain of shadow in front of him. The alien sound was its breath, pulsing through a grotesque body that Caspar could sense but could not see. He felt its pitiless eyes rake over him.

"We came so close, Caspar."

Caspar jumped so hard the restraints cut through his skin. He whipped his head around, searching for the source of the voice.

There. Sitting on a low ledge ten feet in front of him.

The Lady in the Veil turned to Caspar, her eyes glittering like cracked jewels. "We came so *very* close."

She was perched on the edge of a small pool that extended into the shadow. Her hand brushed through the water. Its black surface bubbled with each exhalation of the great hidden beast behind her.

Caspar tried to say something, but only a croak escaped his dry throat.

"We did everything we could, Caspar," the Lady said. "And yet, the tyrant still sits on his throne."

Caspar coughed. After much struggle he found his voice. "It's not my fault. You have to believe me. Veena is responsible for this mess. I—"

The Lady put up a hand and stood up, smoothing her silk blouse. "The responsibility lies with me."

"We can try again," Caspar said. "You and I. We'll come up with a new plan."

"Will we?" The Lady smiled. "Do you even realize what we're fighting for?"

"For our nation. Our people."

"No, Caspar. *My* nation. *My* people."

She pointed upward. Caspar followed her finger to the rafters, high above, where a small cluster of lights fell along the long, rippling body of the American flag.

Caspar lowered his eyes and met the Lady's gaze. "I didn't realize the UN was hiring Specials to do their dirty work."

The Lady laughed. "Fuck the UN."

Caspar felt an old fear creep up his spine, one that had first found him in Miami. "You're a Redblood."

"No. Although I did admire them once. Before they lost their way."

"I have money." Caspar's voice trembled. "Back home. Enough to change your life. I don't even care who you are. Just let me go."

The Lady paced around Caspar, slipping in and out of his vision like a ghost. "Have you lost faith already, Caspar? For two years you believed in He Who Knows All. You believed that he could change you, guide you to a place you had never been before . . . home."

She looked up at the ceiling, at the flag. "I remember how scared I was when my parents made me leave home. By then the war was all but lost, and they knew I wouldn't survive the aftermath." The Lady closed her eyes, holding in a great anger that burned through her skin. "They were human. I was not. And yet they didn't love me any less. They *believed* in something noble, something that gave them strength when their world was overrun by savages. That every living being, regardless of creed, color, or religion, had the right to live free." She turned away from Caspar, hiding her face in the darkness. "They died for those beliefs. And here I am. A girl with no home."

Caspar watched as the Lady walked over to him. She was ageless; she could have been twenty or forty—it was impossible to tell. She knelt down and held his face. This close, her eyes took on unfathomable icy depths.

"You know what that feels like, don't you, Caspar? To feel so very far away from home."

Tears burned in Caspar's eyes. He was shocked when they arrived. The Lady wiped them away with her thumbs. "And you remember what happened to you when you were lost. After Guillermo tore out your soul. What happened then?"

Caspar sobbed. "He Who Knows All found me."

"Yes, Caspar. You started to believe."

She broke her gaze and Caspar exhaled, relieved to be away from those frozen eyes. He cleared his throat. "He's a lie. He doesn't exist." The words fell out of him, the realization opening up a pit of despair. "Everything you told me about him was a *fucking* lie."

The Lady turned around, her breath frosting in the cold. "Not at all. I assure you, he is very real."

She took two steps forward and smiled, her teeth glinting. "Would you like to meet him?"

Without waiting for an answer, she turned and walked back to the pool. Her finger traced the water, white lights brimming there, a small cosmos burning at her fingertips. "I admit, I did mislead you regarding one thing, Caspar. I told you I was a servant of He Who Knows All. The truth"—she looked into the shadows of the pool—"is that He is a servant of *me*."

She raised her arms, an acolyte welcoming a blessing from heaven. Small lights awoke in the high ceiling, falling like a mist over the water, revealing the black goliath that rose from its depths.

Caspar had seen death before. He had witnessed destruction. But never, until that moment, had he truly laid his eyes upon horror.

His mouth fell open. "Oh, *God* . . ."

He Who Knows All rose to the rafters, a writhing steel tree built by demons. The thick metal cables of its massive trunk slithered through and around each other, a swarm of monstrous snakes studded with spikes and glimmering lights. And trapped between the metal anacondas, Caspar saw four women.

They were naked. Old, young, white, and black, their eyes open, shining like ghost moons. Slim vines pulsing with white lights punctured deep into their shaved scalps and exposed spines, *feeding* off them.

They looked dead, but Caspar knew they were not. They were trapped somewhere between life and death, in a psychic wasteland. Their bare breasts rose and fell, and every few seconds a woman would gasp and the tree would carry them to another section of its trunks where new vines found them, penetrated them, and devoured their fragile bodies.

The Lady glided forward, her eyes falling on the machine like it was the nave of a church. "In the final days of the Immortal War, President Mathias was on the verge of unleashing an experimental weapon against the Specials. An artificial intelligence of a magnitude unseen in the modern world. They named it Omega Rex. By setting Rex free, Mathias would have won the war but perhaps doomed humanity to an even worse fate—the rule of a crueler master. It was a gamble that the president was not willing to take."

The Lady looked at the horror behind her, lovingly. "I, however, know that to win big, you *have* to gamble big."

"No." Caspar shook his head. "Omega Rex is a myth."

"Myths are such strange things," the Lady said. "They so often have a habit of becoming truth. Once upon a time, flying men only existed in our stories. But, there is another story at work here, Caspar. A harrowing tale about a group of dedicated patriots who, seven years ago, ventured deep into the heart of a tyrannical kingdom to steal the source code for a weapon capable of—no, a weapon *designed* to—eradicate the race of Specials.

"Omega Rex . . ." the Lady whispered the name reverently, the way a crusader whispers the name of the holy city, rife with a history of pain and bloodshed, enshrined in a mysticism that perhaps she did not fully comprehend. "I once thought, like you, Caspar, that it couldn't be real. When we finally built it, when I saw what it was—part-machine, part-Special—I understood why the president stayed his hand. But I also saw what happened to him. What your king *did* to him . . ." Her eyes vibrated, and she had to close them as if to staunch the anger from bleeding out. "That won't be the fate of my people. Because, as you can see, Caspar, Omega Rex is not a myth." She leaned in so close to him he could see the onyx flecks in her irises. "He is a God."

One of the women gasped, her body arching. The coils tightened around her and brought her back into the pulsing core.

"Omega Rex sees all," the Lady said. "It devised our plot to kill the King. Combined with the psychic Gift of these lovely Southern Sibyls, it penetrated your mind, penetrated Veena's. We haven't even scratched the surface of its full capabilities yet, but what we have figured out is how to speak to those who are broken. Those who are lost." She put her hand on Caspar's shoulder. They both watched in mute fascination as the lights dimmed and the glossy horror receded back into its dark lair.

Caspar stared at his lap. The strings were on him again. He had been used, a marionette, a fool.

You are easy to fool. Guillermo's taunt. True then, true now.

"You won't get away with this," Caspar hissed.

"We will. And you're going to help us."

"What?"

"Get some rest," she said. "You have a part to play in what comes next."

"Who are you?" Caspar demanded, the words slipping out full of venom but ultimately powerless. "*Who are you?*"

Heavy boots marched up behind him. Strong arms gripped him under his arms and undid his shackles.

"Who are you?" Caspar screamed as the men dragged him away down a dark hallway. The Lady stood very still, eyes gleaming as she watched Caspar recede into the darkness.

"*WHO ARE YOU?*"

*

Nobody would have blamed the Lady if she left Omega Rex's chamber and went straight to her quarters for some well-deserved rest. She had spent the last two years behind enemy lines, living under constant threat of detection and capture, and the exhaustion had seeped into her marrow. If the Gray Faces had discovered her true identity, a quick death would have been too much to hope for.

It had been a foolish risk.

But then, she had always been a gambler.

She chose to forgo rest and go back to work. The work that had sustained her for the last ten years. Consumed her.

Time was running out, and she still needed that one roll of the dice, that one big hand to wipe out the memories of all the losses. She had come so close. Years of painstaking labor had fallen apart at the eleventh hour. The worst part was, she knew that if a few pieces on the chessboard had moved one way instead of another, Patriot Gold would now be dead, and the final part of her masterpiece would be set in motion.

She walked up the stairs and into the courtyard. The afternoon sun burned down, a sodden weight on her shoulders. The inner courtyard was walled in on all sides by the balconies and pavilions of a white mansion with a red tile roof. The heat had driven everyone inside, and the Lady took a moment to enjoy the silence and the sun on her skin, wiping away the cold of Omega Rex's breath.

One of her soldiers saluted her at the entrance to the operations wing. He beeped her through the secured doors, and she climbed the flight of stairs. At the top, another soldier saluted and opened the second secured door for her.

The operations center took up the entire second floor of the wing. It was a long bullpen with boarded-up windows, lit only by the glow of monitors and desktop lamps. An industrial air-conditioner blasted frigid air through the space, diffusing the smell of cigarettes, cheap coffee, and the sweat of men and women who had worked through the night.

The forty-six people in the bullpen all stood when she entered. Every single one, from the intelligence analysts to the soldiers, looked exhausted.

"Sit," the Lady commanded. Everyone returned to their work. She locked eyes with the man standing in the corner of the room. He was tall and rangy, with a long brown beard flecked with white. No matter where he was, he was instantly recognizable by the mirrored sunglasses that he wore at all times, even indoors.

He followed her into her office, shutting the door behind them. The Lady switched on the floor lamp and pointed it toward a giant corkboard on the wall.

"Get some sleep," the bearded man said. Everything he said sounded like an order.

"One of these days, Garrison, I'll get around to taking your advice."

Garrison snorted and crammed a pinch of chaw into his cheek. His forearms were roped with muscle, and his skin was bronzed by the suns of distant lands. His Glock pistol was holstered on his right thigh, his constant companion since the day the Lady had met him over ten years ago.

"Get some sleep," Garrison ordered again.

"Do we have our country back yet?" She smiled at him. He just stared back at her with those reflective lenses, chewing. "Well, then," she continued. "Sleep can wait."

The Lady's eyes scanned the board, pinned with surveillance photographs of all the major players in the failed coup. Patriot Gold, Queen Callista, Veena Sixkills, Caspar Von Arx, Faraz Ibrahim, Lazlo Koyle.

Houston Holt.

"Son of a bitch," she whispered, glaring at the man who had brought her plan toppling down.

"Fly in the ointment," Garrison offered.

"To say the least."

She rubbed her eyes and unpinned the pictures from the board and placed them in a pile on her desk. "Our mistake, Garrison, was that we tried to fight power with guile."

Garrison watched as she pinned the picture of Patriot Gold back on the board, at the very top. "But if our experience has taught us anything . . ." She opened a folder and lifted a new surveillance shot from inside. "If my father's experience has taught me anything, it is this: to defeat great power . . ." She pinned the new picture across from Patriot Gold. "You need great power."

The cruel face of General Sixkills glared from the new picture, facing off against the king—two bulls locking eyes before the charge.

Garrison scratched his beard and tilted his head. "Shit. And how do we plan to lasso those two thoroughbreds into the ring?"

"We need a wedge," the Lady said, picking up a third picture. "Someone we can use to divide them."

She pinned the picture of Houston Holt in the narrow space between Patriot Gold and Sixkills.

"Houston Holt. The man who saved the king but killed the daughter of his most powerful warrior." The Lady turned to Garrison. "Almost poetic, don't you think?"

"Hell of a wedge." He chewed. "What about those Frontier pricks?"

"One enemy at a time." The Lady walked over to Garrison and squeezed his shoulder, looking at her own reflection in his lenses. "This time next year, Garrison, you and I will be planting the Stars and Stripes back on our home soil."

One side of Garrison's lip curled up. "Right on that gold motherfucker's ashes."

"Amen." She turned back to the board. "Call in the analysts. We have work to do."

After Garrison had left, the Lady closed her eyes and inhaled deeply, feeling renewed. Sleep was now very far away; the DNA of a new plan was forming, rising, and crackling within her, laced with dark memories and the fire of vengeance.

Her name was Joanna Valencia Mathias. She was the daughter of Gabriel Constantine Mathias, the last president of the United States of America.

And very soon, she would stand over the corpse of her father's murderer and watch as his kingdom burned to the ground.

ABOUT THE AUTHOR

Reeshi Ray fell in love with stories at a young age, devouring everything from Batman comics to Hardy Boy mysteries in a time when books and imagination were the only cures for boredom.

He published his first novel *The King Between Worlds* in 2015, and his second, *One Nation Under Gods*, in 2018.

Reeshi would love to hear your thoughts about this book. Leave a review at Amazon.com or Goodreads.com.

Or visit www.reeshiray.com to contact Reeshi directly.